EXPLOSIVE TOUCH

C. F. FRANCIS

ISBN: 978-0-9995820-2-2 (ebook)
ISBN: 978-0-9995820-3-9 (print)

This is a work of fiction. The characters and events portrayed in this book
are fictitious or are used fictitiously. Any similarity to actual persons, living
or dead, events, or locales is entirely coincidental.

 Created with Vellum

Once again, Cathy, you have pulled me out of the fire and, sometimes, out of my despair. Thank you for your honest critiques and continued support. I'm fortunate to have a friend like you.

and

To my family, who never batted an eye when their crazy aunt started this journey. You have supported me every step of the way.

Love you all!

1

February...Copperhead Country Club, Tampa, Florida

SHAYNE PETERSON GAGGED as she battled her way out of the darkness that had engulfed her. She recognized the smells of charred wood and spilled liquor. But it was something stronger, more acrid, that had her retching. Attempting to roll to her side to vomit, she stopped when she couldn't move anything below her hips. Trapped. She was trapped. Panic quickly bubbled up inside her, but she forced it down along with the bile in her throat. What the hell had happened?

Her legs were firmly pinned to the floor. Whatever entrapped her also had created a vacuum over her upper body. She couldn't move her legs, but she could feel her toes. *Thank God.* She let out a sigh as a small fraction of fear lifted. Her head hurt like a bitch. Every inch of her body cried out, some parts more than others. The fact that she felt pain was a positive omen. She was still in one piece.

Her back and legs were damp and cold where her clothes clung to her skin. Blood? Please, not blood.

Get it together, girl, her dad snapped. Shaking her head, she tried to clear her thoughts. Her dad was dead. He'd been gone ten years. Still, dead or alive, he was right. Whatever had happened, panic wouldn't help. She gulped in a long breath through her mouth to avoid the nauseating scents. Then a second. A few breaths later, she'd calmed enough to focus on her surroundings.

Think. She'd clocked out and had been leaving the country club when she'd noticed another bartender breaking down a cash bar that had been set up for a charity event. She'd stopped to help. Right after the man left for the storeroom with a case of liquor, it happened. A blast. She'd felt it before she'd heard it. An invisible force knocked the air from her lungs before the unbelievable heat had engulfed her. Then blackness.

Shayne blinked several times, ignoring the grittiness behind her eyelids. Lights flashed through the rubble to her right, reflecting off droplets of water. The water would explain her damp clothing. She'd go with that theory. It was better than the alternative.

Sirens, squawking radios, and shouting broke through the ringing in her ears.

"Help," she croaked. Her voice was raspy, the hoarse whisper staying within the confines of her small tomb. "Help," she tried again but with the same pitiful results.

The debris grew heavier as dripping water added to its weight. How long before someone found her? Would she be crushed before they did? She shoved against the inside of her tomb. Glass and debris, trapped beneath her, tore through flesh and muscle as she struggled to break free. The scream she'd been unable to utter minutes before, now rang out loud and clear.

2

S ix months later...Sanibel Island, Florida

SHAYNE SLIPPED through the rear gate of Sanctuary Gardens. If she was any taller, she would have attempted to leap over it. She felt as light as a feather. As giddy as Scrooge when he'd awakened Christmas morning a changed person, except that her night had been so wonderfully peaceful. No ghostly visitors. No faceless man leaving the scene, or a sound that morphed into an explosion, interrupted her sleep. She'd rested solidly and undisturbed until the buzzing of the alarm. There'd been an instant of panic before she realized it had been the clock that had awakened her and not one of her many nightmares.

Setting the alarm was a precaution, though she'd come to believe she'd never need one again. Not a single night had passed since the bombing that she hadn't been awakened by a manifestation of that horrid night. Once she was yanked from sleep, she would sit silently in the dark until it was time for work. One nightmare an evening was enough, thank you. She refused to try for a daily double. But last night was a personal milestone. She was ridiculously happy. It was stupid to get so excited over something as small as a good night's sleep. But she felt she'd turned a corner—a major one. It was damn well worth celebrating, even if that celebration took the form of some quiet time in the garden she'd come to love.

The early morning sun warmed her shoulders as it filtered through the fronds of the towering palm trees. Had she noticed that before, or had she been so worn out from the lack of sleep that she'd let that little gift go unnoticed? She wouldn't let that happen again.

After filling two large watering cans to give the potted plants in front of the building a good soaking, she took the rarely used path on the far side of the property. She didn't want to disturb the owners who lived next door. She'd arrived much earlier than normal, and the couple preferred she didn't work alone for safety sake. Colton and Catherine James were good people, and like the garden, they had grown on her.

The crimson bougainvillea that hung over the narrow, crushed-shell walk needed a good trimming. Ducking to avoid one of its prickly branches, she looked forward to tackling the thorny problem later. *Amazing.* A bartender with a degree in history, she'd fallen in love with the sweaty job of attending to plants. After a few days of digging in the dirt, she'd shorn off her hair, had her acrylic nails removed and tossed out her makeup. Those steps had been freeing. Still, they didn't beat the euphoria of a solid night's sleep.

The instant she rounded the corner, all plans of pruning disappeared. Her heart lodged in her throat. A man was slumped against the cream-colored building. His long, denim-covered legs stretched out in front of him. Scuffed sneakers pointed in opposite directions. His dirty T-shirt rode up from his waist to expose a well-toned abdomen. A dark green baseball cap sat askew on his head, obscuring most of his face. That same head rested on his left arm, which was propped against a large clay pot that held Mexican petunias and lavender lantana.

The man could be unconscious, sleeping, or passed-out drunk. She had no business determining the reason he had landed on the doorstep of Sanctuary Gardens. Her sweating palms forced her to set down the watering cans. She wiped her hands against her shorts. Her legs were itching to bolt in the opposite direction. But she remembered lying injured, unattended, and afraid, not that long ago. Her stomach dropped. Stupid or not, she couldn't walk away from him.

The man's breathing appeared to be steady. Not that she was an expert, but she didn't recognize any signs of distress or injury. Dark hair had escaped his cap and hung over his brow. Most of his face was hidden by the brim of that cap and the arm his head rested on. By the growth of whiskers along the chiseled jaw that remained exposed, it was obvious the man hadn't shaved in days. He was big. His build resembled Colt and his friends. Rick, Steve, and even Colt's business partner, Gib, were all large, muscular men. With the exception of Gib, all of them had served in the Special Forces. She looked closer at his cap. It was dark green. Army green. She could barely make out the letter *A* above the bill. The rest of the wording was hidden along with most of his face. If this guy was one of their friends, she hadn't met him.

She took a calming breath and shook her hands, hoping to shed the nerves dancing across her fingers. She inched closer. As she did, the smell of whiskey overpowered the sweet fragrance of the lantana he was crushing.

Shit. A drunk.

Shayne reached for the phone she kept tucked in the back pocket of her shorts. *Always have your phone within reach*—a lesson in safety she'd learned while trapped in the rubble. She scrolled down to Colt's number. Before she could call, the man stirred and moaned. She eyed him more intently. He might be drunk but that didn't rule out being sick or injured.

Shayne ordered her hand to stop trembling as she brushed his cheek to check for a fever. Suddenly, her wrist was in his grasp, her hand slammed against the ground. She screamed, but her mouth was immediately smothered by his large palm. Smothered. No. Not again. She struggled harder. His hand slipped. The act allowed Shayne to clamp down on his fingers with her teeth. He yanked his hand away, but his large body kept her trapped. He was solid and firm, and no amount of scrambling could get him to move. Her phone had gone sailing when she hit the ground. She was being crushed beneath a man with no way to call for help. She yelled and swore as her struggle continued. He covered her mouth again.

What did he want? It would be easy enough for him to overpower her. She imagined his hands around her neck or ripping at her clothes. Lights blinked behind her eyes as fear continued to bubble up inside her. She tried to get some traction, hoping to push away from him, but her sneakers would not grab hold on the loose surface of the lot.

Her hands were confined between them. She turned her head away from the smell of alcohol. Being trapped along with the smell of liquor took her back to a place she didn't want to go. She heard a whimper and recognized it as her own.

She wasn't going to be able to push the man off her. He was too big. Too solid. Her small frame was no match for his muscular build. When his hips pressed against her abdomen, she panicked. She couldn't get a breath. The flashes of light behind her eyes increased until she was almost blinded by them. *Fight, damn it. Don't give in.*

Painfully, she managed to pull her left arm free. She dodged his hand while she felt for anything to use as a weapon. She found nothing but the ground beneath her. She dug her fingers into the thin layer of dirt, closed her eyes, and threw the sandy soil at the man's face. He reeled back, trying to clear his eye. It was then she saw the scars and patch covering the other eye. Too bad she didn't care. She raised her knee and jammed it in his groin.

The man dropped his hands from his face to his privates as he curled into a tight ball. She tried to catch her breath, cautiously watching him while she scurried away. For a drunk, the man was a hunk. Ha ha. Why did she care what he looked like? Still she didn't miss his tight jeans, which showed off a mighty fine ass. The muscles of his arms bulged as they cradled his stomach—which she'd already noted, was toned and tanned. The patch and the facial scars didn't do anything to hide the strong jaw. It was a shame he was a drunk asshole.

Shayne spotted her cell—her lifeline—on the crushed shell lot next to her attacker. No way she was getting that close to him again. Her wrist was already swelling—no surprise there. He'd damn near twisted it off.

She shuffled back a few feet as his rocking slowed. If she left him to call for help, he could be gone before she got back. What did it matter? The police would surely find him.

~

THE MOMENT TROY felt a hand graze his face, he'd instinctively grabbed it. He twisted the wrist to break the grip on whatever weapon the enemy intended to use on him. He pinned the arm against the ground. The high-pitched tone told him it was a boy. Not a man, but just as dangerous—maybe more. Not old enough to understand death—his own or those of the innocent. Not that Troy was innocent. Far from it.

His remaining eye refused to focus. The small body beneath him squirmed violently. He followed the sound of the shriek and slapped his hand tightly over the attacker's mouth. He yanked it back when teeth clamped onto his fingers. *God*, he was slipping. He should have slammed his fist into the kid's face. Another stupid mistake. Soon, he'd be no good to the team at all.

"Let go of me, you son of a bitch! Get the hell off me."

English. The kid spoke English. Vulgar but clear. That was important but Troy didn't know why. Their struggle continued. *Christ*, the kid was a fighter. And a screamer. Troy pressed his body against his attacker, using his weight to prevent any means of escape. One hand covered the enemy's mouth, but the boy continually fought off his hold.

He felt the urchin's arm pull free. Troy reached out for it. Suddenly, gravel and sand flew into his face, blinding the vision in his remaining eye. Then a knee impacted his groin. Troy rolled to his side in pain as his captive slipped away.

"What the hell is wrong with you?" The boy continued to sling vulgarities at him.

Whether it was the pain or the constant barrage of profanities, Troy realized he'd been caught in a nightmare. *Jeezus*.

9

The searing jolt from the hit to his balls traveled up his body and settled into his gut. He curled in the fetal position, swearing. He hadn't been in this much pain since he'd awakened in the hospital in Germany.

He could hear someone panting. Whoever it was stood in front of him, but from the sound of shuffling feet, the person was backing away. He couldn't see. One eye gone, the other blinded by sand. He blinked, trying to clear his vision.

Who had he attacked? Some neighborhood kid? He'd come looking for help from his friends and started out by tackling one of the neighborhood kids.

The night before—at least he thought it was the night before—someone had dropped him off at his former commander's home and business. He'd been drunk. Nothing unusual but he'd had enough sense left to know better than to knock on their door in the dead of night. He'd planned to sleep it off before he saw his friends again.

He struggled unsuccessfully to pull himself into an upright position. It took several blinks before he cleared his vision enough to get a glimpse of the person. A figure with a round face, short, brown hair and loose-fitting clothes continued to back away. She wasn't much bigger than Colt's wife. *She?*

"Did I hurt you?" he asked. His vision blurred again just as the angel had begun to take shape.

3

Colt barreled around the corner of the building. The dark-haired man was barefoot, bare-chested, and wearing only a pair of shorts. Shayne didn't miss the gun gripped in his right hand.

"You okay?" Colt's blue eyes darted from Shayne to the man on the ground.

"I'll live." She cradled her throbbing wrist against her waist. "But he might be hurt."

"Cat's calling the police now. EMS, too," Colt told her, turning his attention back to the man whose head and knees were pressed against the building. "You did that?" Colt asked, glancing back at Shayne.

"It wasn't hard. He's drunk." Shayne stepped back a couple more paces as Colt approached the drunk. A little distance seemed like a good thing.

"How did you know where I was?" she asked.

"You were screaming in stereo," he explained, patting one of the pockets of his cargo shorts, presumably where he'd stashed his phone.

"I must have hit the call button before I lost my phone.

The whole neighborhood probably heard me." She was turning several shades of red if her body temperature was any indication.

Colt picked up the phone and tossed it to her. "I thought Cat was the only woman who'd raised swearing to an art form."

Colton James wasn't laughing as he nudged the man's back with his bare foot. "Come on, asshole. Get up. Let me get a look at the damage the lady did."

A WOMAN. His last instinct before blacking out had been right. Troy wasn't sure if that was an improvement over a boy or not. He'd attacked a woman. The alcohol he'd binged on the night before was no longer fogging his brain.

Troy recognized the voice of the man who had shouted the order. Vanishing on the spot wasn't going to happen, no matter how much he wished it were possible. Besides, he'd hurt a woman. He'd have to pay for that. He had to pay for a lot of things.

Using the massive planter for support, Troy managed to get to his knees. Getting to his feet was a harder task. His legs wobbled and his stomach lurched. He focused on the stucco wall in front of him, hoping that fixating on a single spot would stop the world from spinning. Between the alcohol and the hit to the groin, he'd be lucky if he didn't puke.

Time crawled. Maybe he'd be able to one-off this incident. Tell them he'd fallen asleep and had a bad dream. The sirens assured him all hope was lost on that front. A drunk on the doorstep of a respectable Sanibel business, who had also attacked a woman, was going to jail. That he could handle. He'd seen his share of drunk tanks since he'd walked out of Brooks Army Medical Center. No biggie.

He swallowed and turned to face the onslaught.

"Troy?"

The stunned sound of his former commander's voice resonated in Troy's ears as his world again went black.

4

"**Y**ou know him?" Shayne asked Colt as he scrambled to catch the man before he tumbled to the ground. If Colt hadn't had such quick reflexes, their visitor would have landed face-first on the unpaved lot. Colt carefully laid the man out, giving Shayne her first good look at her attacker's face. Scars emanated from beneath a black patch that covered his left eye. The remnants of his injury created jagged trails to his jaw, where they disappeared behind tendrils of his thick, reddish-brown hair. The pain that he'd suffered as a result of the horrific wound was unimaginable.

Shayne's attention was pulled away as Cat came flying across the driveway, followed closely by Gibson McKay. Neither was completely dressed. Cat's oversized T-shirt skirted the top of her knees. She wore flip-flops and was clutching a pair of shorts. Gib was clad in a pair of snug boxer briefs, his long blond hair hanging loose. Too bad the situation didn't allow for a more detailed appraisal of the stunning man.

"I told you to stay put," Colt lectured his wife.

"It's Troy," Cat said, ignoring her husband's comment as

she hopped into her shorts then kneeled next to the man. Cat pulled the cap off his head, tossed it aside, then tenderly brushed the hair from his face. The hat landed at Shayne's feet. The word *ARMY*, stitched in dark thread above the bill of the cap, stared back at her.

"He's had too much to drink. Shayne added to his misery," Colt explained.

"I'm sorry." Shayne's shoulders slumped. "I thought he was trying to break my wrist."

"He probably was," Colt agreed. Both disgust and sadness laced his response.

"You have no reason to be sorry." Cat rose to her feet. "You did what you needed to do. Are you okay?" But she had already taken Shayne's wrist carefully into her hands.

"He's a friend?" Shayne asked.

"Troy McKenzie," Cat confirmed. "He served with Colt. We knew he was having a rough time of it, but he dropped off the radar after his release from the hospital. We've been worried about him but didn't know where he was. He didn't want to be found."

"I didn't mean to hurt him."

"I think most of the damage is self-inflicted," Cat assured Shayne, pulling her close.

The parking lot quickly filled with vehicles. Rick Wilcowski, a friend and detective with the Sanibel PD, arrived seconds ahead of the police and EMTs. Steve Brody brought up the rear. The timing of his arrival may have been a coincidence since his security business shared space in Cat's office building, but Shayne wouldn't have been surprised if Steve hadn't been alerted by one of the members of the group.

Shayne was ushered into the bowels of the EMS unit by one of the techs. He checked her vital signs and asked a litany of questions as he examined her wrist. While he flushed her scrapes, her gaze drifted to the group huddled around the man still lying on the ground.

"Do you think he's okay?" she asked the paramedic attending her. Another EMT was working on Troy while his friends stood by.

"I wouldn't worry about him, ma'am. They'd be prepping him for a ride to the hospital if there was something seriously wrong. On the other hand, it looks like you have a bad sprain. You should have that wrist X-rayed to be sure."

Shayne thanked the medic after refusing transport to the hospital. Once she was out of the unit, Rick stalked over to her. She'd gotten used to the size and stature of these men. They were all tall, toned and protective. A Justice League of sorts. Each one was set apart by a distinguishing feature, making it easy for her to keep their names straight. In Rick's case, it was his military short, silver-blond hair. He looked over his shoulder at his friend. "You'll want to press charges," Rick stated.

"What? No." How could he think she'd file charges against one of their own? These people had helped her—taken her in. None of them would consider this man a friend if he hadn't earned their respect.

"You have every right," Rick assured her.

"I am *not* pressing charges. If I hadn't snuck up on him, this would never have happened. Hell, he could press charges against me. He's the one on the ground. So, let's call it even. Besides, it's just a sprain."

"Is that what the paramedic said?" Rick looked at her swollen wrist.

"He thinks so."

"But he can't be sure," Rick concluded. "I'll take you to the hospital so you can get it X-rayed."

Shayne let out a heavy sigh. "I'd rather not." Thinking about the sterile walls and beeping machines gave her cold sweats. If it became clear she needed more than an ice pack, she'd go, but she'd maxed out her stress level for the moment.

Rick unclipped the phone from his belt. "Let me make a call."

Shayne stood in silence when Rick stepped a few feet away. The others remained by Troy's side. She couldn't hear what they were discussing, but each one wore a look of concern or sadness. She suddenly felt very much alone.

"What's going on?" she asked Rick, when he disconnected.

"You need to get that arm checked out," he told her. "I greased some wheels."

Shayne waited with Rick while the others got McKenzie to his feet. Steve anchored Troy's right arm over his shoulder with his left hand gripping the waistband of the man's jeans. Colt repeated the maneuver on the right. Gib walked a few paces in front of the threesome. They headed toward the rear of Gib's and Colt's photography business next door.

"Where are they taking him?"

"Gib's place," Rick answered as they watched the sad parade.

Shayne was aware of the two condos above the photo studio, Island Images. She'd had dinner with Cat and Colt a couple of times. Gib lived in the unit next to theirs, though she'd never stepped inside his place.

As the men disappeared behind the building, Cat stomped over to join Shayne and Rick. She was not smiling. "I wish Colt would have let him stay with us."

"Troy's lashing out right now," Rick said. "Colt's not going to want you near him, at least for the time being."

"We'll see about that," Cat threatened, and Shayne bet she'd eventually get her way. The woman was tenacious and had a temper that was legendary among the close-knit group. Hovering close to five feet, Cat's temper packed a wallop. Perhaps her emotions were concentrated due to her petite size. Whatever the reason, the guys seemed to get a kick out of watching the fireworks.

"What are you still doing here?" Cat asked Shayne. "Shouldn't you be on your way to the hospital?"

5

Troy's shins slammed against the tread of each step as he was hauled up the stairs by his two friends. He did nothing to alleviate the situation. His legs wouldn't hold him if he tried. He was nauseated, and his balls were still on fire.

"Let me grab his feet."

Troy wasn't so far gone that he didn't recognize Gib's voice. The two of them had shared some friendly competition garnering the ladies' attention during Troy's few visits to the island. It wouldn't be much of a contest these days.

"If he's too drunk or lazy to lift his own damn feet, he deserves black-and-blue ankles to go along with his sore balls," Colt snapped.

Knowing the reason behind the insult didn't stop it from hitting its mark. Troy mentally ordered his legs to move. They may not be able to hold his weight, but he could damn well lift his feet. Why that was important, he didn't know.

"Where to?" Gib asked when they reached his door.

"Bed," Troy grunted.

"Shower," Colt countered.

"Hell," Troy croaked. His mouth was dry as cotton.

"Gib, start a pot of coffee, would you?" Steve asked.

"Just let me sleep it off," Troy begged.

"Suck it up, soldier," Colt snapped, as they pulled him deeper into Gib's home.

Troy endured the humiliation of being stripped by two former officers. Undressing would have been an insurmountable task to accomplish on his own. He wasn't able to hold his head erect let alone stand. He'd face-plant on the bathroom floor if he tried. But the instant Troy felt one of them tug the elastic band that held his eyepatch in place, his hand snapped out, grabbing the intruding wrist.

"Still got your reflexes. Good," Colt commented.

"Leave it be," Troy snarled.

"We've seen worse," Steve assured him.

"I said, leave it be." Troy held his hand over the patch.

"Sorry, but unless you have another one of these on you, we're going to need to keep this one dry." Colt slipped the elastic over Troy's head and pulled his hand away.

"Son of a bitch," Troy muttered.

"Upsy-daisy," Steve said, as he and Colt led Troy into the large walk-in shower and lowered him onto a wide, tiled bench. Who the hell had a built-in bench in their shower? He squinted at the room, and without asking, he knew he'd been deposited in Gib's bathroom—a bathroom built for entertaining women. He almost laughed at the idea of sharing a shower with a woman until a spray of cold water hit him directly in the face.

"Stop it, you bastards." Troy tried to stand but was forcefully pushed back on to the bench.

"Sit," Colt ordered him. "You'll break your goddamn neck if you try to go anywhere in your condition."

"Who'd care?"

"Cat, for one. She'd skin me alive if I let anything happen to you."

"My wife, for another," Steve added, tightening his grip on Troy's shoulder.

"They shouldn't care," Troy said, no longer fighting the stream of icy water. Cat and...Josie—hooray, he remembered her name—shouldn't care about him.

"Then what possessed you to come to Sanibel?" Colt asked, shoving a washcloth in Troy's hand. "You knew you'd be among friends here."

Sober meant feeling and remembering. Troy wasn't sure he wanted to do either. He rubbed the soapy cloth over the upper portion of his body. If he didn't make the effort, one of his friends would be bathing him next.

"I came for that job Steve promised me." Not a lie. Not the complete truth. He stared at his feet. Did he dare bend over to wash them? He'd probably land on his head if he tried. Fuck it. He laid the cloth on the bench next to him.

"The job offer was to a sober man who didn't attack women." Steve shoved a bottle of shampoo into Troy's hand.

"She snuck up on me. I thought I was back in Afghanistan."

"I'm sure you did, coming off the bender you tied on," Colt snapped. "Now lather up so you look halfway human when you apologize to Shayne."

"Shayne." Troy tried on the name. Rolled it around on his tongue. Different. "Is she all right?" he asked, sticking his head under the stream of water which was now lukewarm. Apparently, the more he sobered, the more hot water he was allotted.

"Haven't heard from Rick yet. He's dealing with that end of things. You did a hell of a number on her wrist."

"I reacted the way I was trained," he defended himself

while he dumped shampoo over his head. He hadn't had a haircut since he returned stateside. His hair was long. Longer than he'd ever worn it. He hadn't cared.

"I'm sorry I hurt her." Troy stuck his head beneath the stream of warm water to rinse out the shampoo. As he wiped the soap from his eyes, his left hand jerked away from his face as soon as it made contact with the scar tissue. Would he ever get used to that?

"You can tell her yourself and make amends by doing her job while she heals," Colt told him.

"What job?"

"She works for Cat. In the garden center."

"I'm not a damn gardener. I came here to work for Steve."

"You'll do Shayne's job until she's able to do it herself," Steve stated. "Cat can use the help, and you'll cover for Shayne because she had the decency to check on a drunk. You owe them both. Then we'll talk about a security job. I'm not risking my business on you until I know you can stay sober."

"There's a VA center in Cape Coral about thirty minutes from here," Colt informed him.

Troy bristled at the thinly veiled order. "I don't need a friggin' doctor screwing with my head," Troy snapped. "I had enough of that shit."

"Apparently, you didn't. You bailed, didn't you?" Colt asked.

Troy remained silent. Once he'd received his medical release, he had bailed out of counseling. The counselors wanted him to come to terms with the events that had resulted in his disfigurement. All he wanted to do was forget.

"We'll take this one step at a time," Colt assured him.

"The next step being a razor. Can you shave without cutting your throat, or do you want one of us to do it for you?"

Troy managed to get out of the shower under his own power, but dropped his full weight onto the closed lid of the toilet as soon as he did. Resigned, he held out his shaking hands for the two men to see. "What do you think?"

TROY SAT at the table in the bright, sunlit kitchen, doing his best to raise a cup to his lips without spilling any coffee. His hands still trembled. Some Jack Daniel's would steady them, he'd learned, but he hadn't come all this way for a drink. His mind was clearing. Keeping it that way was his current challenge.

Gib had dug up a pair of sweat pants and a T-shirt for Troy. He didn't have his duffel. He'd left it behind on one of his stops. He vaguely remembered having it with him last night, but he wouldn't swear to it. There would be nothing in it that was remotely clean, anyway. When was the last time he'd felt clean—physically or emotionally?

Troy's focus remained on the cup and his hands that surrounded it. He'd yet to look at the men gathered around the table. They were waiting for him to tell them what had brought him to their doorstep. He didn't know where to start. When he'd reached the bottom of his barrel, he'd looked upward and only seen two choices. Remain among the living or end his suffering.

The second option would have been easier, but training, stubbornness, or the desire to continue to inflict damage upon himself had him taking the harder route. He was alive —and wishing he wasn't.

He hadn't believed it possible to sink this low. He'd

witnessed others in the military succumb to stress or traumatic events, but he'd thought himself too strong to become one of the fallen. He should have known better. Colt had suffered, although not to the degree Troy had sunk. If the man he'd admired for over a decade could be knocked on his ass by the carnage they'd witnessed, why should Troy think he'd be any different? But Colt had been successful in taming his demons instead of allowing them to consume him.

"What's the story with Shayne?" Troy asked, avoiding the reason for his appearance on the island.

"That information is need-to-know. You don't need to know." Colt's voice was firm.

Troy's temper flashed. The remark had its intended effect. He was now looking Colt in the eye. "Seriously?"

"Seriously," Colt confirmed. "She works for Cat. She's a good person and a good employee. She stays off the radar. Everyone's radar." The former captain's teal-blue eyes didn't give anything away as Colt pushed a strand of jet-black hair behind his ear.

Troy searched the faces of the other men sitting at the table. He didn't know another team of Green Berets that got into as much trouble outside of a combat zone as this one.

Steve had retired from the Army last year and was building a business with the love of his life at his side. He hadn't been out long enough, though, to lose his military bearing. He sat with his back ramrod straight.

Gib, however, was relaxed, one arm thrown over the back of his chair. With a ruby stud in his ear and his long blond hair, he appeared harmless. Troy knew better.

"What are you guys into now? Does this have something to do with your investigation business?" he asked Steve.

"Look, Troy," Steve replied, "when you get your act together—"

"You don't trust me?" Troy slammed his fist on the table. Any one of them could have taken a knife to him, and it would have hurt less than their lack of faith.

"At the moment? No. You haven't given me reason to," Steve told him, ignoring the outburst. "You were passed out on the street. Drunk. Then attacked a woman. If the situation were reversed, would you be sharing intel with me?"

For the first time since he'd joined the unit, Troy felt ostracized from the team. He craved that sense of belonging again. As much as it irritated him, though, he retained enough of his skills and training to understand. He nodded. "Will you let me know how she's doing?"

"We'll pass it along," Colt told him. "Now, I think it's time you explained what brought you here."

6

Troy never got the chance to explain his reasons for returning to Sanibel. His tremors had quickly increased until he could no longer hold his cup. Beads of perspiration dripped from his temples onto the table. Eventually, he lost the fight and emptied the contents of his stomach. Fortunately, he didn't humiliate himself further by not making it to the bathroom in time.

He knelt there like a child while Colt used a wet cloth to wipe his face. By then, Troy was shaking so badly that there was no way he was going to make it to a bed under his own power. He eyed the plush bathroom rug, ready to crawl into a ball on the floor. Before he followed through with that thought, Gib and Steve appeared. The three of them managed to haul Troy's ass to the guest room and get him into bed.

He woke periodically to find one of his friends sitting in the chair in the corner of the room. Rick, Steve, Gib, and Colt had apparently taken the responsibility of sitting with him. Whether they believed he would hurt himself or choke on his own vomit, he refused to guess. He recognized the side effects of coming off a binge. This wasn't his first experience with it. But on this trip, each time he opened his eye, he saw that one of his friends had his six.

Eventually, light forced its way through Troy's matted eyelashes. He fought off the remnants of his restless sleep. The sun, streaming through the east window, confirmed his suspicion that it was morning. Not that the time or the date were important. He had no place to go. Nowhere to be.

Troy raised a hand to his face. It was no longer trembling. In another sign of progress, he needed to take a piss more than he wanted a drink. He had vague memories of one or two trips to the latrine with assistance, but this time his faculties told him he'd be able to make it on his own. He threw the covers aside and was hit by the smell of sweat. It had been a long time since the odor of alcohol did not accompany the familiar smell.

He sat on the edge of the bed and glanced at the empty chair in the corner. His caretakers were gone. Weak but steady, he managed the trip to the bathroom. After relieving himself, he braced his arms against the countertop and stared at the image in the mirror. His instinct was to turn away from the scarred reflection, but he stood his ground and stared back at the distorted man. He hadn't made it this far to turn away from his goal.

Troy could recall bits and pieces of his journey to Sanibel, much of it muddled by alcohol. But his awakening, the moment he'd realized the purpose of his pilgrimage, remained clear in his mind. How many days or weeks had it been since he'd found himself slumped over the steering wheel of his car, halfway down a ravine? The deflated airbag had told him the collision had been significant. He'd managed to get the damaged door open and had fallen out onto the rain-soaked earth. He'd scrambled up the steep slope, following the gouges his tires had left in the soft soil. Instinctively, he made a search of the immediate area and found no sign of man or animal—injured, dying, or dead. He remembered sinking to his knees and burying his face in his hands. He hadn't killed anyone—at least not that day.

The damp earth had soaked through Troy's clothing, chilling him to the bone. Still, he'd sat there until darkness fell, lost in guilt and regret. The headlights of a passing car distracted him from his inner demons. When he raised his right hand to shield his eye, his Special Forces signet ring flashed brightly on his finger. At that moment, he'd known where he needed to be.

Troy zeroed in on the place where his left eye should have been, much like the first day he'd managed to make it to the bathroom of his hospital room under his own power. The massive bandage that had covered the left side of his face had been removed. He'd been fitted with a patch to cover the missing eye. Mutilated flesh descended from beneath the black patch. It resembled tentacles of the stinging jellyfish that floated in tropical waters. The doctors had told him that, when he was ready, plastic surgery could repair most of the damage although they would never be able to replace the eye he had lost.

His desecrated features were hard to stomach, but they hadn't been the primary reason he was driven to drink. The memory those scars resurrected served that purpose. The image imprinted on his brain seconds before he was blown across the small Afghani marketplace flashed before him every time he looked in the mirror. He desperately wanted to erase it. But there was no eraser that could rub that deep. No eraser that could expunge the past.

He continued to stare at the reflection, trying to look past the physical damage and find the man he'd once been.

Was he still there? Buried somewhere deep? As he'd known when he began this leg of his journey, he wouldn't find that man without help.

Troy had spent the months since his release from BAMC running from that memory. He'd been hellbent on killing himself without being the one to put a gun to his head. He'd picked fights with anyone who looked at him sideways, driven recklessly until he crashed his car. He was damn lucky—and grateful—he hadn't killed anyone.

Whether he deserved to be free of his demons was still up for debate. He'd come to seek advice from a man he knew fought a similar battle and won.

Troy spotted the razor that Steve had used to shave him. This time he picked it up with a steady hand. Studying the growth of his beard, he figured he must have been out of action for days. He needed a shower to rid himself of the stench of sweat, and then a shave.

CLEAN, shaven, and in a fresh pair of sweat pants and T-shirt that had appeared on the bed, Troy made his way to the kitchen. Gib's place was the mirror image of Colt's. Troy had spent enough time at his former commander's home to easily maneuver his way through Gib's living space. Now if he could find the makings for a pot of coffee...

Colt was at the kitchen table with his phone to his ear when Troy entered the room.

"Feeling better?" Colt asked as he disconnected from the call.

"Hungry," Troy heard himself say. He hadn't realized he was hungry until he'd spoken the words aloud. The aroma coming from the oven most likely had something to do with it.

"Not surprised. Think you can keep some food and coffee down?"

"I'd better or I'll pass out again. This time from starvation."

Colt headed for the oven and Troy reached for the coffeepot and a cup on the granite countertop. He held the cup near the rim with the fingers of one hand while he poured with the other. A trick he'd grudgingly learned from his therapist to help him judge the distance and location of the cup since the loss of his eye. It was either that, continually scald himself, or give up coffee. Some choices were easy.

"Cat sent this over." Colt used a dishtowel to pull a square metal pan from the oven. "Be grateful Gib had to leave, or you'd be out of luck."

"Where is he?"

"Photo shoot," Colt answered as he put the coffee cake, plates, and utensils on the table.

"And Steve?" Troy salivated over the smell of cinnamon as he cut a chunk of cake out of the pan.

"Out with a prospective client."

"I assume Rick's on duty?" Troy mumbled, his mouth now full of moist cake.

"What's with the attendance?"

"Putting off the third degree while I eat." He knew it was coming, and he wouldn't feel much like eating once the conversation started.

"It will wait until you're done. You haven't eaten in two days."

"At least," he agreed. When was the last time he'd eaten? "How's the girl? Shayne?"

"You remember her name. Good. At least your brain isn't pickled."

"I thought the lecture was going to wait." Although there was really no point in putting it off, Troy did want to know about the woman he'd injured.

"She has a badly sprained wrist. She's going against the doctor's orders and working at the garden center. Cat hasn't been able to stop her. You will."

"How am I supposed to do that?"

"You will be taking over her duties until she's able to complete them without doing damage to her arm. That is, as long as you stay away from the bottle."

Both of Colt's eyes bored into Troy's good one. He'd found his patch on the bathroom vanity, so his damaged eye was now covered. It hadn't taken him long to realize that when he wasn't wearing the patch, people tended to look at the missing eye instead of the remaining one.

"That's my intention," Troy told him. It would be too tempting to crawl into the bottle and never come out.

"Wanting to be sober and staying that way aren't the same thing."

"No, it isn't," he admitted. Troy considered the beer Gib probably had stashed in his refrigerator. He didn't want one. More importantly, he didn't need one.

"I am giving you one order. You're to stay away from the women if you decide to drink yourself senseless again. Do I make myself clear?"

His former commander's voice was loud, clear, and left absolutely no room for doubt. Troy would get the shit kicked out of him if he disobeyed that order. He'd find himself on the other side of the causeway with Colt's boot still stuck up his ass.

"Roger that." Troy reached for another slice of coffee

cake. He was ravenous. Besides, it was damn good cake. "You going to tell me the story behind Shayne?"

"No, I'm not, and you're not going to ask anyone about her. She's off the radar—including yours."

"What? Are you insinuating I'd make a pass? Like any woman would be interested in this face."

"Feeling sorry for yourself?"

Was he? He had a lot to deal with, but thought he'd convinced himself that his looks weren't one of them. Maybe he hadn't gotten past that yet.

"I have zero interest in women. I don't need that kind of distraction." And that was the truth. He needed to focus. Women had always been a distraction—a delightful and intentional distraction.

"I said the same thing when I left the service." Colt smiled sympathetically.

"How'd you do it, Colt? How did you bury your demons?" They all knew Colt had found peace here. Troy desperately wanted to find some measure of peace within himself, assuming that was possible.

Colt pushed back his chair and walked over to the counter. "What is it you want?" he asked, refilling his cup.

And around to the million-dollar question. Colt had healed emotionally after he'd arrived on Sanibel. Was Troy hoping to absorb some of the magic Cat believed this place held within its shores, or learn from the man who'd suffered a similar wound to his soul?

"I don't know. Forgiveness?"

"From whom?" Colt's eyes narrowed.

Troy felt the weight of his guilt on his shoulders. "Does it matter? I can't raise the dead and ask for it."

"No, you can't," Colt agreed, still eyeing Troy. "Maybe you ought to start with yourself."

None of the members of the team had seen Troy since his injury. He had refused all contact with his friends. The hospital mental health professionals had encouraged him to communicate with his teammates. He'd been adamant. The hospital staff assumed his anger was the result of his disfigurement. Troy felt his injury was deserved.

"That monkey on your back isn't going anywhere until you wrestle it free."

"How did you rid yourself of the weight? The death of those villagers was never your fault, but you saddled yourself with that guilt," Troy blurted out. "How did you get your life back?"

A shadow seemed to pass over Colt but quickly disappeared. Troy was an ass for the way he'd blundered onto the subject that had prompted Colt to end his career in the army. While every member of the team deeply mourned the deaths of the innocent villagers at the hands of the enemy, Colt had blamed himself for the loss of life. He wasn't responsible for the bad intel or the Taliban who had laid the trap. On the contrary, his actions had saved the lives of every member of the team and most of the villagers. Yet he'd carried the guilt of the dead for years. Anxious to know how his commander and friend had managed to shed the mantle of blame, Troy hadn't given any thought how to broach the subject.

"I shouldn't have asked that," Troy said.

Colt waved him off. "It's not something I'll ever forget, nor should I, but with Cat's help, I've managed to put it in a place so it doesn't rule my life and turned it into something positive. Is that why you came? To see if I had a magic elixir?"

"Do you?"

"I wish I did. I came close to crawling into the bottle and

never coming out, but fortunately for me, I didn't get that far."

"But how?"

"We're different," Colt said before retaking the seat across from Troy. "We're all different. The reasons we are affected by situations and the way we process that damage is different for each of us. Luck or fate, as Cat would call it, had me stumbling into that gift shop, where I met Gib. The day after our meeting, he had me taking pictures with a camera instead of obsessing over the ones in my head. Then I literally ran into Cat. She lit a fire under me and within me.

"I do know this," Colt added, his voice as hard as steel. "What happened wasn't your fault, but it won't make a damn bit of difference until you believe it."

"How do you know it wasn't my fault?" Troy asked, daring Colt to contradict him.

"It wasn't." Colt waited a heartbeat. "But me saying it didn't make a dent, did it? I don't know how many times people said that to me. I stopped listening after a while. I took their concern as sympathy or pity. I didn't want either. I wanted what you want. Forgiveness. But those who could absolve me were gone.

"Gib gave me the hand I needed to crawl out of the pit of despair, but it was Cat who taught me the difference between guilt and grief. When you're ready to talk, let one of us know."

"Can I have Cat?" Troy joked. He felt a smirk creep across his face. The muscles were tight. They hadn't been used in a long time. He hadn't found anything remotely funny.

"No." Colt smiled. "You can't. But I have no doubt you'll be hearing from her. Remember what I said. You stay sober, or keep your distance from the women. Have I made myself clear on that point?"

"Crystal," Troy affirmed.

"You are part of this family." Colt stood. "Family can be a pain in the ass at times, but they are never a burden—at least not in this one. You come to one of us if you need help or want to talk. We'll always have your six."

7

Shayne should be happy. She wasn't. After her ill-fated meeting with Troy, Rick had arranged to get her through the back door of an orthopedic surgeon's office. The doctor confirmed the bad sprain, put her wrist in a brace, and added a sling for good measure. Until it healed, she'd been relegated to supervising Troy.

She was certain her shitty attitude had shown during the past few days. It had nothing to do with the fact that the big man had body slammed her to the ground or that her wrist still throbbed on occasion. This garden was *her* sanctuary. After the bustling life she'd lived in Tampa and her close call with death there, she relished the peace she found here. That peace did not include instructing a very large and contrary man on how to do her job.

Instead of sulking, she should be grateful she was still employed. When Cat told her Troy would be taking over her duties and asked Shayne to show him the ropes, she'd assumed her time at the nursery had come to an end. Cat quickly apologized for the clumsy manner in which she'd broached the subject. She explained that the change was temporary while Shayne's wrist healed. She went on to say that Troy needed to work. Being sedentary wouldn't help him heal, physically or emotionally.

Shayne understood the need to keep busy. After her release from the hospital, she'd had too much time on her hands to relive the events of that night. Since the bombing, she'd had that single blissful night when she hadn't been awakened by the imaginary sound of an explosion or the sight of a faceless man. But the nightmares had returned the evening after her encounter with Troy. So yes, Shayne empathized with the need to focus elsewhere, and based on Troy's physical scars alone, she guessed his memories were a hundred times worse than hers.

Working together was awkward. She felt foolish giving instructions to a Green Beret on how to pull weeds. To his credit, he hadn't complained. Hadn't said much of anything since the apology he'd offered her upon their formal introduction. Mostly, he grunted when given instructions. "Withdrawn" was the best description of his persona she could come up with as they'd slugged through the garden together. Since he wasn't speaking, she didn't know how he felt about working at her side, but Shayne was trying to figure out the quickest way to force a break in this unhappy union.

Normally she wasn't one to be truculent. Before the bombing, she'd been downright sociable. Now she had trouble spending long stretches of time with any one person. Troy was fighting an inner struggle, and his friends had reached out to help. Regardless of the circumstances of their initial meeting, Troy deserved her respect, instead of a crappy attitude. If a man of war could lower himself, metaphorically speaking, to yank weeds from the ground, she should be able to get past her foolish need for isolation.

Shayne left Troy on the far side of the garden, uprooting unwelcomed homesteaders she'd identified to him as weeds. Puzzling out problems was something she did best while working alone. So while Troy weeded, she made a beeline to the garden shed. Watering the potted plants out front would give her a few minutes alone and allow her time to get her head screwed on straight.

Once filled, she shut off the faucet then reached for the can. A large hand firmly grasped her good wrist from behind. She jumped.

"Shit! Don't do that again," she snapped.

"Sorry," Troy said. "You're not supposed to lift things."

"I have a sprained wrist. That doesn't make me an invalid," Shayne declared when she was able to breathe again.

"I have one eye. That doesn't make me a pariah," Troy countered.

Shayne tucked her chin in, staring hard into his strikingly green eye. "Why the hell would you say that? I've been at your side all damn day."

"It's pretty obvious you'd rather be anywhere but next to me. You haven't said two words. You just point this way or that."

Shayne fisted her hands on her hips. "Well, you're not exactly Chatty Cathy, either," she accused him. Did she detect a slight twitch of his lip? Impossible. She left the watering can on the ground and stormed toward the front of the building. She didn't doubt her shadow would follow.

"Then what's with the silent treatment? You still angry about your wrist?" Troy asked, catching up with her and carrying the full can of water as if it weighed nothing. "I apologized for that."

"I haven't been angry with you since they hauled your ass up those stairs."

"Then what's your problem with me?"

Shayne came to an abrupt halt when they reached the large planter Troy had been using as a pillow when she'd found him. She pointed to the potted plants in a silent order.

"I don't have a problem with you other than the fact that you're here," she told him, her attention fixated on the water flowing out of the spout of the can instead of addressing the man holding it.

"What's that supposed to mean?" He stopped watering the plant and looked at her.

"All of it," she told him. "The water," she huffed. "Empty the can."

"You'll drown it," Troy argued. His stance told her that it was another dare.

"Since when did you become an expert on plants? They teach you that in boot camp?"

"Can you two hold it down? I'm on the phone." Cat poked her head out the front door.

"Yes, ma'am. Sorry."

Cat looked more amused than angry when she shut the door. Shayne, however, was pissed. She'd worked herself into a stupid, silly snit over nothing but her selfish desire for isolation.

"I've grown accustomed to my own company. Now I can't do my job. I can't even go off and sulk by myself," she said, narrowing her eyes at him.

Troy emptied the remaining contents of the watering can into the planter. "Sulking?" Troy snorted. "Is that what you were doing?"

"Hadn't gotten a good start before you interrupted me."

Troy walked several steps behind the obstinate woman as they returned to the dense garden. The last time he'd visited, Steve and Josie were living in the house while they looked for their own place. Troy knew from emails prior to his injury that the residence had been rezoned for business, and that Steve and Josie had a home nearby. The old Copeland place now served as an office to both Cat's garden center and Steve's investigations and security business. Everyone had moved on and appeared to be thriving. Everyone but Troy. He'd been headed in the opposite direction. Currently, he was stuck in neutral, which was actually an improvement.

His immediate issue was to figure out how to work with the recalcitrant female currently swinging her hips in front of him. She was a conundrum. His apology for hurting her had been quickly accepted. If she had a problem with his appearance, she hid it well. Then again, maybe she had a problem with drunks. No one could blame her for that. He didn't have much use for them, either—even when he was one of their ranks.

"Did I apologize for the condition I was in when you found me?"

"You mean drunk?"

The woman didn't split any hairs. "Yes. I'm not drinking anymore."

"Good." She sounded sincere. "I spent enough time tending bar to know it can be an easy crutch," Shayne added, as she sank into one of the chairs in the small gazebo at the center of the garden.

"You worked in a bar?" Troy didn't follow her into the

small ornamental structure but stood on the crushed shell below the steps, eye level with Shayne.

"Why don't you finish weeding," she suggested, ignoring his question. "When you're done, come find me, and I'll teach you a few things about pruning."

"What's a bartender doing working in a garden center?" He wasn't specifically defying Colt's instruction. He was curious, though. How did a woman go from tending bar to digging in the dirt?

"You have a problem with that?"

Was she hiding something or just plain hiding? Curiosity was an elixir. He'd find a way of learning the secret. A puzzle would keep his mind busy and off his unexpected physical awareness to the enigma now staring at her nails.

"So, your plan is to sit on your ass?" he asked.

She grinned, and the unexpected smile knocked the wind from him.

"Sure. Why not? I'm on the mend, remember?" She displayed her wrapped wrist. "Don't yank out any full-grown plants and we're good."

"You plan on doing your nails while I'm working?" he asked, getting his voice back along with a bit of his long-lost sense of humor.

"Do I look like a woman who worries about a manicure?" She showed off her hands with her clipped, dirty, unadorned fingernails.

She didn't paint her toenails either, he'd bet. He suspected she styled her short, russet-colored hair with her fingers instead of a comb or brush. She wore no makeup. It wasn't necessary. Her face was smooth and tanned. The sun-bronzed skin accented the golden flecks in her whiskey-colored eyes. Her baggy shorts and loose cotton shirt were, to be kind, less than flattering. Her entire build was more boyish than shapely. It was no wonder he'd mistaken her for a boy in his drunken rage.

"You don't spend much time on yourself, do you?"

"Is that supposed to be an insult?" Shayne's eyes narrowed as she straightened in her chair.

"No." Troy almost smiled, again. She looked ready to take him on. "Just an observation. It's kind of refreshing." The admission surprised him.

The women he bedded usually wore cloying perfumes, elaborately decorated acrylic nails, and cosmetics so thick he imagined some of them had to scrape it off with a trowel. He hadn't cared. They were looking for a quick lay with a Green Beret. A slogan he should have had tattooed on his biceps instead of the homages to his Gaelic heritage.

The parade of willing women had been a diversion from the battlefield. The sensual game had allowed him to retreat from the nightmares of war. He'd always made it clear he was promising nothing more than a single entertaining evening of casual sex. Bed sport with no encores. Assuming a woman could look past his disfigurement, he no longer had the desire for a distraction. Instead, his desire was to make things right—an unattainable goal.

"Hey, Mac." Shayne snapped her fingers. "You still with me?"

"Huh?"

"If you're done daydreaming and insulting me, go finish the weeding. Afternoon storms are looming. Chop. Chop."

Troy did crack a smile then. The woman didn't take any prisoners. She shot straight from the hip.

42

8

Shayne was enjoying her solitary time when she heard the rear door to the building shut. The gazebo was surrounded by the lush garden, so while she couldn't see who had exited the business, she had a good idea who it was and that she was headed in Shayne's direction. She sighed. So much for her quiet time.

"Where's Troy?" Cat asked as she popped out of the organized jungle, confirming Shayne's suspicion.

"Over there"—Shayne pointed toward the far corner of the garden—"tackling weeds. He doesn't need a prison guard watching over him."

"I thought you might have buried him under the compost pile the way you two were going at it."

"I am sorry about that. We're not what you'd call simpatico."

"Why is that?"

Shayne shrugged. "My fault, I guess," she admitted. "I'm having a hard time relegating my duties. It surprises the hell out of me, but I love working with my hands and getting them dirty. I'll do better."

"Your position is safe here as long as you want it," Cat assured her. "But your injury gave us the excuse to put Troy to work. He has issues to resolve." Cat paused. "Can I ask a favor? Would you stick with him when one of us can't?"

"Are you afraid he'll hurt himself or start drinking again?" Shayne asked, suddenly concerned. Troy didn't strike her as the type who would harm himself, but what did she know about the damage his tour had done?

"Drinking was his way of hurting himself. He admitted to Colt that he came here for support. We need to keep him busy and talking."

"I can do the first but the second may be difficult. He's about as talkative as a garden gnome."

"I've never known Troy to have a problem carrying on a conversation, particularly with a woman." Cat cocked a brow. "He's been known to charm more than socks off them."

"Maybe that's because he doesn't think of me as a woman."

"He said that?"

Cat's jaw clenched and her eyes pinched as she looked toward the corner of the property where Shayne had left Troy. Uh-oh.

"No," Shayne answered the question quickly before Cat's temper had time to reach a boil. "He made a comment regarding my lack of concern for my appearance. Look at me." Shayne plucked at her baggy T-shirt in an effort to defuse Cat's simmering temper. "I'm a mess. I look more like a street urchin than one of the women who probably chase after him."

Whatever Cat was thinking as she rose from the chair, she kept to herself, but her frown had been replaced with an impish grin. "He's a good guy, and you don't give yourself enough credit. I'm sure you'll work it out."

"He seems to be intrigued by my background," Shayne said as they rose from their chairs. "I can keep him entertained by dropping a breadcrumb here and there. A puzzle might be what he needs to keep his mind occupied."

"Everyone in this group is the curious type," Cat commented as she stepped off the gazebo. "I've got orders to place if I want to get plants in for the Mason project. Make sure you and Troy drink that water." She indicated the bottles she'd placed on the table. "I don't want either of you getting dehydrated."

"Will do." Shayne uncapped one of the waters as she shouted toward a section of the garden where she'd left her ward. "Hey, Mac," she barked. "Get your ass over here. It's time for your next lesson."

Shayne didn't miss Cat's smirk as she walked toward the office. What was that about?

TROY'S INSTRUCTIONS for weeding had been simple and quick, but the project had been easier said than done. Shayne had identified weeds, pointed out the plants he wasn't to touch, and left him to his task. The loss of one eye affected his depth perception. That loss had improved over the months, but still there were times his fingers reached for one of the green invaders and he missed the intended target entirely. What should have been a mind-numbing, demeaning chore of pulling weeds had become a physical therapy exercise in orientation. Each time he'd grab one of those invading suckers on the first try, he gave himself a mental fist pump.

Now he was being schooled in the "art of pruning." This task had become a lesson in concentration. He wasn't having as much success at this one. Shayne was too close. So close he could smell her fragrance. The mixture of feminine perspiration and whatever spicy bath soap she'd used had him imagining them sharing a shower and sliding the bar of soap into interesting places. Listening to the cadence of her voice mesmerized him. While her manner of speech was educated, she'd tended bar and was happy digging in the dirt. Naturally intuitive, she kept to his right as she tutored him, and did so without asking or commenting about his limited vision.

She was a puzzle. Troy felt a rush. He used to thrive on challenges. Now he had two. Redeeming his shattered soul, assuming that was possible, and figuring out the mysterious woman currently waving a pair of pruning shears under his nose.

"Mac, you in there?"

His lips curled up in a smile. "This would be a lot easier if we grabbed some hedge trimmers and just went at them," he replied, knowing the statement would irk her. Pricking her temper could be enlightening as well as entertaining. She touched the pruning shears to his chin, but sadly, didn't take the bait. Instead, she pulled back and began to meticulously explain the reasons pruning with a sharp tool prevented disease and how each cut could encourage growth. He could feel his smile growing while she talked. He congratulated himself on withholding a laugh.

Shayne must have noticed his amusement, because she brought the shears close to his chin for a second time. "You're here to learn how to care for plants, not destroy them."

"We both know this is temporary. My penance for

injuring your wrist," he reminded her, cautiously watching the shears. If they got any closer, he'd have another scar to add to the ones already littering his face.

"And mine for being stupid enough to care whether you needed help. I've told Cat I'm not happy handing my chores over to you, but I promised her I'd keep you busy. I'm doing this for her, not you. If you want to crawl back into the bottle, there's the gate. Go find one. If you're serious about staying sober, then it should be a snap to deal with my snarky attitude for as long as I'm relegated to this sling. Do I make myself clear?"

Troy couldn't remember any woman ever being as brutally blunt as this one—assuming his mother didn't count. And whether Shayne knew it or not, she'd just given him another reason to stay sober.

"Give me the damn shears," he said, holding out a remarkably steady hand.

WHEN THE PREDICTED rain rolled in, the two of them ducked inside. Shayne ran her hand through her wet hair as she and Troy walked toward the front of the building. Two large picture windows framed the entry door and looked out onto the parking area that faced Periwinkle Way. Both were currently being pelted with fat, heavy raindrops. The lobby walls were adorned with the awe-inspiring photographs Colt and Gib had taken of various plants in the garden. A small grouping of comfortable chairs was nestled in the far corner should any clients of Cat's or Steve's businesses need a place to wait.

As Shayne had expected, the lobby was empty. Most people in southern Florida ran their errands and made appointments early in the day this time of year to avoid the afternoon downpours. Opposing genres of music emanated from opposite ends of the former ranch-style home. Cat preferred spa-like music when she worked on designs, while Steve normally had classic rock pumping from his office when he was alone. Troy didn't say a word as he headed toward the music of Bruce Springsteen.

With the afternoon thunderstorms rolling in, Shayne was done for the day. She considered telling Cat she was leaving but decided not to disturb her. The Zen music flowing from her office meant Cat was in her *zone*. Shayne glanced toward Steve's office. The door was closed. If anyone needed her, they knew where to find her. She returned to the kitchen, grabbed her keys and umbrella from the cabinet underneath the microwave, and headed out the back.

Because Shayne's job didn't require her to interact with customers, her working hours were not set in stone. Her job was to tend the garden. Period. When her work was done, she was free to go. The single restriction that had been placed on her was that she never be at the business alone. After stumbling onto Troy, she wouldn't be violating that request again.

Instead of heading home, Shayne sought out the shelter of the gazebo. She wanted some quiet time in the garden. Watching the storm through the window of her small apartment wasn't the same as experiencing it within the realm of this tiny ecosystem. She relaxed at the sound of the rain as it slapped against the large leaves of the Colocasia plants. The scent of jasmine filled her nostrils as the tiny white flowers were jostled from the delicate grip of the mother plant by the wind. The air was so thick that it wrapped itself around her. Her worries began to slip away. No pressure to identify a mysterious man. No bombs exploding. No stench of burned flesh. Instead, she inhaled the aroma of damp earth as the shower began to cool the air. Shayne pulled a second chair closer then rested her feet on it. Only then did she allow her tension to wash away with the rain.

A BRIGHT FLASH of lighting was followed by a booming clap of thunder that shook the pictures on the wall. The lights flickered then went dark. In the silent seconds that followed, Troy cocked his head toward the door. "Did you hear that?" he asked Steve. They'd been tossing around ideas for one of Steve's prospective security clients when the power went out.

"Everybody heard that."

"No, not the thunder." Troy raised a finger toward his lips. With the loss of power, the air-conditioning had stopped humming along with the music. "I think someone screamed." Troy pushed off his chair.

"It came from out back," Troy said to Steve, who'd followed him out the door. There was only one person he could think of who would be anywhere near the garden in this weather.

"Where's Shayne?" Troy asked Cat as she came out of her office, slapping an unlit flashlight against her palm.

"She should be home by now. Why?"

Adrenaline had Troy double-timing it to the rear. The door whipped out of his hand and slammed against the outside wall of the building as the wind caught it. The simple metal chain connected to the doorframe snapped under the force of the gust.

Troy dove into the small hurricane. Rain pelted him

with such force it stung as it beat against his skin. He shouted Shayne's name but heard nothing but the rumble of thunder and the rain as it pounded against the dense foliage. The garden wasn't large—less than a quarter of an acre—but its wandering paths resembled a Victorian maze, giving anyone who explored it the feeling that it went on forever.

"Get back in the house, Cat," Troy said as Steve and Cat followed him out into the garden. "Lock the door. See if you can reach Shayne."

As the door slammed shut, Troy shouted to Steve, "I'll go this way." He pointed at the path that led to the gazebo.

Steve took off in the opposite direction.

Troy sprinted toward the small shelter where Shayne had rested earlier. He heard Steve call out her name, but there was no response. She'd probably gone home. They were getting soaked for no good reason. He quickly dismissed the assumption. Whether it was Shayne that screamed or someone else, he recognized the sound of distress. He quickly rounded the tall planting bed and raced to the gazebo. The solid structure was untouched, but the table and chairs had been tossed around by the vicious wind. The sturdy furniture hadn't been a match for the microburst that had blasted them.

He took the two steps onto the platform in one stride, tossing a chair behind him and onto the pathway to join its mate, but there was no sign of Shayne anywhere near the structure. His sneakers slapped against small puddles of water dotting the garden's path as he approached the gate at the back of the property.

"Nothing?" Troy asked Steve as he shot out from a second garden path. Both of them were soaked. The violence of the storm was letting up but the rain continued to pour.

"Nothing," Steve said. "Shayne might be home."

"I know I heard something..." Troy stopped midsentence as an opened umbrella cartwheeled past them and continued down the alley.

9

The instant his feet hit the ground, Troy spotted a lump of clothing near the end of the narrow alley. He sprinted the short distance then knelt next to the unconscious woman. There was a small, jagged wound on her temple. Blood, mixed with rainwater, trickled into her short hair. Her head rested on her outstretched arm. Her injured wrist lay against her chest, as if protecting it.

Troy would have preferred to assess Shayne's injuries without moving her, but the weather was his deciding factor. Lightning still lit up the nearby skies as a light rain continued. He carefully lifted her into his arms.

"I'll take her."

"I've got her," Troy snapped at Steve as he retraced his steps to the garden center. It rankled him that his friend didn't trust him on an issue as small as carrying a woman to safety.

Troy walked through the open garden gate and took the shortest path to the building. He stepped aside when they reached the rear door so that Steve could open it. Troy carried Shayne into the breakroom and kitchen area of the building. He lay her on the small love seat and tucked a throw pillow under her head. The silence in the room registered with him.

Steve whispered something to Cat. Whatever it was, she didn't like it. She stomped from the room with a worried look on her face. Steve pulled out his phone and said a few short words to the party at the other end before shoving the phone back into his pocket.

"Did you call 911?" Troy asked.

"No, that was Rick."

"What the hell is going on? Why didn't you call the paramedics?"

"We will if we have to," Steve said but didn't volunteer anything further. He was concerned about something. His set jaw and scowl telegraphed as much.

"You didn't have a problem the day I showed up," Troy pointed out.

"That was different." Steve didn't reflect any further.

Cat returned to the room with a first-aid kit and damp cloth. The instant the cloth was placed on Shayne's forehead her eyes flew open, and her legs pumped frantically as she scurried up the cushions of the small couch. Her feet continued to pedal after her back hit the wall.

"It's okay, Shayne. It's okay," Cat said. "You're safe."

Troy took a step forward but Steve stopped him. "Give her a minute."

Cat continued to repeat the mantra as Shayne's ragged, gasping breaths tapered off to gulps of air then dropped another notch into deep, long pulls for oxygen. Sweat beaded on her brow and upper lip. Her fingers trembled.

"What the hell?" Troy muttered.

"You don't have to be a soldier to suffer from PTSD," Steve told him.

The comment shouldn't have broadsided Troy, but it did. How did he, of all people, not recognize the signs? Shayne's reactions were symptomatic for someone suffering from the disorder. Two hours ago, he would have never suspected it. The woman who had been barking at him didn't come close to resembling the one barely holding herself together.

"What happened to her?"

Steve ignored the question. Instead, he joined Cat at Shayne's side. Troy didn't move for Shayne's sake. She remained skittish. Crowding her wouldn't help the situation.

While Steve and Cat checked her for injuries, Shayne sat rock-still with one exception—the golden flecks in her pupils seemed to dance as her eyes darted from the windows, to the room, and then went back to the windows again. She was scared, but after her initial panic attack, she was doing a damn good job of concealing it. Eventually, her breathing slowed to a normal rhythm. As Cat pressed antiseptic against her wound, Shayne winced. She was fully back in the present.

"What were you doing out there in that storm?" Cat asked Shayne before Troy could pepper her with questions.

"It was just raining when I left here," Shayne replied. "I stopped in the gazebo so I could listen to it. I do that sometimes. I hope that's okay."

"I don't mind, but you should have come back inside until that storm cell passed."

"I dozed off. The storm woke me," she answered without making eye contact. She looked embarrassed by the admission. Her fingers trembled slightly as she stared at them.

"You screamed," Steve pointed out. "What made you scream?"

Troy had the urge to uproot Cat, push Steve aside, and

pull Shayne into his arms. She was still frightened. Damn it. He fought the unfamiliar desire and stood his ground.

"Once I was awake, I headed home. I heard something in the bushes as I passed them in the alley. I didn't think too much of it, but I looked to make sure it wasn't some critter that required a wide berth. As I turned, a man jumped out. I screamed. I think I screamed again when he raised his hand. There was something in it. I ducked." Shayne touched the side of her head. "I guess he got in a pretty good lick, because that's all I remember. Did any of you see him?"

"No one was around when we got to you," Steve answered. "Can you describe him?"

"He was wearing one of those dark, heavy rain ponchos. The hood was pulled low over his head. His face was in shadows. I couldn't see it."

Shayne wrapped her arms around her waist and began to rock. Something had happened to her, and she was flashing back to that event. Troy recognized the symptoms all too well now. He was ready to put a stop to the questioning when Cat spoke up.

"That's enough," she scolded Steve. "Come on, Shayne. Let's get you into some dry clothes."

"Rick will be here shortly. We'll talk more then," Steve told them as they left the room.

Troy watched the interaction between the three unfold. They knew Shayne's history. He was the outsider here, but his training told him that Shayne had been involved in something big. And that *something* had followed her to Sanibel.

"What's going on?" Troy demanded as soon as the two women were out of the room.

"Later. We need to check the area. You recon the garden and the alley." Steve looked at Troy. "I want to check next door, since Gib and Colt are gone. Meet me where you found Shayne."

Adrenaline pumped through Troy as soon as Steve had given him the assignment. You'd think he was marching into battle, not looking for a trespasser. *Trespasser.* That was putting it lightly. Whoever he was, he'd assaulted Shayne. Troy knew nothing of her background, but he'd put enough together to guess that her reason for being on the island had something to do with her safety.

Troy searched the garden then hopped the fence a second time. The rain had stopped, allowing puddles to form and fill depressions in the mixture of sand and dirt where he'd found Shayne. The depressions were the result of footprints. They were too big to belong to her. There was no sign of her passage. Her lighter weight and casual stride had been washed away.

Troy's blood rushed through his veins as he followed the tracks until they disappeared on the asphalt of the street that ran perpendicular to the alley. *Damn.* Troy made his way back, scanning the area as he did. When he reached the spot where Shayne had fallen, he noted the shrubbery that lined the alley had been disturbed. Several small branches had been snapped off the bushes that lined the east side of the drive. Moving the branches aside, he saw deeper depressions in the soil. Someone had been waiting for her.

Again, he scanned the alley. This time he spotted a second, less distinctive, set of prints. They were softer, therefore, harder to discern but they were there. Interestingly, they came from the opposite side of the shell drive and followed the first set of prints out of the alley. Had the two planned to double-team her? Had the second person run when Shayne screamed? Troy rose from his haunches to take a closer look at the resting place of the second individual when Steve returned.

"What is it?"

"This was an ambush," Troy spat out the words, indicating the broken branches that led to the depressed muddy soil behind the shrubbery. "And he wasn't alone."

10

Shayne was holding a cold compress to her head when Steve knocked on Cat's office door and asked if Shayne could manage the walk to his office. The question irritated her now that her fear had subsided. Silently, she got to her feet and walked past him, despite her rubbery legs. She managed the hallway but dropped into one of the guest chairs before her legs outed her. Her heart was racing. She'd thought this shit was behind her.

"Do you need a doctor?" Rick asked as he settled into the chair next to her. He lifted the cool cloth, taking a long look at her injury. "You don't need stitches, but Steve said you were out for a few minutes."

"I have a headache, which I suspect is going to get bigger, but I'll pass on another doctor." She'd reached her limits for doctors and hospitals. She wanted to know what the hell was going on. "Can we not argue about my head? It just makes it hurt more."

Rick didn't push further.

"You think this has something to do with the bombing?"

Shayne asked Rick, jumping over any preliminary questions and diving directly into what she feared most.

"I don't know."

"Not a particularly comforting answer. You suspect there's more to this than a simple mugging, or you'd have a posse with you."

"We've got units checking the area," Rick told her. "I understand you saw one man in the alley?"

"Yes." She noticed the two men exchanged glances, but neither followed up on the question.

"Did you recognize him? Can you describe him?" Rick asked.

"Like I told Steve, I didn't see his face. Nothing struck me as familiar. I wouldn't recognize him anymore than I can the man from the country club." She threw her hands in the air then grimaced when her sprained wrist flopped against her thigh. She'd removed the sling so she could slip on some clean, dry clothes she kept at the nursery for emergencies. Due to the dirty and sometimes wet nature of her job, there were times when it was necessary for fresh clothing.

"Hell, as a witness, I suck," she admitted, once the stinging subsided.

As they talked, Steve had one eye on his computer monitor. He clicked the mouse a few times. "Nothing on the surveillance cameras, but I didn't think there would be. After reconnoitering the area, I didn't think anyone had passed this place after Shayne left."

Rick plucked his phone off his belt. He scrolled through his contacts, punched a number, then put the phone on Steve's desk as it began to ring.

"Hernandez." His voice boomed across the room from the phone's speaker. Even though she'd briefly wondered if the attack might be connected to the bombing, she was surprised to hear the voice of one of the FBI agents who'd worked on the case. She hadn't talked to him or his partner, Morgan, since she'd left Tampa.

"Rick Wilcowski here. Shayne and Steve are with me," Rick informed the agent. "There was an incident."

"What sort of incident?"

"I'll let them explain. I arrived after the fact," Rick told him.

"Where are you now?" Hernandez asked.

"My office," Steve answered. "Shayne was assaulted."

"Is she okay?"

"A knock on the head. She says she's fine." Rick shot a quick look at Shayne.

"Tell me what happened."

"Shayne was on her way home when someone jumped her in the alley. Troy and I didn't waste any time getting outside after we heard her scream. She was already on the ground. No one else in sight." Steve's voice had an edge to it Shayne hadn't remembered hearing before.

"Troy?" Hernandez asked.

Shayne ground her teeth in spite of the fact that she'd known this would be a long, tedious conversation as soon as Hernandez had identified himself. No matter which agent Rick had reached, he would tear each statement apart.

"Troy McKenzie. He was here last summer when Cat had that issue. He's out of the service now," Steve explained.

"Can you trust him?"

"Yes, we'll bring—"

"Whoa. Whoa. Whoa," Shayne interrupted, holding her hand up to Steve. "Let's back this bus up." Her wits were returning—and along with them, questions. "Can they trust Troy with what, Agent Hernandez?" Her head hurt, her wrist throbbed, and she was officially out of patience.

"The circumstances behind your move to Sanibel."

"Hell, I'm no longer sure what those circumstances were," Shayne snapped. She looked at the two men in the room. For the time being, she would assume they were in the dark too. "If you'd like to explain, I think we're all ears."

"One issue at a time," Hernandez suggested.

"Okay. Pick one," Shayne lashed out, her ire directed toward the phone on the desk. "Do you want to talk about what happened to me today? Why Troy needs to be trustworthy, or perhaps you can tell us why you were so helpful in finding me a place to live when I decided to leave Tampa?" She no longer believed it was the norm for the FBI to be so involved in relocating a victim.

Steve's cheeks puffed out and his eyebrows rose. Rick remained stoically silent, leaving Hernandez out on the limb with a saw. Shayne waited.

"What happened today?" Hernandez asked, a heartbeat later.

"Okay. Door number one," Shayne declared, maintaining control of the conversation. "We can start with that." She proceeded to explain to Hernandez what Steve and Rick already knew.

"You didn't get a look at this guy, either?" Hernandez asked.

Shayne sucked in some air and let it out slowly. What the hell had happened to her patience? She took another second before responding, hoping it would take the edge off her rising temper. It didn't.

"I know you must think I'm either blind or stupid, but no, I didn't see this guy's face. The man at the country club had his back to me. This guy wore a heavy, dark, hooded poncho. It concealed his face. My best analogy would be the Caped Crusader. I seriously doubt that Ben

Affleck or George Clooney is stalking me but one can always hope."

Hernandez ignored her sarcasm. "He didn't say anything?"

Shayne wanted to reach through the phone and grab him by the lapels. "No. We didn't strike up a conversation. All I can tell you is that he was Caucasian and taller than me. I was focused on the hand that was raised as he came at me. I ducked and screamed. That's all I remember."

"Steve? What did you see?" Hernandez asked.

"Troy was the first to get to her. We'd all assumed Shayne had gone back to her apartment until we heard the scream. I went one way. Troy went the other. Neither of us saw anyone."

"How the hell is it that three Green Berets—make that four with McKenzie—couldn't keep one woman safe?"

"Fuck you," Steve growled, pushing away from his desk. "Rick and Colt weren't here. Now, what the hell did you hold back about Shayne?"

"Nothing."

"Bullshit."

"That's enough," Rick broke in, silencing the room.

"Will someone please tell me what is going on?" Shayne shot out of her chair. Her ears buzzed. Her skin crawled.

"Well, *Special Agent* Hernandez?" Steve asked. "Any answers for the young lady?"

The silence that followed, tripped a switch somewhere deep within Shayne. She'd been an idiot—a deaf, mute, and blind idiot. She'd jumped at the FBI's assistance to relocate her. She hadn't questioned the reasons behind placing her on the Southwest Florida coast, surrounded by former Special Forces soldiers. Stupid.

"Where are you going?" Steve asked when she headed for the door.

"To the bathroom," she lied. She made the excuse assuming neither man would follow her. "He might be more forthcoming if I'm not in the room."

She'd been ignoring the feeling that something was off. Why *was* she here? What did the feds know and had, or hadn't, shared with the people she now considered friends? Did the FBI think she was keeping secrets? She would never be able to identify the man who left the ballroom. Was she being protected, watched—or working herself up over nothing? Her mind and head whirled. She didn't have the patience or boots to wade through the pile of shit that was accumulating in Steve's office.

WHEN THE DOOR to Steve's office slammed shut, Troy was sitting next to Cat at the breakfast bar that had been part of the original kitchen in the Copeland's home. A few seconds later, Shayne stormed into the room, ignoring its occupants, and headed straight for the rear door. Troy knew women well enough to know the one marching by them was not a happy one.

"You okay?" Cat called out to her.

"Fine." Shayne waved off her employer. "I'll see you tomorrow."

Troy pushed away from the bar. He'd felt childishly rejected when he'd been excluded from whatever discussion was going on in Steve's office, but now he suddenly had a purpose.

"She shouldn't be leaving here alone." Troy slid to his feet.

"You read my mind," Cat agreed. "Go. She shouldn't be walking home alone."

～

TROY CAUGHT a glimpse of Shayne as she turned onto the side street. He sprinted to catch up with her.

"You shouldn't have left on your own," he said when he reached her side.

"Why do you keep intruding on my sulks?" she asked.

"Good timing, I guess." He fell into step on her left. He moved his head from side to side, surveying the surrounding area before taking a quick look at the sky. The rain had stopped, but the sun was fighting a losing battle against dark clouds rolling in from the east.

"Not in my opinion," she snarled. "Go away."

"After I see you to your door," he responded. This time, he was dead serious.

"What are you? A gentleman or a guard dog?"

"Why would you think you need guarding?" he asked.

"I don't know. Do you?" She pulled up suddenly, turning to face him.

"I have no idea," he answered. The gold flecks in her eyes shimmered, even in the limited sunlight.

"Shit." Shayne's shoulders slumped. "You're of no use to me at all."

"I resent that." Troy tried to sound indignant as he slapped the flat of his hand against his chest. The veiled attempt to lift her spirits covered his reaction to the direct hit she'd landed.

"Tough. If you can't answer my questions, you can't help me." Her voice held no malice, but her frustration was evident.

"You asked if I was a guard dog. You didn't say why you needed one," Troy said as they started walking again.

"That's what I'm trying to figure out."

"I'm confused." Troy shook his head. The woman was talking in circles.

"That makes two of us." Shayne stopped in front of a single-story stucco building. The long structure had four doors, each individually numbered with a deadbolt lock, indicating single residences. A metal mailbox with matching numbers rested on a pole close to the street, confirming his assumption. Shayne dug a key chain out of the pocket of her shorts. Apparently, she was home.

"Give me the key," he told her, holding out his hand.

"For God's sake," she swore, her fingers tightened around the small chain. "Are you attaching yourself to my hip?"

"I have no intention of leaving you until I know that you're safely tucked away. Now give me the damn key." Troy stood his ground. Why was he angry at Shayne? Anger wasn't anything new to him. He got angry often—too often since his discharge. He'd pick fights at every opportunity, but none of those flashes of anger were directed at anyone other than himself. Instead of sex, he'd turned to fighting to release the valve on his internal pressure cooker. A good fight also served as a means of self-punishment, since he couldn't literally kick the shit out of himself. Why hadn't he let one of his targets pound him into the ground and leave him there? In hindsight, the soldier in him hadn't been trained to accept defeat. But none of that explained why he was angry at the stubborn woman currently staring him down.

Shayne stood with her hands on her hips, one fist still

wrapped tightly around the key. Thunder rumbled behind them.

"We're both going to get soaked if you don't give me the key. And if you think you can beat me to the door, think again." Other than some physical therapy with the mobility specialist at Brooks Army Medical Center, and his frequent bar fights, he hadn't done any training since his discharge. There was a good chance he was going to find out what sort of shape he was in because Shayne's determined stance told him she was ready to accept his challenge.

Then lightning lit up the sky, once again followed immediately by a clap of thunder. As the ground trembled beneath them, Shayne's eyes change from defiant slits to wide with fear. Apparently, loud noises were a trigger. He could relate.

"Give me the key. Let's get you inside where it's safe."

11

Shayne unrolled her fingers, allowing Troy to take the ring that held the keys to her home, office, and bike lock. Her hands shook, so inserting the key into the door lock wouldn't have been a sure bet. Twitches and shakes during the day were something new. Normally, she only battled them after one of her nightmares. She wasn't looking forward to the night ahead. Would she now associate every storm with the attack or an explosion? Would she have dueling nightmares? One from the night of the bombing and another from today's attack? What a delightful thought.

"Number one," she told him, indicating the door at the end of the structure with a nod. The apartment building was nondescript—old Florida-style with stucco plastered on cinder block. It had been painted pink, which had paled considerably under the tropical sun. A white Spanish-tile, pitched roof, in desperate need of a good pressure wash, hung over the entrances. Currently, the parking spaces in front of the building were empty. Shayne had not used the crushed shell lot since shortly after her arrival. Her second-hand bike was parked in the middle of her living room.

"I'll check the place out." Troy walked past her as he unlocked the door.

"I don't think that will be necessary." Embarrassingly, she heard her own sigh of relief when the solid door clicked closed behind her, a barrier between her and the thunder god. Shayne disarmed the security system using the keypad next to the door.

"Jeez Louise," Troy said. "A squirrel couldn't nest in here."

Safe now, Shayne could smile at the disbelief in his tone. She looked at the room that greeted him. The place had come furnished with a futon, which was tucked beneath the side window. An end table sat between the futon and a single chair in the corner. Also crammed into the L-shaped living area was a miniscule kitchen table with two chairs. She suspected someone had stolen them from an old-fashioned ice cream parlor. The kitchen contained a shrunken stainless-steel sink and a stove that looked oversized compared to the pint-sized refrigerator that fit under the counter. Her storage space consisted of two cabinets—one above the sink and another under the countertop. Above the stove, a shelf had been installed to hold a compact microwave. Her bicycle took up the middle of the room. The unit was more suitable for a hobbit. Definitely not for a man his size. Gulliver in Lilliput.

"As I said, I don't think you need to check the place out."

"What's through there?" Troy asked, pointing to the closed door next to the kitchen area.

"Closet. The bathroom is on the other side," she answered. "Don't worry about it. My phone would have notified me if there had been a break-in." She caught Troy's quick appraisal of the alarm before he walked through the entrance to the closet. The man was definitely stubborn.

"You're all clear," he confirmed, returning to the living room a few seconds later.

"Thanks," was all Shayne could think to say, embarrassment hopping to the forefront of her brain. The closet served as a pathway to the bathroom. It also doubled as a dressing area. A single rod for the few items she still owned that required a hanger. There was built-in shelving that took the place of a dresser as there was no room in the small studio for a cumbersome chest of drawers. Her shorts, jeans, and shirts took up the lower shelves. Her undergarments sat openly on the top shelf. She hadn't expected to receive company here. Ever. There was no way Troy could have missed her bras and panties on his way to the bath. Her skin warmed.

"Do all the units come equipped with an alarm system?" Troy eyed the keypad again.

"I have no idea. What you see is what I got." She hadn't questioned the accommodations that had been arranged on her behalf. She was grateful to have a place on the island she could afford.

Her guest visually circled the room a second time. Initially, the tight space had bothered her, but Shayne had grown accustomed to the postage-stamp-sized unit. With Troy in it, however, it again felt claustrophobic.

"You don't own a car?" he asked, indicating the bike.

"Not anymore."

"What the hell is going on with you?"

TROY WASN'T JUST FRUSTRATED by the cryptic answers but

genuinely curious about Shayne and the situation that surrounded her. His stance was intentionally intimidating. His single eye bored into hers with little effect. After today, he expected to get the full story on Shayne from his friends, but the subject of his interest was currently staring back at him. She was not easily intimidated.

"If you're that interested, Google me," she told him.

"What?"

"Google me. You've got a phone, don't you? Go ahead. It'll save me the trouble of explaining some things."

A crack of lightning followed by a roll of thunder had her reaching for the back of the small kitchen chair. Its scrolled wired backing appeared delicate compared to her steel grip. Scared. For all her bravado, she was scared. He waited until the color returned to her knuckles before he dug into the pocket of his jeans and found the one item he hadn't managed to leave behind after one of his binges. He keyed her name into its search engine and waited.

"Do you want some coffee?"

"Huh?" He glanced up from his cell.

"Would you like some coffee or something to eat?" she asked. She was standing in front of a coffeemaker that seemed too large for the short countertop. "No point in leaving until the storm passes," she added.

"I could use some coffee," he answered. Being hungry or marching through a storm was no big deal. Neither was a stranger to him, but he suspected her suggestion had more to do with the need for company or a reason to keep busy than any concern for him. Too bad. Shayne was beginning to intrigue him. Not that the interest would be reciprocated.

As Shayne pulled items from the compact refrigerator, Troy dropped into the armchair as articles began to pop up under her name. He clicked on one from the *Tampa Bay*

Times. A bombing. *Christ.* She'd been the victim of a bombing. Cold sweat beaded across his brow as images ran through his mind like a slow-motion video. He flinched as he instinctively reached for the patch over his eye.

"You okay?" Shayne asked as he continued to stare at the screen. "Troy?"

"Yeah. I'm fine," he snapped, coming out of his fugue state.

"I didn't think to warn you. My story must hit close to home." No one had told her what had caused Troy's injuries, but it wasn't hard to guess.

"I said I'm fine," Troy replied. He'd found that he hated the pity as much as he did the stares.

Shayne eyed him closely for another minute before she shrugged and resumed whatever she was doing. Troy forced himself to return to the article. There'd been a bombing at a country club in an elite suburb of Tampa. It must have been where Shayne had tended bar. The fact that he didn't remember the incident wasn't surprising. It had taken place in February, around the time he'd been discharged from the hospital. He'd done his best to hide from the world. If he had seen it on the news, he would have turned away or switched it off. Too reminiscent of his own experience.

He finished the article and glanced at the woman in the tiny kitchen currently occupied by something at the counter. He resumed his electronic search and clicked on another link. She'd been hospitalized, but her condition had been listed as good. A miracle, the press had dubbed her survival. Initial reports had attributed the explosion to a possible gas leak, but those were quickly thwarted as all evidence pointed to a bomb. No credible group had claimed responsibility, and the authorities had not offered any theories. As usual, the press had plenty of their own, most of them speculating that a congressman who had been present earlier in the evening had been the target. If true, Troy couldn't find any explanations in the online stories as to why the public official was considered a target. With no new developments and more interesting stories to chase, the news regarding the attack quickly faded.

"It's not cordon bleu, but it should fill the hole." Shayne set a plate with a ham sandwich and chips on the small table next to him. Whether she'd ignored Troy's declination of food or didn't hear him, it had given her something to do.

"Are you in some sort of protection program?" he asked, then took large bite out of the sandwich. He was hungrier than he'd realized.

"You were able to Google me, weren't you?"

Right. No way they'd let her keep her given name if she were under government protection.

"Do you know who was behind the...bombing? What do you know about the investigation? Why are you here?"

"No. Nothing. I don't know."

"You don't know why you're here?" She was one mystery on top of another.

"I needed a change in scenery. The FBI hooked me up with Cat and found this place for me to stay." She made a gesture to encompass the room. "I believed they were being helpful. Now, I'm wondering why."

"What's going on with you?" Troy asked. They didn't have muggers on Sanibel, particularly one who would wait in a thunderstorm in a seldom-used alley. She'd been targeted. The question was why?

"I'll work it out." Shayne reached for the door. "Thanks for walking me home."

"You okay with being alone?" Troy rose to his feet.

"I'd prefer it."

Troy had one hand on the doorknob when his phone rang. "McKenzie," he answered, stepping over the threshold. "I'm looking at her now. Why?"

Shayne's ears perked up.

"She's fine. I'm just leaving." He gave a quick nod to Shayne, pointed to the lock, then closed the door after him.

12

Troy listened to Steve while he waited to hear the snap of Shayne's lock.

"Don't leave," Steve told him. "Not until I get there to keep an eye on the place."

Walking away from the building, Troy stepped behind a large shrub. Some of its saucer-shaped leaves still held water from the rainstorm that had passed. The dense bush shielded him from the front of the building. "I'm out the door but have her place in sight. What the hell is going on?"

"Stay put. I'll be there in a minute."

"Why don't you bring me a gun and I'll stand watch? I don't have anything better to do, and you've got a business to run. An explanation would be nice."

"I don't know if that's such a good idea," Steve hesitated.

"What? The gun, me staying, or the explanation?" Troy shot back. He waited, gripping the phone tightly as the silence continued on the other end of the line. "If you don't trust me, say so."

"I'll bring you a weapon," Steve agreed.

The concession on Steve's part was a victory, and

perhaps, a veiled invitation back into the fold. Troy would take one and hope for the other. He texted Steve his exact location then waited.

Steve arrived on foot a few minutes later. He handed a small canvas sack to Troy. "There's a thermos of coffee, some water, a flashlight, and insect repellent in there," Steve told him. "Or you could knock on her door and ask if you could spend the night."

Was that sarcasm Troy heard? The question was on Troy's lips when Steve slapped his SIG Sauer into his palm.

"Where did this come from?" Troy had known it was his personal weapon the instant the metal touched his skin. He could field-strip this baby in the dark.

"You left it in your duffel at the VFW post in Fort Myers. The bartender dug through the bag when no one returned to claim it. They found Colt's business card inside."

Troy was grateful to the vets he'd tripped over since his release. Once he'd decided to seek out Colt and the others on Sanibel, he'd hopped from one VFW or American Legion post to another. Some had given him shelter and food. Others a drink. *God.* It was a miracle he'd managed to land on Colt's doorstep.

Troy checked the magazine on the P320. "Can you at least tell me why she needs guarding? Am I to keep her in or someone out?"

"Both," Steve told him. "She's not to leave unless one of us is with her. She shouldn't have any visitors so if you see someone approaching the place, stop them and call me or Rick."

Those instructions begged for answers. "Come on, Steve. What the hell is going on with her? Does it have something to do with the incident in Tampa?"

"How'd you learn about that?"

"Google. She can't be in a witness protection program if her name is plastered all over the web. She knows something's up."

"What are you? Her father confessor now?" Steve cocked his head, indicating the stucco building.

"Digging in the dirt doesn't make her stupid. She strikes me as the opposite. And," Troy added, "I wouldn't be the least bit surprised if she didn't bolt. She's scared."

"You make sure she doesn't."

"Why? What is going on?" Troy asked again, keeping his voice low. Shayne didn't need to know she was being watched. It would make her all the more anxious.

"We're working on getting answers."

Steve's response had an edge to it as he looked over his shoulder toward Shayne's unit. Was he angry at Troy or the situation? Didn't matter. "What more can you tell me about the bombing? How badly was she hurt? Is she okay?"

Steve studied Troy. "Why the concern? Why are you worried about her?"

Interesting question. Why *was* he worried about her? He barely knew Shayne. She was an intriguing mystery, and that alone drew him in. She reached out to help him, and he might have killed her for her effort had she not managed the knee to his privates.

Shayne was also in trouble. That much was obvious. He should walk away before history repeated itself. *Damn it.* Why couldn't he walk away?

"Who was that guy today?" Troy asked, ignoring Steve's question.

"No idea. It would help if she was better with details."

"What is that supposed to mean?" Troy slipped his gun into the waistband of his jeans.

"She can't identify either of her attackers."

"And that's her fault?" Troy still had some work to do on controlling his temper, but he wasn't shouting, and he'd managed to keep his fists at his side. Both an improvement.

"None of this is her fault," Steve said. "Look, we're still digging. We'll fill you in when we get more details, but if you want to take this watch, then we need to end this discussion before she gets wise to us. You picked a good spot," Steve continued, looking around. "I'll let Rick know where you are in case someone calls into the station to report a Peeping Tom." Steve smirked. "One of us will take over for you later."

"One more question. Did loud noises bother her before today?" Troy had seen her jump a half-dozen times since the attack. It would be helpful if he knew her triggers.

"Not that I've noticed or that anyone has mentioned. She's either been good at hiding her reaction or this is new." Steve glanced up at the clearing sky. "No more rain expected tonight. You both should be good."

With that, Steve slapped Troy on the shoulder and headed off in the direction he'd come.

Troy was mildly jacked at the realization he was part of the team again. He quickly settled into position. It felt good. He hadn't been on a mission since before...

No. he couldn't go there. The guilt and absolute terror of that day would overwhelm him. His mind had to be focused solely on keeping the woman living in that hamster cage safe from harm. If the team believed Shayne required protection, he would damn well make sure she got it. He had a goal now. It felt good.

Thin strips of light escaped through the closed blinds of the apartment windows as the sun set. Shayne occupied an end unit, so she had the benefit of an additional window on the side of the building. The bathroom, he'd noted earlier, had a small, opaque jalousie window set high in the shower wall. A child would have trouble fitting through it.

He'd accessed the bathroom through a passageway Shayne had referred to as a dressing room. Her description was exceptionally generous. It was a small, tight hallway connecting the living area to the bathroom. It contained shelves and a short rod for hanging clothes above a stunted water heater. He hadn't missed the small quantity of clothing or the lingerie items. She didn't have much, which was a good thing considering the size of the place. He'd been in bedrooms that were bigger than her entire unit.

Troy settled back against the rough bark of a large pine tree, but not before he made a quick check of the ground for fire-ant mounds. It was a lesson he'd learned after his encounter with the vicious insects during his first visit to the island. The insect was well named. A bite from one was akin to being stabbed with a small, red-hot needle—and when the insects showed up, they tended to do so en masse.

His eyesight adjusted easily to the waning light. He'd swear the vision in his right eye was stronger—keener—since the loss of his left. His peripheral vision sucked, though. He was still learning how to compensate. Initially, his neck developed a crick from continually turning his head. The hospital's mobility specialist had developed exercises to help deal with the loss. He'd carried out the perfunctory tasks, directing his anger toward his therapist as he did. Now that his anger had tempered, he'd begun practicing some of the exercises and posture positions she'd pushed him through in spite of his nasty attitude. He owed the therapist an apology.

It was past midnight before Shayne's unit went dark.

Troy hoped she'd be able to find peace in her sleep. She'd been strung as tight as a piano wire when he'd left her hours earlier. He could relate to the terror each night might hold. Nightmares were a bitch. It was one of the reasons he'd volunteered to take this watch. It wasn't unusual for him to stay up for days in an effort to avoid the sights and sounds that invaded his sleep. He'd taken to binge-drinking when his body cried out for rest. Passed out, he rarely entertained the visions he'd been trying to bury. Now he'd either have to endure them or find a way to put them behind him. He wouldn't binge while in the company of his friends. Hopefully, not ever again.

Rick texted to say he'd take over the watch at midnight, but Troy had declined. It felt good to be focused. He wasn't anxious to give that up. Standing watch beat pulling weeds, though he expected he'd be at it again tomorrow—assuming Shayne didn't skip town.

Troy uncapped the second bottle of water. He was leaving the coffee untouched in the event he needed the jolt of caffeine in the early hours before dawn. The temperature had cooled with the sunset, but the summer humidity had yet to drop. He needed to stay hydrated. He also needed to pee. While he was accustomed to relieving himself outdoors, he didn't think the residents of Sanibel would approve. The other option was to knock on Shayne's door and ask to use her bathroom. Therefore, he had no choice.

As he watered a nearby shrub, the thought of interrupting Shayne's sleep stayed with him. What did she sleep in? Something sexy? Doubtful. She wasn't the sexy type. The underwear he'd seen on the shelf was as utilitarian as the clothes she wore to work each day. A T-shirt was more her style or nothing at all.

His cock stiffened. It obviously didn't care that Shayne didn't come close to the well-endowed women it usually homed-in on. Shayne wasn't unattractive, but he wouldn't call her sexy. With her cropped hair, heart-shaped face, and slim figure, he'd call her cute. He didn't do cute. Besides, his friends would kill him if he tried to seduce her.

Why the hell was his mind running in that direction? Nothing was going to happen, even if they both wanted it. It had been a long time since his mind had wandered to that physical need. While it was always an enjoyable diversion, he didn't need, or want, a diversion now. He was on an assignment. You didn't screw the assignment.

He carefully zipped up, all the while keeping his eye on Shayne's building. The compressor on her air-conditioning unit finally quieted. It must be close to freezing in there the way that thing had been running. Her nipples were probably hard.

For Christ's sake! What the hell was wrong with him? Sex should be the last thing on his mind. He snatched the opened bottle of water from the ground. He was half tempted to pour it over his head. Instead, he took a long pull, followed by a few deep breaths. He needed to get the head on his shoulders in gear and keep the brainless one tucked away. It was going to take some doing now that he had pictured Shayne without any clothes.

Shayne may not be a beauty queen, but he hadn't missed her toned arms and shapely legs. He'd never been drawn to a woman simply because she was physically fit, although stamina in the bedroom was a plus. Pretty face? Check. Rounded breasts? Most definitely. If the woman's interest was mutual? Find the nearest respectable bed and have at it. Shayne was none of those things, so why did his dick keep pointing in her direction like a divining rod?

Maybe he was simply beginning to feel human again, and she was the only single female within radar range. Since his face could now easily slip into the infamous cantina scene in the original *Star Wars* movie, without the grotesque makeup, who the hell would want to share a bed with him unless he paid them? He wasn't that desperate. Sex had been an enjoyable distraction. Not a necessary one.

Before he could settle back into his position next to the large pine, he heard a muffled thump come from Shayne's unit. Silently and quickly, he made his way toward her apartment, but before he reached the building, a crash sounded from inside. He forgot all need for stealth and made a mad dash to her door. He tried the doorknob. Locked, of course.

"Shayne! Open the door," he said while keeping his voice low so he wouldn't bring his presence to the attention of the neighbors. Three cars were now parked in the lot in front of the building. The other tenants had come home to roost.

He waited, but when she didn't respond, he tapped on the door. "Shayne. It's Troy. Open up," he said a bit louder. If she didn't answer this time, he'd break it down. That would get half the island's attention.

A few seconds later he heard the lock click and the deadbolt unlatch. Shayne opened the door a crack and peeked through it. "What are you doing here?" she asked.

Troy didn't wait for the invitation he knew wouldn't be coming. He shouldered his way in. Shayne scurried back. He quickly shut and locked the door behind him.

"What the hell are you doing?"

Ignoring her question, he walked past her to check the dressing area and bathroom. Both were empty.

"Reset the alarm," Troy told her when he returned. He

noticed the small lamp that had sat on the end table earlier. It was now in several pieces on the floor next to the futon.

"Why?" Shayne stared back at him. Her injured arm rested against her waist. Her left arm, however, was planted firmly on her hip. A defiant stance in contrast to her pale skin and quivering lip.

"I'm not leaving, so you might as well set the alarm," Troy told her.

"It's the middle of the night. Have you been watching me?"

"I've been watching your *place*. Not you." If he had been peeking through the blinds, his earlier supposition would have been confirmed. She did sleep in a T-shirt, or had she taken the time to throw one on before she'd answered the door?

"You're being obtuse. What are you doing here at"—she glanced at the clock on the kitchen stove—"at two o'clock in the morning?"

"Making sure things stayed quiet. You were attacked today, remember?"

Shayne touched the small cut on the side of her head. "I remember. Has this been going on long? Has someone been watching since I arrived?"

"To my knowledge, this is the first time," Troy answered. "The guys were concerned after the attack on you. I offered to take the night watch. I don't sleep much." He looked at the remnants of the lamp again. "And it appears you don't sleep well."

"Bad dream," she explained. "I'm fine. You can leave now."

"I don't think so. Why don't you go back to bed? I'll take the chair." He silently started counting. He didn't get to three.

"The hell you will. This is my place. I say who stays here. Not you."

"True. But I can either stay inside or out. I'd prefer the air-conditioning to the bugs." Rubbing his arms, he asked, "Why do you have it so cold in here?"

"None of your damn business. Just leave."

Troy studied her for a few minutes. There was a lot going on in that head of hers. She could pretend bravado, but the hand on her hip was clenched, and the fingers attached to the injured wrist trembled slightly. She was frightened.

"If that's what you want," he told her. He wasn't going to press the issue of staying inside with her for several reasons. The least of which was the fact that he could see her nipples poking through the thin T-shirt. "Lock the door and reset the alarm when I leave. Yell if you need anything."

"You're serious? You're going to stick around outside?" Shayne asked, her eyes widened.

"It's either me or one of the others. Gib is scheduled to pick you up in the morning for work. He's supposed to text you before you leave."

"And you? Is he picking you up as well?"

"You weren't supposed to know I was out there. I heard the crash. Figured I'd better check on you. Steve will have my ass."

"Sit down," Shayne huffed as she walked over to the tiny refrigerator. "Do you want a water?" she offered, holding out a single-serve bottle.

"No, thanks. Let me retrieve my stuff. It will only take a second but lock the door behind me anyway."

"Now you're really scaring me."

He caught the tremor in her voice as he headed toward the door. *Damn.* First he was fantasizing about getting her naked and now he was scaring her. *Asshole.* He changed directions and grasped her by her shoulders. "It's going to be fine. We may not know what's going on yet but we'll find out. Until then, we have your back." He tightened his grip. "You got that?"

13

Shayne slumped against the locked door as she pressed her fisted hand over her galloping heart. Between Troy's sudden appearance and her night terror, it was racing. *Breathe.* She inhaled deeply, letting the breath out slowly. *Again.*

Her earlier premonition had come true. The bombing and today's attack had morphed into one terrifying dream. In it, a blast had sent her flying through the air, clothes aflame, only to be caught by a hooded man lurking in a dark rain. While she scrambled to escape the faceless monster, her healing wrist had hit the wall. The pain had yanked her from her nightmare, but it was preferable to being trapped with the demon.

The lamp from the end table lay in pieces on the floor next to the futon. Its shade was still attached but lay at an awkward angle, resembling a broken neck. She'd been frantic to escape her imagined tormentor. As she lashed out, she must have knocked the light to the floor. The crash had added another layer to her anxiety.

Now she had to deal with Troy. She preferred to come

down from the stratosphere without a witness. This freak show would make it twice he'd seen her at her worst. She resented being viewed as a bundle of nerves. She'd been confident once but had been zapped of that self-assurance. She'd done her best to hide that loss. She'd been making progress. Then today happened.

Even though she'd been expecting it, when the rap on the door came, Shayne jumped. *Get it together*, she lectured herself as she reached for the lock. She realized she was still in her worn-out sleep shirt. What the hell did it matter? Troy had made his opinion of her clear. She could probably dance nude in front of him and he wouldn't take notice. Still, it made her feel more vulnerable.

When she opened the door, Troy stepped inside so quickly she had to dodge him to get out of his way or get knocked over. She locked the door then activated the alarm system.

"Thanks," Troy said. "I didn't mean to scare you earlier. I heard the noise and couldn't let that go without making sure you were okay."

"It would be insulting if I got pissed because you cared enough to check on me. I guess we're even in that department."

"Far from it. How's the wrist?" He was looking at the arm she continued to cradle against her stomach.

"I banged it on the wall. It'll be fine. Why don't you take the futon?" she suggested, redirecting his focus. "I got a few hours' sleep. I won't be getting anymore tonight."

"Doesn't work that way," Troy said. "I stay awake while you sleep."

"I doubt I'll be nodding off again tonight between the dream and having you sitting next to me."

"I can move the chair over to the door," Troy suggested.

Shayne studied the muscular man. He may have recently spent some time in the hospital, but the stay hadn't cost him much lean meat. He was solid despite his pale skin and the hollow look in his eye. It was a wonder the old chair hadn't collapsed beneath his weight earlier in the evening.

"You're being stupid. Set this thing in an upright position for me." She indicated the extended futon. She had no intention of bending over so she could turn it back into a sofa. He'd already seen enough of her. Opening the futon into a bed had been a dumb move anyway. She'd known sleep would be fleeting after her day.

"I'll make some fresh coffee in a minute." First, she wanted to put on something so she wouldn't feel so exposed.

"You won't be fit for work tomorrow if you don't get some rest."

"That will make two of us, then." She didn't need to hear the lecture. It wasn't uncommon for her to go to work on a few hours' sleep. She'd survive. After closing the door to the dressing area behind her, she slipped on a pair of yoga pants and the single sweatshirt she possessed.

When she returned to the living area, the futon was still in its opened position. Troy was in the corner of the kitchen, returning the broom to its niche. All evidence of the broken lamp was gone.

"You don't follow directions very well, do you?"

He turned at the sound of her voice and glared at her. "Why did you get dressed? You need to get back in bed."

"If you think I'm going to start taking orders from you, you can take that chair and sit your ass back outside. I'm not going to sleep whether you're inside or out. Up to you where you stay." She was being a bitch. Too bad.

When he pulled the covers from her bed, she'd expected anger or irritation. Instead, she caught his brief smile. A butterfly took up residence in her stomach. "Toss the linens over the back of the chair for now. I'll put them away later," she told him, ignoring the unfamiliar feeling.

Once the coffee was started, she adjusted the thermostat.

"Do you always keep it like a walk-in cooler in here?" Troy asked, rubbing his arms.

"Only at night. I sleep better when I can snuggle under the covers." Did she just say "snuggle" while talking to a hot guy? "Coffee black, right?" She pulled two unmatched mugs from the cupboard.

"Black," he confirmed, lowering himself onto the upright futon.

"I don't imagine you have your choice of fancy creamers and such when you're deployed."

"I'm not in the army anymore, but no, you get used to drinking it black."

"Sorry. I seem to be good at bringing up bad memories." She grabbed the carafe and poured two cups.

"It looks like we both have some bad memories we deal with." He glanced at the spot the broken lamp had occupied on the floor.

"Yeah, well, I didn't go to war, and while I might have a few psychological scars, I don't carry physical ones to go with them." She added sugar with her usual copious amounts of cream to her cup. The real stuff. Crossing the room, she handed him his black coffee.

"You cut right to the chase, don't you?" Troy took the cup from her hand.

"I can be diplomatic," Shayne said. She returned to the kitchen counter to prepare the coffeemaker for the next morning. "If you work in the service industry and want decent tips, you have to be charming. It would seem I lost that filter. I got pissed today. Haven't done that in a while. Sorry if I took out my frustration on you."

"You were a bit stressed."

"Ya think?" she asked, crossing the room with her coffee in hand. "If I'd been a spider, I'd have been halfway up that wall before Cat calmed me down."

"We all have our triggers," Troy admitted. His lips pressed against each other until the formed a thin line.

Shayne caught the glance he'd given her. He'd inadvertently opened a door and was waiting to see if she would walk through it. He had a right to his secrets.

"Agreed. We'll leave it at that. Okay?" She heard his breath as it slowly escaped his lungs. She sat down next to him.

"Agreed," he answered, relaxing his back against the cushion. "Can you tell me what happened in Steve's office? What set you off?"

"It came to me in a blinding flash today that I've probably been played. The feds led me in this direction. I assume so your friends could keep an eye on me. I don't know why. If I hadn't lost my temper and stuck around, I might have gotten an answer."

Shayne felt Troy stiffen next to her. She adjusted her position and waited until he faced her before she continued. "I'm not saying your friends did anything wrong. They may be as much in the dark as I am. I don't know. Before I fell asleep, I was wondering whether that question bothered me enough to collect my things and leave or if I'm willing to let things play out." Shayne sighed.

"Don't you like it here?"

"I do. I initially hadn't thought of it as a long-term move. Never thought I'd like the job. But I found peace here. I admit, I was getting comfortable."

"Do you have family?"

"None in the States. My mom moved back to Ireland after Dad passed away. That's where they met. Grandmama has Alzheimer's so Mom is where she needs to be. Besides, I think she'd always been homesick for the Emerald Isle."

"Sorry about your grandmother," Troy said. "Is Ireland a goal? Do you want to be closer to family?"

"Some might say my problem is that I have no goals. No goal lines." Shayne took a sip of her coffee.

"Why not stay here until you make up your mind?"

"You're assuming that will happen." Since they'd lost her dad, she'd been adrift. She loved her mother and her grandmama to the moon, but the relationship with her dad had run deep. They'd been kindred spirits. She didn't just love and respect him, but could talk to him about anything. He'd kick her butt when she warranted it and give her a shoulder when needed. Perhaps she'd leaned on him too much. His sudden death while she was in college had knocked the wind from her sails.

"I should have questioned the move from Tampa when it was so easily pulled off. I figured I got lucky. Now, I'm not so sure. How did I happen to land in the lap of a bunch of former Green Berets?"

"If it means anything to you, I've trusted those men with my life. I would do it again," Troy assured her. "And Cat and Josie are two of the best people I know."

"From my short time here, I can't disagree with you, but I don't know if it's enough anymore. I won't be a pawn, and that's what I feel like." She didn't want to leave but wasn't sure she could stay. Where would she go? Would trouble follow her? What would her dad tell her? That wasn't hard to figure out. He'd tell her to stop feeling sorry for herself.

"I wouldn't recommend running. If there *is* a problem,

you'd only get so far before it caught up with you," Troy warned her. A shadow had passed over his face. Was he speaking from experience?

"Give it a couple of days," he added. "Knee-jerk reactions aren't usually the best."

"I feel like I'm crawling out of my skin," Shayne admitted, running her right hand up and down her left bicep. "There are times I wish I could go back to the night of the bombing and keep walking past that bar."

His silence had Shayne turning toward her unexpected guest. Troy's jaw was set. His right eye closed. *Shit.* She was grumbling about a bombing that she'd been lucky enough to virtually walk away from. How shallow was that? Shayne didn't know exactly what had caused Troy's mental and physical scars, but whining about an explosion that left her with minor injuries was pretty damn tactless.

"Stupid thing to say. Sorry. The conference call with Hernandez today got under my skin. I wasn't thinking —again."

"Hernandez?"

"He's one of the agents working on the bombing investigation," Shayne explained.

"I knew a Hernandez once."

"Unless he's with the FBI, I doubt it's the same guy."

Troy sipped his cooling coffee while he calculated the odds that two different federal agents with the same last name would be involved with people he knew. If this was the same Hernandez who had handled Cat's case last summer, Shayne might be in more trouble than she could possibly imagine.

Bait. It was the first thought that jumped into Troy's head upon hearing Hernandez's name. His gut told him that his friends would never go along with using Shayne as bait. Then again, Colt would do just about anything to damage or destroy the murder-for-hire organization that had accepted a contract to kill his wife. Troy was tempted to wake him and ask what the hell was going on, but he wanted to see their reactions when he confronted the team. It could wait until morning. Shayne was safe with him.

Shayne's cup, which appeared to contain more cream than coffee, rested in her lap. Her hands loosely gripped the mug. Since she was seated to his right, a slight turn of Troy's head confirmed her eyes had drifted shut. He waited and watched. Once her fingers began to slide down the sides of the cup, he removed it from her grasp and set it on the small end table. She didn't blink.

He should stretch her out on the futon, but he was afraid he'd be pushing it and wake her. She'd have a stiff neck in the morning if he left her where she was, but she'd also have a bit more sleep under her belt. Gib was scheduled to pick her up around eight o'clock. Troy would make sure she had thirty minutes to get ready. Shayne was a minimalist—a unique trait in the women he knew. Thirty minutes should be plenty of time for her to prep for the day.

Subconsciously, she tucked her feet beneath her then rested her head on his shoulder. Her breathing softened as she fell into a deeper sleep. He silently chuckled. He couldn't remember ever having that kind of effect on a woman unless he wore them out first.

Troy carefully slipped his arm from between them then rested his hand on her hip, anchoring her gently against the back of the futon. He was torn between wishing she hadn't changed out of her paper-thin T-shirt and being grateful that she had the sense to cover up. The firm muscles of her legs were obvious under his hand and accentuated by her tight leggings. The bulky sweatshirt, however, hid the firm, toned arms he'd noticed while working with her in the garden. Tending bar and the current physical nature of her work in the nursery kept her fit. He'd bet she'd once had a gym membership. She wasn't the type to remain sedentary.

With a little makeup and some decent clothing, Shayne could push the scale from cute to attractive. Cute or attractive, she was off-limits. Even if that wasn't the case, she had more than her share of problems. A disfigured, mentally unfit ex-soldier was the last thing she needed. When she snuggled closer and dropped her injured hand into his lap, his cock twitched. He didn't do cute.

14

―――――

Shayne fought to remain in her dream. A dream where she felt warm and safe. She nuzzled her head deeper into the firm pillow.

"Shayne. Wake up."

Her eyes flew open. *Oh shit!* She scrambled to sit up, digging her elbow into Troy's thigh as she did.

"Ouch!"

"Sorry," she muttered. How the hell could she have fallen asleep on him? She averted her face as she untangled herself from Troy's grasp. Dried saliva was crusted on the corner of her mouth. She fought her inclination to check Troy's shirt for drool. Did she snore? God, she hoped not.

The last thing she had expected to do was fall asleep after one of her nightmares. That in itself was rare, and to do so cuddled up against a man she barely knew? She couldn't digest that. She slipped off the couch and crossed the room, pressing the brew button on the coffeemaker before heading to the bathroom. She didn't say another word to the man she'd spent the night using as a mattress.

Shayne took a deep breath as she leaned against the

small sink before glancing in the mirror. Her short hair stood straight up on the left side of her head. The side that had rested on Troy's shoulder. *Suck it up.* She couldn't rewind the clock any more than she could spend the rest of her life in this bathroom, as tempting as the thought was at the moment. She brushed her teeth, splashed some cold water on her face, then used her wet fingers to plaster the gravity-defying strands of hair against her scalp. She bypassed the shower for now. Troy would need to use the facilities. As she exited the dressing area, he confirmed her assumption when he slipped by her and closed the door to the bathroom.

Sipping the hot coffee, she second-guessed the intake of caffeine. It cleared her head, but it also ratcheted her nerves up a notch. What the hell was she going to say when Troy reappeared? Apologize for using him as a pillow? Thank him for allowing her the safety of his arms?

She still hadn't settled on an answer when he exited the bathroom. Her breath caught in her throat. Droplets of water trickled down the hard planes of Troy's chest. He wiped them away with his bunched-up T-shirt before pulling it over his head. She caught a glimpse of some tats on his biceps before they were covered. He grabbed his small satchel that had contained his thermos and headed for the door. "I'll be outside. Gib will be here shortly to pick you up. See you at work," he said, disarming the alarm.

She shook her head, dislodging the masculine vision. "What? Why?" she asked as it hit her that he knew her alarm code. She should change it.

"Why what?" Troy stopped, one hand on the doorknob.

"Why do you have to wait outside? Can't you call Gib and let him know you'll walk me to work?"

"They'll know I spent the night in here and that your surveillance is blown. Neither will make me look good."

The words stung, but anger was preferable to hurt. "I'm sorry if the perception of spending the night with me might embarrass you," she snapped, allowing her blood to simmer. "I'd offer you coffee, but Gib might get here early."

"Shayne—"

"I won't tell anyone you were with me last night," she spat out, storming toward the door. As soon as he was on the other side of it, she'd damn well would be changing the alarm code. "Now if you'd leave so I can get cleaned up before my ride gets here, I'd appreciate it."

"Shayne." Troy was standing so close that she could feel his warm breath tickle the soft hairs on the back of her neck.

Steeling herself, she pulled open the door and stepped aside to let him pass. Troy reached over her head and firmly shut the door.

"What did you do that for? You need to leave."

"And you need to listen and not make assumptions," he barked.

"And what exactly am I assuming? You made your position perfectly clear."

Troy had her back plastered against the door in an instant. He loomed over her, one hand still pressed against the wooden panel. With his other hand, he'd grasped her chin with his fingers, forcing her to look at him. His lungs worked like bellows, blowing more warm air over her face. He wasn't happy, although she didn't know why. She was the one who'd been insulted. She caught herself glimpsing around the room, looking for an escape.

"No," he said. In addition to good looks and a ripped body, Troy apparently possessed the ability to read minds. "Neither of us is going anywhere until I've had my say."

"Then say it. This standoff isn't getting us anywhere. You want out. I want you to leave. I don't understand why you won't go."

"Because of this," he declared, covering her mouth with his.

SHAYNE'S SOFT, unadorned lips tasted of coffee and cream. He tongue licked the sweet liquid from the corners of her mouth then followed the taste deeper when it opened in surprise.

So much for his determination to keep his distance. But her pouty lips had begged to be kissed. She believed he'd be embarrassed if anyone thought he'd done more than act as her pillow last night. She had no idea he'd stroked her arm softly while she'd slept. It was all he could do not to wake her and ask for permission to do more. He'd been hard and hurting most of the night.

Dismissing all the reasons why this was wrong, he wrapped his arms around her and deepened the kiss. If his mouth hadn't been preoccupied, he would have smiled when her hands tentatively made their way up his chest before circling his neck. It was obvious she wasn't very experienced. It made the taste of her that much sweeter.

He ran one hand through her boyish cut, coaxing her mouth closer to his. The taste of innocence was an elixir. Troy wanted more. Her little moans and sultry movements against his body had him lost on a path different from any he'd been down. Her fingers inched up his scalp, pulling him closer. Then he felt it. The tug on the strap that held his patch in place. A cold shower couldn't have cooled the fires that burned within him any faster.

Troy pushed her away, grasping her arms as he did. Shayne hissed when his large hand encircled her sprained wrist. He took another step back, releasing her completely.

"I'm sorry," he muttered, securing his patch in place as he continued to put distance between them. "I'm sorry."

Shayne stared back at him, wide-eyed. He didn't miss the quivering lips before she turned away. Unlocking the door, she wiped a tear from her cheek with the back of her hand. "Please leave."

After that kiss, how could she think he didn't want her?

"You don't understand," he began.

"I understand this... You're in my place and I don't want you here. I won't say anything to anyone. You don't have to worry. Your precious reputation will remain intact."

"Give me the chance to explain."

"You made yourself clear. Goodbye, Mr. McKenzie. I don't think I'll be needing any further assistance at work. In fact, I'm sure of it."

She spun on her heels, leaving the door open and marched toward the bathroom. "Lock the door on your way out," she shouted as she disappeared into the dressing area. The bathroom door slammed, punctuating her point.

Well, fuck. Troy studied the plain white door that now separated the two. How had he managed to screw that up so well? He hadn't wanted to put Shayne in the awkward position of having to explain why he was in her apartment instead of outside where he'd been stationed. He also did not want Steve to think he was incapable of handling the simple assignment of standing watch without seducing the subject of that surveillance. Instead, he'd insulted her with his off-the-cuff remark about not looking good if it was known he'd spent the night at her place.

Before he'd had the chance to explain the badly worded

comment, the sparks that had been building within him all night overran the limits of containment. He'd kissed the scowl from her face. And Lordy, what a kiss. He'd felt it in his toes. It had stunned him but hadn't stopped him. He'd wanted more. Kissing had always been a means to an end— a necessary foreplay on the path to seduction. But kissing Shayne had been different. Spellbound by the taste and sensory overload, he'd forgotten the repulsive looks he'd seen in the eyes of strangers. He'd forgotten the disfigurement and reason behind his scars during those blissful moments of kissing the blazes out of her. Until she'd brushed the strap of his patch.

Fuck, fuck and triple fuck. He should never have gone near her. He was damaged goods. But when his lips had touched hers, she'd kissed him back with such vigor and sincerity that it reached something deep within him. Right or wrong, he wanted her.

From the spot he occupied in her tiny apartment, he had no trouble hearing the running water in the shower. Picturing her in naked was not a good idea. He had no business fantasizing about her. She was off-limits. He was damaged goods and she was in trouble. The combination was toxic.

He fought his animalistic urge to seek her out—to see her unclothed and dripping wet. Instead, he opened the front door and stepped out into the hot, humid summer morning. It did little to jar the vision now stuck in his head.

15

The scar tissue ached as his knotted muscles pulled at the damaged skin. He'd double-timed it back to the complex of buildings that included Cat's nursery. The short workout did not distract him from his irritation. The minute he'd watched Shayne cheerfully greet Gib as he helped her into his truck, Troy's jaw had locked into place. She hadn't even bothered to scan the area to look for him. Her attention had been fully focused on her escort as they drove off. Troy got the message. He'd been dismissed.

His gut tightened. Regardless of her reaction, he'd hurt her. She hadn't understood his apology, which could be a blessing in disguise. Her anger could serve as a shield between them, but he'd seen the tears she'd wiped from her cheek. His fingers knotted, making a fist. He couldn't beat the shit out of himself, but he knew where to find a few targets who might deserve to have the crap knocked out of them.

Troy heard Shayne and Gib's voices coming from deep within the garden as he passed the rear of the property. His run up the stairs to Gib's unit was filled with silent curses. If charming people were a business, Gib would own the goddamn world. Was he interested in Shayne? She'd been on the island for months. Surely, Gib would have made a move by now. That image had Troy slamming the bathroom door behind him. He took small solace in the fact that Shayne wasn't alone in the garden—but did she have to be with him?

He took a shower, washing away Shayne's fragrance before he changed into clothes that someone had laundered for him. He bypassed the pot of coffee on his way through the kitchen. It would only remind him of the taste of Shayne on his lips. Would he ever drink coffee again without thinking of her? He almost slapped himself. He was acting like an adolescent.

As he reached the kitchen door, he pulled up short. Shayne would still be in the garden. If he left through the front, his chances of being seen would be minimal. He wanted to talk to Steve, and whoever else he could round up, without making Shayne aware of the conversation.

As he let himself in the business next door, Troy quickly reached up and silenced the old-fashioned bell that hung above the door, intended to announce visitors. He made an immediate left and barreled through the open doorway at the end of the hall. Steve was on the phone. He held up his index finger, giving Troy the *hold on a minute* signal. Troy ignored it. "We need to talk," Troy demanded, shutting the door behind him.

"What the hell is your problem?" Steve asked, the phone still pressed to his ear. "Grumpy from lack of sleep?"

"You might want to get Rick and Colt over here for this discussion, but if they aren't available, you'll do."

"What's wrong with you? What discussion?" Steve

paused to tell the party on the other end of the line that he was needed in Steve's office.

"Was that Rick or Colt?" Troy asked.

"Colt." Steve leaned back in his chair. "Have you been drinking?"

"Not a drop, but thanks for the vote of confidence." Troy pressed his palms flat on Steve's desktop, putting his considerable weight against it. "What I *have* been doing is talking to Shayne."

"You were supposed to watch her. Not question her." Steve rose to his feet.

"I did watch, until a nightmare had her crashing around her place. While the chances were slim anyone got by me, I checked on her anyway. Your secret guard dog routine is in the latrine."

"That didn't take long."

"Don't go there. If you'd heard her thrashing around, you'd have done the same thing." Troy leaned in farther. "It was only a nightmare, but waking her was preferable to leaving her stuck in one. We've all been there."

"Yes, we have," Steve agreed. His tone softened slightly as he dropped back into his chair. "What did Shayne tell you that's got you so riled up?"

The door to Steve's office opened. Colt stepped through and quickly shut it behind him.

"Did you send for Rick?" Troy angled his head so he could see Colt clearly.

"I could hear you down the hall," Colt said, ignoring Troy's question. "What's going on?"

"Hernandez," Troy spat out.

"What about him?" Steve's eyes narrowed.

"What has Hernandez got to do with Shayne?" Troy demanded. He looked from one man to the other. Both were professionals at interrogation. Neither gave away what they were thinking.

"How does he know about Hernandez?" Colt asked Steve.

"I'm guessing Shayne let the name slip." Steve straightened in his chair.

"He was supposed to be on guard duty."

"He was."

"Knock it off. I'm right here," Troy interrupted. "It doesn't matter how I know. I know. Why is he on this case?"

"He works a lot of cases," Colt explained.

"Hernandez just happens to be investigating a bombing that killed two men. He just happens to place a potential witness in the care of former members of the Special Forces who have a score to settle with a particular murder-for-hire organization. An organization that Hernandez is determined to put out of business. What the hell is going on?"

"Troy..." Steve started.

"Are the two connected? Tell me you guys aren't letting them use Shayne as bait." Troy pounded his fist against the wall. "Damn it. Tell me."

The office door suddenly swung open, hitting Colt squarely in the back. When Colt stood his ground, Cat popped her head through the crack in the door. Troy wasn't surprised when she forced her way through it.

"What's going on? What's all the shouting about?" Cat scanned the room, sending a questioning look at each man.

"Nothing for you to worry about, Kitten," Colt said with affection as he leaned forward, closing the distance between them. He dusted a kiss on her forehead.

Cat pulled away from her husband, her eyebrows rising. Colt's wife did not do the *little lady of the house* routine, and

Colt knew it more than any man in the room. His kitten had claws.

"I'll worry about what *I* decide to worry about," she said. "Now one of you needs to answer my question." Her hair flew from around her shoulders as she spun to face the others in the room. "What's going on?"

"You'd better tell her now, Colt," Troy suggested as he took a step back from the pistol of a woman. The corner of his mouth kicked up in a sly grin, despite his concerns. "She doesn't have any sharp objects in hand."

Cat glared at Troy before she turned back to Steve then faced her husband. No one spoke. "Someone better tell me what the hell's going on before I *do* go in search of something sharp," Cat said.

"We were discussing Shayne," Colt told her.

"And why the FBI was so hot to have her on Sanibel," Troy added.

"I understood we were doing them and her a favor. Is there something more to it?" Cat's deep brown eyes narrowed at the man she'd married.

"Yeah. Is there more to it?" Troy asked.

"You're jumping to the wrong conclusion."

"What other conclusion am I supposed to jump to when Hernandez is involved?"

"Hernandez?" Cat's eyebrows almost reached her hairline. "Hernandez is on Shayne's case? Does this have something to do with my old case?" Troy was glad he wasn't on the receiving end of the look currently directed at her husband.

"No," Steve answered for his friend. He'd already taken the precaution of moving his office chair several feet back by the time Cat directed her laser focus on him.

"Hernandez is involved. What makes you so sure?" she growled.

Troy put one foot flat against the wall behind him, crossed his arms over his chest, and leaned back. He'd let Cat take point. There was an Amazon warrior trapped inside her pint-size body. While Troy might get a need-to-know response, neither Colt nor Steve would use that line on her.

"There's something going on, and we're going to find out what it is, but I promise you, Kitten, it has nothing to do with what you went through," Colt assured her.

"But there's more to Shayne showing up here than a simple request for help." Cat didn't back down, her hands on her hips.

"I'm not going to argue that after yesterday," Colt admitted. He clutched Cat's shoulders gently before pulling her to his chest.

The bell over the front door jingled. Cat scowled as she untangled herself from Colt's arms. She shot her husband a look that could have melted steel. "We'll talk later."

Colt caught her by the chin and pressed his lips to hers. "We will," he assured her with more tenderness than tension in his voice.

"Troy?" Cat looked over her shoulder at him as she reached for the doorknob.

"Yes, ma'am?"

"You take care of Shayne. You understand me?" It wasn't a request.

"Uh... She's not happy with me at the moment."

"Then do what you have to do to make her happy." The door shut firmly behind her.

Troy would have to leave town in order to make Shayne happy. He couldn't do that. Not until he knew she was safe.

16

Why the hell wouldn't Gib go away? His constant chatter made Shayne's ears hurt. Troy, at least, had worked with her in silence.

Troy. She hoped he would heed her wishes and remain unavailable. How could she have been so stupid as to think he'd be attracted to her? She'd heard his friends talk. Beautiful women fell at his feet. Why the hell had Troy kissed Plain Jane Shayne? From the shocked look on his face as he'd pushed her away, he was probably wondering the same thing.

"Don't you have something better to do?" Shayne snapped at Gib. She was at the potting bench, dividing one of the groundcover varieties of bromeliads. It was an easy way to increase Cat's inventory of the plants. It also didn't require any lifting or significant use of her wrist, which had been Gib's initial explanation for being at her side. Slamming the joint against the wall during the night had set her back a day or two, but she didn't require an assistant for her current task.

"You don't like my company?" Gib grinned as he settled his hip against the potting bench.

"You. Are. Not. Needed," Shayne said. "Don't you have photos to take or some woman to charm?"

"You mean I'm not charming you?" Gib asked, cocking his head.

"Look, if I promise I won't use my arm, will you please go away?" Shayne shoved her trowel into the bag of potting mix and sprinkled it around the transplant.

"You didn't chase Troy away," Gib teased.

"There are two major differences between you and Troy," Shayne replied, crushing the soilless mix into the pot.

"Only two?" Gib's grin widened.

"With regard to working in this garden...yes," Shayne said. Gib was enjoying himself. His gray eyes sparkled almost as much as the ruby stud in his ear. "One," Shayne began, "he was being punished. And two"—she paused for effect—"Troy doesn't talk much." This time, her grin came naturally.

Gib stumbled back a couple of steps as if he'd been hit. "You wound me, madam."

Shayne shook her head. He was incorrigible. In the short time she'd been on the island, she'd learned that behind his extraordinary good looks, there was a wicked since of humor and a heart of gold. You didn't stay mad at Gib long.

"I'm perfectly capable of potting plants without assistance. Is this bodyguard routine because of what happened yesterday?"

She'd spent her time in the shower that morning trying not to think about Troy and her idiotic behavior. She hadn't been very successful. When she wasn't thinking of Troy, she was theorizing why someone would attack her and why Steve and Rick suddenly felt she needed around-the-clock guards—one of those being Troy.

Or was it sudden? Had someone been keeping an eye on her since her arrival? Had her every move been tracked, or worse, recorded?

Just stop. No point in driving herself crazy. She'd talk to Steve or Rick. Find out what she missed when she'd stormed out of Steve's office yesterday in a huff. It was her own fault she hadn't been around to hear the end of the conversation with Hernandez.

"Do you know why the guys are huddled together in there?" She'd seen Colt tear out the back of the studio before he zipped around to the front of the business. Steve's car was parked in the lot. Troy wasn't anywhere to be seen. It wasn't hard to put things together.

"What guys?"

Gib wasn't any more successful at acting dumb than he'd been at playing the insulted male. Shayne dipped her head to look at him over the top of her sunglasses.

"Can't say," Gib answered, when she continued to stare.

"Or won't?" Shayne dumped potting mix around the base of another plant. "Is Troy in there?" Hopefully, Gib hadn't noticed the unnecessary force she used to press the mix into the pot.

"I have no idea," Gib told her.

"They had him watching my place last night."

"I heard," Gib responded, no longer playing innocent.

"I think it's time I moved on."

"Why would you say that?" Gib hefted a second bag of soilless mix onto the bench. He moved the items around to give her more room to work. The man charmed even when he didn't realize it.

Shayne blew out another long, slow breath. "If the attack on me yesterday wasn't random—and I'm guessing no one here thinks that it was—it's probably not safe to have me around." But where would she go? She had no roots here in the States since her dad died and her mom returned to Ireland. Would she be putting her mother and grandmama in danger if she joined them? It might be better for everyone if she took off to places unknown. She could manage. People reinvented themselves every day—or so she'd heard.

"Do you like it here?"

"Does that matter?" Shayne stopped staring off into space to answer Gib. His arms rested casually on the surface of the potting bench. He was totally focused on her. Not only was he stunningly handsome, but he made you feel like you were the center of his world.

"The guys will figure it out." Gib laid his hand over hers.

The guys will figure it out. Shayne stared back at Gib. When had she started letting others run her life? Yesterday, she'd let her temper flare. It had been about time. It was past time to take control of her life again. What was there to stop her from leaving? The urge to do so was suddenly over-whelming.

"Shayne?"

Tight, thin lines creased Gib's tanned brow. All his trade-mark charm had evaporated. Whether it was because of concern or suspicion, she wasn't sure. "What?"

Gib grabbed the last of the potted bromeliads from the bench and set them on a cart with the others. Shayne's mind was no longer on gardening. Her presence could be putting these people at risk. Gib laid a hand on her shoulder. "We can handle this. It's not our first rodeo."

Sighing, she glanced back toward the garden center. She needed to start making plans, just in case. She looked at her dirt-stained clothes and beat-up sneakers. A trip to the laundromat was in order. If she decided to leave, she didn't want to start out looking like the homeless person she might become.

17

"Why did the FBI approach you about Shayne? I know you wouldn't take her in without asking questions." Troy's head pivoted slightly so he could look at one man then the other. Colt's forearms rested on his solid thighs, his fingers locked together. Steve leaned back into his chair, arms banded across his chest. Neither had lost any of their fighting form since leaving the military—nor did they answer his question.

"Well?"

"What's happened to your patience?" Colt asked Troy.

"Left it behind at Brooks." Troy glanced at the door again. *Fuck it.* He got to his feet. He needed to check on Shayne. He didn't want the responsibility Cat had thrust upon him, but he damn well wouldn't shirk it, either. "I'll be back in a minute."

"Shayne's fine," Colt assured him, reminding Troy of his uncanny ability to read people.

The sound of Rick's truck pulling into the parking lot explained the stalling. His friends had been waiting for another player.

The entrance bell rang. Troy overheard Rick and Cat, although he couldn't make out the conversation. A few seconds later, the door to Steve's office opened.

"Do you know what's going on?" Troy asked Rick as he moved into the corner of the office so he could see everyone more easily. Rick nodded, sinking into the chair Troy had vacated. "Okay, then. Who's going to start?"

Colt straightened. "Hernandez contacted us a few months ago. They had a subject who didn't fit the parameters for a security detail. She'd survived—"

"I know about the bombing and the two deaths," Troy interrupted. "What else can you tell me that wasn't on the Internet?"

"There's something peculiar about one of the victims," Rick said.

"Peculiar? How?" Troy's right eye narrowed as he focused on the former lieutenant.

"His background is a bit too neat," Colt answered.

"A plant?"

"Can't say. I'm being honest with you," Colt continued. "If it hadn't been for yesterday, we wouldn't have gone back over the info we had. We need to dig deeper."

"And the other victim?"

"Male. Single," Rick responded.

"Everything we have is in this file." Steve unlocked his desk drawer and pulled out a thin manila file folder.

Troy began to leaf through the miniscule amount of information.

"After the wasted phone call with Hernandez yesterday," Rick said, "we started digging deeper. Haven't gotten much more info than we already had. We need time."

"We need Don," Troy muttered, then looked at Rick, hoping he hadn't caught the comment. Don Volpe was a freakin' genius at the keyboard and breaking through fire-walls. A skill not exactly supported by law enforcement. He was currently deployed with the other members of the team. "When do we expect the guys Stateside?"

"Soon," Colt answered. "But we won't know until it's go time."

Troy hoped they were wheels-up sooner rather than later. Don would be a major asset to information gathering, and they might need the additional manpower.

"While she was opening up to you last night, did she happen to mention the guy she saw leaving the banquet room seconds before the explosion?" Steve asked.

"What?" Troy pushed away from the wall.

"The authorities questioned her six ways from Sunday, but she only saw him for a split second. His back was to her," Rick explained. "She had a concussion. That memory took a while to resurface."

"But she's still a witness?"

"Not one they consider viable." Rick shook his head. "Race, height, and hair color. That's all she could give investigators. Given what she knows, it is unlikely she'd be called to testify if they find the guy."

"Did he see her?" Troy's stomach churned at the possibility.

"No way of knowing," Colt answered.

"Any idea of how this relates to yesterday?"

"It may not," Colt told him, "but we damn well need to find out for sure. The ball is in our court, and we're going to run with it."

Troy noted the thin, grim line of Colt's mouth. Someone had brought trouble to their door. That trouble was directed at a woman who had been entrusted in their care. It could also put Cat and Josie in danger. Colt was doing a good job of restraining his rage, but Troy recognized the anger that boiled behind those teal blue eyes.

"Do you know why the FBI tapped you to help Shayne?" Troy asked.

"We may be a pain in their ass at times, but they trust us," Rick answered. "They asked us if we could take Shayne in. She has no family nearby, and she wanted to move away from the area of the attack."

"Did it occur to any of you they were casting her out as a lure?" Troy growled. "Goddamn it. They could be using her as bait." Troy paced to the window and lifted one of the slats on the blinds, looking at the cars in the parking lot. Someone was after Shayne.

"Take it down a notch. It's a possibility we considered briefly," Rick told him, "but we've dismissed it."

"Why?" Troy turned away from the window.

"Shayne needed a place to stay. People who cared what happened to her," Colt added. "The FBI wouldn't ask us, of all people, for help if that was their plan. They would have placed her somewhere else or left her on her own and watched her themselves. Doesn't make sense they'd plan a sting here."

"Then how the hell did that asshole find her yesterday?" Troy's voice rumbled with anger. "Who else knew she was here?"

"Don't go off half-cocked just because you're pissed," Rick warned him. "Morgan and Hernandez aren't the only ones who know where Shayne is. Other agencies have access to the same information."

"Either way, it's not going to happen again," Colt said. "The next move is ours, and we're going to make it."

"And what is our move?"

"Get Shayne some place safe and find out who the hell is behind this," Colt told him.

"The last part sounds pretty vague."

"We've started off with less information," Steve reminded him.

True. Troy had been along for those rides.

"Shayne's questioning just how much you know," Troy warned them. "She's wondering if you guys are in on some plan she's not been made aware of."

Colt's head snapped up as if he'd been hit. Steve's fist slammed against the surface of his desk, while Rick stared at Troy. He wasn't surprised the accusation hit a nerve. They were men of honor.

"She confided that to you?" Colt asked.

"She was hurting and tired. I told her you wouldn't be a party to anything that would put her in harm's way—not that she has any reason to take my word for it." Troy glanced toward the office door again. He was anxious to get outside.

"She must trust you," Steve said.

Trust him? God help her if that was true. Troy had done nothing to earn it and everything to prove himself unworthy.

"She hit bottom last night and let shit slip," Troy explained. "I've never met a more contrary woman." He wasn't going to tell them about the kiss. He needed to forget that kiss. At the same time, he knew he'd never forget the sweet taste of cream on her lips.

The three men stared back at Troy.

"What?"

"You never met a woman you didn't like," Colt pointed out.

"I didn't say I disliked her. I said she doesn't like me. I

body-slammed her to the ground. Remember? Kind of hard to get past that."

"She hasn't said a word about that morning." Steve pressed back into his chair. The corners of his lips ticked up. "She did ask about you several times."

Troy didn't like the direction this was heading. "Do we have a plan or not?" he asked.

"I'm waiting on a call," Colt said as he got to his feet. "Regardless, we need to be ready to move. I wouldn't be surprised if the next conversation with the feds was face to face. Shayne needs to be gone before that happens. In the meantime, you're her shadow."

"Why me?" Troy asked. "I guarantee you, she'd prefer anyone else but me."

Colt was reaching for the door when he abruptly stopped, turning to face Troy. "What's going on between the two of you?" He crossed his arms over his chest.

"Nothing," Troy answered quickly.

"I don't buy it," Colt told him. "What happened?"

"Not what you're insinuating." Troy had a history with women. It was no secret. What they hadn't figured out was that the man they'd known no longer existed. "She doesn't like me. It's that simple." Which wasn't a complete lie. Colt continued to stare at him, his jaw set. Apparently, he didn't buy it. Too bad. He wasn't getting anything further from Troy. He had no intention of embarrassing Shayne or confessing about the clumsy pass he'd made. Instead, he folded his arms across his chest, mirroring his former commander.

"You'd best find a way of getting along with her, because if this plan works out, you're going to be her sole protection. You up for that?" Colt reached for the door again.

Troy moved quickly, shutting the door firmly before Colt could escape. "Trust me, this is not a good idea."

"What's the problem?" Steve asked. "You've been working in the garden with her for days. You appear to tolerate each other well enough from what I can see," Steve continued, propping his feet on his desk. Suddenly, he seemed to be enjoying the debate if the grin on his face was any indication.

"Why can't the four of us rotate until we get more back-up?" Troy asked. "That's the way we've worked it before."

"If my plan doesn't pan out, that will be an option," Colt said. "Right now, I want her away from here if it can be arranged, and you're the only one free to take off. So, if tolerating one another is the best you can do, then that's the way it will have to be. We've got Cat and Josie to consider."

"And the baby," Steve said, sporting a wide grin.

"What?" Colt asked.

"We're expecting," Steve replied. "Josie wanted to make the announcement, but I figured I should let you guys know under the circumstances."

"Josie's pregnant?" Rick stared at his friend.

"*Baby* plus *expecting* equals pregnant. Yes." Steve's chest puffed out. He was already the proud father. His smile quickly vanished as his feet hit the floor. "Which is an additional reason to move Shayne."

Troy's arm dropped from the door, and his head sank to his chest. *Damn.* "Fine. Work out the details, and let's get her away from here." Josie had saved Troy's life at the risk of her own. He owed it to her and Steve to keep them and their child safe. He'd get along with Shayne and keep his distance, even if it killed him.

After backslaps and handshakes, Steve warned them not to say a word to Cat until Josie had the chance to talk to her.

"Then I suggest you get Josie on the phone and tell her to break the news to my wife now," Colt said. "Cat will drag me over hot coals if she finds out I withheld that kind of news."

Troy broke into a smile at that point, because he could picture Cat doing just that. Josie was her closest friend. He stepped aside so Colt could slip out the door.

18

As soon as Troy cleared a small outcropping of plants, he spotted the top of Shayne's head over Gib's shoulder. Her hair spiked at the crown. He hadn't noticed that before. Why did the fact that she had a cowlick intrigue him?

Gib's right arm dropped to his side as soon as he saw Troy. He'd been reaching for a gun. While Gib was trained in the use of firearms, it was common knowledge he wasn't fond of them. The fact that he was carrying a weapon telegraphed the depth of their concern.

Shayne quickly turned away and moved to the shed where the gardening supplies were stored, ignoring Troy's arrival.

"Rick and Steve need to see you," Troy informed Gib.

"What's up?"

"They'll explain," Troy answered offhandedly, staring at the back of Shayne's head. As she was wearing a tank top, her boyish haircut allowed a view of the taut muscles of her neck and shoulders. "Thanks for sticking around."

"Don't screw this up," Gib warned him in a hushed tone.

"What's that supposed to mean?" The edge in Troy's voice could have sliced through metal.

"You know," Gib answered, tipping his head in Shayne's direction. "She's not your usual," he added softly. The grin he'd been sporting when Troy had arrived was gone.

"Would you care to elaborate?" Troy asked, turning to face Gib. He'd been watching Shayne as she rearranged items in the shed. She was doing her damnedest to ignore him. Unfortunately, she was going to have to get used to his presence.

Gib took a few steps toward the house then waited. Troy got the message and joined him.

"I'm saying she's a friend," Gib said.

"And you're telling me to keep my distance? Why? Have you made a move on her?"

Gib's normally bright smile was gone. His gray eyes narrowed. "I'm telling you she's not one of your distractions."

The reprimand brought back memories of Shayne's kiss. No, she wasn't a one-night stand. Another reason he had to keep his hands off her. "She's different," Troy admitted.

"She is, and she doesn't need heartache to add to her headaches. I can't tell you what to do." Gib slapped a hand on Troy's shoulder, grasping it tightly. "It's not my business. Just letting you know that we consider her one of us."

Troy took a step back. "I've got enough issues to deal with without adding another one to the heap."

Gib started to turn away but stopped abruptly. "You said it yourself. She's different. That doesn't mean she's off-limits, but it damn well means you'd better not hurt her."

"I have no intention of hurting her." Troy stopped short of saying *again,* but he couldn't keep himself from taking a glance in her direction. "Things have changed for me, if you haven't noticed."

"You think your scars or jackass attitude matter to her?" With that, Gib was done with the lecture. He disappeared into the organized jungle.

Troy waited to hear the rear door of the business slam shut before he addressed Shayne. She was doing a fairly good job of pretending he wasn't there, but the tension in her shoulders telegraphed otherwise. "Shayne?"

Her shoulders hunched up as she sucked in a deep breath then fell on her audible exhale. "Yes?" she answered.

"We need to talk," Troy started. What could he say? This morning shouldn't have happened, but he couldn't change that. He'd managed to bungle everything from the kiss to the apology. Now she was in a shitload of trouble, and he was going to be responsible for keeping her safe. The best thing to do was let her continue to think he was a bastard—which wasn't much of a leap. Still, he needed to earn some form of trust if she was to be his responsibility.

"About wha—" Shayne was cut off by the sound of the back door slamming again. This time the sound was followed by a high-pitched squeal.

"What the hell?" Shayne jumped.

Troy's mouth ticked up at the corner when he saw Cat come flying toward them.

"We're going to be godparents!" Cat grabbed Shayne's hands then jumped up and down like a giddy child before gracing Troy with a tight squeeze. "We're going to be godparents!" she repeated before dancing her way through the garden gate and toward the studio, shrieking in delight.

"What's that all about?" Shayne asked.

"Josie and Steve are expecting a child," Troy explained, watching the woman who had just chewed the men out prance across the driveway. He stopped fighting his grin when Cat literally skipped the last few steps to the studio door.

"Josie's pregnant?"

"Steve let it slip." Troy chuckled. The seriousness of the situation lightened for a moment. "I'm sure he was on the phone to Josie the minute Colt left, telling her to call Cat." Shayne's face softened at the news. The gold flecks in her eyes sparkled again in the morning sunlight. Did they sparkle in the moonlight or when she made love? *God.* What the hell was wrong with him? He couldn't allow his mind to stray there. She was off-limits. Troy pinched the bridge of his nose and inhaled slowly, attempting to calm his inner beast. Instead, his nostrils filled with her scent. He'd caught the hint of her woodsy fragrance last night when she'd rested her head on his shoulder. It had been the most peaceful night he could remember since returning from overseas.

"You okay?" Shayne asked him.

Troy allowed himself one last whiff. "Yeah. I'm just great," he answered, shaking off the spell she'd cast. When he again looked at Shayne, the flashes of gold were no longer visible in her eyes. Wrinkles in her forehead reflected her concern. For him?

"What was it you needed to..." Shayne started.

Troy audibly groaned when their conversation was interrupted again. This time by Gib's whoop as it carried across the dense foliage from the back of the building.

"I'm going to be a godfather!" Gib shouted proudly as he burst into sight. He grinned at them before he, too, hopped the fence and took off toward the building next door.

"How many godparents is this kid going to have?" Shayne asked as Gib disappeared from sight.

"I expect he, or she, will have at least one godmother and somewhere around a dozen godfathers." Every member of the team who had served with Steve would adopt this kid. *And if it is a girl—God help her.* The men would terrorize any boy who looked her way. Hell, they'd put her in a nunnery, if such places still existed.

"Twelve?" Shayne's voice rose. She looked up at Troy, her brow creased.

"Yep. Eleven team members plus Gib," Troy explained. Her stunned look had the corners of his mouth ticking up again. Her face was so expressive. He'd known the minute the hurt had registered with her this morning. *How would she look in the throes of passion? Enough.* He had to put an end to this.

"Look," Troy stated sternly. "Whether you like it or not, you're going to be spending the foreseeable future with me."

SHAYNE KNEW THEY WERE WORRIED, but the depth of that concern hadn't truly registered until she'd seen Gib hike up his shirt and reach for the gun tucked in the back of his jeans. The last person on earth she'd expect to see carrying a gun was the fun-loving, charismatic charmer. She'd been momentarily sidelined by the news of Josie's pregnancy. Now her feet were again firmly planted on the garden soil.

"Why you? And what happened to bring this on? Was it the attack on me yesterday?" How the hell was she going to develop a plan to slip away with Mr. Tall, Dark, and Handsome looking over her shoulder?

"I don't have all the details yet," Troy said. "Colt is making some calls, but I suspect we'll be leaving shortly."

Shayne's heart sank—which was plain stupid. She'd just

convinced herself that it was time to strike out on her own. It would protect her new friends, and as the decision had settled over her, it gave her a new sense of freedom. Now that freedom was being snatched out of her hands before she could taste it. Could she refuse? Would that be stupid?

"Why you?" she asked again. "I'm sure you didn't volunteer for this assignment."

"Doesn't matter whether I did or didn't. Colt and Steve won't be leaving Cat and Josie, especially now that Josie is expecting. Rick isn't free to take off, and Gib doesn't have the skills. They're scraping the bottom of the barrel, but I'm the one available at the moment."

Shayne's immediate instinct was to contradict the low opinion Troy had of himself but she didn't dare. It would signify empathy for him, which he would probably throw back in her face.

"Any idea when we leave and where we're going?" Could she slip away before they put their plan into place?

"I don't know anything more at this minute other than it will be just you and me, and that it will be soon."

"I need to do some laundry. I'll meet you back here in a couple of hours," she told him, turning to shut the door of the shed. She'd been organizing items in anticipation of her leaving.

"You're not going anywhere alone. If you need clothes washed, we can walk back to your place, get what you need, and throw your laundry in the washer next door, assuming we have time." He stood erect, his stance defiant.

Shayne stepped around him and walked toward the back gate. She didn't bother to look over her shoulder to see if he was following. He was too stubborn and too loyal to his friends to let her have her way.

They walked in silence the short distance to her apartment. After she disarmed the alarm, she glanced around the small unit while Troy locked the door behind him. The space was pitiful. Small, crowded, and nothing to make it feel like a home but it had somehow become one just the same. Shaking off the morose feeling, she grabbed one of the reusable grocery bags from underneath the kitchen sink.

"Help yourself to some water," she told Troy. "I'll be ready in a few minutes." She pulled the door to the dressing room closed behind her. Suddenly, the door pushed back at her.

"Leave it open," Troy ordered her, his hand clasping the edge of the door.

"The hell I will," Shayne snapped. "I want some privacy."

"You don't need privacy to throw your stuff in a bag."

"Did it occur to you that I might want to do more than pack? There's a bathroom in here, remember?" Shayne knew her blood was close to a boil. Her skin heated as she stared at the large hand still clutching the door.

"Leave it cracked, then."

In response, Shayne raised her foot and slammed her heel against the wood panel with all the force she could muster, crushing Troy's fingers against the jamb. He howled a few swear words. She didn't care. She was tired of being told what to do. She'd reached her limit of being maneuvered, regardless of whether it was for her own safety.

Troy's fingers disappeared, only to be followed by a loud grunt as he shouldered the door open again.

"What the hell were you trying to do? Break my fingers?" he shouted as she jumped back to avoid the swinging door.

"If that's what it takes to get some privacy. Get the hell out of my apartment. Wait outside if you want, or leave altogether. I don't give a damn." Her head was going to pop off if her blood pressure rose any higher, but she was done with this shit. She hadn't gotten an explanation as to why everything had changed so drastically after the run-in with the hooded man, but she was so mad at the moment that she didn't care. She wanted to be away. Away from it all. A plan was forming in her mind but she had to lose her bodyguard.

"Leave," she snapped as she entered the bathroom. "I'm not a prisoner of war or a criminal in custody. If you're going to be my shadow, we set some rules, and one is no voyeurism."

"You think I'm doing this so I can get a look at you naked?" Troy's tone sent chills down her spine.

"No. You made that perfectly clear this morning." Shayne hoped the hurt didn't show through the anger. She felt both. Throw in some embarrassment and she'd pretty much run the gamut of emotions with this man. She could not tolerate spending an undetermined length of time with him. It was past time she took matters into her own hands.

"Shayne..." Troy started, his voice softened as he rubbed the knuckles of the hand she'd squashed in the door.

"Leave. Please," she added, her voice cracking. "Give me a few minutes."

She noted his hesitation then his nod. "I'll meet you out front. Don't be long."

As he exited the tiny dressing area, Shayne shut the door then waited until she heard the outside door click shut. Quickly, she tossed what little clothing she possessed into the cloth sack, along with the envelope that held her personal papers, identification, and a measly stash of cash. Finally, she emptied the contents of her bathroom cabinet and threw it all in the bag. She did use the facilities then took the small bathroom trash can, dumped its contents on the floor, and turned it upside down under the small window in the shower.

Balancing on the bottom of the overturned can, it was still a stretch to reach the small window. She unlatched the screen, cranked the window open, then started removing the three opaque jalousie panes, one at a time. Getting through it was going to be a tight fit. Hopefully, sweating in the garden had cost her a few pounds. She tossed the bag through the window then hefted herself up on her elbows onto the sill. There was only one way to accomplish the escape and that was headfirst. She might break her neck but if she didn't, she'd be on her way to freedom. Until yesterday, she hadn't imagined herself a captive. Oh, how things could change in the span of a few hours.

She managed to get her head and shoulders through the opening then let gravity do the rest. Bracing herself for the fall, she bit her bottom lip to keep from making any noise that would garner the attention of the gatekeeper out front. Her knees had just cleared the opening when two massive hands encircled her waist.

19

"Going somewhere?" Troy asked, grasping Shayne by the hips, letting her head dangle just above the ground. He was caught between laughing and railing at her for the stupid stunt. He'd known she was contemplating something when he talked to her this morning. Even the news of Josie's pregnancy hadn't put him off the scent. She was an easy read. Her face wasn't just an open book, but one with pictures and diagrams. She'd talked about setting out on her own. He'd warned against the dangers of such a move, but it would appear she didn't like having her back up against a wall. Particularly if he was the one pinning her there.

"Put me down!" she growled. Her sunglasses slipped from her nose, but her quick hand caught them before they hit the ground. A pendant slipped from her shirt and bounced against the tip of her nose. "Will you please put me down?"

Troy considered letting her dangle a while longer. She'd had the sense not to struggle. All that would do was increase her chances of being dropped on her head. Besides, she was doing her best to keep her baggy shirt from slipping over her breasts. He considered waiting to see if gravity won that battle.

"I ought to paddle your butt for pulling such a stupid stunt." He wanted to shake her. Hell, if he hadn't suspected she was up to something, he'd have been standing idly out front while she broke her neck diving out the tiny bathroom window.

"I'm not into S&M," she retorted, in spite of her precarious position.

Troy muttered a few swear words while he reined in his temper and lowered her carefully to the ground. Maybe he should have dropped her on her head. It might have knocked some sense into it. The damage would have been minimal. Shayne might have thin skin, but she had a thick skull.

"What the hell did you think you were doing?" he asked while Shayne got to her feet. She braced one hand against the wall of the building as she did so. He wasn't surprised she was lightheaded.

"Shortcut to the laundromat," she said without hesitation, slipping her sunglasses back on.

He didn't like the shades, Troy decided, ignoring her nonsensical remark. They hid those expressive eyes, not to mention the gold flecks that changed with her mood.

Turning away from her, he snatched clothing and toiletries off the ground. He'd been rounding the corner of the building when her belongings flew out the tiny bathroom window. He could have put a halt to her escape plan then, but he was curious to see what her next move would be and how far she would go. He didn't think she could make it out the window. Apparently, she was smaller or more determined than he'd imagined. When her momentum had her sliding downward, his heart lodged in his throat. The crazy woman was going to break her neck.

As Shayne stuffed the last of the items back into her sack, Troy's phone rang. He pulled it out of his pocket while he indicated to Shayne that she needed to move.

"McKenzie," he answered sharply, watching Shayne's narrow hips sway as she headed toward the front of her apartment. Yeah, he needed to get laid, then maybe his attraction would fade.

"Where the hell are you?" Steve snapped. "Is Shayne with you?"

"We're at her place," Troy said. "She took off. I followed. She says she has laundry to do."

"You should have notified us."

Troy didn't respond to the statement. The truth was he hadn't thought to call. He'd been so focused on Shayne that he hadn't considered what the guys would think when they both disappeared. He followed Shayne through her front door, and locked it.

"She's gathering her stuff now," Troy lied. She already had a sack full of clothes, but he needed time to fix the window she'd bailed out of. He didn't have any intention of telling them his ward had almost slipped away.

"We'll be back there shortly," he replied as he watched Shayne pull the small trash can from under the kitchen sink then yank the door to the shrunken refrigerator open. She pretended to ignore him, but even with his limited peripheral vision, he caught the occasional flicks of her head in his direction.

Troy made his way to the bathroom, leaving the door open and Shayne in sight. The condition of the jalousie windows she'd removed needed to be assessed. The type of window was no longer commonplace, but some older homes in Florida still had the narrow crank windows. Each pane was held in place by simple clamps and provided privacy as well as fresh air. Fortunately, they were intact and could easily be clipped back into place.

"The incident yesterday is bound to make someone nervous," Steve told him. "We want to get her moved before the feds do."

"You don't trust the FBI?" Troy asked, slipping the first pane into its tract.

"We're playing it safe. We don't know where they stand at the moment. We should have a better feel once we talk to them, which could be anytime now. We'd like Shayne to be out of reach while we sort this out."

"Do we have a destination yet?" Troy asked, slipping the last pane into place and cranking the window shut.

"Yes. Gib should be here any minute with a safe vehicle for the two of you. We'll go over the details as soon as you return."

The sound of breaking glass reverberated from the small unit's kitchen and into the bath. It was loud enough that Steve could hear it through the phone. "What the hell is going on there?"

Troy returned to the main room. Shayne was tossing items from the cupboard into the trash bag that rested against the tile floor. The small refrigerator door remained opened. It was empty. "Shayne's dumping her perishables. She's not happy about the move or that I'm to be her watchdog. I warned you."

"How did you manage to get under her skin so deep? That's not your style."

"I don't have a 'style' anymore," Troy told him. If Shayne

wanted to share the details of their encounter, that would be her decision. She could easily get him kicked off this assignment if she reported he had his tongue down her throat.

"You need to deal with that chip on your shoulder and learn to deal with her. We don't have the time to find someone else who can disappear without being noticed."

"The FBI knows I was here," Troy reminded Steve. "If we both disappear at the same time, I think they're bright enough to figure out that she took off with me."

"It won't matter if they can't find you. Where you're going, you won't be a blip on their radar screen. Get back here and we'll fill you in." Steve disconnected.

"Leave it," Troy told Shayne as she headed for the door with a trash bag that was ready to burst at its seams. "We'll take it out together when we leave."

"I'm getting tired of taking orders," she responded, the trash bag still dangling precariously above the floor.

"You take orders every day from Cat. You don't like taking orders from me."

"Bingo."

This was not going to be easy. Troy intercepted her at the door. "I get that you don't want me around. I even understand why. But I'm trying to keep you safe and my friends from worrying about you. Can we call a cease-fire for their sakes?"

Shayne's shoulders sagged as she set the plastic garbage bag on the floor. Resignation was etched in her expression. "For their sakes," she agreed. "And neither of us speaks a word about what happened."

"You never let me explain—" Troy began.

"Agreed?" Shayne interrupted.

"If that's the way you want it," Troy nodded. He would

have liked to set the misunderstanding straight, but leaving the chasm between them was as good as a wall.

"Is that all you want to take with you?" Troy asked, indicating the bag that sat on the futon. The sack was half empty. "We're headed out, but I don't know to where or for how long."

"I don't have much." She glanced at the garbage bag filled with the contents of her kitchen. "It seems I have more garbage than I do possessions." She shrugged.

"Have you always lived this lean?" Troy asked, truly curious. Most women he knew carried more in their purses than she'd thrown in the sack.

"In spite of what you think, I am a woman." She wrapped her arms around her tiny waist before turning back toward the small kitchenette. "I used to have a nice apartment chock-full of shit I didn't need."

"Shayne—"

"No. We agreed not to talk about it."

Troy stayed glued to his spot on the floor. He wanted to hold her, shake her, and kiss the living daylights out of her. None of which he could do, but he could make one thing clear.

"The person I kissed this morning was all woman." She might be a bit willowy and short-tempered, but she was definitely a woman.

"Did you run into someone after you left here?"

"Knock it off. Are you looking for pity or are you outright stupid?"

That got her attention. She wheeled on him, her hands knotted into fists. "I don't need anyone's pity, especially yours. I like who I've become. The events in Tampa changed my perspective on life and possessions. It's rather freeing."

"I imagine it is," Troy sighed. "I haven't got to that point yet." He stroked his hand over the scars on his face.

"Sorry. That was an insensitive thing to say."

Troy ignored the apology. He didn't want her pity. He wanted her—but that wasn't going to happen.

20

Steve's office was a tight fit for all the players involved. Shayne had taken a seat in one of the guest chairs. Rick, Steve, Colt, and Troy were squeezed into the remaining space. They were all big men. What appeared spacious on previous visits felt claustrophobic now. Rick stood by the single window that faced the street. The blind had been drawn. Steve was seated in his desk chair, and Colt sat in the chair next to Shayne. Troy loomed behind her.

A set of car keys landed on the desk, rattling Shayne. She felt Troy's hand rest on her shoulder, reassuring her of her safety. The gesture shouldn't have been welcomed, but regardless, she settled at his touch.

"Where's the car?" Troy asked Steve, who had tossed the keys.

"Parked at Bailey's General Store. No one will connect it to this place."

"I'll drop you both off once this briefing is over," Rick added.

"I still need to get my stuff," Troy reminded them.

"Gib took care of it," Colt told him. "It's in the car."

"Would someone mind telling me what's going on?" Shayne asked. She felt like she'd arrived in the middle of a movie and had yet to catch up with the plot. She absently began to massage her temples, closing her eyes. She was tired. Tired and frustrated with a tinge of anger and fear mixed in for good measure. She wasn't a pleasant person to be around at the moment.

"Okay." She raised her head and studied the men in the room. "I'd like someone to tell me why I landed here in the first place and where we're headed." Her starry-eyed dream of escaping this nightmare had been busted.

Shayne pushed out of her chair and took up a position near the corner of the room where she could watch all the men, including Troy. He was staring back at her with that emerald-green cat's eye, silently questioning her actions.

"Why did Hernandez and Morgan want me here on Sanibel and under your watchful eyes?" Shayne asked, crossing her arms under her breasts.

"To put it in a nutshell, the FBI contacted us and asked if we would help you out," Colt told her. "It's that simple."

"I know Hernandez and Morgan have held on to the hope I'd remember something significant regarding that night. Is that why they felt the need to shove me off on you?"

"You weren't 'shoved off' on us," Rick answered. "We're glad to have you. You wanted to move, and they wanted someone to look out for you."

"That worked out well, didn't it?" Shayne huffed.

"That was our fumble," Steve said. "There'd been no issues since you came here. We should have been more vigilant. We can talk more about this later. Right now we need to move you."

"I knew you were in a hurry, but what's happened to

make this so urgent?" Troy said, asking question that had been on Shayne's lips.

"Hernandez and Morgan are on their way. We want Shayne out of here before they show up," Colt answered. "For the time being, you'll be safer if no one knows where you are except for us."

"And so will Cat and Josie," Shayne added, glancing at Steve then Colt.

"It is a factor. I won't deny that," Colt agreed, surprising Shayne when he took her hand in his. "But your safety is just as important. It's the reason we're sending you with Troy." She felt the gentle squeeze of his hand. Shayne was doubly surprised when she felt Troy's hand on her shoulder. Her skin sizzled at his touch. Not good.

"I suspect we're wasting time," she said, stepping away, distancing herself from Troy.

"Where are we headed?" Troy asked.

The question had been directed at Colt, but Troy's focus was locked on Shayne. He was frowning again, his eye narrowed. *Why?* Because she didn't want to be physically close to him? She would get along with him for the sake of her new, albeit short, friendships. She'd trust him with her safety but nothing more. She didn't want his compassion, and she certainly shouldn't want a physical connection. The expression on his face when he'd broken away from their kiss would be emblazoned in her memory for a long time to come.

Shayne broke the staring contest and looked to Colt for an answer to the question Troy had posed.

"A photographer friend has some properties tucked away on the edge of the Everglades. A cottage and bungalow sit behind his gallery off US 41 between here and Miami. During season, the properties are available for rent but not at this time of the year. The main house is out of commission due to hurricane damage. The bungalow is in good shape and even deeper into the Everglades, so you'll virtually be isolated. Go straight to the bungalow. The manager of the gallery has been told to unlock the place and leave the key on the kitchen counter. There should be no reason for anyone to venture back there this time of year."

Steve lifted a backpack from the floor. "Some things you may need, plus a satellite phone."

"Do you have your cell phone with you?" Rick asked Shayne.

"Always." Shayne reached into the back pocket of her jeans and pulled out her phone. Ever since the bombing, it rarely left her body. It had been in her purse the night all hell broke loose. That feeling of panic when she realized it was not within reach so she could call for help was imprinted on her soul.

"The feds issued that one," Rick reminded her. "Leave it here so they can't use it to monitor your location."

Shayne's heart rate ratcheted up a notch at both the idea of being tracked and the loss of her lifeline, but Rick was right. "Can I get a different one?"

"Where you're going, cell service is spotty," Rick said. "You'll have the satellite phone, and Troy still has his cell—if you're lucky enough to have service."

"And supplies?" Troy asked.

"The car is packed with everything you should need. There's a cooler with perishables and some MREs in case of an emergency," Steve said.

Shayne was familiar with Meals, Ready-to-Eat. Not an appetizing prospect. It was also frightening. "How long do you expect us to be there?" Shayne asked in dismay. Being isolated with Troy for an indefinite period of time was not good. Not good at all.

"We'll sort this out as quickly as we can, but I can't give you a time frame. Not yet." Colt rose to his full height.

"Can I at least say goodbye to Cat?" Shayne asked, unable to hide the tremble in her voice as the finality of the situation hit her.

"She's not here. She left with Josie. They're shopping for baby items," Colt explained then grinned. "Gib's with them."

"Oh," Shayne murmured. "Tell her I'm sorry to leave her shorthanded." She then looked to Steve. "I should have congratulated you sooner. Let Josie know I'm happy for the both of you."

"You can tell her yourself when you get back," Steve assured her.

"Sure." Shayne stepped toward the door. "I guess we're ready, then."

"I need a second to check this stuff out," Troy told Shayne. "Can you grab us some cold water out of the fridge?"

As soon as she left for the breakroom, Troy reached for the backpack to check its contents, but it wasn't the main reason he'd wanted Shayne to step out. "How serious is this?"

"We honestly don't know," Steve told him. "It could all be for nothing. We'll know more after we talk to Hernandez and Morgan. I can assure you of that."

"She doesn't believe she's coming back," Troy informed them as he inspected the contents of the backpack. As he suspected, it was stuffed full of goodies. The satellite phone, a second gun, ammunition, combat knives, night-vision goggles, and a first-aid kit, among other things.

"How is it you've gotten such a good read on her?" Colt asked. "She's normally a quiet one."

Troy didn't miss the narrowing of those turquoise eyes. The others in the room remained silent, waiting for his response.

"She's not that hard to read. You saw how she was acting. She's usually full of sass." Troy zipped the backpack closed and slung it over his shoulder.

"What are you smiling about?" he asked Rick.

"You. I haven't seen this many sparks since Colt met Cat."

"I don't know what the hell you're talking about," Troy said as he left the room.

21

Shayne gazed out the passenger window of the Jeep Wrangler as they traveled south on US 29. They'd passed through the small farming town of Immokalee, and since the community had disappeared in the rearview mirror, she'd seen nothing but saw palmettos, melaleucas, palm trees, and alligators.

Shayne was semi-amused when she'd spotted her first "panther crossing" sign. Could panthers read? Why did she find that, or anything else, humorous? She was sitting next to a surly man who had lost his voice after Rick had dropped them off next to the four by four in the supermarket parking lot.

Rick had given her a hug before stepping back to talk to Troy. The two men shook hands and had some parting words, none of which she caught. At the end of the conversation, Troy had held the passenger door open while she attempted to buckle up. She'd fumbled with the latch, partially due to her wrist, but nerves helped make the easy task more cumbersome. Troy had to reach across her to complete the act then slammed the door shut. He hadn't uttered a word since they'd driven off the island.

The humming of the tires against the asphalt seemed to grow louder along with the tension. Shayne considered breaking the silence but couldn't think of a safe or common subject to discuss. Troy didn't know squat about plants and had made it clear he couldn't care less. She knew nothing of war, unless the bombing counted, and she doubted he wanted to reminisce about his brush with death. She had no desire to delve into his personal life. She could imagine what filled his nights and days when he wasn't deployed. Stories from Shayne's previous job as a bartender didn't seem appropriate, given his recent issues with alcohol. She could bring up the four years she wasted obtaining a degree in medieval history, but the subject bored her. The weather? It was Florida and it was summer. Hot, humid, with afternoon thunderstorms. It rarely changed, making it easy to predict and not much to discuss. She kicked herself for not running into Bailey's supermarket so she could grab a book or magazine, assuming she wouldn't have been blocked by one of her guardians.

As if her wish had been conjured up by her subconscious, a lonely convenience store appeared on the horizon.

"Can we stop up ahead?" Shayne indicated the business on the other side of the sole intersection. "I want to pick up something to read and use the facilities."

At first, Troy looked dismayed when she spoke. Had he forgotten she was in the vehicle? He glanced at the rearview mirror then checked the vehicle's GPS. "We have another twenty miles or so to go. Can't you wait?"

"Obviously, you don't have any sisters. No, I can't."

"I don't like the idea of you being seen." His focus returned to the road, a scowl plastered on his face.

"Well, I'm sorry, but I'm not going to squat behind some bush just so an alligator can take a bite out of my ass." She squirmed in her seat to make the point.

She thought she caught a ghost of a smile cross his stern face, but she probably imagined it.

He took off his ball cap and tossed it to her. "Put that on and wear your sunglasses," he told her. "That damn shirt fits too tight or we might be able to pass you off as a boy. I'll grab one of my shirts for you to throw over yours."

Shayne smacked his bicep with the back of her hand. *Ouch*. Her knuckles stung. She might as well have hit a board.

"What the hell was that for?" Troy asked, rubbing the spot on his arm where she'd made contact.

"You're lucky there's not a tire iron under the seat," she snarled before tugging the bill of the cap down over her eyes and slumping deeper into the passenger seat.

TROY STOOD across from the restroom waiting for the very pissed-off woman he'd followed into the store to exit. He'd insulted Shayne—again. But damn it, her clothes were too tight. Of all the days for her to change out of her baggy T-shirt and shorts. Was she teasing him or was that her normal choice of clothing when she wasn't at work? A snug tank top and skinny jeans. *Damn*. He scanned the customers in the convenience store. There weren't many at this remote station. Troy was probably drawing more attention than Shayne had when she'd stormed into the store demanding to know where to find the bathrooms. A large, scarred man with a patch over one eye lurking by the ladies' room was sure to arouse attention. Still, he wasn't moving until she came out.

He wasn't surprised at Shayne's reaction when she emerged from the restroom. Seeing Troy waiting for her, she yanked the shirt he'd given her tightly around her middle, her eyes narrowed to slits and her lips formed a straight line, punctuating her irritation as she slipped by him without saying a word.

The shirt that he'd pulled from his duffel was long enough to cover her ass, for which he was personally grateful. Still, its fabric clung to her as she walked away from him. It was a struggle, but he managed to keep his eye off those swaying hips and on the customers meandering through the store.

As Shayne approached the front of the store, she stopped at a magazine rack to peruse its contents.

"Head on out to the car," Troy told her. "We need to get out of here."

"I'm getting some reading material first. Our titillating conversations can't last forever." Sarcasm. He should be used to it by now.

"People are beginning to stare," Troy pointed out.

"Well, that might be," Shayne said, picking up a book and turning it over to read the jacket cover. "They're probably wondering why I'd be wearing a flannel shirt ten sizes too big when it's ninety-five degrees outside, and why the man I'm with doesn't leave my side and keeps glowering at me."

She had a point. Everyone wore T-shirts, tank tops, and shorts. A few patrons were starting to study him rather than Shayne. He could be anything from a purveyor in the sex trade, which he knew was big business in these parts, or an abusive partner. "Fine," he agreed. "Grab something quick and let's go."

Troy wanted to shout as Shayne picked up a half-dozen paperbacks before selecting two. If she was drawing this out just to get under his skin, she was succeeding. She grinned as she handed him the books and a couple of magazines.

"Here you go. I assume you have funds." Troy looked at the books and groaned. She'd picked up two romance novels with some very steamy cover art. "I'll meet you in the car," she added.

"No, you won't. You go where I go and vice versa."

Shayne's eyes pinched again as her jaw tightened. "No one is going to grab me out here in the middle of nowhere. I'd like some space to myself."

"You'll get it when we reach the cottage. It's remote enough that I won't have to be with you every minute. For now, do as I say."

Shayne let out a huff as her shoulders dropped. "Go on. I'll be right behind you."

She kept her word as he approached the register. A haggard, sun-wrinkled man in his mid-fifties held court behind the grimy counter. It was obvious that some of the patrons were regulars, hanging by the register swapping fishing stories. They'd probably been coming in for coffee or beer for years. Their skin was more weathered than the clerk's. Troy had noted that the few vehicles parked outside were pickup trucks with beds loaded with fishing gear. The clerk gave Troy an assessing glance then looked at the purchases and laughed.

"Wouldn't have guessed you were the type." The clerk held up the books for his cohorts to see, which resulted in another round of laughter.

"Ring up the damn sale," Troy ordered the man who

smelled of tobacco. Troy pocketed his change and almost elbowed Shayne as he did. A minute ago, she couldn't get far enough away from him. Now she was crowding him. When she slipped her arm around his waist, he wasn't at all sure he'd been able to suppress his surprise. He grabbed the items off the counter and led her out the door.

"What was that show about?" Troy asked, ignoring her protests when he buckled her into the passenger seat again. This time, he was able to place the fragrance that he associated with her. Sandalwood. It was intoxicating. *Crap.*

"I didn't want them to get the wrong impression of you." She shrugged, checking the purchases in her lap.

"You couldn't care less what they thought of me. Why the act?" Troy stood in the open door on the passenger side. He still felt the jolt of her touch, and now she was waving him off like a pesky fly.

Shayne puffed out her cheeks before letting the air escape. She looked at the convenience store. "Would you mind getting in so we can get out of here?"

Troy checked over his shoulder and saw the two men who'd been hanging out at the counter had exited the building. Instead of walking to their trucks, they stood in front of the store watching Troy and Shayne. He shut the door, hightailed it around the vehicle, and slid into the driver's seat.

"Do you know them?" Troy asked as he pulled out onto the highway.

"Seriously? No. I don't know them, and you need to put on your seat belt."

Troy reached across his body and managed the task one-handed, quieting the complaining vehicle. "What was going on back there? Why the ruse?" He'd wasted time when they'd reached the car. He should have been paying more attention to their surroundings instead of focusing on identifying the scent that emanated from the woman next to him. He had a job to do. He checked the rearview mirror again. No vehicles followed.

"So, we're talking now?" Shayne asked.

"Cut the crap."

"Okay." Shayne tossed the books and magazines onto the floorboard. "I'm surprised you didn't figure it out yourself."

"Will you spit it out?" He took another glance behind them. Nothing.

"Those men," she started. "While you were busy exchanging barbs with the clerk, they were busy undressing me."

"What?" Troy gave her a quick visual check. "Explain."

"You of all people should know. Don't tell me that you never mentally stripped a woman of her clothing? You may not think of me in that way, but I imagine those guys don't have a lot to pick from out here at the edge of a swamp. Trust me. A woman knows what that feels like."

"Son of a bitch." Troy's hands fisted around the steering wheel. He wasn't sure what angered him the most: the fact that he'd missed the scrutiny those scumbags had given her, that she still believed he wasn't attracted to her, or that she was right about the way he'd looked at members of the opposite sex. How many women had he sized up, imagining them naked and figuring out how fast he could get them that way? He'd never given any thought to how the woman felt if the attraction wasn't mutual. He'd simply brushed the rebuff off. There were plenty of fish in the sea. How often had that appraisal demeaned them?

"You should have said something," Troy snarled.

"And what? Make a scene? Draw more attention to ourselves?"

Another good point. A pretty woman and a disfigured man were already enough to draw the attention of the locals. Getting into a fight would have meant cops, a report, and their location pinpointed.

"You're wrong, you know," Troy said as Shayne reached for one of the books on the floorboard.

"I'm often wrong about a lot of things." She forcefully flipped the pages of the paperback.

After a split second to check the rearview mirror, Troy slammed on the brakes. Shayne's book went flying as she lurched forward, straining against the seatbelt. The screeching of the tires was punctuated with his booming voice. "Stop it!" Troy demanded.

The gold flecks in Shayne's eyes flashed as they locked onto Troy. The furrows between her dark brows deepened as her eyes widened. Her right hand grasped the passenger door handle as she quickly looked around them.

"Let's get one thing straight, right now," Troy growled. "Stop putting yourself down. There's not a damn thing wrong with you. Any man would be lucky to have you."

She remained silent as he stepped on the gas. Traffic was headed toward them from the east. They'd best be on the move. They'd brought enough attention to themselves for one afternoon.

"You're right," she responded, her voice, soft and hesitant. "I'm not normally down on myself. I was convinced I'd gotten my priorities straight."

Troy waited for her to continue but she remained silent. She stared out the passenger window at the dense tropical foliage that lined the road. He wanted to hear more. He wanted to know how she had changed after the bombing. How had she dealt with survivor's guilt and to what she attributed to her low self-esteem. He settled for a simple question: "How?"

"How what?" she asked.

Apparently, she'd lost track of their conversation. "Your priorities. How did they change?"

Another deep exhale was followed by a soft chuckle. "You will be surprised to know that I was once a very girly girl. My much-longer hair was professionally styled with just the right amount of highlighting. My makeup was meticulously applied. My fingers and toes, perfectly mani-cured. I'd even reward myself with an occasional trip to a spa. Oh, how I loved massages—the pampering, the atten-tion, the Zen-like peace that surrounded me."

"But the bombing changed that." Troy checked the rearview mirror again. A truck was fast approaching.

"It did but I'm guessing you know that. It made me realize how unimportant those things were."

She slipped the convenience store receipt in the book to mark her place and laid it on her lap. "I was actually thrilled the FBI had found me a place to work that didn't require the frippery, to use an old term, that I once put so much stock in. I didn't want or need it anymore."

Troy listened as he watched the vehicle coming up behind them. It wasn't one he'd spotted at the convenience store. As traffic cleared in the oncoming lane, the vehicle's turn signal came on and it sped past. He relaxed a bit.

"I get that," he responded. He understood the impact a life-shattering event could have on someone.

"No, you don't."

"Why the hell would you say that?" Troy was instantly peeved. How could she look at him and think he hadn't changed?

"Oh, I get that things are different for you. Your face is

damaged, and you weren't in the habit of drinking yourself into a stupor. You also didn't have that chip on your shoulder before you were injured."

"How would you know that?" Troy sent her a quick glare. She wasn't looking at him. She was again staring out the window while she unconsciously feathered the edges of the paperback. He wondered what else she knew. Did she know how he became disfigured and the ugly story that matched his scars?

"Your friends care about you. I pick things up," she answered.

"You eavesdrop."

"Occupational hazard. I tended bar, remember?" She adjusted her position so she could face him.

"All right. What is it that I don't get?" Troy asked.

"You won't like it."

"Then that should make your day."

A small grin ticked up the corner of her mouth. He wondered what it would take to get an outright smile out of her.

"It might but I think I'll pass." She picked up her book, dismissing him.

22

B right yellow banners fluttered in the breeze, alerting Shayne to the upcoming gallery. They seemed so out of place in the midst of the tropical landscape. The banners were the only signs of civilization they'd seen since they'd turned onto the long stretch of US 41.

Troy drove past the main building, following the narrow roadway leading around the back of the gallery. Shayne was thankful Gib had gotten his hands on a four-by-four for their escape. Debris from the recent tropical depression littered the single-lane road. They made their way past the first premises, its roof still covered with a blue tarp to prevent further water damage. Shayne assumed the roadway was better maintained when the buildings were available to the public.

About a half-mile later, their final destination came into view. The bungalow was built on stilts and was small. So much smaller than she'd imagined.

Troy maneuvered the vehicle between the substantial posts the building was perched on before popping the latch on the back of the Jeep. As Shayne stepped out onto the solid but damp ground, she felt her imaginary shackles slip away. She might be stuck in a swamp with a man who couldn't tolerate the sight of her, but there was some freedom the isolated location would allow her.

It took two trips to get everything up the stairs. Shayne unpacked and stored the groceries. Troy took off to survey the area. She didn't know how long they'd be there, but she suspected it was going to be more than a few days based on the amount of food that had been packed for them.

Once that chore was complete, she took a look around the bungalow. Her breath caught in her throat when she saw that Troy had placed her bag of meager possessions on the bed and his duffel on the floor at the foot of the same bed. One bed. Two people. *Shit!* That wasn't going to work. She grabbed her sack of personal items and headed out to the living room. The couch would have to do. No way Troy could squeeze his bulk onto it. She gave the piece of furniture a closer look, lifting up the cushions to confirm what she'd suspected: it didn't convert into a sofa bed.

"What are you doing?"

Shayne literally jumped at the sound of Troy's voice. The man moved like a cat. She hadn't heard a sound when he reentered the house.

Taking a deep breath, she ordered her heart to slow from a full gallop. When she faced him, she no longer had to hold her fist to her chest to keep the thumping organ from breaking through.

"I was checking to see if this was a sleeper sofa. It isn't, so you can have the bed."

His emerald-green eye flashed with fury. She'd angered him again. *Damn.* How the hell were they going to get along if a simple explanation set him off?

"You're in the bedroom. I'll be out here." It was an order.

"That doesn't make a lick of sense." Shayne planted her feet, fisted her hands on her hips, and stared back at him, mentally damning him for being such a stubborn asshole. "You won't fit on the couch. I will."

"The bedroom is yours. I'm out here. This isn't up for debate." Troy met her stare for stare.

"Why?" Shayne wasn't surprised when Troy huffed. Apparently, he wasn't used to having his orders questioned.

"Someone would have to get by me to get to you. That's why. End of discussion."

"You seriously believe someone is after me?" She no longer felt defiant. Still, logic argued with fear. "Even if that premise were true, who the hell would be looking for me in the middle of the Everglades?" The hairs on the back of Shayne's neck prickled. Something was going on, and she wasn't very good at fooling herself about it. Her bravado escaped like air from a balloon as she plopped onto the couch.

When Troy sat down beside her and took her hand, she almost jerked it free.

"I frightened you again. I'm sorry." He gave her fingers a comforting squeeze. "The relocation is only a precaution until we figure out what's going on."

Troy had adjusted his position so he could watch her more intently. Worry lines now etched his brow, replacing his temper. She'd rather have him angry. He was a little less appealing when he was mad. Not much, but a little. She took her hand back. "So, we wait here?"

"The team will be grilling the feds and digging hard for information. And you and I will be going over every second of that night at the country club."

Shayne stood. Every inch of her skin itched. She needed to move. "Do you know how many times I've been over it?"

she asked as she retreated toward the open kitchen. "Not just with the authorities but in my head?"

"Every night, I imagine."

Reaching in the fridge for a bottle of water, Shayne froze. Between anger, worry, and her battle against her attraction to him, she'd again forgotten Troy shared a similar, if not uglier kind of hell. "Sorry."

"No need," he replied, getting to his feet. He approached her, taking both her hands this time. "And maybe, just maybe, because we share similar experiences, we can look at that night another way."

Shayne stared at their hands, stunned by his statement and the empathy it held. She'd been able to steel herself against him since the kiss in her apartment, but if he started to care, the wall she'd been building between them might never be completed.

"Now, what was in that cooler that we can eat for dinner?" Troy asked.

Troy KNEW Shayne had come close to breaking down twice since the two of them walked in the door of the bungalow. Changing the subject seemed like the best way to avoid tears. And he avoided tears like the plague.

He rested his arms on the railing of the large deck, scanning the unforgiving swamp. He'd stepped outside, needing to put some distance between him and the woman inside. To his right, a grill stood in the corner—a new propane tank attached. They wouldn't be firing it up. Gib had thrown some steaks in the cooler, but Troy had discovered they shared an aversion to the smell of charred meat. Shayne had opted to prepare pasta.

The Jeep had been loaded with enough provisions to hold them for at least two weeks. He sincerely hoped they wouldn't be there that long. Jeezus, he had to get his head screwed on straight and keep his other one in his pants. Shayne did her best to play down her looks, but she couldn't hide the sparkle in her eyes when she smiled, the freckles on her nose that gradually disappeared into her cheeks, or those lips that looked like a cupid's bow.

Shayne had a warrior's spirit. She'd been fighting back when he'd mistaken her for the enemy. She'd stood toe to toe with him even when he'd dented that spirit. She suffered from night terrors, yet still got up every morning and put one foot in front of the other and got through each day. She found beauty in nature and joy from digging in the dirt. She was intelligent, sarcastic, strong... *Crap!* He was in deep shit.

"Everything is set in here," Shayne announced from the other side of the screen door that led to the deck.

Even through the mesh of the screening, Troy saw the gold in her eyes sparkle in the late afternoon light. Shayne's mood had improved, and that smile robbed Troy of his breath. But he wouldn't forget that look of shock as they parted from that single kiss, her fingers having brushed against the strap of his patch. He understood her revulsion. He was a stupid, adolescent fool for thinking of her as anything more than an assignment.

When Troy returned to the house, his mood was much less charitable than it had been when he'd stepped outside. Shayne was in the kitchen with her back to him as she poured tea into glasses filled with ice. Troy eyed the food that had already been placed on the table. He silently moved his plate of food along with the setting so that he would be sitting to Shayne's left. Vanity wasn't the sole reason, although he couldn't deny that wasn't partially behind the change in seating. She wouldn't be subjected to the picture he cast while eating dinner. People had a tendency to stare at his patch or the scars that escaped it. It was disconcerting and maddening.

"Something wrong with my seating arrangements?" Shayne asked as she returned to the room.

Troy's fork hovered over his dinner. "You have a problem with me sitting next to you?"

"No, but *you* seem to," she countered.

"You want to explain?"

Shayne had picked up her eating utensils then quickly set them on her plate to give Troy her full attention. "You don't want to be here—at least not with me. You've made that clear. So, I have to wonder why you moved closer. It's because you don't want me looking at your scars, right?"

Troy grunted. She called a spade a spade.

"My face can be a distraction to some people," he muttered. He felt like he'd gotten caught stealing from the cookie jar.

"I've worked with you every day. Why do you think your injury would suddenly bother me?"

"It's become a habit. If you want me to move, I'll move." He'd promised he'd not bring up that kiss again. If he reminded her of her reaction to it, he'd be breaking his word.

"Doesn't matter to me. Eat before your food gets cold," Shayne told him. "Let's save our discussion for after dinner. No point in ruining both our appetites."

The two ate in silence. The clinking of silverware against the dinner plates was magnified by the silence in the room.

He managed to finish his meal with only an occasional glance over at Shayne. Apparently, being aware of the upcoming conversation was enough to ruin her appetite.

She'd only taken a few bites before she spent the rest of the meal pushing the food aimlessly around on her plate.

"You need to eat," Troy commented as he headed toward the kitchen with his empty dish. He heard silverware clang as it hit her plate hard. Shayne's shoulders were as straight and rigid as a T square. His statement had come out sounding like a command and had not landed well.

"If you eat some more, you can have dessert," Troy offered in a poor attempt to lighten the tension. A few seconds passed before she laid her head into the palm of her hands.

He dropped his dish in the sink and returned to her side, crouching next to her chair. "What's wrong?"

"Nothing. Everything." Her fingers massaged her forehead. "I have a headache. Can you handle the cleanup?" She grabbed the wrist support she'd taken off before dinner and pushed back her chair. She didn't wait for Troy to respond. "I'm going to lie down."

Her head and shoulders drooping, Shayne silently left the room. All the fight had gone out of her. Troy looked back at the table and her plate of barely touched food. His own meal settled like a brick in his stomach. A headache? Something was definitely off. Should he check on her? Demand to know what was wrong? With the exception of Cat and Josie, Troy didn't *talk* with women. Too messy.

He blankly stared at the closed door. What did it say about him that he couldn't carry on a conversation with a member of the opposite sex? Since he regained consciousness in the hospital in Germany, he'd been learning a lot about himself. He didn't care for much of what he discovered as the layers slowly peeled away.

He fought the urge to make sure Shayne was okay. He'd fix a sandwich for her later, or a big breakfast in the morning. She needed to put on some weight. The tight jeans and tank top she'd been wearing were appealing, but they also showed her need for a few more pounds. She looked delicate. Not weak or sick, but certainly not the contrary woman he'd spent his days arguing with in the garden.

After tossing the remnants of Shayne's meal into the trash, he rinsed the dishes and placed them in the dishwasher. With that done, he decided to assess the property and area surrounding the building while it was still daylight. Snatching the satellite phone off the coffee table, he exited the rear of the building via the screened-in porch. The informational brochure left on the kitchen's breakfast bar described the bungalow and the area that surrounded it— thirteen acres of private, uninhabited land that backed up to Everglades National Park. Other than the gallery and the damaged cottage they'd passed on their way in, there was nothing, and hopefully no one, for miles. That situation made the location both good and bad. The gators, snakes, and even the pesky mosquitoes would act as a deterrent to unwanted visitors. But there also was no way he could patrol such a large area without backup when he needed to stay close to Shayne. Backup he suspected wasn't going to get here anytime soon. Troy cursed the fact that he'd known so little about this property before their expedited exit off the island. Too late now. He'd have to make do with what he had.

The croaking of alligators told him one or more were near. Mosquitoes buzzed and bit. In his rush to get outside, he hadn't stopped to apply insect repellent. He'd been bitten by worse and lived. There'd been times after the attack that he would have welcomed a place such as this so he could walk off into the abyss and be lost forever. Troy looked back toward the small house and the bedroom window glowing from the warm light within. He was glad that he hadn't come close to making that choice. He was needed.

WHEN SHAYNE HEARD the back door shut, she slipped from the bed and padded across the cool bamboo flooring to the solitary bedroom window. Peeking through the wide slats of the plantation blinds, she watched Troy stalk toward a dense stand of native trees and shrubs. Tension radiated from him. The intensity of it sent waves of concern pulsating in her direction.

Nerves had been tingling under her skin like an electrical storm since Troy had taken the seat next to her. Contrary to what he had surmised, she hadn't wanted him to move. She'd wanted him closer. She wanted to reach out and brush the back of her fingers against his cheek. His jaw had been covered with a coarse, dark stubble from a day's growth of beard. How would it feel against the softness of her skin? Instead, she'd tightened her grip around her fork. Better to stab him with the utensil than show any sign of affection. Was that what this feeling was? Or something more? Why the hell was she so attracted to such a jackass and why, of all times, now?

Once they'd sat down to dinner, her appetite had disappeared. The memory of the kiss, the taste of his lips on hers, had soured the meal. Then he teased her about dessert. Whether he'd meant to or not, his coaxing had come close to crumbling the last of her defenses. If she hadn't left the room, she'd have done something idiotic—like kiss him again. Now, while she was mooning over the jerk, he was patrolling the property looking for...what?

As soon as the focus of her attention disappeared

around the corner of the building, Shayne slipped across the hall into the bungalow's single bathroom. Pulling out her toiletries, she found the bottle of pills prescribed for stress.

She'd had the prescription filled after her release from the hospital but decided to face her demons on her own. But tonight, she'd hit a wall. She didn't have it in her to fight the onslaught of emotions. She wanted to forget about the bombing and whatever threat was hanging over her—and she wanted to forget Troy. If she could get a solid eight hours of sleep, perhaps she'd have a clearer head in the morning. She took one of the pills then quickly readied herself for bed.

TROY AGAIN SURVEYED the area for footprints or any other evidence of human activity. Not all his team's deployments had been to dry deserts. They'd seen their share of swamps and the creatures that called them home. As a result, he'd immediately recognized the alligator tracks he came upon in the boggy soil. The creature that had left them must be one big sucker. With laser focus, Troy swept his gaze across the hammock of live oaks, pines, and cabbage palms. He could hear the skittering of some of the smaller inhabitants of the ecosystem. He inhaled the smell of damp earth as he stood on the edge of knee-high water leading into the swamp. It was summer in the tropics. As Shayne liked to point out, it was rainy season. The thick brush that had become kindling during the dry winter months was now thriving in brown, brackish water. Grasses and ferns attached themselves to root stumps or downed trees that remained above the water line. The bromeliads and orchids grew higher up in the canopy, sucking up nutrients from the thick, tropical air.

He finished his patrol of the property then went to the simple wooden shed that sat adjacent to the house. The narrow, six-foot-tall structure was built on a thick slab of solid concrete, raising it above ground level. A cinder block acted as a single step. He slipped the key he found on a hook inside one of the kitchen cabinets into the lock. When Troy yanked the door open, cockroaches scurried into the darkened corners while several brown anole lizards escaped toward the light. Ignoring the shed's inhabitants, he scanned the interior. Rope, wire, screening material, and other odds and ends were stashed against the walls or sat on shelves. Keeping these items on the property would save a handyman a long trip to God knew where to find the needed supplies. Yet for all the crap stored in the shed, the only tool he found was a pair of rusted pliers.

Troy took the pliers along with some wire and rope, before heading back to the bungalow. By that time, the sun was casting long shadows through the trees as it began to set.

He placed the procured items on the floor next to the dining room table then headed toward the bedroom. It was past time he checked on Shayne. He tapped lightly on the bedroom door then waited. His hearing, which had always been keen, seemed sharper since the injury. He should be deaf and blind on the left side, but he'd fortunately lost only one of the two senses. No sound emanated from the room. He reached for the knob and let out his breath when it turned freely in his hand. The unlocked door saved him the trouble of deciding whether to force his way in.

The bedside lamp cast a yellow hue over the room. Shayne had fallen asleep with the light on. She was curled up on top of the bedcovers. She'd changed into one of her baggy T-shirts and what looked like a pair of men's boxer shorts. Were they? He pushed that thought aside as he gently covered her with a throw from the foot of the bed. He remembered she liked the temperature low when she slept. He'd adjust the thermostat before he called Rick. He switched off the lamp and stepped back into the hallway, leaving her door slightly ajar.

Troy made a stop by the bathroom. Shayne hadn't spent all her time sequestered in the bedroom while he'd been outside reconnoitering. She'd taken the time to set out her toiletries on the small vanity. The small number of items she considered necessary shouldn't have surprised him. He already knew she traveled light. But for some reason, he felt she deserved more. Much more. Moisturizer, sunscreen, and face wash along with toothpaste and a toothbrush, were bare essentials for most women. Was it because she couldn't afford the fripperies, as she'd called them, or did she prefer the minimalist lifestyle? And why should it matter to him?

The last question followed him down the hall. He had work to do, but first he had a call to make.

23

"'B out time," Rick answered.

"You learn anything new?" Troy didn't want to waste time on small talk.

"Is Shayne there?" Rick asked.

It was obvious from the background noise that Rick had put his phone on speaker. Troy gripped his cell phone tightly in his hand. Fortunately, they'd had no trouble getting a signal since they arrived.

"She's asleep—which is surprising. She's strung as tight as a garrote, and I'm betting you're going to tell me something that won't improve her condition." How much more could Shayne take? This wasn't her fight. A simple act of kindness had become an unending nightmare for her.

"Who's at your end?" Troy asked.

"Steve, Colt, Gib, Cat and Josie," Rick boomed over a chorus of answers.

The fact that Cat and Josie were present didn't surprise Troy. Cat would hardly be left out of the fray, and Steve's protective instincts wouldn't have permitted him to leave Josie alone, especially now that she was expecting.

"Okay," Troy said more to himself than those at the other end of the line. He wiped the perspiration from his brow with the back of his forearm. This was a mission. He'd been on plenty of missions. "Fill me in, and tell me exactly how long you expect us to remain in this swamp. The alligator that left the tracks I saw outside could swallow Shayne whole."

"Snaggletooth," Colt said. "He's been a resident there for over twenty years and is very territorial. Keep your distance."

"Damn straight," Troy huffed. "Now, where do we stand?"

"Hernandez and Morgan showed up here shortly after you took off. They suggested Shayne should return with them."

Troy had been sitting on one of the dining room chairs. His intent had been to clean his pistol as soon as the call was complete. Shooting out of his chair, he began to pace the small living area. The scar tissue that trailed over his left jawbone throbbed as the muscles in his neck tightened.

"They aren't getting her." Troy recognized the laughter that immediately followed as Gib's. It wasn't funny. "I'm serious. They can't have her."

"They didn't press. Didn't argue. That is telling on its own," Colt told him.

"Could they be listening in on this conversation?"

"Doubt it. Your disappearance was unexpected," Rick said. "They can't just tap a phone or bug a place without a warrant, and they'd have to have reason to get a judge to sign off. I don't see one, and even if they did, it would take time."

"What did you tell them?" Troy asked.

"Only that the two of you left together."

"They've got to know that you know." Troy continued to pace. The living space seemed to grow smaller as the conversation continued.

"We didn't deny it," Steve told him. "But we didn't confirm it, either."

"They'll be back."

"They never left," Cat said.

"Right now, they're cooling their heels in their car outside. We'll deal with them," Colt said. "They're probably deciding how much they can or want to share. They appeared genuinely concerned for her safety. We questioned them on the leak of Shayne's location. I don't believe they're behind it. If we can get the suits to share anything, that could save us a lot of time."

"Did you get anything out of your visitors other than their desire to take Shayne back with them?" Troy asked.

"Not a whole hell of a lot," Colt admitted. "I expect we'll see them in the morning, but other than your location, we don't have much of a bargaining chip."

"You're not giving that up. Right?"

"I gave you my word we wouldn't," Colt assured him.

"We're working some other angles," Steve said. "Don should be on this soon, and Josie has put out some feelers as well."

"I don't want Josie involved in this." Troy's pacing came to an abrupt stop.

"Tough."

Josie's Southern drawl was recognizable in that single word. Steve's tall, dark-haired wife hailed from North Carolina. A freelance journalist, she had a network of contacts and friends she could tap for information. Information that led to the arrest of a state's attorney the previous year.

"I don't like it," Troy countered.

"Trust me," Steve assured him. "We've got her covered. Besides, there was no way to keep her from poking her nose into this."

"Hey!" Josie said.

Steve was right. Josie would have gone behind her husband's back once she was aware of a mystery that needed solving. She wouldn't be able to resist.

"Tell me what you learned today," Troy said. "Are we sure they weren't setting her up? Trying to draw out someone?"

"I have a hard time believing they'd use her as bait any more than we would," Rick answered. "We don't always see eye to eye, but they're honest, by-the-book agents."

Troy gave a glance at the bedroom door, fearing his raised voice might have awakened Shayne. By her own admission, she didn't sleep well. He headed out to the screened porch for the added sound buffer and the extended space to prowl.

The night was hot and muggy. His eye tracked the darkened landscape upward as it bled into the night sky where stars sparkled in abundance. They reminded Troy of the golden flecks in Shayne's eyes.

"We'll tackle them tomorrow," Rick said. "They brought this to our doorstep. They damn well better enlighten us."

"You've got a lot of feelers out—" Troy began. He was concerned one of those feelers could lead back to Shayne.

"We know the drill," Colt answered Troy before he could complete the question. "No one knows where you are. We plan on keeping it that way."

"How's Shayne holding up?" Gib asked.

Of course Gib would be the one to ask about Shayne.

"She claimed she had a headache. Went to bed early. She didn't eat. The woman's skinny enough as it is."

The silence that hung in the air told Troy he'd revealed too much. "Call as soon as you know something more." Troy disconnected as he headed toward the bedroom.

24

Shayne raced down the uneven trail. It was dark. She couldn't see but she could hear the heavy pounding of feet behind her. He was gaining on her, the distance between them shrinking. *Run! Don't look!* She looked. The simple turn of her head started her free fall. The man, his face in shadows, dropped to the ground next to her before she could regain her footing. When his massive hands reached for her neck, she screamed.

The blast snapped her head to one side, sending the man flying into oblivion. She covered her eyes with her arms and tightened into a ball, waiting for the searing heat.

"Shayne!"

She heard her name as her forearms were tugged away from her face. As she blinked against the light, Troy's face broke through the thick fog. Her mind sluggishly switched from fantasy to reality.

"Nightmare?" Troy asked.

She nodded, her lungs still sucking in air. "Sorry."

While she fought the battle against tears, Troy squeezed her arm then left her side. She watched as he quickly checked the closet and stopped to look through the slats of the blinds. "I'm going to double-check the rest of the place. Don't move. I'll be right back."

Shayne didn't think it was possible for her to move. She hadn't gotten past the trembling and seriously doubted her legs would hold her. *Damn it!* She'd taken that pill to avoid such an incident. Glancing at the bedside clock, she saw she had managed a few hours of sleep. In addition, her headache that had been brewing was gone. She couldn't gather much enthusiasm for either of those successes. Now, she had to deal with Troy.

The place was so small that it didn't take long for Troy to return to the confines of the bedroom. Scooting up on the bed, she leaned back against the headboard.

"We're locked up tight. Is there something I can get you?" he asked, turning on the bedside lamp. Troy was standing so close to her that she could feel his heat.

"No, I'll be fine." Shayne pulled her knees up to her chin.

"You've had a rough couple of days. Don't you have something to take the edge off?"

Shayne slapped her hand against the mattress. "I took something earlier and look where it got me." When she looked up at him, his striking green eye was staring worriedly into hers. "I'm fine now."

"You don't look fine."

When had she ever looked good to this man? She reached for the book that she'd placed on the nightstand before going to bed. "I'll read some. It may put me to sleep." She lifted a hand that was steadier and shooed him away. "Go. Do whatever it was you were doing before my stupid nightmare."

Troy kept surprising her. He crouched next to the bed.

"We all have nightmares, Shayne. It's nothing to be ashamed of."

"What makes you think I'm ashamed?"

"The way you're chasing me out of the room. Talking could help. Not only your state of mind but sometimes they hold keys to actual events."

"What are you? A psychologist now?"

"No. Just been there, done that."

Shayne felt that twinge of guilt stir again. Why did she keep forgetting he'd been through something much more frightening than she'd experienced? "I can't see you opening up to counselors." Skepticism laced her words.

"If I wanted out of the hospital, I had to talk to the shrinks."

"Did it help?"

He offered more of a sneer than a smile. "I wasn't interested in help."

"So, the short answer is 'no.'" If he'd answered yes, Shayne would have been dumbstruck. He'd apparently spent months prior to turning up on Sanibel trying to drown his issues in alcohol. "I'll pass on the therapy," she told him, making a show of returning her attention to the book.

When Troy's large hand covered hers, her head snapped up.

"Damn, you're as cold as an icicle." Troy grabbed her other hand and began to rub them between his palms.

God, it felt good. She let her eyes drift closed as heat from his hands seeped into her. The man was a furnace. She hadn't realized how cold she was until he'd touched her. When those warming hands moved up her arms, her eyes flew open. As had become his habit in the last twenty-four hours, he kept his face averted. It angered her that he still believed she found his scars disturbing. It also hurt that he'd think she was so shallow. Of course, there could be another reason he didn't look at her, which was almost as hurtful.

"Does it kill you to look at me?" she asked, pulling away from him. Her arms slipped from his grasp.

"What?"

She had his attention now. "Am I that hard to look at, or are you suddenly shy about your appearance?"

"My face…"

"Is a badge of honor," Shayne blurted out, surprising herself.

"There is no honor in this. Trust me."

He'd quickly stood and turned his back to her. She studied his broad shoulders beneath the taut T-shirt. They were arched with tension. The injury went deeper than the physical scars, but she had no right to pry. He wasn't going to talk, and she wasn't in a position to do anything about it, even if he accepted her offer of a shoulder. She was in a mess, and all bets were off as to whether she'd be successful putting her own life back together again. The steel backbone that her dad had been so proud of was again bending. She was tired. Her instinct was to take her chances and walk away. She could sneak out to the highway when Troy fell asleep—he'd eventually have to—and hitch a ride to the Keys or Miami. She could almost hear her dad tell her that was a stupid idea. She missed him. If he were here, he'd lecture her on feeling sorry for herself then he'd give Troy a swift kick in the ass and tell him the same. Nope. She was too messed up to go digging into Troy's issues.

"If you say so," she murmured, letting his statement go. "But if you plan to grill me on the bombing, we're going to have to occasionally look at one another."

Shayne stood so she could pull back the comforter she'd been sleeping on. "Do you think we could return to tolerating each other? I'm sorry I got you and your friends involved in this mess." She crawled into bed. "If I had a way out, I'd take it."

Tossing her book on the bedside table, she reached for the light.

"This isn't your fault," Troy told her.

When she flicked the switch, the room was engulfed in darkness. Surprisingly, she yawned. "I don't want to talk anymore tonight." To punctuate her statement, she turned her back to him. The shot of adrenaline had faded, and with any luck, her tranquilizer still had a little juice left in it. She was so very tired.

25

Troy dodged popping grease to remove crisp slices of bacon from the frying pan. He placed them on a baking sheet he'd covered with paper towels. He eyed the portions and decided it wouldn't hurt to cook a couple more slices. Shayne needed to put on some pounds.

He broke a half-dozen eggs into a bowl, added some salt and pepper, and then, for good measure, added more eggs before he began to beat them. A loaf of bread sat on the granite countertop next to the toaster, ready to go once Shayne made her appearance.

After he'd left her last night, he spent his time constructing some simple defenses with the items he'd procured from the shed. When those tasks were completed, he'd allowed himself to slip into a half sleep in the large living room chair. Rest was necessary if Shayne's protection was to continue to fall solely on him. Still, he was up at daybreak, patrolling the small patch of land the bungalow was located on. The tripwires he had set in place at the base of each staircase were still strung tight. Animal tracks were evident in the boggy soil surrounding the property, but there was no sign of human activity.

After that detail was done, Troy had slipped back into the house and quietly looked in on Shayne. He showered and shaved before she awoke. With the cooking done, he leaned against the counter and sipped his coffee, debating whether to check on Shayne again. By her own accounts, she was an early riser. The sound of the bedroom door opening saved him from having to make that decision.

He heard the toilet flush, then the shower. Apparently, Shayne could live without a shot of caffeine right off the bat. Though, to be honest, she drank more cream than coffee. He still remembered the taste of the sweet liquid on his lips. That wasn't smart. He hated that she believed he didn't want her, but her continued assumption would serve as a firewall between them. *Fire.* Funny. He felt the heat when she was near, and damned if he could explain why or convince himself otherwise.

When the shower shut off, he poured coffee into a cup of cream. He was tempted to taste it to see if he got the ratio of cream to coffee right, but then he'd be in deep shit again. The door to the bathroom opened. He waited. She didn't strike him as someone who ran from a fight, but the last few days had been rough. She needed to eat, and if she didn't come around the corner momentarily, he'd be dragging her out of the room.

It wasn't necessary.

"Good morning." She smiled as she entered the kitchen. Shayne reached for the coffee he slid toward her on the counter. A small grin lit up her face when she saw the light brown color of the coffee in the cup. He'd scored. *Damn.*

After a sip Shayne's eyes grew wide as she glanced at the counter. "Are we expecting company?"

"It's called breakfast," he explained, pulling the pan of crisp bacon from the oven.

"You've made enough for an army."

"You didn't eat last night," Troy reminded her.

"I'm hungry, but not *that* hungry." Shayne grinned. "Hopefully, you are."

The invisible band forcing Troy's shoulder blades together loosened at her cheerful tone. All might not be forgiven, but she wasn't snapping at him. He scanned the counter loaded with food. He *had* overdone it. What started as a silent chuckle surprised him when it became a full-fledged laugh.

SHAYNE SAT with Troy at the table they'd shared the evening before. Instead of taking the seat next to her as he had last night, he'd set his plate, piled high with bacon, eggs, and toast, directly across from her. They seemed to be making progress.

The aroma of the hickory-smoked bacon made her stomach growl. "Have you heard anything?" she asked while she munched on her food.

"That's right. We haven't discussed last night's call." Troy shoveled up a forkful of eggs.

"What call?" She dropped her eating utensil.

"Keep eating and I'll tell you," he told her.

The statement was given casually enough. Some panic left her. "What call?" she repeated, taking a bite of toast.

"I heard from the team last night." He paused. "Cat and Josie say hi, by the way."

"Hi back. Now, what was the call about?"

"Hernandez and Morgan showed up. They want you

back," Troy answered, his attention still directed at the breakfast in front of him.

Shayne's appetite dropped with her stomach.

"They're not getting you."

His statement was firm and quick—delivered before her heart had missed a single beat. When she looked up at him, he was watching her intently. "Eat."

The confidence in Troy's voice steadied her. "How can you be so sure? Won't your friends get in trouble for hiding me?"

"What sort of trouble? You're not wanted for a crime, are you?" He smirked. "You're not under arrest. There is no law being broken simply because they haven't shared your whereabouts. The FBI could eventually track you here if they put enough effort and resources into it. You've been pretty low on their list of priorities, so I expect that will take a while, assuming they're even working on it."

Troy continued to eat. Shayne found herself mesmerized by his ability to put away food—and by the confidence of his statements. "Assuming Hernandez and Morgan are looking for me, how would they find us?"

"They'd probably go through rental car agencies to see if any names click with cars rented in the last few days. If that panned out, they'd track us through the GPS on the vehicle."

"Shit," Shayne swore, pushing back from the table.

"Finish your breakfast," Troy ordered her. "And stop worrying. No way Gib went through normal channels to get our ride. Besides, even if he did, that sort of trace takes time and people."

That made sense. She hadn't been thinking clearly since the incident in the alley. She picked up her fork. "Will you ask?"

Troy nodded. "When I talk to them later on."

"So, what did you learn last night?" Shayne asked, relaxing a bit.

"Not much. The feds are hanging around and the guys are digging deeper into the bombing. The team is back on U.S. soil. We may have additional backup, if needed." Troy walked his empty plate to the kitchen and refilled his cup. He lifted the pot in a silent offer to her. Shayne shook her head.

Troy dumped the remaining coffee into the sink then rinsed the pot. "I'd like to go over everything you remember about that evening. I know you've done this before, but maybe I can trigger an elusive memory. You game?"

Shayne wasn't sure what was happening between the two of them. She didn't know what had happened to change his attitude, but he was no longer distant or resentful at being her caretaker. They'd talked of a truce. It would appear they'd reached one. She would do her best not to break it, but with the wall between them crumbling, would her emotions do the same?

26

Before they got into the details of that deadly night, Troy left to make another pass around the perimeter of the building. In addition to checking the area, it gave him the time needed to get his head screwed on straight. They were going to be discussing a bombing. Instinctively, he reached for the patch covering his eye but stopped himself midway through the movement. This wasn't about him, no matter how close the subject came to his past. He'd been avoiding the memories and the ache that accompanied them. Until recently, he'd drowned them in drink. Eventually he would have to face those memories if he was to move on with his life. It was the reason he'd sought out his friends. The woman waiting for him had more guts than he did. She didn't back away from a fight, while he'd spent the last six months running from his demons.

In addition to the memories their discussion would resurrect, he'd be fighting another battle. He'd clearly seen the change in her expression, a softening in her reaction to him, as they'd policed the kitchen. Troy struggled against his ongoing attraction to her, despite the fact that she'd resumed her habit of wearing baggy clothing. It didn't matter to him. This desire to get close to her was something more than physical attraction. An attraction he didn't understand.

Inhaling the scent of brackish water instead of Shayne's spicy scent, he ordered his mind back to the reason for his trek outside. There were no signs of human activity since his pre-breakfast reconnoiter. He stood on the edge of the saturated hammock and studied the wilderness in front of him. It was beautiful, in its unique and unforgiving way. He hoped Snaggletooth was too busy with the ladies to bother them during their stay. He had no desire to wrestle with the monster. The best-trained and most physically fit soldier would wind up on the losing end of a fight with the prehistoric descendant.

Troy checked the simple traps he'd set up last night. A professional would spot them in a heartbeat, but they might give a rookie pause. The rope he'd strung across the drive to their bungalow blended into the brown and green landscape. The wires he'd strung between the posts on the front and back steps gave him little confidence but you worked with what you had—and he didn't have much.

He looked back toward the house. Personally, he'd prefer to be with the team, solving the puzzle and searching for Shayne's pursuers. But logically, this was the best place for her. His skin prickled as he scanned the surrounding area. He had a bad feeling. His gut told him something was brewing.

Troy tried to shake off the feeling as he returned to the bungalow. When he entered, Shayne was sitting lotus style on the floor next to the couch, a pad of paper on the coffee table in front of her. She was chewing on the end of a pen, concentrating hard on the notepad. She looked up as the door shut behind him.

"Hi," she said, smiling softly. "All safe and sound?"

Troy instantly felt like he'd been sucker-punched. The gold flecks in her eyes shimmered in the daylight. Her soft voice held a hint of laughter. When she cocked her head, he remembered to breathe.

"We're good. What are you doing?" he asked, tearing his eye from hers and focusing on the pad.

"Making notes. Key points I remember. I've given every agency a statement, but I've yet to make notes for myself. It might help."

Troy crossed the room and glanced over her shoulder, keeping his hands in the pockets of his jeans. The urge to lay a hand on her shoulder and give her a supportive squeeze was strong, but he managed to fight it.

"Has it helped?"

"No," Shayne huffed. When her shoulders slumped, he fought the urge to reach for her. He was either a jerk or a man of steel.

"Okay," Troy said. "Then let's go over it together."

He pulled a couple of bottles of water out of the refrigerator and handed one to Shayne. He swiped the notes off the table then fell back into the chair he'd dozed in the night before.

"There's not much here," he said.

"There's not much to tell. At least not from my perspective. I readied the dining room bar for the next day then stopped to help the bartender break down one of the portable bars set up for the event. Then everything went boom. Ten minutes, max." Shayne twisted the cap off her bottle. "I didn't notice anything unusual until then. That was kind of hard to miss."

"What about the man who left the room?"

"What about him?" Shayne scowled.

He was tempted to kiss her pouty mouth. "Did anything stand out?"

"He was just a man walking. He wasn't running. There was nothing unusual about him. They even had me work with a sketch artist, and we put together a good resemblance of a man striding away in a suit. It was a waste of time. The description matches a quarter of the white male population."

"You're sure he was Caucasian?"

"Yes. He had short, dark blond hair. I could see the back of his neck."

"How long between the time you saw him and the explosion?"

Shayne let out a long breath. They weren't going to get very far if she lost patience this easily. Troy put her notes back on the coffee table and rested his forearms on his thighs. "What was your day like?"

"Huh?" Deep furrows etched Shayne's forehead.

"Back up a bit. You've been repeating the same events. Let's start somewhere different," Troy explained. "How'd your day begin?"

Shayne cocked her head. "Like any other day, I guess."

WITH ALL THE emphasis directed to what she'd seen that night, she'd forgotten the time that preceded it. The investigators had picked apart every second after she'd arrived at work to the moment she was pulled from the rubble. No one, including herself, had torn into the time before she'd arrived.

"I don't see how that's going to help," she muttered, literally scratching her head.

"You never know," Troy said. "Anything unusual happen that morning?"

Shayne almost said no. She hadn't thought anything about that day except for the time that framed the bombing. It was as if everything that had come before her decision to stop and help had taken place in another lifetime. What had she done that day besides survive?

"Shayne?" Troy asked. "You okay?"

"I'm trying to remember."

"You can't remember?"

"God, it's like the bombing erased the first part of the day." She paused, struggling to organize her thoughts.

"Do you remember going to work?"

"Sure." She let out a small breath. "Yes," she answered, more firmly this time, relieved as the memories began to return. "I remember getting to the club and thinking it was going to be a long night."

"Why?"

"As I pulled around the building to the employee parking area, I didn't see many cars in the public parking lot."

"What time did you get there?" Troy took a slug of water.

"Around three o'clock that afternoon."

"That would be kind of early to be busy, wouldn't it?" he asked, capping his bottle.

"We were rarely very busy that time of day, but I could pretty well gauge the evening crowd by the number of people that hung around after playing golf or tennis. If the bar stayed busy after lunch, we tended to be busy in the dining room that evening."

"Why was that?"

"Couldn't tell you. It was a pattern I'd noticed."

"No, I mean why were things slow that night?"

"Because of the gala," Shayne answered. "The residents were never fond of the big events the club hosted. They understood the income they brought into the community and were always supportive of the charitable causes, but the bigger ones interrupted their routines. Regular guests tended to go out to dinner elsewhere or stay home." Shayne leaned against the back of the couch.

"So, everyone in the community knew the fundraiser was scheduled?"

"Hell, I think everyone in Florida knew about it. It was a huge event. In my opinion, it should have been held at one of the larger hotels downtown." Shayne pulled her knees up to her chest.

"Why wasn't it?"

"Hell if I know. They didn't make a habit of consulting bartenders when I worked there."

"Might be a question for the guys to dig into," Troy said. "From what I read, it was a charity fundraiser. Not a political event, right?"

"Right. The club hosted the event annually. It has always been a well-supported fundraiser for local shelters helping abused and battered women. In previous years, the attendance was good but didn't bust the seams of the club. They had to open up the adjoining ballroom to accommodate the additional tickets sold for that night. I suspect the breakthrough of the MeToo movement had something to do with the increased interest." And it was about damn time.

"Were a lot of politicians there?"

"I can't help you with any information concerning the actual event. I don't know who was invited or who attended. I worked the dining room bar all night. Stopping to help the bartender was my only connection. If I hadn't stopped, I suspect I wouldn't be here now." Standing, Shayne walked to the picture window and stared out at the dense wetland. Even though she'd been over every detail a hundred times, she still couldn't get past the fear that bubbled up inside her with each telling.

"I wonder if there are any ghost orchids out there," Shayne said, taking a minute to gather herself. "They're endangered, you know."

"No, I didn't," Troy responded.

"No reason you should." Shayne glanced at his reflection in the window. He'd moved to stand behind her. "Sorry. I should be used to this by now."

"I don't think you ever get used to it."

She'd done it again. "How do I keep forgetting that you went through worse?" she asked as she turned around.

"Good question. There's a neon sign on my face."

27

Shayne's head snapped back at his slashing remark. "What the hell prompted that? I've never called attention to your injury."

Troy wasn't sure why he'd thrown that at her. He'd told himself he'd gotten past the loss of his *GQ* model looks. Why did he care what she thought of him? Yet he continually pointed the scars out to Shayne, almost begging for a response. "No, but you've made your disdain for me clear."

"You don't know shit." She stormed into the small kitchen and disappeared behind the refrigerator door she'd flung open.

"What are you looking for?" Troy snapped, annoyed she'd walked away from him.

"Wine would be good," she shouted back.

"It's barely noon."

"It's five o'clock somewhere," she said. "And since when did the time of day ever stop you from drinking?"

That stung. He hadn't had a drink since the day he'd arrived on Sanibel, and to his surprise, he hadn't had the desire for one. Now he had a mission. He damn well wasn't going to screw it up with alcohol.

When she reappeared from behind the open door, she was glaring at him. "What the hell has gotten into you? This was supposed to be a discussion of what happened at Copperhead, not some damn commentary on our looks."

He noted a soft drink in her hand instead of the sought-after wine.

"There's nothing wrong with your looks."

"We agreed not to talk about that." She popped the top on the soda can.

"No, we agreed not to discuss the kiss," he said, approaching her.

"What kiss?"

Troy stopped. He had to give Shayne credit. She hadn't missed a beat with her return volley. She even stared back at him with a look of wide-eyed curiosity. He was tempted to kiss her until those eyes filled with passion. He took a step back.

"Why do you put so much effort into looking unappealing? You're not very successful at it. Remember those miscreants giving you the once-over at the convenience store?"

"They'd have probably considered a heifer appealing."

"Knock it off."

"You're right," Shayne agreed quickly, surprising him. "Look. I don't care what you think of me or my choice of clothing...and I don't see why it matters."

"It doesn't matter but for a pretty woman to hide..." Troy stopped, a fear suddenly broadsiding him. "Did something happen to you? Has anyone touched you inappropriately?"

Troy reached for her, but she backed away.

"No one has touched me. Not in the way you mean." Shayne pressed her back against the kitchen counter.

"If anyone did, I want to know." He'd kill the son of a bitch.

"No one touched me," she repeated. "Why do you insist on analyzing me?"

"Analyzing situations and people is what I do. Or did."

"Fine. Then let's get back to analyzing my last evening at Copperhead."

SHAYNE STUDIED the condensation as it trickled down the sides of her soda can. She'd returned to the living area, this time taking a spot on the couch instead of the floor. Troy didn't sit. He paced back and forth like a caged tiger. He'd questioned if she'd been molested. She suspected he was walking off the fire that had flared within him. Her heart melted at his concern. Not good.

"You ready?" Shayne asked.

"Huh?"

"Are you ready to finish reviewing the events of my big night?" she asked.

"Right." Before he joined her in the living room, he grabbed another water from the refrigerator then settled into the living room chair. He picked up the notes she'd made earlier.

"What did you do before you went to work that day?" he asked, after reviewing the items she'd listed. They obviously told him nothing he didn't already know.

"What difference does that make?"

"Probably nothing, but let's start at the beginning," Troy said, reaching for the pen that had been next to the pad.

Shayne couldn't imagine her day would have any significance, but they were back under a cease-fire. She went along with it.

"I don't remember anything specific about that morning."

"It was a Saturday. Did you have a routine?"

"I worked every weekend, so I hung around the apartment those mornings. I went to the gym and did my shopping during the week while the rest of the world was at work."

"No phone calls or visitors?" Troy asked.

"No. This has nothing to do with me."

"It has everything to do with you now. You were targeted on Sanibel. We're clearing the slate—making sure we're not being led in the wrong direction."

"You have a suspicious mind," Shayne told him.

"Remind me to tell you sometime about Cat and her stalker."

"What?"

"Anything unusual that morning?"

"No. Wait. What happened to Cat?" How the hell could he drop that tidbit and expect her not to be curious?

"Later, I said. What happened when you got to work?"

"The normal stuff," Shayne snapped, annoyed at his refusal to answer her question.

"What was normal? Walk me through it." Troy had flipped the page on the pad.

Shayne let her curiosity regarding Cat slide away then closed her eyes, picturing the day. It had started out so normal, but it had ended by changing her life.

"I clocked in, then went to the dining room to set up for the evening."

"Where was the time clock located?"

This was going to be more tedious than questioning by the authorities. She went over every step she'd taken prepping for the day.

"The evening was uneventful?" Troy asked when she'd finished.

"It was normal. Slow but normal."

"Did you talk to anyone?" Troy asked as he made some notes.

"I filled drink orders. My regular foursome came in an hour before closing." Shayne paused. "One of them, Mr. Russell, lost his son in the explosion."

Troy stopped writing to stare at her. "You knew one of the victims?"

"No. But his dad would stop by the bar most nights with his friends for a drink. I never met his son. I only saw him from a distance when the family ate together in the main dining room. I never got the chance to give his dad my condolences. I should have sent a card, at least."

"You had your own shit to deal with at the time. I'm sure he understood." Troy leaned back in his chair. "And the other man who was killed? Did you know him?"

"Never heard of him before the names of the victims were released."

"How long did you work at the club?"

"I started part-time while I was in college then went full time after I graduated. I guess it was close to five years." Her eyes narrowed as she leaned back and crossed her arms over her chest. "What difference does that make?"

"You didn't go to college to learn how to tend bar."

It was a statement—one Troy, apparently, expected her to explain. Why did people look down their noses at individuals who chose a job in the service industry over one behind a desk? It was as if they settled for some lowly position because they were incapable of finding one in the more prestigious white-collar world. It pissed her off when people made those sanctimonious assumptions.

"I discovered that tending bar paid a hell of a lot better than being a librarian or a historian. Besides, I had student loans to pay off."

"Did you plan on finding a job other than tending bar?"

"This shit has nothing to do with the bombing. Why the hell do you care what I do for a living? You had nothing against bartenders before we met."

Troy flashed her a look that had chills racing down her spine then freezing into one solid, inflexible rod. Her heated anger was replaced by uncertainty, fear, and regret.

THE SECOND CRACK about his drinking hit him just as hard as the first. A few weeks ago, if she'd been a man, he'd have taken her on with fists flying. Now, he allowed the words to sink in and simmer below the surface. As his temper cooled, the comment that preceded the cutting remark cracked opened a door, giving him an insight into her thinking. He was beginning to figure her out—which should scare him. Shayne lashed out whenever the opportunity presented itself because she didn't want him getting close. Was she fighting to keep her emotional distance? When you were at war, you used the weapons you had at hand. Words were her weapon.

Something akin to kindling lay between them, so he understood her need for distance, even if she didn't. One spark would set off a forest fire. One that could consume them both. So he backed off. Let the hurt slide away. With Shayne's life in play, he wouldn't engage in the battle.

Yet there was more than worry for her safety involved. He felt an unfamiliar flutter deep in his gut. He cared for her. God help him. He more than cared.

Now what? He had no idea how to react to that revelation. He was too stunned to speak, which was just as well. There was too much going on. Too many distractions for him to dwell on what he felt. This wasn't the time or the place. Shayne was his responsibility. Being distracted could get her killed.

"I'm sorry," Shayne said, breaking the silence. "That was cruel and uncalled for."

"But true." Troy tore his eye away from the gold dust shimmering in her eyes. He hadn't realized he was staring until she'd spoken. Had he looked like some lovestruck teenager? This wasn't happening. He couldn't let it happen. She was an assignment. She would never be anything more.

"Doesn't make it any less cruel."

"Apology accepted." Troy picked up his water, tilted his head back, and finished off the bottle. He tossed it into the recycling bin as he passed the kitchen. Instead of burying his memories in alcohol, he'd recently been drowning his emotions with water. A bathroom was in order.

When he reentered the living room, he almost laughed. Shayne had retrieved two more bottles of water from the refrigerator. She held one bottle in her hand. The other sat on the table in front of his chair.

Troy glanced at his watch. He was surprised it was after noon, and he still hadn't heard from the team on Sanibel. "We'll pick this up later. It's time I took another walk around the property." And it was past time he'd checked the vacant house that sat between them and the studio. He tucked his pistol into the waistband of his jeans. "I should be back in an hour or so," he told her before escaping through the screened porch. "Stay inside and lock the doors."

THE INSTANT TROY stepped on the ground, his mind was focused on the task at hand. He walked the property's perimeter, searching for signs of visitors, both human and animal. He recognized the tracks of a raccoon in the soft soil, and at the water's edge, imprints made by some sort of frog. No sign of Snaggletooth or any human activity. Nothing large enough to cause him concern. It drove him nuts that he didn't have the gear or the men to search the swamp. At the same time, chances of finding anything in the wet environment would be slim unless their suspect tromped around like the Hulk.

He headed back toward the building, checked the car, then sprinted toward the cottage.

Troy didn't have a key to this property. He'd make the decision whether he'd have to resort to some breaking and entering after he took a closer look around the building. There was no reason to think it was inhabited, but it was the nearest shelter to the bungalow. It was better to be safe than sorry.

The plot of land was larger and higher than the one the bungalow stood on. Troy found tracks from a variety of wildlife, including panther tracks at the outer edges of the property that dropped off into the boggy soil. Another reason to be cautious. The soil and patches of grass showed no tire tracks or human footprints.

The doors to the enclosed parking area beneath the building were secured. The guests of the rental were apparently given an electronic garage door opener when they checked in. The ground-level entry door was locked tight.

Troy examined the area around the lock but saw no signs of tampering. He made his way around the building, looking through each of the windows. Nothing appeared out of the ordinary. He hiked up the stairs to the living area, examining each tread carefully as he went. As he expected, the door at the landing was also locked—double bolted. There were no obvious signs of forced entry.

Anxious to get back to Shayne, he double-timed it down the steps. As he hit the ground, his cell rang. Finally.

"McKenzie."

"We just left Rick's office," Colt told him. "Things have gotten a bit more complicated."

"How much more complicated?" Troy could hear the roar of Steve's Mustang in the background, but it didn't hide the tension in Colt's voice.

"We knew the FBI, ATF, and Homeland Security were investigating the bombing. We discovered there is another player. One whose involvement hasn't been released."

Troy's grip tightened on the phone. "Spit it out."

"The Drug Enforcement Agency," Colt told him.

"The DEA?" Troy stopped in his tracks. "What the fuck does the DEA have to do with this?"

"We don't know. Hernandez and Morgan volunteered that information with the warning if we told anyone they'd deny we heard it from them."

"So what good does it do us?" Troy resumed his trek to the bungalow.

"It gives us another area to look into."

"As if we didn't have enough already," Troy said.

"Josie is in contact with an investigative reporter in Tampa. He should be getting back to her this afternoon, and Don is working this from his end," Colt told him. "Has Shayne come up with anything more?"

"Not yet." Troy had the bungalow in sight.

"The suits are on their way back to Tampa," Colt said. "We won't hear more from them unless it's life or death. They do want to be kept informed if we find out anything."

"So, we're doing their legwork?" Troy asked.

"They shared what they could. More than they should have," Steve answered. "We'll get this. Stay low and out of sight."

Troy looked up at the screened-in porch as he approached the rear of the building. Shayne sat in one of the two deck chairs reading. Definitely not "out of sight." He quickly looked at the swampy hammock behind them. Nothing, not even the ever-active anole lizards, moved. He didn't like it.

"Roger." Troy disconnected the call.

28

Shayne heard Troy coming before he'd rounded the corner of the building. He'd been talking on the phone but disconnected quickly when he saw her. His expression went from stern to seriously pissed. His eye narrowed and his jaw firmed. She seemed to have that effect on him. She'd been sitting peacefully, soaking up the quiet, lush landscape surrounding her, but the stunning man with the chip on his shoulder was an expert on how to ruin a decent day. A small hurricane continually churned inside him.

"What the hell are you doing outside?" he barked as he let himself in through the screen door.

"Are you always so charming?" she asked.

"Anything beyond those solid doors is considered outside. Are we clear on that?"

"I wasn't aware I was a prisoner," Shayne said through clenched teeth.

"No. You're a target. Let's get inside. We need to finish our talk." Troy held the door open, eyeing the landscape as he waited.

Whether it was his blunt statement or tense body

language, Shayne's skin prickled. She followed his gaze but saw nothing but the greens and browns of nature. Silently, she walked past Troy and headed for the open kitchen.

"What happened? Is something wrong?" She'd planned on making sandwiches—a peace offering—when he returned. After all, he'd made breakfast, but her stomach wasn't going to hold anything down. "Who were you talking to?" She didn't attempt to hide her anxiousness.

"Nothing has happened," Troy said, locking the door behind him. "I talked to the team, and they added some interesting info to what we already know. You and I need to finish our discussion. Too many pieces to the puzzle are missing."

As much as she didn't want to relive the events of that night, she also hated to drag Troy through them with her. She hadn't missed his subtle reactions when discussing the subject. That single, intense green eye would briefly break contact as the conversation neared the explosion. His expression would darken. It was as if he ceased to exist for those few seconds before he reclaimed himself.

"Would you like something to eat before we get started?" While she couldn't stomach anything, he was a big man. Based on the dampness of his T-shirt, it looked like he'd sweated off a few pounds.

"I'll get something later," he answered, yanking off his shirt.

Holy shit! You wouldn't know from his chest and arms that he'd been injured in battle. She'd gotten a glimpse of him back in her apartment, but she could now confirm that Troy was rock solid. She spotted a scar beneath a tattoo that banded his left bicep. It didn't look recent. Not like the scars on his face.

He tossed the shirt over the back of the dining room

chair and reached for his duffel. His back muscles rippled as he dug through his bag. She took time to admire his sculpted form. God knew when she'd get another opportunity to feast upon a physique like the one before her.

Troy pulled a clean shirt over his head. "What the hell are you looking at?"

She closed her eyes for a second, just long enough to break the spell. "Ah...those tattoos on your arms. They're different. Something to do with the army?" *Good excuse, right?*

"Gaelic," Troy responded, his head cocked. He wasn't buying her story.

"What do they mean?" she asked, trying to wipe the memory of those pecs from her mind.

"My left has the armband of a Celtic warrior. The right is the translation of McKenzie in Gaelic."

"What does it mean?" She reached into the refrigerator, her wits returning.

"McKenzie?"

"Yes. What does it mean in Gaelic?" She pulled out a soft drink and handed him a water.

He took the bottle and uncapped it. "The Fair One."

"Seriously?" She grinned.

"What's so funny?" Troy chugged some of the water.

"With your dark hair and green eyes, I wouldn't call you fair."

"The other definition of fair."

"Oh. Sorry." Well, she'd insulted him again. So much for her attempt to be pleasant. "You ready to get on with this?"

He stared at her for a moment then nodded.

"Go ahead. Ask away." Shayne took a seat on the couch while Troy dropped into his chair. He set the phone on the coffee table and seemed to study it. He was hesitating. Not good.

"Before we finish going over the events of that evening, what do you know about narcotics?"

"Excuse me? Are you accusing me of having something to do with drugs?" She'd taken a tranquilizer last evening. Did he think she was in the habit of doing that? Son of a bitch. "What the hell was that call about?"

"The DEA is involved in the investigation," Troy told her. "Do you know of any reason why that might be?"

"You haven't answered my question. Do you think I take drugs?" She wondered how much it was going to hurt when she hit him.

His single eye bored into her along with his silence.

"I took one damn tranquilizer!" Her hands fisted, ready to do battle.

"Have you always jumped to conclusions? I didn't insinuate that you were taking something illegal, but the FBI revealed that the DEA is part of this investigation. The question is why?"

"I never noticed anyone using drugs or heard any rumors of that nature. Does that answer your question?"

"Yes, but it doesn't help." Troy got to his feet and again began to pace the living area like a panther.

"If there was an issue with drugs at the country club, I didn't know about it." Shayne, her skin no longer sizzling, reached for her drink and took a sip. She watched Troy circle the room over the rim of the soda can, his pace slowing with each pass. Eventually, he returned to his seat.

"Okay," he said. "Let's pick up where we left off. See if we can give Josie and Don more information to work with."

"I hate that Josie is involved with this. That any of you are, for that matter." Shayne rested her head in her hands.

She was overwhelmed with guilt. What if something happened to one of these people? What if something happened to Troy?

"Steve will make sure Josie stays safe. Trust me on that one." Troy flipped a page on the pad in front of him. "You were telling me a customer lost his son that night."

"Mr. Russell. He'd given his tickets to his son, since he didn't want to go. How does someone get past that?" Shayne couldn't stop her eyes from tearing up.

"You said he had family. I'm sure they were there to support one another." Troy was watching her cautiously. Whether he wasn't one for tears or was truly concerned about her, she couldn't tell. Either way, it didn't matter.

"And you?" he asked.

"What do you mean?" The question caught Shayne off guard. Troy had her full attention now.

"Who was there for you?"

"I don't understand." What was he getting at?

"Where were your family and friends after you were injured?"

Shayne was silent while she digested the question and the possible reason behind it. Nothing came to mind. "Why do we keep diverging to my personal life?"

WHY *DID* Troy keep veering in that direction? He pictured her alone in the hospital bed with no one but cops pounding her with questions. She mentioned she had family, but they lived overseas. A boyfriend?

"Who was with you when you were in the hospital? Who took care of you when you got home? Did your mother come stay with you?" What mother wouldn't?

"I can take care of myself, if it's any of your business."

It wasn't his business and he knew it. He remembered lying alone in a hospital, though, with nurses and doctors invading his sullen mood. He hadn't wanted to see or talk to anyone. But those hours of silence only allowed him to dwell on the horror and his failings. It was what he deserved. Shayne didn't.

"I've no doubt you can take care of yourself, but I know what it's like to be in a hospital. They can be long days."

"I didn't spend all that much time in the hospital. I was lucky," she told him. "Mom needed to stay with Grandmama. She would have made arrangements to come if I'd asked."

God, she was stubborn. "So, you went through your hell alone."

"Didn't you? Look, I don't want to discuss it. Can we get back to the business at hand?"

If they didn't, she'd probably wall herself off in the bedroom and pick up one of those happy-ever-after novels he'd purchased for her.

"Okay." He leaned back in his chair and let out a slow breath. They had work to do, and he needed to rein in his emotional response to her and concentrate. Troy uncapped another bottle without taking a drink this time. "You policed your station then left to clock out?"

"Yes. It was a quick cleanup since we were slow."

"Do you always leave the club by the route you took that night?"

"No," Shayne answered, then let that digest for a minute. "Normally, I go out the door near the employee lounge, but it was blocked."

"How?" Troy asked, his back straightening.

"Don't get too excited. It was nothing nefarious.

Someone left a hand truck in front of the exit. It was stacked high with cases of water and soft drinks. It was too heavy for me to move so I headed toward the exits near the ballrooms. That's when I spotted the bar and the guy who was tending it."

There were an awful lot of coincidences that put Shayne in the wrong place at the wrong time. Troy made a note of items to relay back to Sanibel in a later call. Sometimes things were simply coincidence. Sometimes not.

"Did you run into anyone else after you clocked out?"

"Nope. I didn't expect to see anyone on my way out of the building. The event must have kept the bar hopping because he should have finished his cleanup by then. Someone from the maintenance department moves the monstrosity in the morning if it isn't needed for a luncheon the next day." It was that monstrosity that had probably saved her life.

"Did you ask the bartender why he was running so late?"

"No. Figured they'd been busy. The guy was either new or a temp called in to help. That's the only reason I can think that he'd be so slow at cleaning up. I offered to help…"

"What?" Troy prompted, when she hesitated.

"Well, if we're being specific…"

"We are."

"I didn't offer. I set my purse on the shelf under the bar and started picking up trash left on the countertop."

"How did he react?" Troy cocked his head.

"I think I surprised him. He didn't voice any objections."

"What then?"

"He picked up a box of unopened bottles and headed for the stockroom."

"How do you know he was going to the stockroom?"

Shayne shrugged. "He told me."

"Did he say anything else?" Troy continued to read Shayne. She'd completely abandoned her relaxed position curled up on the couch. Now, the bare heel of her right foot softly bounced against the wood floor. The palms of her hands slid against her jean-covered thighs. Every movement telegraphed the ratcheting up of her nerves.

"No. Just 'thanks,'" she answered. "I didn't even ask his name."

Shayne had turned her head to gaze out the window toward the dense foliage surrounding the building. The rhythm of her breathing was steady but picking up pace.

"So the guy left," Troy said. "What did you do next?"

"I got rid of the rest of the trash on the counter—cocktail napkins, stir sticks. Stuff like that. The fruit that had been prepared for mixed drinks was shot so I tossed it out. It was right after that when I saw the man everyone is so anxious for me to identify."

She was going to have road rash on the palms of her hands if she didn't stop rubbing them against the denim fabric. Troy reached over and placed his rough hands on hers. She stilled.

"Back up a bit. Let's break it down further. Picture the events as if you were watching a movie. Start from the time you first spotted the bar."

Shayne took a breath so deep it seemed to suck all the oxygen from the room, closing her eyes as she did so. Troy waited. Her stubbornness wouldn't allow her to back away.

"I was headed for the doors near the banquet rooms. They are the next closest exit to the employee parking area."

"And you saw the bar?"

"Yes," Shayne answered, opening her eyes.

"What was the reaction of the bartender when he saw you?"

"He seemed a bit surprised by my offer to help but didn't say no. He finished putting bottles of liquor in a box and headed toward the storeroom."

"You're sure he headed straight for the storeroom?"

"Yes. No. He came back for his cell phone. I forgot that."

"Then what?"

Shayne exhaled audibly before she answered. "Like I've said before, I disposed of the clutter, gathered the unused plastic cups and cocktail napkins, and put them in another box to be returned to the storeroom."

"Is that when you saw the man in the hallway?" Troy was no longer covering her hands but clasping one of them. She was holding on to it as if it were a lifeline.

"No. That was after I'd dumped the unused fruit."

"You didn't see him exit the room?"

"I'd ducked behind the bar when I disposed of the fruit. There was a lot of juice in the container. I wanted to be sure I didn't get any on the carpet. When I stood up, I saw the man walking away. That's when I heard the muffled voices and realized there were still people in the ballroom."

Her hand was slick with sweat. "Let's stick with the man you saw for the moment," Troy said. "Describe him. How tall was he?"

Again, Shayne closed her eyes. "I can't give you inches but he was around your height."

"How did he walk? Don't just tell me what you saw but your impressions of him as well."

"I didn't see him for more than a minute," Shayne said, turning to face Troy.

"You can see a lot in a minute. If you had to guess his age..."

Shayne hesitated. "Somewhere between late twenties

and early forties. That's a guess. I wouldn't take it to the bank."

"That's fine. Keep going."

"There was nothing leisurely about his stride. Confident, I'd say. He had broad shoulders," Shayne added.

"See? You're remembering details. What else?"

"He had a full head of hair. Dark blond. And his suit..." Shayne paused.

"What about it?"

"That's another reason I think he was younger. It was tailored narrower at the waist. Older men tend to have a square cut to the jacket. His shoes were dark. Black, I think."

"His suit color?"

"Navy."

"Did you see him leave the building?" Troy's hand remained wrapped around Shayne's.

"No. I got distracted once I realized the room wasn't empty. I heard voices but I couldn't make out what they were saying." Sadness was in her eyes. "If only I'd gone in and suggested they leave, they'd still be alive."

"You'd probably be dead."

She looked at the floor. "I was trapped under the bar when the force of the explosion slammed it to the ground. They told me that's what saved me."

"Then I'm glad you didn't check on them," Troy told her. He knew what it was like to be filled with *what ifs*. It was those questions that had driven him to drink.

"Do you remember the explosion?" Troy felt her short nails dig into his palm. "I know this isn't easy for you," he started, but stopped as her eyes grew wide.

"Me? What about you? How can you possibly want to talk about this? Hell, I can't forget the sounds or smells of that night but you..." Shayne choked. "You..." A tear ran down one cheek.

Troy kept Shayne's hand in his. It wasn't only stupid but an enormous mistake when he pulled her into his arms and held her tight. He let her cry, holding back his own tears. He'd shed his share in silence, lying in the darkness of his hospital room. Not for himself but for the people who had died due to his arrogance and incompetence. Now Shayne was hurting, and damn it, he wanted that hurt to go away.

APPARENTLY, she hadn't mastered the ability to wall off her emotions when relating the details of that night. By the time she'd left Tampa, she'd been able to answer the endless questions without turning into a blubbering idiot. But this was Troy. His experiences had to be far worse than her memories, yet he was willing to walk down that road to hell with her. Now he was holding her—and it felt so damn good. *God*, she was so fucked up.

She brushed away the tears with the back of her hand. Sniffling, she pulled away from him. Troy gave her some space but continued to gently grasp her arms, dipping his head so he could study her face.

"I'm fine." She sniffled, wiping a tear away from her other cheek. "Let go. Please?" She'd rather have him mad at her than pity her.

Troy's hands fell away as he rose to his feet. Without a word, he disappeared but quickly reappeared with a box of tissues.

"Thank you. I'm not sure why I broke down like that."

"You've been through a lot these past few days. Stress

affects us all differently," Troy told her, returning to his chair.

"How do you deal with it?"

"I got shit-faced drunk, remember?" Troy ran his hand through his shaggy hair.

"You're not drinking now. How do you do it?" Shayne pulled another tissue from the box and wiped her eyes. "I don't understand how you can stand to be around me. I must be a constant reminder of what you went through."

"I don't need you around to remind me." Troy's voice was cold as ice.

"Sorry." Of course he didn't need her to serve as a reminder.

"Will you stop saying you're sorry?" Troy snapped. "This"—he brushed his knuckle across his scarred cheek —"has nothing to do with you. Save your pity for those who died due to my arrogance."

29

Shayne eyed Troy as she would an untethered pit bull. With fear and apprehension. She scooted away. Just an inch or so. She didn't get up and run, although common sense told her that would be a smart move. She'd inadvertently poked an open wound. What had happened to scar him so badly, both physically and emotionally? The physical scars were evident. The emotional ones were obviously more severe. None of this was her business.

But Troy was here, protecting her when he had no reason to feel responsible for her. Hell, he didn't even like her. Revisiting her brush with death only served to remind him of his own close call, yet his ingrained sense of duty to help others took precedent. She didn't believe he'd put others in danger. Not knowingly.

"I'm..." She stopped before she repeated the same apologetic words. Empty words he didn't want to hear. Whether he was calling her on her thoughtless comment or he interpreted the apology as pity, he wanted neither. She didn't blame him.

Troy's eye continued to drill into hers. His fists were

clenched tight, yet he remained silent. What was he waiting for? A reason to call a halt to this forced imprisonment? They couldn't continue to walk this precipice. They had a truce that continually faltered. What they needed was a peace agreement or a total severing of their ties. But how?

Troy's phone rang, shattering the icy wall between them.

"McKenzie."

"Who is it?" Shayne asked.

"Okay if I put you on speaker?" Troy asked the person at the end of the line.

Shayne's skin warmed as her blood pressure rose. "If it concerns me, I don't care whether they're *okay* with it or not."

"It's Rick," Troy told her as he set the phone on the table.

"Hi, Shayne," Rick said.

"Hey," she responded, but her focus remained on the muscular man in the chair next to her. His features gave nothing away, but because she had been watching him so closely, she noticed his jaw had slackened slightly. His lips no longer held a tight, straight line. Apparently, he preferred talking business, no matter how serious, to more personal conversations.

"What's up?" he asked.

"Josie and Don have been busy," Rick said. "I wanted to bring you up to date on what we have so far."

"Don's there? On Sanibel?" Troy asked, reaching for the pad they'd been using to make notes.

"No. He's working from Bragg."

"And he's already found something?" Troy asked, a note of skepticism in his tone.

"More or less. It's the 'less' part that has our radar up," Rick said.

"What the hell does that mean?" When Rick didn't

respond quick enough, Troy said, "You either have something or you don't. What's going on?"

Shayne's fingers were clasped together, her right thumb rubbing circles in the palm of her left hand. She was pretty sure she wasn't going to like what she heard.

"One of the two victims seems to be a ghost."

"Not Russell," Troy said.

"No, not Russell, but how did you know that?" Rick asked.

"Shayne knew his father. The dad was a regular at her bar."

"Interesting," Rick said. "I'll get to Russell in a minute. The other victim, Sunderson? None of Josie's contacts have come up with anything more than basic, superficial information, which she finds odd. After a quick search, Don agreed. The backstory on him is suspicious."

"The feds should have been all over that," Troy said.

"Oh, yeah," Rick agreed. "We don't know if they're responsible for the absence of information or if he's a mystery to them as well."

"Shayne?"

"Still here," she answered, turning her attention again to the phone.

"Did you know the other victim? Lawrence Russell?" Rick asked.

"By sight alone. He didn't live at Copperhead."

"Is there something interesting in his history?" Troy asked. He leaned forward, his forearms now planted firmly on his thighs. His fingers were locked together as well.

"At this point, not a lot. Single. Other than one DUI, nothing. We're digging deeper there," Rick told him.

"We need to know what he was on when they pulled him over for DUI."

"You'll get it when we do."

"Russell gave his fundraiser tickets to his son," Troy said, turning to Shayne. "Do you know why?"

"I overheard Mr. Russell say he was glad he wasn't going to the event. He was sick of getting 'all gussied up,' to use his term. I'm sure he doesn't feel that way anymore." Shayne's voice cracked.

"What can you tell us about the father?" Rick asked.

"Not much. They'd come in for a drink most nights."

"Who came in with him?" Troy asked.

"I called them the Gang of Four. Golfing buddies. After the dinner rush, the four of them would meet up at the bar and nurse their nightcaps. They'd bullshit about normal stuff. Golf, of course, politics, weather, whatever. They were always polite to me, tipped well, and occasionally liked to tease me about being single." Shayne paused. "I hadn't realized I missed that. I'm so sorry he lost his son." An emptiness she hadn't felt since moving to Sanibel began to fill her. She knew what it was like to lose someone close.

"I want the names of his drinking buddies," Rick told her.

"Why?" The request stopped Shayne from drifting into the melancholy state. She liked the old guys. She didn't want them harangued, especially Mr. Russell. He didn't need the added pain.

"Just following threads. If we don't have to contact them, we won't. But we need the background of everyone with a connection to that night, no matter how thin it appears."

"Have you learned anything else regarding the DEA's involvement?" Troy asked after Shayne had given them the names of the three other men.

"No. Not yet. They have to be tied to one or the other

victims. I'd bet my shirt on it," Rick told him. "As soon as we come up with something else, one of us will call."

"Hold on a minute." Snatching the phone off the table, Troy headed out onto the back deck and through the screen door.

≈

"WHAT IS IT?" Rick asked.

"Will someone be coming to relieve me or give me some backup?" Troy stepped onto the soft soil. He'd taken the phone off speaker. Shayne was already testy. He didn't know how she'd interpret Troy's request. He lowered himself to one of the bottom steps.

"What's the problem? Can't handle one woman, or is there something else we need to know?" Rick's tone had become serious.

"The problem is that there's a lot of geography for one person to cover and at the same time stay close to the target. And, as I've pointed out, she does not like me. Trying to get information out of someone who constantly wants to argue isn't easy."

"Use some of that infamous charm of yours," Rick suggested. "It appears to be getting somewhere."

Not as far as Troy would like to get, and that was a major problem. "If you want someone to charm information out of her, you'd best send Gib. She and I argue more than we talk."

"Well, you'd better find some of that charm, because for the time being, you're on your own. With the DEA involved, I'm assuming this is worse than we originally suspected. None of us are comfortable with the possibility of leading someone to you. At the very least, the FBI has eyes on us."

"Shit! Do you know how much territory there is surrounding this outpost? I can't keep my eyes on her and patrol it too."

"We got you out of here fast. No one had the chance to follow you. But the Feds are on alert now. There's only one way in and out of that place. I don't want to give your location away by sending out support." Rick paused. "Stay close to Shayne."

That was Troy's problem. He wanted to be close. The idea of being intimate with her sent trickles of sweat running down his back. *What the hell?* Sex was sex. Nothing more.

"Troy? You still there?" Rick asked.

"Yeah." Troy shook his head, clearing it. "I have a bad feeling about this." For the umpteenth time, he scanned the landscape behind the building, watching and listening.

"Can you be more specific?"

"I wish I could." Something was off and he didn't know what. He shouldn't be here. His instincts could be off or skewed because of his unfamiliar animalistic desire for the woman waiting at the top of the stairs. "Have you considered that Shayne might be better off with the FBI?"

"That wasn't the impression we got from them," Rick told him. "Do your best."

"What if it's not good enough? I'm not the man I was," Troy admitted. It was the first time he'd verbalized those fears.

"No, you're different, but that doesn't mean you're less of a man or less of a soldier. Only different. Stop doubting yourself. We have your six. If it comes to the point you feel we need to get you out, send up a flare."

Troy looked up at the bungalow. He wasn't going to let anything happen to Shayne. Not on his watch. "Use the satellite phone from now on to communicate. It's unlikely anyone would track my phone, but I don't want to take that chance."

"I'll let the others know. How's Shayne holding up?" Rick asked.

"Bad night last night, but doing her best to push it behind her. She's tough as nails." Troy caught sight of Shayne as she walked by the large windows on the interior side of the screened porch. He'd have to tell her to keep her distance from them. He could picture that argument already. "We don't get far without one of us setting the other off."

"You've interrogated insurgents. You should be able to handle one recalcitrant woman. What the hell did you do to piss her off so badly, anyway? Colt's right. She's not one to be contrary. You must have said or done something."

"If I find out anything more from her, I'll report in," Troy said, avoiding the question. "That all you got?"

"For the moment."

After Troy disconnected the call, he disabled the locations setting on his phone then switched it off for good measure. As far as they knew, the FBI was the only agency who could put him and Shayne together but leaks happened. Better to be safe.

Troy scanned the room as he entered. Shayne was in the kitchen, her back to him.

"I'm making some grilled cheese and bacon sandwiches," she said, glancing over her shoulder. "We had plenty of bacon left over from that breakfast you fixed."

Okay. She wasn't snapping and didn't jump on him for his desire to finish the conversation with Rick in private. A new truce? He'd do his best to maintain it.

"Sounds good. Need help?" He'd planned to tell her to

stay away from the windows, but he suspected that would set her off, so he'd pass for the moment. Unfortunately, he couldn't just drop the blinds to rectify the situation. There were none on the porch side of the building. The owners probably decided against them due to the property's isolation and the fact that the screened-in space shaded the interior of the bungalow. There was the option of the two of them holing up in the bedroom. Nope. Not a good idea.

"Grab something for yourself to drink," she instructed him as she sliced the sandwiches in half on the cutting board.

Troy, again, had to shake the image of the two of them together in bed. As much as he wanted her, he broke out in a sweat at the possibility of getting that far. What the hell was wrong with him? He was a seducer. Sex was a game played among mutually consenting adults.

He grabbed a bottle of water from the refrigerator, he uncapped it, and took a seat at the table. Shayne hadn't put out place settings. Would she sit across from him or take the seat that would obscure the view of his scars?

When she took the seat opposite him, his mood lightened more. She didn't say anything as she snatched a napkin from the holder on the table and took a sip of water. "What did you and Rick discuss? Are we staying here? Am I getting a different bodyguard?"

The questions were asked casually and without rancor. She'd gotten a handle on her anger. He could do the same.

"We're staying and there will be no backup. They don't want to take a chance of anyone being followed here." Troy took a bite out of the gooey sandwich then wished he'd waited when the hot cheese burned his tongue.

"Don't you think we're overdoing this cloak-and-dagger stuff?" Shayne asked.

If Troy had the choice, he'd get her even farther away from the shitstorm that seemed to be building. He didn't like what he'd heard from Rick. He suspected he'd like Don's report even less when it came.

"Considering the attack on you and learning that one victim appears to have a covert background, I think the precautions are warranted." He chanced a second bite of the sandwich. When he looked up, the smile she'd been wearing was gone. She was picking at the crust of her sandwich, rolling the bread into tiny little balls between her fingertips. She'd been looking for confirmation of her suspicions.

"I'd be lying if I told you otherwise. I don't think you want that, do you?"

"No," Shayne answered. "I don't understand my part in this. I didn't see anything. Why would someone be after me?"

"That's what we're trying to find out. Finish eating. We'll get back to picking your brain after we're done." He reached across the small table and clasped her good wrist. "We'll figure it out."

30

―――――

Shayne managed to finish her meal, but had done so mechanically. It had been childish to hope for one of two outcomes from the private conversation between Rick and Troy—they'd come to the consensus their concern was unwarranted or she'd get a new guard dog.

When Troy's large hand had encircled her wrist, the warmth had done more than calm her. The touch set off a sensual reaction within her that had her squeezing her thighs together. She'd retrieved her limb and spent the rest of the meal silently cleaning her plate. Now she wished she hadn't.

She was spending too much time wishing for things she couldn't have. Her dad would give her hell if he were still around. *Work with what you've got. Make the best of a bad situation.* Mantras he'd drummed into her head. She was spending too much time dwelling on her needs, her wants, rather than the problem that had brought them here.

Someone believed she knew something. She wouldn't be a target otherwise. What, or whom, had she seen that made her worth the trouble of tracking her to the ends of the earth?

She glanced at Troy. He was dealing with the weight of his own issues while he took on the assignment of protecting her. She owed it to him and the families of the men that died at Copperhead to deal with this shit.

Carrying their plates to the kitchen sink, she asked, "Do you want to pick up where we left off this morning?"

"You up to it?" He joined her at the sink.

When she faced him, he was watching her closely, trying to get a read on her. She suspected the whole team possessed that skill. Doing what they did, it probably saved lives. She'd learned to read some people while she was tending bar, or she'd just gotten to know them better. Either way, her life hadn't depended on it.

"Might as well get it over with." They finished putting the rinsed dishes in the dishwasher and returned to the living room. She noted Troy's long look out toward the porch. "What is it?"

"You're not going to like it," he declared. She swore she saw the wisp of a smile touch the corner of his lips.

"Does that surprise you?" This time there was no doubt he was fighting a grin. "Go ahead. Spit it out. I won't bite your head off. Promise."

That ghost of a smile disappeared. "I need you to stay away from the windows," he told her.

"Why?" she asked, but she knew the answer before she'd asked the question. "You think someone is out there?"

He reached for her. "Unlikely, but we don't want to take chances."

Shayne snatched her hand back. No touching. If they were stranded together, there could be no touching. Too easy to make a fool of herself. "That doesn't leave me much room to roam. First, you tell me to stay off the porch. Now I'm to stay away from the windows. Next, I'll be locked in the bathroom."

"Just the back windows. They don't have shades," Troy responded, all emotion stripped from his expression. He walked over to the nearest window and closed the blind. He continued the process throughout the building. As the natural light disappeared, she began to feel trapped again.

TROY JERKED at the cord on the last window, lowering the blind. He'd meant to reassure her when he'd instinctively reached for her hand, but she'd yanked it away as if she'd been scalded by his touch. Just as well. As much as he wanted to get her clothes off, the notion scared the hell out of him. He didn't understand it. The fact that she couldn't stand his touch saved him the trouble of figuring it out. Besides, they had a crime scene to visually reconstruct.

"You ready to go over the details again?" Troy asked when he came back into the room. He took the seat across from her. He needed the distance, and he knew she preferred it.

"Sure," she answered without much enthusiasm. "I don't know what more I can add. After the explosion, I was knocked out. Police, fire, first responders were everywhere when they pulled me from beneath the overturned bar."

"Did you hear anything as you regained consciousness —before the rescuers arrived?"

"My ears were ringing. The first sound I remember was the sirens."

"What are your first memories?"

She dropped her head into her hands.

"Smells. Smells that I wish I could forget. Then the absolute fear that the moisture seeping through my clothes was my own blood. Relief when I realized it was water. There was pain from the glass that was cutting through my clothes and my skin when I struggled to get free." She took her head out of her hands to look at him. "None of this helps. It hurts us both."

Troy clasped his hands together before he found himself reaching for her again. It did hurt. God, it tore him to pieces. He wanted to walk away. Not only was she reliving her worst nightmare, so was he. Smells. That was one of his strongest memories. He'd never forget the odor of charred flesh.

"How did they find you?" Troy asked, forcing his memories behind him.

"I didn't ask, but I suppose they heard me scream."

"What about the guy who was tending that bar? Could he have pointed out your location?"

"I suppose he could have, but I never laid eyes on him again." Shayne quieted. "I assumed he was okay, since I understood no one else was hospitalized."

"He didn't check on you?" Troy clenched his fists. The asshole would have been buried under the rubble instead of Shayne if she hadn't stopped to help. The least he could have done was visit her in the hospital.

"He didn't know me. Why should he?"

Because it was the decent thing to do...or could there have been something more to it? "We'll find out his name and check on him," Troy told her. "Did you see anything or anyone that seemed out of place that night?"

"No. Everyone who came into the dining room or sat at my bar were residents of Copperhead."

"And the delivery person who abandoned the hand cart? Did you see him?"

Shayne bit her lip while she gave the question some thought. He couldn't take his eyes from the soft pink flesh. *Damn.*

"Unless I lost part of my memory of that night, no." She looked at Troy. "Other than the guy leaving the dining room, the only other person I didn't recognize was the guy behind the bar. But it's not unusual for the club to bring in additional help for a big event. There's only so many employees to go around, and like I told you, this event was busting our seams."

The new guy might have been just that—a temp employee or a new hire. Either way, he picked the wrong night to join the staff. He was worth looking into.

"That's enough for today. We'll go over it again tomorrow. Something else may come to mind." Troy didn't miss the brief closing of her eyelids, as if lowering a shade so he couldn't read what she was thinking. It wasn't necessary. His own thoughts mirrored hers every time the bombing was discussed.

Shayne excused herself and puttered around the kitchen before closing herself in her room. She'd withdrawn emotionally again, but they'd managed to get through the afternoon without jumping down each other's throats. He'd take that as progress.

He picked up the pad full of notes, flipped to a blank page, and began making a list of questions and things that needed further investigation. The team already had the names of Shayne's Gang of Four. Troy didn't expect anything to come of them, but it gave them another angle. He was more interested in digging into the backgrounds of the two victims. The DEA was involved. There was something off with the bartender. Where did he go? Did he come back to look for Shayne, or did the bastard take off without making the responders aware of her location?

Troy glanced toward the closed bedroom door. He pictured her curled up under the covers reading about a lady in distress being rescued by a handsome prince. He was certainly no prince and no longer qualified as handsome.

He needed to get his mind back on the business of keeping this woman safe. Walking to the rear windows, he stared out into the wetlands thick with cypress and pine trees. Shadows were getting longer. Still, he could make out the shapes of nature's work. There was a time when he would have seen the swamp only as a place that could give ample cover to the enemy. But he'd seen the photographs Colt and Gib had taken. The pictures highlighted the beauty of what he once would have considered a dangerous wetland. *Damn it.* Not a year out of the service and he was getting soft.

Once blackness fell, he'd take the high-powered flashlight and night goggles and scan the area. Things not seen to the naked eye in daylight could be spotted by the artificial light in the darkness. Hunters routinely used the method to hunt alligators when it was open season. The eyes of the gators were luminescent when hit by the beam. And who knew? He might surprise someone.

The ringing of the satellite phone snapped Troy's attention from his plans for the evening. "McKenzie," he answered. The larger phone felt awkward in his hand.

"McKay," Gib responded, a lilt to his voice.

"What the hell do you want? Where's Colt?" Or Steve or Rick, for that matter. The last person Troy expected to hear on the other end of the line was Gib.

"Temper, temper. You got a problem hearing from old friends?"

"I'm looking for information," Troy snapped. "Not a social conversation."

"I'm looking for information as well. How's Shayne doing?"

Troy's knuckles tightened around the phone. "Why do you want to know about Shayne?"

"Because I care what happens to her."

"Like I don't?" Troy barked.

"Touch a nerve? Based on your pent-up frustration, I'd say you've not made your move on her." There was a hint of laughter in Gib's voice.

"She's an assignment."

"One that you're having a hard time keeping your hands off, I'd guess, based on your sunny temperament."

"Why the hell are we having this conversation? Put one of the others on the phone before I hang up," Troy growled as he prowled the room.

"You're not going to hang up. You want the information they have. Now, how are things really between you and Shayne?"

"Did you become a therapist while I was on tour?" Troy said. "She's fine. I'm fine."

"And still celibate." Gib laughed.

"Why is that any of your concern? You said the two of you had nothing going on. Besides, you told me point-blank to keep my hands off her."

"No. I reminded you that she wasn't your normal lay."

"You think I don't know that? I'm not going to make a move on her. She deserves better. Not damaged goods. She needs support—help. She has nightmares most nights. Where the hell is her family? Why is she going through this alone?"

"She's not alone. She has us. She has you," Gib reminded him.

Troy huffed, "Some support. She doesn't like being in the same room with me."

"You're wrong. I've watched the two of you work together. I've seen the sparks. Could be it's that snarly attitude of yours that's putting her off. Try losing it."

"You don't know squat about me anymore. Just because we used to be friends doesn't mean you can lecture me."

"Sounds like you need one. And we're still friends. Get your shit together. You're eventually going to have to face whatever it is that's eating you. Cat helped Colt back into the world of the living. Have you considered that you and Shayne could help one another? You're a good man, Troy. Don't let the past destroy your future."

"Are you insinuating I have a future with Shayne? You are crazy."

"I'm not sure what signals you're picking up from her, but I'm willing to bet you're not reading them correctly."

"Can we get past the high school conversation and get back to the investigation?" Troy glanced toward the bedroom. "Have they found out anything?"

"Hang on a sec. I'm downstairs. I snatched the phone while they were clearing the dinner dishes. Cat's gonna have my hide. I told her I'd help with cleanup."

"You skipped out on KP duty?" Troy could picture Cat twisting Gib's ear. He almost cracked a smile. "You're right. Cat will have your ass."

31

"How's it going?" Colt's deep voice resonated across the speaker.

"It's going. I've got a couple of things for you to look into."

"Is Shayne with you?" Colt asked.

"She's in the bedroom. Do you need her?" Troy took a glance over his shoulder into the hallway. The door remained shut.

"Not for this conversation," Colt told him. "What do you have?"

"Do we know anything about the guy Shayne stopped to help? She can't even give me his name. She says she never saw him before, but the club often hired extra help for big events."

"We don't have it, but that shouldn't be hard to get," Rick chimed in.

"He may not be involved in any way, but he's an unknown," Troy.

"We have a list of employees, but if he was a temp, he wouldn't be on the country club's payroll. They'd probably be paying him through an employment firm. We'll check it out. What else?" Colt asked.

"This probably has nothing to do with anything, but someone left a hand truck in front of the exit used by employees. The only reason Shayne went by the banquet hall was because she couldn't move the deliveries. Too heavy. It's probably a coincidence, and I can't see any reason it would make a difference, but it might be worth looking into why that exit was blocked."

"Got it," Colt confirmed.

"We plan to go over that night again tomorrow. See if anything else rises to the surface. That's all I got," Troy said. "What do you have?"

"Sunderson is dead," Colt told him.

"I think we're all aware of that," Troy said. Sunderson's remains had probably been spread over half of Tampa. He knew exactly what an explosive device was capable of doing to the human body. His stomach curled.

"He's been dead for over thirty years," Steve said.

"What? He was a plant?" Troy was on his feet. "That's an old trick."

"Still works even in this age of technology," Steve replied.

"Good guy or bad guy? Do we know?" Troy asked.

"Pretty sure he was one of the white hats," Steve said. "His backstory is too solid according to Don. I'm guessing it was a cover set up by the government."

"I think we can safely guess he was a DEA agent." Rick added.

"Have you confirmed with the FBI?" Troy ran his fingers through his hair then yanked them back when they touched the band for his patch. Would he ever get used to the damn thing?

"We can ask but we won't get an answer. They weren't supposed to tell us about the DEA," Rick reminded him.

"Why'd they do it, then?" Troy and the gang had a love/hate relationship with the two agents.

"Their hands are probably tied, and they were looking for some outside help," Rick answered. "If the bombing was part of a DEA investigation, then we've all been heading in the wrong direction looking for a motive. The congressman may not have been the target at all."

"Investigators would like to keep that plate spinning as long as feasibly possible," Josie said. Stories concerning congressmen are sexier and would keep the reporters' attention directed elsewhere."

"That would certainly fit. Thanks, Josie." If anyone knew journalism, it was Josie. "And congratulations. Didn't get the chance to tell you before we left. You doing okay? Steve better be pampering you, or I'll have his ass." Troy thought he'd forgotten how to tease.

"I'm fine and when you and Shayne get back, we'll all celebrate together."

"We need to discover who that guy was and what he was doing there," Troy said turning the discussion back to business. "Where is he now? And what about the other victim? Russell? Was he working with the DEA? Was he a target? Or in the wrong place at the wrong time?" The questions tumbled out of Troy.

"There's nothing showing up in Russell's background other than the DUI," Steve said. "We're going to have to go beyond the records. Josie has a few contacts looking into that end."

"Anything you can tell me about the person posing as Sunderson?"

"Nothing yet. Don says he's hidden behind a steel firewall."

"Can we get more info out of Hernandez or Morgan?"

"I doubt they'll tell us more, but we'll push them," Colt assured him.

Troy picked up the pad and scanned his notes. "Have we learned anything interesting about the three men who were with Russell's father?

"All are retired," Steve answered. "Each owned or ran successful businesses. None of them seem to have any other connection to each other except for the fact that they're living in the same community and play golf together."

"So, we're back to why the DEA is involved and one of their agents was killed. I think you're right. Unless the Congressman was involved in something fishy, this has nothing to do with him." Troy tapped his pen against the pad. "We need more info on the son, Russell, and that bartender. My mind keeps circling back around to him. Why was he so slow getting his bar broken down? You'd assume for a big event they'd only hire experienced people."

"Could be that's all who was available but we'll do some more digging," Steve said.

There was something Shayne had said. What was it? Troy flipped through the pad. "Do we know how the bomb was detonated?"

"That much we do know," Rick told him. "Cell phone."

"Damn it. We need to find that guy." Troy circled the words on the page. "Shayne remembered he made a point of taking his cell phone with him to the stockroom. Why would he do that if he was coming back? He still had his work at the bar to finish up."

"Could be lots of reasons," Steve said. "He might have been taking advantage of Shayne's good nature and didn't plan on returning, didn't trust her, or he might have been expecting a call."

"All possible but I'm not buying the coincidence. Shayne says she surprised him. What if it wasn't her offer to help that surprised him but the fact that he now had a witness?"

"We'll find him," Colt promised. "We haven't gotten any more information on the man who left. Did Shayne come up with anything new on him?"

"No. Description is consistent with what she told the authorities. She got the impression that he wasn't in a hurry. Look, what if the bartender was the bomber? Then the guy leaving the room could be a nobody that doesn't want to get involved..."

"Or the other half of a DEA team," Rick interrupted. "They tend to partner up. I think it is time to push our friends in Tampa."

"We need to find his partner, assuming he had one, and talk to him."

"If we're right, and that was an undercover DEA agent, it's not going to be easy finding out who the partner was, let alone talk to him."

Troy knew Rick was right. Undercover operatives were not given up voluntarily.

"See what you can flesh out," Troy said. "Anything on the guy from the alley?"

"Nothing. Other than the two pairs of footprints, we couldn't find any trace evidence," Steve informed him. "We've seen no sign of a return visit, either. We've rotated watches."

"For Josie and Cat's sakes I'm glad." Troy sighed. He didn't want any harm to come to those women any more than he would allow something to happen to Shayne. "How did the guy find her in the first place? Could her location have been leaked?"

"No matter how tight the organization, there's always a possibility of a leak," Colt answered. "Hernandez said while she wasn't in any formal witness program, they wanted to keep her location buried as much as possible."

"If the people tracking her are half as skilled as Don on a computer, they could have found her through her bank account."

"We were asked to pay her in cash to avoid the bank issue."

"And that didn't raise your antennae?" Troy asked.

"Hindsight is twenty-twenty," Rick said. "She was still connected to an investigation. Keeping her off the front pages and off the radar, didn't seem all that unusual. It was one of the reasons she wanted to move. When she first arrived, we kept a close eye on her. There was no unusual activity."

"Can you check with the country club? See if anyone has been asking about her?" Troy asked.

"I'll add it to our list," Colt answered. "Anything else?"

"I'd like the key to the cottage that's under repair. I want to check it out and make sure we don't have squatters. I could get past the locks, but the property belongs to a friend of yours."

"I'll see if I can reach Clyde. In the meantime, if you feel the need for some B&E, do it. We'll cover any damages," Colt assured him.

"That's it for me."

"We'll touch base in the morning. Rick has the sat phone tonight. Call if something comes up."

"Will do."

Troy ended the call and faced the short hallway. Darkness had fallen during the conversation, but no light emanated from beneath the bedroom door. Shayne was supposed to be reading. Why wasn't the light on? Was she okay? She'd been holed up in there a long time. He should check on her. *God.* Now who was acting like a teenager? He wanted to see her. If only for a minute. How juvenile was that? Still, he found himself reaching for the doorknob and silently slipping into the room.

He had yet to turn on any lights, so his vision didn't need time to adjust to the darkened space. He zeroed in on the small form on the bed. Again, she lay on top of the covers, legs stretched out before her. Pillows were stuffed behind her, supporting her back while her head hung forward. A book lay on her lap with one thumb acting as a bookmark. Her other hand rested next to her side. Despite the awkward position, she looked relaxed and at peace. A rarity since the beginning of this exile.

He should have left, yet his feet remained glued to the floor as he watched her chest rise and fall. As Gib had reminded him, she wasn't his usual. Then again, it wasn't his habit to get to know the women he took to bed. He hadn't sought a long-term relationship with any woman. He'd seen how deployments could tear them apart.

Sex, on the other hand, had been a delightful distraction from the stress of those deployments. He continued to stare at the woman who was totally unaware of his presence. How would he feel if she'd been used as a distraction? His hands fisted. He'd kill the bastard. She was long term. Troy wasn't.

His last thought was the motivation he needed to step back and quietly shut the door. Like he'd told Gib, she deserved better than a broken-down soldier.

Troy grabbed the flashlight and sat phone he'd left on

the breakfast bar then headed out the back door and into the humid night.

SHAYNE BLINKED, trying to rid herself of the darkness that surrounded her, fighting the panic of being trapped. A solid thud sounded next to her. She blinked several times, trying to adjust to the darkness. She took a deep breath and let it out gently.

She wasn't trapped. She didn't lie in a puddle of water from sprinklers and fire hoses. She'd fallen asleep and slept deeply. Without looking, Shayne knew the sound she'd heard was her book hitting the floor. She'd been reading when she lost her battle to exhaustion. Her body and mind had finally had enough.

Unlike after the bombing, where the air had been filled with shouts, sirens, and the squawking of radios, her room was silent. In fact, the whole house was deathly quiet. What time was it? The bedside clock must have been acquired at a thrift store. It had no light source, the time indicated only by a pair of hands. It was useless in the dark. She got out of bed and peeked through the blinds. A light flickered in the distance. It disappeared for a second then was back. A flashlight? Who'd be out in a swamp in the middle of the night? As she watched the light swing from side to side, she remembered reading a story she'd read about frog giggers. Frogs were hunted at night and spotted by shining a light in their eyes. Their legs were considered delicacies. Yuck.

The light blinked out again. When it didn't return, she got nervous. Where did they go?

Uneasy, she carefully made her way toward the door, leaving the lights off so she wouldn't advertise her presence.

Had Troy seen it? Her mind could have been playing tricks on her or was the light a remnant of a dream? If Troy was asleep, she'd wake him, tell him about the light.

By the time she reached the living room, she knew Troy was gone. The house was empty. He wouldn't leave her. Troy was tenacious and stubborn. She was a job. He wouldn't quit a job.

She looked for the satellite phone. It wasn't on the counter where she'd last seen it. The flashlight was also missing. The absence of both items explained her vision. Troy was patrolling the property.

The realization should have made her feel less tense. It didn't. Since the attack, she'd felt adrift, alone, and frightened except when he was near. He couldn't wait to be rid of her. What the hell was wrong with her? The silent question did not evoke any words of wisdom from her dad, which made her feel that much more alone. She didn't want to be alone. She'd spent the years since her father's death and her mom's return to Ireland turning herself into a self-sufficient woman who didn't need anyone. She'd been convinced she had succeeded. Obviously not.

Troy's cell had been left on the counter. She lowered herself to the floor in the small galley kitchen, clutching the phone. Troy had turned it off so it couldn't be tracked but simply holding it made her feel securer.

When the humming of the refrigerator stopped, she strained to listen for any sounds coming from outside or within the bungalow. Nothing. Where was Troy? What was he doing? What if he'd left? She'd been a royal pain in the ass. The tinge of fear that she'd been left behind bubbled to the surface. She tamped it down. He hadn't abandoned her. He wouldn't abandon her. He'd given her his word.

32

Troy stepped over the tripwire strung across the bottom tread then bounded up the remaining stairs. His night patrol had yielded nothing significant. He'd identified animal tracks in the wet soil that skirted the property. His sweep of the marsh with the high-powered flashlight confirmed what he'd suspected. The beam reflected off a pair of iridescent reptilian eyes. Snaggletooth was near, guarding his territory and his harem.

"Shayne?" As soon as he entered the living room, he sensed Shayne's presence. He scanned the room quickly, searching for her.

"Here," she answered, popping up from behind the breakfast bar.

"What are you doing? Are you all right?" he asked, rushing toward her.

"I woke up, and you were gone," she answered, avoiding his direct question.

"I was checking the area." He dipped his head to get a look at her face, her expression. It was impossible in the darkened room. "I'm going to turn on a light."

Instead of turning on the brighter overhead fixture, he opted for the low-wattage bulb in the hood of the stove. Even with the warning and the dimmer light, Shayne still shielded her eyes, her head bent low. She stood there in silence, looking at the floor, not making a sound.

"Are you sure you're okay?" Troy asked.

Shayne nodded ever so slightly. "I wondered if you'd left."

"What? You thought I'd leave you?" Troy grasped her shoulders, fighting the urge to shake her while he brushed back the insult.

"No." Her head dropped. "Yes," she admitted, "but only for a second."

Troy cupped her chin softly then tilted her head back. "I'm not leaving you." His gut tightened when he saw the single trail of a tear reflected in the faint light. "What is it? What's wrong?"

"Nothing. I'm fine." She wiped the tear from the corner of her eye.

Troy placed his hand on Shayne's elbow and guided her out of the kitchen and to the sofa. "Relax," he said. "I'll be right back."

He grabbed some tissues from the bathroom and a bottle of water from the refrigerator before returning to her side. He handed her the tissues as he took the seat next to her.

"Did something happen while I was gone? What upset you?" Was he voluntarily talking to a crying woman? A first for him. He uncapped the water and took a sip before remembering he'd intended to give it to her. He wiped the neck of the bottle with the hem of his shirt before handing it to her. Stupid. He'd had his tongue down her throat. Drinking out of the same bottle shouldn't be a big deal. "Did you have another bad dream?"

Shayne shook her head. "I'm fine. I don't cry," she said, then took a sip.

"You'd be the first woman I've known that didn't." When the corners of her mouth ticked up, the tightness in Troy's shoulders slackened. "Are you going to tell me what happened?"

"I woke up. It was quiet. I didn't know where you were. I guess I was a little frightened."

"Is that why you were hiding in the kitchen?" he asked.

"It gave me a choice of doors if I needed to run." She shrugged. "Stupid, I guess."

"Actually, it was brilliant." Troy placed his hand on her knee and gave it a reassuring squeeze before he remembered she disliked his touch. He quickly pulled his hand back.

"Why do you do that?" she asked.

"Do what?"

"Never mind." Her eyes found a spot on the floor that appeared to deserve her attention more than he did. Her shoulders dropped.

"Why do I do what?" Troy asked.

That underlying tension resurfaced. It had been there since that kiss. A kiss that was seared in his memory for reasons he still didn't understand. He never should have touched her. He couldn't change that fact any more than he could breathe life back into the bodies of the dead. But Shayne was here. Could he make this right? He'd been running from his past. If he continued to let issues slide, how would he ever face the bigger one that had sent him on a search for help? Troy blew out a breath.

"Shayne?" It seemed to take forever before she raised

her head so she was looking at him.

"Yes?"

As she swung around, the almost nonexistent light reflected in her eyes like gold dust. Mesmerized, he stared back at them.

"What did you want?" Shayne asked. Her tone had softened, so he took his shot.

"I keep saying and doing the wrong things around you." He'd never been this frank with a woman. He felt the uptick in his heart rate and a slight shortness of breath. He'd marched into battle and never felt this unsure of his next move. Shayne could hurt him in ways the enemy never could. Regardless, he plunged ahead.

"What am I doing that keeps upsetting you? I don't know how to make a stronger apology for hurting you the day you found me." He looked at her wrist. "I've tried to stay away from you since that morning in your apartment, but..."

"Wait a minute. What do you mean, you've tried to stay away from me?" Her eyes narrowed as she studied his face.

"I'm attracted to you. Damn it."

SHAYNE'S HEAD SNAPPED BACK. Was Troy admitting an attraction or damning one? A thousand questions ran through her mind, but she blurted out the first thing that came to her: "I can't tell if that's a good thing or a bad thing."

"I'm not sure myself," Troy admitted.

Shayne took a minute. "Could it be because I'm the only female in the vicinity?" Wrong question. If his eye had been a laser beam, she'd have been cut in half. "I'll assume that's a no."

"Hell of a time for this to happen."

"Sorry to inconvenience you."

"You deserve better. Damn. What is wrong with me?" Troy raked his fingers through his hair.

"I'm not sure if you're insulting me or the opposite. What are you trying to say?"

"This is wrong." Troy walked away from her.

"Hold it," she told him, rising to her feet. "If you're going to insult me, do it to my face." But he either didn't hear her or ignored her. He mumbled to himself as he circled the combination living and dining area. He appeared confused, edgy, and angry. What was wrong with him?

"Hey," she shouted. No response. No indication he was aware of her presence any longer. He continued pacing and muttering. A thousand questions ran through her head. Was he experiencing a flashback? Did he learn something and was afraid to tell her?

"Troy! What the hell is going on? Do I need to call someone? Do you need help?" One of the questions must have gotten through, because he stopped then glared at her.

"What do you see when you look at me?" he asked.

"Huh?"

"What do you see?"

Shayne hesitated not sure of his mental state.

"Answer the question."

"A man," Shayne responded. "I see a troubled man, at the moment."

"That's it? That's all you see? Are you blind?"

"Will you stop insulting me?" She could feel her skin flush. Troubled or not, he was pissing her off. "I see a handsome man with scars on the inside and out. I see a man who is angry. I see a man fighting his way back from something horrible. What is it I'm supposed to see? What do you want me to see?"

"A man who wants you."

Shayne stared back at him. "We're both blind," she whispered. "Why?"

"Why do I want you?"

"Yes. Why do you want me?" She was lucky to get those words out. She wrapped her arms around her waist, waiting for his answer. Afraid of his answer.

"Honestly, I don't know."

Shayne again stared at Troy. She wasn't sure what she'd expected, but his confused expression told her he was being truthful. His brow was furrowed. His lips formed a straight line while he continued to rake his thick hair with his right hand.

"I can't explain it. It has me tied up in knots. I've not wanted a woman the way I want you."

"That seems to be a problem for you." How was she supposed to interpret that? "Maybe it's time to ask again if one of the others can take your place here. It might be easier on both of us."

"No," he responded, walking toward her.

"I could leave. I'm sure I could hitch a ride in the morning, assuming I can't have the car."

"No," he said again. This time the word was sharp as a knife.

"You can't force me to stay," Shayne said, throwing her shoulders back. She gave herself points for not retreating.

Troy reached for her before she had time to reconsider her decision. His hands quickly encircled her upper arms. While he didn't hurt her, his grasp was firm as he pulled her against him. His lungs moved like bellows against her chest. The heat of his breath washed over her face.

"Wanna bet?"

33

The street urchin in front of him had a backbone made of steel. Not many people would stand up to him when his temper flared. There was an instant when she gave the exit a glance, but she'd stood her ground. Again, those gold flecks sparked with heat. Heat directed at him.

His blood began to sizzle, but not from anger. His nostrils flared at her scent. She was so close, and it was too late. He should have stepped back when she didn't retreat. He was committed now. Tired of fighting a battle he didn't understand.

Shayne began to pull away. Shifting one hand from her shoulders, he clasped her chin gently between his calloused fingers and looked into her eyes. "You never let me explain." His words came out in a rough whisper. "I wanted you back at your apartment. I've wanted you ever since."

"Why?" Shayne repeated. Her voice cracked.

"I told you, I don't know. I can't explain it." Troy touched his forehead to hers. "I'm scared as hell of wanting you, but here I am, wanting you all the same."

"But you pushed me away."

"Not for the reasons you thought. Never because of you," he said then pressed his lips to hers.

In spite of his hunger for her, Troy curbed his appetite to nip seductively at the corners of her mouth. Her tension and misgivings gradually ebbed away, and her lips softened. He deepened the kiss then opened his mouth, allowing his tongue to tease her lips where they met. The seal opened, inviting him in. She was void of the taste of cream he'd been unable to forget. Still, the taste was sweet. He pressed her closer, deepening the kiss. One hand cradled her head while the other traced the length of her spine until it reached her waist. He pulled her closer, pressing her hips against his need. He was hard, hurting, and the intent was to transmit that message. He would never force her. She was free to walk away, but a small mewing sound passed her lips as she moved her hips against him.

Damn. He knew this was a bad idea, but he was past caring. Taking one of her hands into his, he guided it upward. Shayne didn't need further instructions. She wrapped both arms around his neck, bringing them closer together. Her fingers raked against his scalp. He flinched when she touched the elastic that held his patch in place. The strap would remind her who she was getting involved with. Would she continue? Instead of backing away, she used that hand to pull his mouth closer as her tongue dueled with his.

The palm that had been pressed against her lower back inched up until he could feel her bare skin under the surplus material of the T-shirt. It felt like silk beneath his calloused fingers. He stroked her back, relishing the texture of her skin. He followed her spine like a path until he reached her shoulder blades. It dawned on him that nothing had stopped his trek. The softness of her chest against his registered.

Lifting his mouth enough to allow a whisper to pass between them, he stated the obvious: "You're not wearing a bra."

He was still so close that he felt her smile. "Hate the damn things."

His grin was brief as his lips moved to more important matters than talking. The hand that had traced her spine now wandered to her small breast. He cupped it, using his thumb to stimulate her nipple. Her moan was his reward.

Shayne pulled her head back, but not in retreat, and like he'd just done, only far enough to speak. "Not what you're used to, I'm sure."

"Better." He wanted to strip her naked, to take her up against the wall he'd backed her into, but she deserved more. So much more. He didn't want to examine why he felt that way. Instead, his hands dropped to her hips, and he lifted her off the floor, forcing her to wrap her legs around him or fall.

"We need a bed." And then it hit him. "Shit!"

Her eyes widened, and she immediately began to struggle to break loose. "No!" he said. "Don't think that. Not again." He kissed her hard to make the point. "I don't have any protection," he explained, almost in a panic. He couldn't remember the last time he'd had sex. He knew there were no condoms in his dopp kit. Even if he had any, they'd probably expired. Then he remembered who'd packed his stuff.

"Hang on," he told her, tightening one arm around her waist as he dipped his head for another kiss. Carrying her across the room, he held her tight as he reached for his duffel bag next to the couch. The first compartment he dipped his hand into, he struck gold. God bless Gib. It felt like he'd stuffed the entire contents of a box of condoms into the zippered compartment. He owed Gib—big time. Troy grabbed a handful of the packets.

Hitching Shayne up higher on his hips, he pressed her head against his shoulder as he walked toward the bedroom. He wanted to run but it might be seen as a little overanxious and a bit frightening. Reaching the bed, he tore back the covers then lowered Shayne to the mattress. When he tossed the half-dozen condoms onto the nightstand, her eyes widened. He couldn't contain his smile.

"Rather presumptuous, wouldn't you say?" she asked.

Troy chuckled. Her timid smile was precious. He leaned over to kiss her until her nervousness slipped away. As she relaxed, he reached for the hem of her shirt, and pulled it over her head.

"You're beautiful," Troy whispered, admiring the sight in front of him. Her build was small but perfect. She was more beautiful than all the women who had previously disrobed before him. These desires, these feelings for Shayne, baffled him. He'd never had to cajole a woman into his bed. They were either interested or not. With Shayne, it was different. He needed her to know that this was different for him.

When Troy raised his head, Shayne stared back at him. "What? You don't agree?" he asked, brushing the back of his hand against her cheek.

"I've never considered myself beautiful. Average—and that's okay with me, but I'm sure you're used to women who are more, shall we say, sensual. I don't understand this interest in me."

"We'll discuss the opinion you have of yourself another time." He stopped stroking her cheek and cupped her head behind her ear. He didn't want her to look away. "I'd explain this if I could, but in all honesty, this is new to me. I want you but only if you agree."

When she hesitated, Troy dropped his hand and started to rise. *Damn.* He didn't know how to say the right things to her. Didn't even know what those things might be. "Is it because of my face?" he asked.

"Now who's the one with the negative opinion? Your scars have never bothered me." She reached up and clutched the fabric of his shirt, pulling at it until he was eye level with her. "But I don't want to be a notch on your bedpost."

Troy rested his forehead against Shayne's. "Can we forget my sexual history and trust what I'm telling you now? What is happening between us is different for me."

She brushed her hand gently over his hair. The motion was soothing and erotic at the same time. He could have stood there indefinitely, but as she remained silent, Troy began to pull away.

Shayne reached out with her other hand. She ran her thumb along the elastic band that held his patch in place. Troy didn't back away this time, although he couldn't swear he hadn't reacted at all. Summoning the courage that had never been an issue on the battlefield, he looked into her eyes.

"Common sense tells me this isn't a good idea," she murmured, pulling his face close to hers and pressing her lips against his forehead. "We'll probably be scrapping with each other in an hour or so but until then..."

Troy's head jerked upward. His eye danced over Shayne's face. His eyebrow quirked up with the unspoken question. He looked nervous, not the reaction she'd expected, knowing his history with women. Reaching for the tail of his shirt, she began to pull it up and over his chest. His confused look transformed to one of desire in an instant. He finished the task for her and tossed the T-shirt to the floor.

It was Shayne's turn to lose all speech. The broad shoulders Shayne had noticed gave way to a toned and tanned chest. His upper arms bulged with taut muscle.

"Are you sure?" he asked.

Her sexual history wouldn't fill a thimble. She had nothing against sex, but she'd always left the encounter wondering why people thought it was such a big deal. Looking at the bare torso in front of her, she was reconsidering that opinion. She touched the hard planes of his chest and felt his muscles tighten under her fingertips. With hesitation, she caressed his skin, allowing her hand to drift lower as she did. When her fingers touched the waistline of his jeans, she pulled her eyes from the sculpted form and looked up at his face. His eye was closed.

"I suggest if we want to go any further, we might want to shed the remainder of our clothing."

Troy was quickly on his feet, reaching for the button of his jeans and at the same time leaning into her for a quick kiss. He unzipped his pants then stopped when he noted Shayne hadn't made a move to slip out of her legwear.

"What are you waiting for?" he asked.

"You." And that was the God's truth. If the rest of him looked anything like his chest, she'd be damned if she'd miss him stripping bare.

He gave her a cocky grin before reaching for her. "You first." He fumbled with the snap on her jeans, eventually unhooking it. The zipper followed. As the fabric slipped past her hips, his attention was drawn to the dark patch of hair at the top of her thighs. He stopped to stroke the tender spot. Her anticipation had to be evident by the dampness pooling between her legs. He bent over her and inhaled the musty fragrance. Shayne felt like she might explode with the sensual action. She struggled to kick off the jeans that bound her ankles. A crooked smiled graced Troy's face before he took mercy on her. He pulled her jeans over her ankles and dropped them to the floor.

For all her bravado, Shayne felt like crawling under the covers as Troy stood by the bed visually exploring her naked form. She reached for the sheet he'd tossed aside, but he caught her hand and gently clasped her wrist. "Don't," he said softly.

"I'm feeling a bit exposed here," she admitted.

"Then we should even the playing field." With one smooth motion, he had his jeans over his hips. He sat on the edge of the bed to tug the pants over his ankles.

Shayne was a bit disappointed that she didn't get the show she'd been expecting. His back and buttocks were nothing to sneeze at though. His wide shoulders spread to his muscular upper arms. She ran her hand along his spine, stopping at the tan line. She was so tempted to stroke the skin below the demarcation line but her timidity held her back.

She continued to caress the tan skin. The action was both comforting and exhilarating. As her fingertips feathered toward his waist again, Troy reached behind him, stopping her. He twisted so he could bring her hand to his lips, brushing a kiss against her knuckles. *Shit*. She was in trouble.

Why did he remain propped on the edge of the bed instead of crawling into it with her? "Are you having second thoughts?" Shayne asked.

"Hell no." Troy's voice was deep and sharp. "I don't want to screw this up."

Nerves. It must have been nerves that had the giggle

bubbling up her throat. There was nothing funny about their position. *Oh, shit.* She covered her face with her free hand as she tried to muffle the laugh. She was on the verge of having sex with a man who could be cover material for a men's magazine, and she was giggling like a schoolgirl.

Troy reached up and removed her hand from her face. "What's so funny?"

"Nerves, I guess," she told him.

"Don't be nervous. I won't do anything you don't want me to do," he assured her.

"I think it's got more to do with me living up to your expectations that has me rattled," she admitted.

She wasn't sure how he'd moved from the edge of the bed to covering her with his body so quickly, but there he was, blanketing her and whispering against her lips. "My only expectation is to make love to a beautiful woman who has graciously consented to share her body with me."

His mouth covered hers. The day-old beard chafed her cheeks, but she quickly forgot the whiskers as Troy deepened the kiss. Their tongues battled as he ran one hand over her hip then under it, gently grasping her cheek. She could feel the hardness of his body. His chest hairs tickled her breasts as his erection pressed against her sensitive flesh. Then suddenly she couldn't breathe. She was trapped, choking on dust. She wrestled her mouth away from his and pushed against his shoulders.

"Air. I need air."

Troy quickly backed off. Leaning back on his heels, her legs between his knees, he waited. His eyes narrowed.

"Sorry," she said between gulps of air. "Sorry." When Troy started to move from the bed, she put her hand to his chest. "No. Stay."

Troy patiently waited for her to explain. She was touched that he didn't get up and run from the room.

"A small flashback to being trapped. It scared me. I'm okay now."

"You sure?" he asked. He brushed an errant hair from her forehead. "We can stop. I'm a bit out of practice, myself. We can call this a dry run and try another time."

"It would certainly be a 'dry' run for you." She smiled. "I'm fine now. The memory surprised me." She stroked his chest. "Did I ruin the mood, or can we continue?"

Troy bent over, careful not to cover her completely, then took one of her breasts in his mouth. Question answered.

$\sim$

HE'D BEEN an idiot smothering her like that. Of course she'd felt trapped. Normally, he didn't think. He didn't plan. He improvised depending on his partner. But Shayne was different. He couldn't screw this up. It was too important. He felt the tension leave her body as he began to suckle her breast. When his ministrations elicited a moan from her, he brought his other hand to her free breast. After giving it the attention it deserved, he seductively moved his hand toward her hip. She jerked a little when he touched her waist. Ticklish. He'd remember that. When he reached her hip, he spread his fingers and touched the curls above her thighs. Her hips arched up.

He dipped his fingers deep into the valley between her legs. *Fuck*. She wasn't damp. She was wet. His cock hardened to steel. He'd forgotten what it was like. No, you couldn't forget something you'd never experienced. This was more than just a fuck. God help him—this was making love.

He took her breast into his mouth and lightly bit the

nipple as he increased the pace of his stroking. He curled one finger inside of her while his thumb continued to caress the nub at the entrance. Her hips pumped against his hand. He inserted a second finger, increased the pressure on her clit, and nipped at her breast again. She screamed as her spasms overcame her. He covered her mouth with his, inhaling her passion.

"You okay?" he asked, running his finger down her cheek.

She nodded, still catching her breath. A whisper of a smile was on her lips when she looked at him. "Yes. Thank you."

"My pleasure." He kissed the corner of her mouth. He couldn't remember another time that pleasuring a woman had affected him as that moment had. He was lost in these emotions that were swirling inside him.

"And now it's mine." She reached for a packet on the nightstand and handed it to him.

"I don't want to frighten you again." He couldn't believe he was offering her an option out.

"You won't."

Before Troy could open the packet, Shayne wrapped her fingers around his erection. Her strokes were tentative and slow—and excruciatingly erotic. His neck arched and his muscles tightened while he endured the sensual torture. When it was either embarrass himself or stop her, his hand snapped out. He brought her hand to his mouth and placed a kiss on the soft skin.

Once he had the condom in place, he knelt between her legs, brushing the insides of her thighs with the back of his hands. *Don't screw this up.* He raised her hips and guided himself to her entrance. He smiled when she raised herself to meet him, allowing him to glide into the warm, moist heat of heaven. *Crap*. This wouldn't last long.

He wrapped his arms around her thighs, anchoring her as he began to move. He didn't hover over her again, not wanting to close her in. Stroke after blissful stroke, he watched her face for any signs of stress. None appeared, so he quickened his pace. Her back arched further, and he felt her tighten around him. The response took him over the edge.

34

Troy collapsed beside her. Neither of them spoke. They were too busy sucking air into their lungs. While this hadn't been Shayne's first experience with sex, she'd had no idea that the act could be so intense and still so intimate. Shayne watched Troy's chest rise and fall as he caught his breath. She couldn't stop the grin. She was the reason for his exhaustion. She wanted to shout.

Troy's breaths became shallower. He let go of her hand and rolled off the opposite side of the bed. When he trotted out of the room without a word, her heart sank. She'd read too much into the interlude. She knew he was a player. Contrary to his claims, why did she think she'd been any different? She wanted to crawl under the covers and hide. Damn it, she wouldn't.

Getting to her feet and staying there was risky. Her knees wobbled. Muscles that hadn't been used in eons objected to the weight of her body. She wanted the bathroom but was damned if she'd leave the room tonight. It would take the rest of the evening to get her spine back. She shuffled over to the dresser, opened the drawer she kept her nightclothes in, and pulled them on. Turning back toward the bed, she stared at the rumpled sheets. Assuming she wouldn't spend the rest of the night berating herself, how the hell could she fall asleep in the same bed they had just set on fire?

The bench seat at the foot of the bed was too small to hold her. Childish idea anyway. She wasn't that much of a coward. As she sat on the edge of the bed, her eye caught the condom packets on the nightstand. Jerking the small drawer open, she swept the packets into it and slammed it shut.

"What are you doing?" Troy asked, his large form filling the doorway.

She clasped a hand to her chest, surprised by his appearance. "You're back."

He stalked over to her. "You figured I got what I wanted and left?"

"You left and didn't say anything…"

"We really have to do something about your problem with self-esteem." He squatted before her. He was still naked and a sight to behold.

"I'm not the only one with issues," she reminded him.

"No, you're not." Troy took one of her hands into his. He gulped air before he added, "Do you think we can work on them together?"

The question stunned her. She looked up from where their hands were joined, to the man who was now staring back at her. His jaw was firm, his eye scrutinizing her face. Trying to read what she didn't say. He was willing to open himself up to her. Could she do the same?

"We can try," she answered.

"Not tonight." He opened the drawer she'd slammed shut. "Tonight is a good night to forget."

They made love twice again that evening. Each time was more tender than the last. The urgency she'd initially felt in both of them had dissipated into a slow-moving dance. He'd been careful not to box her in, even suggesting she straddle him. The position was new, exhilarating, and empowering. She fell exhausted onto the mattress and curled up beside him, only to be surprised at suddenly being lifted into his arms and carried across the hallway.

"What are you doing?" she asked as he set her naked bottom on the cold granite vanity top. He reached around her and turned on the faucet. He remained silent as he took one of the washcloths off the stack of toweling on the shelf behind them. After testing the water with the back of his hand, he ran the cloth under the cascade then used it to clean himself. Shayne watched the movements, trying to anticipate what came next. She should have lost most of her shyness during their gymnastic session in the bedroom, but sitting under the harsh lighting fully exposed, proved that she still maintained a good portion of it. She reached for a towel from the bar over the toilet, but Troy stopped her, gently bringing her hand back to her side.

Still silent, he ran the cloth under the water for a second time before shutting the flow off. Then he leaned over to kiss her and as he did, he pressed the warm cloth to the tender skin between her legs.

"You've got to be sore." He lifted his lips to hers.

The warmth of the cloth soothed tissue that was sensitive, but still, apparently, combustible. As he tended to her most private parts, toiletries hit the floor as she leaned back and spread her legs wider.

The warm cloth was suddenly gone. She opened her eyes to find him smiling at her. "If that's an invitation, neither of us would be walking tomorrow if I accepted it." He took the towel from the rack and used it to dry her.

Then, as swiftly as he'd done the first time, he swept her up and carried her back into the bedroom.

"I'm going to get the satellite phone." He placed her on the bed. "I'll be right back, so make room for me."

She scooted over as soon as he disappeared from the room. She fluffed both pillows that had been battered from the lovemaking then tossed the covers over her. This time, she didn't bother with her nightclothes.

When Troy returned to the bedroom, he was wearing boxer briefs, with a pair of jeans slung over his shoulder. In his hands were a bottle of water, his gun, and the sought-after phone.

He'd set the phone and gun on the nightstand and draped his jeans over the chair in the corner. "Here," he said, uncapping the water. "We both need hydration."

She propped herself up on her elbow, taking several gulps. When she raised her head to hand the bottle back to him, he was holding her T-shirt and night shorts out to her. She reached for them, silently questioning the reason he wanted her dressed.

"Precaution," he said, answering the unspoken question.

"Against what?" she asked, pulling the T-shirt over her head.

"Needing to move quickly, if necessary."

She'd forgotten the reason that they were holed up in this retreat. At least Troy had kept his wits about him.

He joined her in bed, but propped his pillow against the headboard then rested his back against it.

"You're not going to sleep?" she asked. The sensual high was wearing off. A bit of fear was creeping back in.

"I'll doze." He leaned over and kissed her softly on the lips. "Get some sleep."

Turning onto her side, she rested her head on her pillow

as Troy feathered his hand over her upper arm. "If you go outside again, will you wake me?" she asked, the soothing motion lifting the tension.

"I'm not leaving you, honey, so stop worrying."

"If you do go out, be careful. I saw a light in the distance. Could belong to some hunters. If they don't know what they're doing, they could mistake you for something other than human."

The caressing stopped. "Where did you see a light?" he asked.

"Straight out the bedroom window. I'd guess about a quarter mile away." She yawned.

"Get some sleep." He resumed stroking her arm.

She didn't fight as her eyelids drifted shut.

TROY DIDN'T SLEEP or doze. Shayne, on the other hand, was out like a light snuggled up next to him. Another first. He'd never slept with a woman. He had sex. No entanglements. Yet tonight he'd made love to this woman, and it had felt natural and right. He loosened the chain that appeared to be digging into her neck. The chain and the pendant attached to it had been the single item that remained after she'd been stripped of her clothing.

He laid the pendant against her skin. A martini glass with a swizzle stick skewering a small diamond. An olive? Appropriate. He pulled the covers over her shoulders. He'd adjusted the thermostat on the AC, remembering she liked to sleep in a cold room. When had he become so conscious of a woman's wants and needs?

He'd have to sort out his feelings another time. At the moment, her remark about the light outside had him concerned. The property wasn't located on the north side of US 41 where it would be part of the Big Cypress Preserve and hunting was legal. This piece of property was tucked into the Everglades, a national park. Hunting anything but the invasive python was illegal within its boundaries. You didn't hunt those monsters at night. He couldn't rule out a park ranger or one of the members of the Seminole or Miccosukee tribes but that was improbable this far from any ranger station or reservation.

He was itching to get back outside and check the area, but had promised he wouldn't leave without telling Shayne. He didn't want to wake her or scare her. So he held her, listening for sounds in the night.

35

The aroma of coffee brought Shayne out of a sound sleep. She was alone in the bed but the sound of Troy's voice drifted into the room. She lay there listening. Had reinforcements arrived or was he on the phone? Based on the fact that he'd left the door to the bedroom open, she assumed he was on the phone.

She swallowed a groan as she slipped out of bed. Muscles that were rarely used had gotten a workout last night. She was paying the price this morning. It had been worth it.

Grabbing some clean clothes from the dresser, she headed directly for the bathroom. She showered and changed then was stopped short by her reflection in the mirror. Her skin was flushed, her cheeks pink. From the heat of the water or residual effects of last night's lovemaking? She washed her hair, but out of habit, had only ran her fingers through it. She loved having it short, but perhaps she could find a style that was less boyish and more feminine. She looked under the sink to see if the owners provided a hairdryer for their guests. She jumped when there was a tap on the door.

"You ready for some coffee?" Troy asked from the other side.

Shayne gave up her search and opened the door. A smiling Troy stood in the hallway with two cups in his hands, one dark the other the color of caramel. She took the lighter cup and sipped before smiling at the first man who'd ever brought her coffee. He leaned in for a kiss. He took his time before ending it by tracing her lips with his tongue.

"I've been waiting for that taste since the first time I kissed you." He grinned.

"What do you mean? We've kissed since then." A lot.

"You taste of cream and coffee," he explained. "I haven't forgotten that first taste of you."

Shayne stood there speechless. The same kiss that had her hurt and stressing had been a wistful memory for him. She didn't know how to respond.

"Come on." Troy took her arm. "We've got some things to discuss. We can do it over breakfast."

"You made breakfast again?" she asked, picturing what she'd find piled on her plate.

"I restrained myself," he said with a slight grin. He must have showered and shaved before she awakened. In spite of the smile and his fresh look, his face telegraphed some tension. His eye narrowed, and his grip on her arm was tight as he led her to the dining area.

"Something wrong?" she asked, after she noted the boxes of cereal he'd placed on the breakfast bar, along with milk and juice.

"Get something to eat then we'll talk."

She filled a bowl with cereal from the box nearest her. She

wasn't paying attention. Her nerves had ticked up a notch. Eating might not be the best idea at the moment, her stomach warned her. Still, she poured milk into the bowl then joined Troy at the table, skipping the juice. The acid would not sit well.

"Did you eat?" she asked.

"Long time ago."

"Did you sleep?"

"Some."

Shayne couldn't tell if he was being truthful or saying so to appease her. "What's going on?"

"Got some updates from the team. A few things have popped up you may be able to help with."

"Is that who you were talking to this morning?" she asked, forcing herself to swallow a spoonful of cereal.

"And last night as well," he added. "I forgot to mention it. You and I got distracted with other things." The corner of his mouth ticked up again.

"Well, spit it out. You're making me nervous,"

"Can you tell us any more about the guy you stopped to help?"

"All I can do is describe him. Why don't you contact the club or the temp agency? They should be able to give you anything you need." It should have been a simple search. Obviously, it wasn't.

"The agency assigned a contracted employee to the club. He never sent in his time sheet, and they haven't heard from him since. Our team hasn't been able to locate him."

Shayne dropped her spoon into the bowl as the impact of that statement hit her. "You think he's the guy behind the bombing."

Troy reached across the table and took her hand. "It's a possibility."

"But why? From where he was stationed, he'd have

known the congressman was gone. What was his reason?" Shayne pushed her bowl to the center of the table. She couldn't concentrate on food while questions swirled through her head.

"There's also the possibility that the man the agency sent wasn't the man you saw."

"Shit." His thinking was becoming clear to her. "I wasn't supposed to be there. If what you're saying is true, then he knows I can identify him. That's what this is about, isn't it?"

Troy got out of his seat and crouched next to her, taking her hand. "We need to figure out who he is and why he was there. Do you think you can help us with that?"

"I have no idea what he was doing there. I'd assumed he was tending bar." She searched Troy's face. "The man I saw leaving the room had nothing to do with this?"

"We think he's with the DEA. We suspect the other man who was killed was a DEA agent as well. We're digging, but that will be hard to confirm without the government's help." Troy pulled a chair closer to her as he continued to hold her hand.

"So this has been about drugs the whole time?" Shayne asked. "I told you before, I never overheard anyone discussing drugs. Never."

"Nothing?"

Shayne's eyes narrowed. "There were a few cryptic conversations I suspect were about marijuana but didn't think anything of it. I put it off to social use, like drinking."

"I don't think cannabis is the issue. Once Josie's contacts heard the DEA was involved, they were all over it. It seems that the Port of Tampa has been the subject of a major investigation by the agency. We're waiting for more information."

TROY REMOVED the dishes from the table and placed them in the sink. It was obvious she wasn't going to eat any more that morning.

"What's the connection to Copperhead?" she asked when he returned to the room. He set a Coke in front of her. The sugar would help, and she'd still get her dose of caffeine.

"We're working on it." He popped the top on the can.

She took a sip of the soda, which she immediately followed with a soft hiccup. "All this time I've been having nightmares about the guy walking down the hall. Couldn't someone have told me? I believed I was unconsciously suppressing the damn key to solving the murder of two people—and he was a friggin' government agent?"

Troy's eyebrows rose a notch. His lady was pissed. Good. He'd rather have her mad than scared. "It's an educated guess. I suspect that's why they let you go. They knew there was no point in you identifying him."

"What about the goddamn bartender? I saw him. They let me walk away knowing I saw the bomber?"

"Take it easy. The agents on the scene questioned the man. His story dovetailed with yours. They took his statement and contact information—contact information that belonged to the missing bartender. They're probably kicking themselves now that they can't locate the man who was actually hired to tend that bar. If they haven't put two and two together yet, they will shortly. Your official statement didn't mention the incident with his phone. That's what clicked for us."

"How do you know what was in my statement?" she asked.

"I told you we had a maestro with the computer keyboard on our team. We have a copy of everyone's statement regarding that night." Troy grinned. "Describe the man."

"I didn't pay close attention to him. I'm not sure I can."

"Yes, you can." He kissed the corner of her lips. "You've been so fixated on the mystery man, you haven't taken the time to recall the details of the bartender." He paused. "Close your eyes and picture him. You had a longer look at him than you did the man walking away. Start with what you already told the authorities."

Shayne did as he asked and closed her eyes. Damn. He was tempted to lay a kiss on each eyelid. Was this what it felt like to fall? It broadsided him, and he was in damn poor shape to deal with it, but he wasn't going to fight the pull any longer.

"C'mon, honey. How tall was he?"

Her eyes flew open. "You called me that last night."

"You have a problem with it?" He held his breath. He'd never used the endearment before, but it came naturally when talking to Shayne.

"I don't think so." But the answer didn't stop her brow from furrowing.

"Let's get back to the bartender. Height, weight, hair color, etcetera."

"He was a few inches shorter than you." Her eyes drifted shut again. "He was bulky but not overweight. He was fit. He lifted that full box of liquor like it was filled with paper cups." She opened her eyes. "He had dark brown, curly hair."

"What was he wearing?" Troy leaned forward, placed his hand behind her neck, and began to massage it. Her shoulders dropped as he loosened the tension that had been building.

"Standard for a barkeep. White shirt. Dark trousers."

"Eyes?"

"I didn't pay attention to the color. It mustn't have been distinctive." Her eyes widened. "He wore a ring. Not a wedding band but something like a class ring on his right hand. Ring finger. I noticed it because it was rather large."

"A class ring?"

"It reminded me of one. It had a large blue stone in the middle. I can't swear that it was a class ring. It seems familiar for some reason."

"But you don't know why?"

"No. It may be nothing."

"Let's keep going," he said. "How old was he?"

"Oh, sorry. Obvious question. Early thirties would be my guess. There was nothing much about him that stood out. He was clean-shaven. Average looks. I have to go back to the fitness thing. His shirt sleeves were rolled up and I could see the muscles in his forearms."

"Anything else?"

She reached for the soda can and took a sip. "No."

"You did good. The guys are getting a description of the temp the club hired. This should be enough to know whether it's the same guy." Troy rose from his seat.

"If it's not?" she asked, looking up at him.

"Then we'll make sure the FBI knows. We don't have the people to trace a missing employee."

"He could be dead."

"The temp? Yes. It's a possibility." Troy didn't want to worry her but didn't want to lie, either.

"I can't wrap my head around this," Shayne said.

"We'll get there." Troy came up behind her and began

massaging her shoulders more vigorously. "Will you be okay if I take off for a while?"

Shayne's head snapped up. "Where are you going?"

"To check the perimeter, then I want to go through the cottage we passed on the way in here." Colt had come through. During their last conversation, Troy was told he would find the key taped beneath the bottom tread of the front steps. The gallery manager was probably wondering about all the cloak-and-dagger stuff. It worried Troy a bit, but Colt trusted his friend, and by extension, his employees.

"Why do you need to check that place?"

"Precautions. I don't expect to find anything but it should be cleared." He tilted her head so she was looking at him, and he feathered a kiss to her lips. The action surprised him, but damned if it didn't feel right. "Will you be okay for an hour or so?"

"I think I can manage," Shayne answered on a sigh of relief. "I'll clean up the dishes. When do you expect to talk to your friends?"

He almost corrected her. She didn't appear to realize that the team had accepted her into their circle of friends. But she had enough to digest at the moment between the new suspicions regarding the bombing and the change in their relationship. She was smart. She'd figure it out.

36

Shayne cleaned up the dishes and wiped the table and breakfast bar. Now she stared at the notepad, a blank sheet of paper staring back at her. She'd planned to make a list of things she remembered about the bartender. It was busywork. Troy, she was sure, had the description imprinted on his brain. He'd relay every detail to the others whether he had her written notes or not.

Her mind kept returning to activities of last night. The two of them had made love not once but three times. Hell, she could hardly move this morning. She was still deliciously tender, and thinking about the evening had her wiggling in her seat. Troy seemed to have no regrets—a thought that had crossed her mind once or twice while she showered. The question was, did she?

Her defensive wall had crumbled to the ground last night. A large pile of metaphorical bricks now lay at her feet. Too much debris for a wall she'd quickly assembled. But the construction hadn't begun because of her feelings for Troy and her perceived rejection of those feelings. He'd been the impetus to complete the invisible wall she'd already begun.

She closed her eyes. She'd been kidding herself. Her heart ached at the admission. The building had begun the day she'd lost her dad. His sudden death had torn her apart. She'd withdrawn. She'd expected the ache to eventually pass. It hadn't. She loved her mother, but every visit home she expected to see her dad walk into the room. Sadly, she'd been relieved when her mother had returned to Ireland. Years later, Shayne still continued to put off the trip to see her grandmama before her relative didn't recognize her at all. How selfish was that?

Her dad would be angry that she still mourned him. He'd also be pissed that she'd wasted her college years. Instead of putting her degree to work, she'd taken the part-time job tending bar and made it full-time. She'd *checked out*, so to speak. She'd had friends but never close friends. Having them meant losing them. Why was this suddenly clear to her?

Shayne had the sudden desire to call her mom. Talk to her and be her little girl again. Tell her mom she'd met someone and that she was scared and excited at the same time. Troy's phone sat on the counter. He'd switched it off for security reasons. She wouldn't put them at risk just so she could feel better. If she got out of this mess in one piece, then she'd have a nice, long chat with her mom and make that trip she'd put off.

She redirected her attention to the pad in front of her. That night at the club had taken on a new perspective. Had she spoken to the bomber? Was he the man who'd attacked her in the alley? She mentally pictured the bartender, trying to remember his every move. The only additional item she could add to what she'd told Troy was he wore dark, soft-soled shoes, which were standard attire for the job. She could say even less of the man in the alley. Their heights were similar, but all she'd noticed was the dark poncho and his raised hand as he ran toward her. She could add that they were both Caucasians. She concentrated on the hand. She couldn't vision what he'd held in it, but she suddenly remembered a flash of something bright. *I'll be damned.*

WHEN TROY RETURNED to the bungalow, Shayne sat at the dining room table. She was scribbling furiously on the pad. She didn't acknowledge his entrance. Her focus was on the page in front of her.

He'd come up with nothing new on his patrol of the perimeter and inspection of the vacant cottage. He found no signs of trespassers. Tracks from species native to the area were abundant, but none of the human variety. The house showed no signs of a break-in or squatters.

Peering over Shayne's shoulder, he asked, "What are you doing?"

"Shit! You scared the hell out of me." She held a hand to her chest.

"Sorry." He bent over and gave her a quick kiss. "I'm not sure how I could have avoided that. What's got you so distracted?" Looking closer, he saw she'd drawn a line down the middle of the sheet of paper. Words filled each column. One had considerably more than the other. At the bottom was some sort of drawing.

"The guy that hit me in the alley?"

"What about the bastard?" Troy brushed his knuckles against her forehead where she'd been hit. He had plans for that son of a bitch.

"I remembered something."

"You said you couldn't make him out."

"I didn't. But I saw his hand the second before he whacked me. He was wearing a ring on his right hand." She handed her notes to Troy. "That's what I remember about both men. I didn't see much of the guy on Sanibel, but what I did see tracks with the man from the bar. I was playing with a drawing, but it's no use. I didn't see enough of either man's ring."

Troy looked at her notes. "There's not much to compare, but nothing disqualifies him from being the same man. It's time we talked to the team."

Steve answered the phone this time, but he and Troy agreed they should round up the rest of the team before they got any deeper into the weeds. Twenty minutes passed before he heard back.

"McKenzie," he answered, hitting the speaker button.

"Troy," Colt responded. "Is Shayne with you?"

"Yeah. Who's at your end?"

"Rick, Steve, and Gib," Colt answered.

"Hey," Cat interrupted. "Josie and I are here too."

"I was getting there."

"How are you doing, Shayne?" Cat asked, dismissing her husband.

"I'm good," Shayne replied. "Sorry I left you shorthanded."

"We're fine. No worries here."

"You two getting along yet?" Gib inquired.

"We're getting along fine. Can we get down to business?" Troy asked.

"So, you took my advice?" Gib continued.

"What advice?" Shayne asked, cocking her head to look at Troy.

Troy pretended he didn't hear her, but it was hard to miss Gib's distinctive laughter coming through the line.

"Can we stay focused? Did you locate the bartender from the agency?"

"No," Rick answered, "and I don't think we will. Not alive, anyway."

"What makes you say that?" Troy asked.

"He's vanished," Rick said. "His name is, or was, Curtis Franklin. He quit his job via text, and his last paycheck was never cashed. He disappeared from social media entirely months ago. His last post said he was taking a break from it. Nobody disappears entirely unless something has happened to them. Besides, he left his stuff in his apartment, and all his bills are past due."

"Josie dropped off the grid last year," Troy reminded them. She'd been running for her life while she searched for Steve. Going underground had kept her alive. Smart lady. She and Troy hadn't hit if off at first, but he admired the hell out of her now.

"She didn't pull it off for months," Rick said. "That takes a special kind of technical knowledge. From what we've learned, he was your average guy."

"Describe him."

As Rick related the physical description of the temp agency's employee, Troy knew the bartender Shayne had seen and the contract employee were not the same person.

"That's not the man I saw," Shayne said loud enough for all to hear.

"While it wouldn't hold water in a courtroom, the man who attacked Shayne matches the general description of the bartender," Troy said. "There is one thing that might help. Both men wore a large ring on their right ring finger."

"Did you see any insignia? Anything that might help identify it?" Rick asked Shayne.

"No," she replied. "And I'm not saying it was a class ring,

but it reminded me of one or something similar to your signet rings. It was gold and the stone was dark blue."

"Are the authorities looking for him?" Troy asked. "A prime witness gone missing is a hell of a red flag."

"My bet is they don't know that he's missing," Rick said. "But they will after I call them."

"How could they not know?" Troy asked.

"He didn't raise any concerns when he was questioned after the explosion. Any further questioning would be done by phone since he wasn't a suspect at the time. That's standard operating procedure. If he kept Franklin's cell, he could easily have stayed in contact with the FBI and continued his charade for as long as it suited him or they figured it out. Somebody's ass is going to be in a sling for not following up on this guy."

"Locating the phone won't be of any help now. I'm certain he's ditched it," Steve added. "After the attack on Shayne, he'd put two and two together and assume it would eventually lead the cops in his direction."

"So, we got nothing?" Troy asked.

"Some of us do."

"What did you uncover, Josie?"

"You already know the DEA is investigating drugs passing through the Port of Tampa," Josie replied.

"Go on."

"To make a long story short, one of the investigative reporters I know discovered that the original DEA agents who were assigned to the case are no longer working it."

"I could think of several reasons that might happen," Troy said. "Why is that significant?"

"Because one of the agents is dead, and the other took a leave of absence shortly after the bombing," Josie said.

Troy turned one of the dining room chairs around and

straddled it. "The dead agent was one of the two killed in the blast, right?"

"You got it," Steve confirmed.

"Shit. And the second agent? Do we know where he is?"

"He recently dropped off the grid as well," Rick answered.

"He's hunting his partner's killer." It wasn't a question. Troy felt it.

"That would be my guess," Rick agreed. "If they removed him from the case because he was too close to it, he might have gone rogue. Any of us would have done the same thing. And if he doesn't want to be found, he has the skills to stay that way."

"Now we have two unknowns wandering around," Troy said. He didn't like it. "What's the missing agent's name?" For all the good it would do them, it made him seem less like a ghost.

"Gardner. Garrett Gardner," Josie added. "He's a FAST Team agent, whatever that is."

"Is he still an agent?" Troy asked. "If he's been AWOL for six months, the DEA might have cut him loose."

"He asked for and received an extended leave," Rick told him. "We're assuming he's still on their team. Regardless, he hasn't surfaced."

"He was navy before he joined the DEA," Josie continued.

"SEAL?" The equivalent of the army's Green Berets. Troy knew some, and they were a real badass group of guys.

"No. Pilot," Josie said.

"How did he go from navy pilot to DEA agent?"

"Don't know the answer to that one. He got his degree in criminal justice while in the navy. I haven't received any information as to how or why he wound up with the DEA, but after his stint in the navy, he's a mystery."

"As he should be," Rick said. "A good agent wouldn't have his name in the news."

This was getting them nowhere. "Do we have any information regarding the investigation they were working on before his partner was killed?" Troy asked.

"Over a year ago," Josie said, "there was a sudden and steep rise in heroin deaths in the Tampa Bay area. This heroin is cut with fentanyl and has proved extremely lethal. The Port of Tampa is the suspected port of entry, or the death trail would have started further south. Most drugs smuggled into the state come through Miami or the Keys. Recently, the DEA upped their efforts in and around the Port of Tampa. Gardner and his partner, whose real name was Stokes, were on the task force and undercover."

"How the hell do you know all that?" Troy asked.

"It's called investigative journalism," Josie answered.

Damn. Troy grinned. You could hear the pride in her voice. Josie may not have Don's hacking skills, but her network of contacts was just as impressive.

"What's the connection between the drugs and the country club?" Shayne asked.

"Still working on it," Colt replied. "Too many unanswered questions. Who was the guy Shayne saw tending bar, and why were Stokes and Russell in that room when the bomb went off? You told Troy you didn't know the younger Russell?"

"I'd only see him from across the room," Shayne said. "His dad, along with his friends, were almost nightly visitors at the bar. They were good customers. I haven't been in contact with any of the residents since that night, but I could reach out to him if you want." Troy noticed she developed a nervous habit of fiddling with the pendant around her neck.

"We're going to delve into the son's history," Colt said. "What I'd like to know is your impression of him. Anything about him strike you as odd or distinctive? Anything noteworthy?"

"Nothing I can put my finger on. I always felt on edge when the Russell family came in for dinner." Shayne's eyes narrowed.

"Why?" Troy asked.

"That's just it. I'm not sure. From my station at the bar, I could see them clearly in the dining room but I couldn't hear them. Their body language was off, particularly between the two men. Mrs. Russell talked nonstop like a nervous person or a loquacious drunk."

"And the father and son?" Troy asked.

"I'd call them *distant*. Although I'm not sure they could get a word in edgewise if they wanted to carry on a conversation with Mrs. Russell present."

"Did the son come in for dinner often?" Colt asked.

"When I first started working there, I saw him a couple of times a year, at most."

"But that changed?" Troy asked her.

"Yes. A few months before I left, the three were coming in almost weekly."

"Do you know why the frequency of visits changed?" Troy continued the questioning.

"His dad didn't comment on it. He rarely spoke of his son at all. Made me think there was some sort of a rift between the two. My guess is that they tolerated each other for the sake of Mrs. Russell."

"We'll give him a close look," Rick told her. "Anything else you want to add?"

"Can you make some inquiries about hunting in this area?" Troy asked. "Shayne saw a light outside last night. I don't know the laws regarding hunting around here. It would be good to know if we might have unexpected visitors."

There was an extended silence at the other end of the line. His friends were a lot more familiar with the national park than Troy. The pause confirmed what Troy had surmised. No one should have been out there last night when Shayne saw the flash of light.

"You sure this was behind the bungalow?" Colt asked.

"A little southeast of the property."

"I'll contact the tribal police and the park rangers," Rick said. "Could be someone was out there poaching. In the meantime, we'll figure out a way to get you some backup."

37

After the call ended, Shayne left Troy alone at the table and numbly walked toward the kitchen. Mechanically, she pulled out a loaf of bread, deli meat, and other items necessary to make sandwiches. She reached for one of the bottles of wine in the back of the refrigerator then hesitated. A glass would calm her jumbled nerves. Would her drinking alcohol be a problem for Troy? She hadn't seen him drink since the morning he'd been assigned to help her in the garden.

"Go ahead," Troy said from behind her.

"Stop doing that!" Shayne slammed her palm against her chest. It was becoming a habit. "Do you always sneak up on people?"

"Occupational training," Troy responded. "I'll try to make some noise next time."

"My mind was elsewhere," she explained, still holding the refrigerator door open.

"On that bottle of chardonnay?" Troy relaxed against the kitchen counter.

"I was, but I'm fine." How did you tell someone you were

afraid to drink in front of them? Would it insult him? Would it tempt him? Was his binge drinking an aberration? Damn. She'd slept with him but was too timid to bring up the subject of his drinking.

"You look like you need a drink. The question about the light scared you, didn't it?" Troy crossed his arms over his broad chest.

"You knew there wasn't a hunter out there last night, didn't you?"

"I figured it was unlikely. Hunters are rarely allowed in national parks. If there was a special permit, the guys will find it."

"You didn't question what I saw. Thank you." She closed the refrigerator door.

"No one is questioning what you saw," Troy assured her as he straightened and reached around her to open the fridge. He grabbed the bottle of wine off the shelf.

"I know. If they didn't, they wouldn't be sending someone to back you up. The news made them nervous." She watched as Troy hunted through the drawers until he found the object he was looking for—a corkscrew.

"That's what hit you, wasn't it? Not the news regarding the missing bartender," he said, as he uncorked the bottle.

"The guys had been so damn adamant about not sending you additional help, but as soon as I mentioned the light, we suddenly need backup. Yeah, I admit, that's got me a bit nervous, but I'm fine without anything to drink."

Troy pulled a water glass out of the cabinet above her head. The place hadn't come equipped with wine glasses. "So am I, Shayne." He leaned over and gave her a quick kiss. "I haven't needed a drink since I woke up at Gib's. A beer would be nice, but I'm going to talk to someone before I give alcohol a try again."

Shayne hadn't planned to discuss his issues with drinking or the reasons behind them. She wasn't sure if she wanted to. She let out a breath and took a sip of the cool liquid. He may not need it, but she did.

"I didn't mean to bring up the subject. I shouldn't have a say in what you do or how you handle what you went through." She looked at the food she'd set on the counter. She'd lost her appetite. "You hungry?"

"No." He shook his head.

Together, they silently put the food away. Shayne took her glass of wine and headed toward the living room. Her stomach flipped when Troy stopped and went back to the refrigerator. When he appeared with a bottle of water, her skin warmed with embarrassment.

"Sit. Please," he said.

Shayne could pretend the doubt hadn't crossed her mind, but she'd seen the moment he realized what she'd been thinking. He'd been sober and at her side since the trouble began. He deserved more from her.

"I'm sorry," she said.

Troy shrugged. "You had no reason to believe me."

"I had no reason to distrust you, either. I was concerned I'd put the idea into your head. I'm not sure how to act. I'm not much of a drinker. A glass of wine now and then, but I've never been close to anyone with..."

"An alcohol problem? A drunk?"

"You're not a drunk," she snapped. "It was stupid for me to even think you might dive back into a bottle. Hell, your friends wouldn't have packed it if they believed that was the case."

"They're good friends," Troy agreed. "They were my lighthouse. When I hit rock bottom, they were the beacon that drew me to a safe port." He chuckled. "Corny and the analogy is better suited for the Navy, but I looked to them because I needed help. I knew they wouldn't desert me, no matter how miserable I made them."

"They were pretty hard on you when you arrived."

"Passed out on their front door, you mean." Troy rubbed his hand across his stubble. "I deserved it."

Shayne brushed her palm on the back of Troy's head before resting it on his shoulder. "I don't think they're going to kick you out." Her heart hurt for him.

"They won't. I'm going to talk to a professional when this is all over. But as long as I'm around them, they won't let me stumble."

"And instead of getting their help, you're stuck with me."

Troy reached behind and grabbed Shayne's wrist, pulling it from his neck. "You think what happened between us last night was the result of me being 'stuck' with you?"

He shouldn't have snapped at her, but her thinking she was a convenient lay hurt. He loosened his grip then slipped his fingers through hers. He pulled her to his side. "Give me a minute."

He had yet to let go of her hand and was relieved she didn't fight him for it. He needed the anchor. "Do you think last night was normal for me?" he asked. He did his best to keep the emotion out of the question. He wasn't sure if he'd succeeded.

Shayne didn't answer. Instead, she stared at the wall across the room.

"That's not a fair question," Troy admitted. "You really don't know." He continued to hold her hand, his thumb rubbing a circle in her palm.

"I know you're a good man," she replied.

"How can you say that? You know about the women. You know I drank to excess. You have no idea what I did to deserve this face." As much as he wanted to walk away from her, he wanted to stay just as much.

"I know you're a good man," she repeated, clenching his hand.

"How?" he asked. "What makes you such a good judge of my character?"

When she faced him, she no longer looked lost but determined. "Because I know your friends, and I know they wouldn't care what happened to you if you weren't worth helping."

"You don't—"

She put her finger against his lips, silencing him. "It took all you had left in you to reach out for help. That's a sign of strength, not weakness. You've protected me from unknown assailants not to mention yourself."

She took her free hand and turned his face so she could see his scars clearly. "I know something terrible happened to you, but I don't believe it's the damage to your face that's left you scarred. Whatever it was, you tried to drown it in alcohol, but you've conquered that beast. You're a strong, good man."

Her gaze drifted to the windows. "You asked me if I believed last night was normal for you. I didn't answer because I don't know what is normal for you. But I want it to be different. If it's not, then I'm the fool, because it was different for me."

Troy released her hand. He pulled her close as he dusted kisses over her cheeks and across her lips, lingering there. Then he lifted her into his arms and carried her to the bedroom. Once he placed her on the bed, he began shedding his clothing. He remembered to check the drawer of the nightstand. A couple of condoms remained. He dropped them on top of the stand.

Deliberately, he began to undress Shayne, slipping her shirt over her head. He tossed it aside and bent over her to taste the buds, still rosy pink from their night of lovemaking. Good thing he could multitask. He had her jeans unbuttoned and over her hips before he found it necessary to remove his mouth from her breasts to finish the task of undressing her.

Admiring the slim figure laid out before him, he asked, "Are you up for this?"

Shayne's coquettish smile took his breath away. "I think *you* are," she answered, wrapping her hands around his erection.

He closed his eyes and threw his head back with a groan. "If this is too soon, let me know and I'll back off." It would kill him but he would do it. "Otherwise, let me get this thing on," he said, holding up the sealed condom. His voice was strained. Hell, he was surprised he could speak at all.

Shayne snatched the packet from between Troy's fingers with her free hand, Shayne tore it open with the aid of her teeth then slipped it over him with excruciating slowness. The minute her fingers reach the hilt, he straddled her. Again, he was careful not to box her in. He reached between them, testing her readiness. At his touch, she began to move against his hand. She was warm and slick. He needed no further invitation.

He made love to her. Slow, tender, all-consuming love. She was under his skin—a part of him—and it felt so damn right. He looked at the woman who lay exhausted next to him. Why now? He was a certified mess. She was in trouble...and he had absolutely no idea what was supposed to happen next.

He sat up, swinging his legs over the side of the bed. A soldier without a battle plan. Not good.

"Is something wrong?" Shayne asked when he didn't move.

Her fingertip traced the Gaelic words on his right bicep. *The fair one.* How ironic. If he was being honest—and he was trying—he wasn't being the least bit fair to her. His life was fucked up, and he had a long way to go before he had anything to offer.

"Troy?"

He pressed her hand against his arm, stilling it. How could he think about a future when he couldn't get by his past? Gib had warned him he couldn't do it alone. Could he share his burden with Shayne? Would it make it lighter or add to hers?

"Troy? You're scaring me."

He tenderly grasped her shoulders and laid her against the mattress. A swath of her hair touched her brow. He brushed it away from her forehead with the back of his hand then continued to stroke her angelic face. "I'm scared too," he admitted, forcing a tight smile on his face.

Shayne's eyes widened but remained locked on him.

"You don't look away," he whispered, absorbing his conclusion. "You've never looked away."

"Is that what you want?" she asked, reaching for the sheet to cover her.

"It's as if you don't see my scars."

"We all have scars. Some we can see. Some we can't."

"Like yours," he said. He still caressed her smooth skin. In spite of the time she spent working outside in the sun, her skin felt like silk.

"I have my share but I don't carry the burden you do." Shayne touched the scarred tissue beneath his patch.

He grasped her hand then kissed the palm. His heart was tumbling. "Can I tell you about it?" He held his breath as his palms grew slick with sweat. *God.* He'd never needed anyone to say yes as much as he needed to hear the word from Shayne.

Shayne scooted up and pressed her back against the headboard. She covered herself with the sheet. "I'm listening."

Troy slid into his jeans. It felt disrespectful to have this conversation unclothed. He returned to the bed and took the hand she offered.

"During one of our deployments, there was this kid," he began. "A boy. He liked to hang around our base camp. Basim was twelve, maybe thirteen, years old. The kid was always smiling. Anxious to help. We gave him odd jobs to do then paid him with food or something else his family could use. We interacted with the locals when it was safe. Building trust was as important as getting the bad guys. It helped to make friends in the local communities. Basim attached himself to me for some reason. I helped him with his English. Kicked a soccer ball around with him. You know, let him see us as the good guys. I got closer to him than I should have."

"Something happened to him?"

"On my last tour, we were in a village. For a second, I saw this kid, a young man actually, moving through a crowded marketplace. A little older and taller but he looked like Basim. As he was moving into the busier section of the market, I shouted out his name.

"I swear to God I remember every second, every miniscule change in his expression. The spark in his eye when he recognized me. The desolation that quickly extinguished that spark and the cold determination that replaced both. The starkness of that look hit me like a kick to the chest. That's when I realized... That's when I saw he was wearing a vest—a bomb."

Troy kneaded his forehead, wishing he could force the images into the deep recesses of his brain and never see them again. But this woman holding his hand had a right to know what she was getting into.

Frame by frame, the pictures came at him. "I bolted toward him. That look... I'll never forget that look on his face. It should have told me everything I needed to know. As soon as his hand slipped into the pocket of his vest, I knew it was too late. People died. I should have been one of them."

SHAYNE HELD back tears as she absorbed his words. He believed he should be dead. From what she'd learned, he might have been successful at completing the deed had he not come to his senses and sought out his friends. She understood survivor's guilt. Boy, did she ever. But there was something more to his death wish. "Why?"

Troy launched himself off the bed, yanking his sweaty palm from hers.

"Why do you think you should have died?"

His neck was corded and his hands fisted. His body language and previous attempted acts of self-destruction signified something more than survivor's guilt. It was stupid for her to play psychologist. She needed one herself. But he was opening up. She'd let the poison spill out. It was a step toward healing.

"I should have stopped him. I should have recognized

the danger sooner. Instead, I was reaching out to someone I considered an old friend."

"Could you have gotten to him in time?"

Troy remained silent. An answer in itself.

"It never occurred to me that he'd become radicalized." He dropped into the corner chair. It was all she could do to stay where she was. But he didn't want her pity. He was looking for something else. Understanding? Forgiveness?

"Did anyone figure out why he changed?"

"Not that I'm aware of." Troy looked at Shayne. "I believed he was a good kid. I must have missed something. What if I could have intervened during the time he spent with us?"

"I gather it was months or years between your first inter-action with Basim and the sighting at the market. You know as well as I do how easily teens are influenced. Perhaps something happened to his family during that time period. Did you or any of the other team members suspect some-thing was off when he first arrived at your camp?" Shayne reached for her clothes and slipped them on as she waited for his answer.

"I never discussed it with them."

"Well, that's stupid. Wouldn't it have helped set your mind at ease if they felt the same way?"

"I was closest to Basim. I should have noticed."

"I bet there was nothing to notice when you knew him. Blaming yourself for something you had no control over is stupid."

Troy's eye narrowed. "You weren't there."

"No, I wasn't," Shayne replied. "But your teammates were. Ask your friends what they saw and how they felt. If they suspected Basim of anything, they would have told you. I'm sure of that. Two years is a lifetime for a teenage boy. You don't know what happened to him during that time. Give yourself a break."

"And the people who died in the marketplace that day? Do I give myself a break because I was so blinded by a former friendship that I ignored the signs of a terrorist?"

He blamed himself because he believed it was his job to save a kid from going over to the "dark side." That guilt was compounded because Basim wasn't the only one who lost his life that day. Troy was a protector.

"You ran toward a bomber in an attempt to save others and almost got yourself killed in the process. You tried to save Basim and others at the risk of dying..." Shayne trailed off.

"I shouldn't have told you." Troy glanced her way, looking tired and pale.

"Why? Because it brings back memories of my own experience?"

"Yes."

Shayne studied Troy. He'd given her an idea. He wasn't going to listen to arguments that excused him. Perhaps if she jumped into the pity party with him, he'd see it from a different perspective.

"You know, you're right," she said, looking past him. "We both could have saved lives if we'd made different decisions. There must have been something I missed that would have helped me stop the bomber. At the very least, I should have chased the two men from the room as soon as I realized they were there. They might be alive today if I had."

"And you could be dead." Troy scowled. "There was nothing you could do. You didn't know he was a killer. You didn't know his plans."

"But I was there and I lived. Based on your logic, I shoulder some of the blame."

"Stop that." Troy stalked across the room. "You're being ridiculous. You aren't to blame." He pulled her up from the bed.

"How is it different?" Shayne met his gaze.

"I knew that kid. I should have recognized the signs. Then when I spotted him in the market, I was too slow to react."

"What are you? One of the Avengers who lost his superpowers? *Savior of the World Fails at Quest.* Makes for a great headline."

Troy's eye narrowed. Anger emanated off him in waves of heat. Good. With any luck, it would burn off some of that self-loathing.

"You have no idea if he was radicalized. He may have been forced into that situation to save a family member. Perhaps his entire family. You said he was a good kid. You could be wrong about your assumptions. I'd like nothing more than my memories to disappear—to be sure there was nothing I could have done to save two lives."

"You weren't trained. I was." Troy glared at her. She didn't budge.

"What's the real problem here? Are you at fault because you didn't recognize that someone was capable of committing a heinous act? Are you faulting yourself for not being able to move at the speed of light? Or are you angry because you feel betrayed? I'd file them all under self-pity." She was poking a tiger and had no idea if it would help or hurt.

Troy pivoted and stormed toward the bedroom door.

"That's it?" she asked. "You can't finish this?"

"Finish what? An argument? I wanted you to know what kind of man you were sleeping with."

"I already knew."

Troy stopped and turned to face her. "You knew what happened?"

"No. Of course not." Shayne sighed. "I knew you were a good man."

"How could you think that?" he asked. That single eye felt like a laser beam. "You couldn't stand me."

"I managed to get my head out of my ass. You care about people. It's written all over you. You care about me. And you're cared for by your friends. You're worth the effort."

38

T roy sat on the living room sofa sipping a cup of coffee. Shayne was in the kitchen, prepping items for an early dinner. They'd skipped lunch, she reminded him. He'd offered to help, but she'd chased him out.

He stared at the pad of paper that had made its way back to the coffee table. The words on it were a jumble of letters. As much as the mystery surrounding Shayne needed solving, his mind kept slipping back to his confession and her response to it. She'd hit every nail on the head and hammered them home. He hadn't entertained any other possibilities as to why things had happened except he'd failed, and that failure had led to the death of Basim and three others. It had also left him scarred inside and out.

Maybe he'd screwed up but, then again, maybe he hadn't. If he had, he wasn't going to figure out how to deal with it on his own. With his friends, some professional help, and, with any luck, Shayne, he could wrestle this monkey off his back. The future no longer looked so dim.

The jumble of letters formed words as his head cleared. It was imperative that they find the man who had tended that bar, but Troy kept coming back to Russell. What was he doing in the same room with a DEA agent? Was it a coincidence? That seemed implausible. Who had the bomb intended to kill? One or both of the men? They still couldn't be sure the congressman wasn't a target, but the federal authorities would be all over that. Troy needed more information on Russell. This time, instead of waiting for someone to report back to him, he picked up the phone.

"What's up?" Rick answered. "Everything okay there?"

"Nothing new at this end," Troy assured him. "Have you gotten any more information on Lawrence Russell or the bartender? My money is on the imposter as being the bomber."

"You're not alone. After we talked to Hernandez and Morgan, he is now considered a person of interest."

"He's a goddamn killer, but if that's what they want to call him, that's fine with me as long as someone gets their hands on the bastard."

"Agreed," Rick said.

"Any word on the man from the agency who was supposed to be tending bar that night?" Troy leaned over the table, ready to make some notes.

"He's going to be more difficult to find, assuming he's alive. His last post to social media was an announcement he was going on a pilgrimage and dropping off the grid. I'm quoting his post here, he needed 'to find himself.'"

"Would seem like a lot of people are doing that these days," Troy huffed. "He's a dead end—literally and figuratively."

"If the bomber took Franklin's phone and continued to use it, masquerading as Franklin, he wouldn't have wanted Franklin around to screw up the facade."

"You're not getting an argument from me on that point,

either," Rick said. "But how did he know that Franklin was working the fundraiser so he could intercept him?"

"It could be as simple as the bomber hanging out at the country club and waiting for an opportunity to slip in," Troy replied. "Which would be risky. This is a lot more synchronized than pure luck would allow."

"You're talking inside job," Rick said. "Which would mean someone at the country club or the temp agency had to be involved. The charity wouldn't have had anything to do with the hiring of the staff."

"The drug operation the DEA is investigating has a lot of tentacles—a lot of people." Troy paused and glanced at the kitchen, where Shayne remained busy. He strode out onto the screened porch so she wouldn't hear. "Christ, Rick. If that's the case, how are we going to protect Shayne?"

"We'll have someone there tomorrow."

"And I appreciate the help, but we can't stay holed up here forever. We need to solve this case more than the DEA does—and faster. As long as someone from the ring believes Shayne can identify them, she'll be a target." And he could lose her. He wasn't sure he'd survive that.

"Trust me, Troy, we're not going to let anything happen to her," Rick assured him, as if he'd read Troy's mind.

"We're not getting very far with the bomber unless we hang Shayne out as bait—which we're not," Troy emphasized. "We need another starting point."

"The victims," Rick said.

"Yes," Troy agreed. "Did we get anything more on the younger Russell?"

"We got nothing from the Feds, but Don's dug up some information."

"Anything interesting?" Troy asked. He glanced into the

bungalow. Shayne had her back to him, concentrating on whatever was cooking on the stove.

"Russell was single. No significant other. He was a partner in a law firm in Tallahassee until he moved to Tampa."

"Lobbyists?" It wouldn't be unusual with Tallahassee being the state capital.

"They have a general practice, which includes some work for lobbyists. It's a well-known and respected firm."

"Do we know why Russell left?" Troy asked. Shayne was setting the table, and he needed to wind up this conversation.

"We contacted his old firm, but no one would discuss his departure."

"What was he doing in Tampa after he moved?" Troy returned to the living room, keeping an eye on Shayne. He liked watching her mumble and talk to herself as she worked.

"He partnered with a local attorney, a former prosecutor."

"That's interesting. Get anything from him?"

"We're still waiting for a return call. In the meantime, Cat has left a message to see if Jason can help out. The partner may be more willing to talk to him."

If anyone could get through, it would be Jason Waters. Before he'd retired, Jason was a prosecutor with the Florida's attorney general's office and was Cat's former boss. Jason and his wife treated Cat as if she were their daughter. He still had connections and wasn't afraid to use them.

"I believe Russell is the link," Troy said. "We need to find out why he was with the DEA agent. Was he a suspect, a source, or just unlucky?"

"If we don't hear from Jason shortly, I'll touch base with

the Tampa PD. They may have some info on him, but he was there such a short time, I doubt it."

"What about his DUI?" Troy looked at Shayne, and this time she was pointing to the table that had been set. Apparently, dinner was ready.

"DUI goes back to his college days. He admitted to it. Paid a fine and did some community service. No record of any further violations."

"Any sign of the DEA agent, Gardner?"

"Nothing yet. He'll be a tough one to find. He could be using any one of the aliases he created while he worked undercover. I'm sure the agency has a list, but there's no way we're getting our hands on it."

"All right. If you get more on Russell, call me ASAP." Troy disconnected.

∼

"Who were you talking to?" Shayne set a plate on the dining room table in front of Troy.

"Rick," Troy answered, staring at his food. "You made this?"

"No. I had it delivered."

Troy's eye widened for a beat before he smiled.

"Didn't you think I could cook?" Shayne had been surprised when she'd unpacked the groceries and discovered more than the basics for meals. She'd half expected more MREs than real food. Instead, the bags were loaded with fresh fruits, vegetables, and baked goods. A well-stocked kitchen gave her options for meals and something else to think about other than what Troy had been discussing on the phone.

"I hadn't given it much thought," Troy admitted, taking a forkful of stir-fried chicken over rice. "This is good."

"Thanks," she said, and took a bite. It *was* pretty good. "Did you learn anything?"

"Not as much as I'd hoped," he answered, around a mouthful of food.

"Are you going to keep it a secret?"

"They're sending some backup tomorrow." He glanced over his shoulder at the living room. "It's going to get crowded in here."

"I guess it will." Her stomach did a flip. How was she supposed to act in front of his friends? She was comfortable with them when she was simply the hired help. Now she was a target and sleeping with a good friend. How would that affect their interaction with her?

"It will be good to have some help." Troy continued shoveling in food, oblivious to her concern.

"I've put a lot on your shoulders. I'm sorry."

"I'm glad I'm here." Troy placed his hand over hers.

She stared at the large, rough hand. What would happen between the two of them when her "situation" was resolved? Would he stick around? Should she? Would she be alone—again? *Don't borrow trouble.* Another lecture from her dad popped into her head. This time, instead of comfort, the words reminded her of his absence.

"Shayne?"

She looked up from their joined hands and was met with a harsh stare.

"What's going on?"

"Nothing."

"Bullshit. You were miles away. You're an easy read. Where did you go in that head of yours?"

Shayne wasn't ready for this conversation. She'd prefer not to have it at all.

"Wondering where we'll put him and if he'll bring more food." She gave him a quick grin. "I imagine they've already figured that out."

"Probably." The solemn look on Troy's face told her he hadn't bought her story.

"I heard you mention Russell while you were on the phone," she said, changing the subject. She was worrying about the future. It was a waste of energy and emotion.

"The team dug up some information on him. Lawrence Russell was an attorney. He'd been with a law firm in Tallahassee until he moved to Tampa. He partnered with an attorney there. The guys haven't had any luck in reaching his partner. I'm assuming Josie is working her contacts as well."

"That's it?" Shayne asked. "That's not much."

"It's progress. Slow, but still progress." Troy leaned back in his chair. "Russell feels like the key to me. The fact that his last partner is a former state's attorney could be a coincidence or something deeper. We're getting puzzle pieces one at a time, and we don't know what the picture is supposed to look like."

"I wish there was more that I could do," Shayne huffed. She rose and picked up their plates. She was surprised she'd eaten as much as she had. She needed to get her emotions in check. This was not the time to feel sorry for herself. She should be dancing on the table after having the best sex in her life.

Troy followed her into the kitchen. "You've done everything you can. We'll get there. Besides, the longer it takes, the more time I have with you."

"And after this is finished, you'll be gone?" Shayne

hadn't meant for that insecurity to find a voice. Damn. She was an adult. Not a pouting child.

"Is that what you think? Is that what was going on in your head over dinner?"

She wouldn't admit it. It would be insulting to both of them.

Troy slammed the skillet he'd been drying against the counter. "Thanks," he shouted, tucking his gun into the waistband of his jeans. "Thanks a hell of a lot for trusting me." He snatched the sat phone off the counter and stormed —there was no other word for it—out the rear door.

39

Distracted, Troy almost went flying when his ankle caught the wire strung across the last step. Fortunately, he managed to right himself before he hit the ground. What the hell was wrong with Shayne? He opened up his heart for the first time in his life, and she didn't trust him to keep his word. That would teach him. He'd head back to Sanibel when his backup arrived. He didn't need this shit.

Until then, he still had a job to do. A job. That was all she was and would be. He looked up the steps and saw the light go out in the kitchen. He couldn't help himself when he circled the house to wait to see if the bedroom light came on. It didn't. She was probably in the bathroom. Screw it. What did he care, so long as she didn't venture near a window? He'd be damned if she'd die on his watch. But as soon as his responsibility was over here, he was gone. Whether he stayed in Sanibel would depend on whether she did.

Fuck. Since when did he let a woman dictate how and where he lived his life?

He made his way up the drive toward the cottage, fighting his anger and forcing himself back into security mode. Anger and hurt had no place in a soldier's life. Not that he was a soldier anymore, but this job demanded the same skills.

His right hand began to throb. It had stung when he'd slammed the pan on the counter. He didn't know he had that much rage left in him. Now, he clutched the satellite phone in the same hand so tight that his joints hurt. He switched the phone to his left hand as he continued down the trail looking for any signs of unnatural visitors. He took his time. He was in no hurry to return.

When his inspection of that property was done, he made his way back to the bungalow. Using the flashlight feature on the phone, he shifted it from side to side, checking for footprints or anything out of the ordinary. The closer he got to their hideout, the harder it was to concentrate on his reconnaissance.

The look on Shayne's face when he'd lost his temper would be seared in his mind for a long time. He'd seen fear. He couldn't hold that against her. He'd been pissed. It was a wonder the handle remained attached to the skillet. He'd never lost his temper at a woman, but he hadn't been hurt by one until today. He hadn't allowed a woman to get close enough to cut out a piece of his heart. But before that flash of fear, he remembered the sadness of her pouting mouth and the moisture pooling in her eyes.

He glanced up at the bungalow. Shayne should have switched on a light by now. While night had not fallen, it wasn't far away. Was she huddled in the dark kitchen again, afraid she'd been abandoned?

Abandoned. Was that a result of her experience when she'd been trapped? He'd been out for days after the explosion. He had no memory of anything that had happened immediately following the detonation. Shayne, on the other hand, was knocked out for a short period of time. She'd come to, trapped and alone. PTSD affected everyone differently. Sudden, loud noises were one of her triggers. Was fear of abandonment another side effect of her ordeal?

He looked out over the swampy hammock. The sun cast a long shadow over the wilderness. A ray of light highlighted the trunk of a partially submerged fallen tree. Ferns, bright and green, had taken root in the decomposing material. A new purpose for the once mighty cypress. Life from death. Something vibrant springing from destruction. Trees would continue to fall and plants would continue to die, but nature rekindled itself if left alone. It didn't give up. This landscape had more guts than he did. Instead of fighting, he'd walked away in anger.

He had no idea what the future would bring, but like this landscape, didn't he and Shayne deserve a second chance?

When Troy stepped into the unit this time, he did not immediately sense Shayne's presence. His heart ramped up. He almost shouted her name but reconsidered. He'd scared her once this evening. Yelling was probably not a good idea.

He glanced in the galley kitchen as he rushed into the short hallway. She wasn't cowered next to the cabinets this time. That left two other possibilities. God help him if she wasn't in the bathroom or bedroom. It could only mean she'd left while he was patrolling the area. But where would she go? And how would she have slipped by him?

The bathroom door was open, signaling she wasn't in there, but he flicked on the light anyway. His breath caught. The vanity had been cleared of all her toiletries. He vaulted the few steps to the bedroom and came to a sudden stop when he spotted Shayne sitting in the corner chair, her knees pulled up to her chest with her head resting on them. She didn't acknowledge his entrance, but there was no way she could have missed his thundering footsteps.

As he approached her, he noted the cloth grocery bag sitting at the end of the bed. It stood upright. He knew it was filled with her things. Had he caught her before she tried to leave, or had she changed her mind?

He squatted in front of her. Unless she sprouted wings, she wasn't getting past him until they'd talked.

"I'm sorry," he started. "I lost my temper. What you said hurt me. Instead of figuring out why, I reacted—badly. I'm sorry."

He heard her sniff but didn't move or acknowledge him. "Do you want me to go?" he asked. He didn't want to leave but here he was, setting himself up for another stab wound. There was the slightest shake of her head, which he interpreted as a no.

"Do you want me to stay?" he asked. He had to be certain.

A nod. His shoulders relaxed a bit. Okay. Now what? They weren't going to get very far if she could only communicate with small gestures. They needed to talk.

He took a deep breath. "Look at me, honey. Please? Look at me."

Her head came up with hesitation. Her forehead was red where it had rested against her knees, but it was her eyes that ripped at his heart. Swollen, red and overflowing with tears. Still, she did as he asked and looked into his eye. Brave or stubborn, he wasn't sure. Both suited her. He used his thumbs to wipe the tears from her face. As he did, her eyes closed and more tears followed.

"Stop crying, honey. I'm sorry."

Shayne hiccupped. "No. *I'm* sorry." The words came out jerky, followed by another hiccup. She dropped her head back onto her knees.

Troy coaxed her chin up again. "We're both sorry. That's a good place to start." As he rose to his feet, he lifted her in his arms. He took her seat in the small armchair. It was a tight fit. He was instantly concerned she'd feel closed in, but she relaxed into his arms. He cuddled her close to him, inhaling her scent as she rested her head against his shoulder.

When her breathing and sniffles slowed, he reached for a tissue from the nightstand, tucking it into her hand. "You up to talking?" he asked.

She made no effort to pull away. He took that as a yes.

"I am sorry for my outburst and for frightening you. No one has ever cut me as deep as you did when you asked if I planned to leave you. I'm new to this intimacy thing. I seem to be doing everything wrong. Did I say or do something that made you think I wouldn't stay? Do you want me to go?"

He felt the deep breath she sucked in before letting it out slowly. "No." Her head brushed against his chest. "I don't want you to go anywhere unless you want to. This is all new to me too. This fear that I'll close my eyes and you'll suddenly be gone is just plain stupid. I know it, but it's there." She held on to him tighter. "And that's not fair to you."

"I'll decide what's fair for me." Troy rubbed his chin against the top of her head. "We'll figure this out together if you're willing to try."

∽

SHAYNE DIDN'T SPEAK—AFRAID if she did, it would break the spell Troy was weaving. It felt so right to be in his arms— safe, secure, and...loved. God, was she in love with him? Was that why she was so afraid of losing him? *Celebrate what you have.*

"I don't know what you see in me," she started. "I'm not a runway model, and I can be contrary and moody."

"We never did have that discussion regarding your self-esteem, did we? The same could be said about me. My face is grotesque—"

"No, it's not," Shayne said, pushing away so she could look at him. "Don't ever say that."

She hadn't expected to be greeted by a smiling face. Hell, he looked like he wanted to laugh. "What's so funny?" she asked.

"You," he answered, still grinning. "Your moods change faster than a drag racer. A second ago you were belittling yourself. Now you're lecturing me."

"I wasn't lecturing," she said.

"Yes, you were, but I can handle it. I'd appreciate it, though, if you applied the same standards to yourself." Troy's tone was lacking all humor.

Gnawing on her bottom lip, Shayne let his words sink in. He was right. Not only was she applying a different standard where she was concerned, but when did she begin to judge herself or others based on their appearance? She was taught better. She knew better. Man, her head was messed up.

"You're right. My emotions have been all over the place. I can't explain it."

"You've been under a lot of stress." He tucked her head under his chin.

"You make me feel like Cinderella at the ball." She nuzzled closer.

"I'm no Prince Charming."

"You're *my* Prince Charming." She lifted her head, raising her hand to stroke his face. "And I intend to break every clock in this place before they strike midnight."

She pulled his head toward hers until their lips met. His mouth was warm, his whiskers rough. Opening her mouth, she invited him in. The kiss deepened until her lips weren't the only part of her moist and ready for more.

He lifted her without breaking the kiss and lay her on the bed. She quickly began to shimmy out of her shorts while he trailed kisses down her neck. His lips moved south to her navel, then began to leave another trail of kisses up her torso as he slowly raised the hem of her shirt. When he stopped at her breasts, she almost screamed. She arched her back, begging him to take one in his mouth. She felt the puff of his breath as he chuckled at her surrender. She didn't care. Kicking away her shorts, she reached for the button of his jeans. He pulled back.

"What?" she asked, breathless from the foreplay.

"Didn't want to damage the family jewels." He chuckled.

He yanked his shirt over his head then did the same with her T-shirt. As he reached for the zipper of his jeans, she could barely keep from reaching down to stroke herself. God, this was taking way too long.

Finally, he was on top of her. He hesitated. "You okay like this?"

Hell yes, she was okay. "I'll be better in a minute." She raised her hips to meet his.

They made love fast and furious, and then a second time, slow and sweet. Her head rested on his shoulder. It rose and fell with his breathing, which was steady and deep. She ran her fingers over his chest. *Celebrate what you have.*

"Where do you keep going?" Troy asked.

"Huh?"

"Your mind wanders," he said. "Where does it go?"

"My dad."

"Your dad? You're thinking about your dad now?"

She felt his neck crick toward her. She could imagine his expression based on the incredulity of his question. She smiled. "He would approve."

"Of what? Sex?"

"Making love," she corrected him, softly swatting his chest. "And he'd probably say, 'It's about time.'" She resumed exploring the contours of his body. "He'd approve of you. He'd also agree with you."

"Is this going to be twenty questions?" His hand dusted her hip. "He'd agree with me about what?"

"My insecurities."

"The bombing..."

"I'm sure that has a lot to do with it. Like you, it wouldn't hurt for me to talk to someone. I never did, even though it was suggested. I dealt with it on my own, convinced I was handling it, but obviously not as well as I imagined."

"But you're insinuating something else played a part?" Troy asked, now stroking her backside.

"I thought I'd gotten over my dad's death, but he's been popping into my head a lot lately. It's like having Obi-Wan Kenobi or Yoda dropping into my subconscious with little bits of wisdom or a lecture."

"Why the lectures?"

Shayne sighed. "I kinda checked out after he died. His death was sudden. An aneurysm. There was no time to say goodbye. The two of us were best friends. I could talk to him about anything. He'd be disappointed in me for the things you mentioned and for settling."

"What do you mean by 'settling'?"

Troy had stopped caressing her backside. Instead, he'd pulled her close. She didn't feel alone.

"I finished college. Got my degree. It would have been insulting to him if I hadn't. But then I let it collect dust. Stayed at my job, tending bar. When my mom had to return to Ireland due to my grandmama's illness, I could have gone with her. I didn't. Instead, I kept a job where I was surrounded by strangers who came and went. I have no idea why this seems so clear to me now. I surrounded myself with people but not friends. I wasn't lonely but I was alone. There was no one left who could leave me." Shayne kneaded her forehead. "I should have my head examined. Who receives advice from the dead?"

Troy touched his lips to her hair. "Was he always there after you lost him, or did he suddenly reappear?"

"I heard his voice as I came to after the explosion. He was telling me to get my act together and stop panicking. I don't remember anything like that before."

"It was because you needed him. You were very lucky to have had a dad like that. Someone who loved you so much that he could come to your rescue even after he was gone."

She was lucky. Instead of missing her dad, she should rejoice in having had him in her life. "When this is all over, I need to go see my mom. It's been too long."

"You two get along?"

"We talk all the time. She's a special lady, but my dad's absence was more pronounced when just the two of us were together. She seemed to understand my feelings. She knew Dad and I had a special bond so she didn't push. Not many mothers would be so patient. It was selfish of me to think of my loss and not hers as well. I'm not very proud of myself."

"As you said, she understood," Troy told her, continuing to stroke her arm.

"Do you see your family often?"

Troy nestled her up against him and told her about his family. His three brothers—all military. His mom and dad who lived in Washington state. He admitted to avoiding his family after his injury. They talked in hushed whispers about growing up, and their dreams, and regrets. Shayne drifted off into a peaceful sleep—until all hell broke loose.

40

"Get out!"

Troy heard the shout seconds after the back door slammed against the inside wall. His pistol was already trained on the doorway when a man came barreling into the room.

"Get out unless you two want to wind up kindling," the man shouted.

Troy took a fleeting look at Shayne. She was awake with the sheet tucked up under her arms. She was staring wide-eyed at the man. Troy kept his Sig trained on the intruder. With his free hand, he reached for the clothes Shayne had left on the chair and tossed them to her. The man's eyes didn't stray from Troy.

"Who the hell are you?" Troy demanded.

"The name's Gardner and if you don't get your asses out of here, you're going to wind up barbecue. Dammit! Look out the fucking window!"

The flickering light should have caught Troy's attention before it had to be pointed out. He lifted a slat of the blind and saw flames lapping up the side of the building. As he stepped into his jeans, Gardner ran back out the door.

Troy looked at Shayne. She was already dressed and headed around the end of the bed. "Go. Head out the back," he shouted. "I'm right behind you." He grabbed his gun then almost tripped over Shayne as he flew down the hall. "What the hell are you doing? Move!"

"I knocked the phone off the counter. I can't find it."

The flames licked outside the living room windows but did nothing to cast light on the darkened floor. "Forget the phone," he shouted, lifting her off the floor. He heard the whoosh of air from her lungs as her diaphragm landed on his shoulder—but no complaints. They needed to hurry, and with his long legs, they'd make it out faster if he carried her.

The minute Troy opened the door, it felt like they were stepping into a furnace. The screening that surrounded the porch was curling and melting under the heat. He sent up a prayer for more time—more time than he'd had in Afghanistan. He kicked open the screen door and ran down the steps, this time remembering the tripwire at the bottom. He dropped her on to her feet on the other side of the step.

"Get behind the shed! Hurry." The small building might offer them some protection from what he feared was to come. His shove propelled her forward as the gas tank of the car exploded. His mind flashed back to the boy he'd failed to save when a loud blast sent him flying, and fiery bits of shrapnel rained down from the night sky.

SHAYNE HUDDLED BEHIND THE SHED, whimpering, her arms protecting her head. Would they find her this time? She waited for the pain, the sirens, and the smell of charred flesh. Nothing but the smell of burned wood. The rest was missing.

It was all missing. She wasn't at the country club. She wasn't trapped under a heavy bar. She looked up and saw a star-filled sky. Her wits returned but her panic increased. Troy. Where was Troy?

Looking back at the house, she saw him, face down on the ground, his large form reflected in the light of the burning building.

She shouted his name as she ran toward him. *Oh, God.* Why didn't he answer? Why didn't he move?

"Troy. Talk to me," she screamed. "Damn it, wake up." It took all her strength to roll the large man onto his back. She shook him by the shoulders as she continued to yell his name. It wasn't having any effect.

She surveyed the scene quickly. The vegetation was highlighted by the eerie orange light from the flames. It also made it clear they were out in the open and easy prey if their would-be killer decided to come back. Her eyes darted to the shadows and then back to Troy. She could see his chest rise and fall, but he wasn't regaining consciousness.

"Wake up. I can't carry you." They had to move. They were sitting ducks. She slipped one hand under his neck. Her palm was immediately covered with a warm, sticky substance. "Troy," she cried, pulling her bloody hand away. He needed help, but she had no way of getting it. The bungalow and car were in flames.

A second explosion had Shayne throwing herself over his face and chest. They were showered by bits of wood and other debris.

"Get out of the way."

Shayne's head snapped to the side. She recognized the silhouette of the man who had warned them of the fire.

"Move so I can get a look at him," he ordered her.

She hesitated as she hovered over Troy. She had to protect him.

"That was the propane tank," Gardner shouted over the roar of the fire. "That was the last of them. Now let me get a look at him."

Shayne quickly moved to the side to give him room. She was putting her trust in someone she'd seen for half a minute, but he'd warned them, and that warning had saved their lives. "The back of his head is bleeding."

Gardner slipped his hand beneath Troy's neck. "He got a pretty good whack," he agreed, checking Troy quickly. "Stay close." He lifted Troy into a fireman's carry. "We need to get you away from here."

Shayne followed the stranger without question. He had Troy, and she wouldn't be leaving him. They sloshed through knee-high water, heading deeper into the swamp. Gooey mud oozed into her sneakers. Ignoring the creatures that brushed against her legs, she focused fully on the man being carried on Gardner's back, watching for signs of distress or awakening. Troy's substantial weight didn't slow the agent's pace. Gardner would occasionally hesitate then change directions before picking up his pace again.

"Where are we going?" Shayne demanded.

"Someplace safe until I can get you some help."

"Someone is supposed to join us tomorrow."

"I'll let 'em know where to find you."

"You're that DEA agent." Shayne struggled to keep up with Gardner's grueling pace.

"So, it was one of your group who was doing a deep dive into my background."

The statement was made without malice, but Shayne wasn't going to admit that Don was probably the culprit. "You were the man who I saw leaving the ballroom."

"Where I left my partner to die."

"I'm sorry," she said. "I should have chased them out of there." Her stomach still tumbled when she wondered if she'd had time to warn them.

"Then you'd be dead too." Gardner didn't appear to be the least bit winded sloshing through the muck and carrying Troy.

"That's what Troy said." She'd been addressing Gardner's back the entire time. He wore a dark, long-sleeve T-shirt that pulled across his wide shoulders. A shoulder holster was half hidden by Troy's form. Like Troy, he wore snug jeans. She'd been right about his build, but she still didn't have the slightest idea of his facial features. Both instances she'd seen him at the cabin, his face had been backlit. Odd how a man who was playing such a pivotal role in her life would still be without a face.

"Smart man," Gardner declared.

"Is he hurt bad?" she asked. Her voice shook. She couldn't hide it.

"Some cuts on his back and a concussion. My guess is he'll live. He's been through worse."

Shayne let out a breath at the matter-of-fact diagnosis.

"How did you find us?" she asked. The trek through the boggish soil was taking all her energy, not to mention she was starting to feel chilled.

"Be glad I was here when that bastard tried to get rid of you." Gardner spat out the words like venom. "That's the second damn time I've let him slip through my fingers."

"Who is he? Why did he try to kill us?" She felt another chill, but it had nothing to do with the dampness.

"He didn't care any more about killing your boyfriend than he did when he killed my partner," the agent answered, skipping over her first question. "It was merely another twofer for him. You're a witness. The guy my partner was with in Tampa was his target. The asshole is cleaning up."

"The bartender, you mean."

"Not his true profession."

"I've figured that much out. What's his name? How'd he find me?"

"Still working on that one. He showed up on Sanibel a few weeks ago."

"How long had you waited for him?" Silence. Next question. "How did you find us out here?"

"Easy. I slipped a GPS tracking device into your boyfriend's duffel. I figured wherever you went, he'd be stuck to you like glue."

"And before that?"

"Are you always this chatty?" he asked.

"You said I'm a target. I think I have the right to ask some questions." She was getting pissed. A side effect of her rising blood pressure was that she was no longer cold. "Where are you taking us?"

"See that chickee hut?" he asked as the hammock's canopy gave way to grassy, water-covered landscape. Shayne leaned around Gardner's large form and spotted the raised wooden platform protected by a thick, thatched roof. "You'll be dry and out of reach of the natural predators until help arrives."

"And the unnatural predators?"

"There's only one you need to concern yourself with, and he took off in the opposite direction. I don't think you'll be seeing him as long as he thinks I'm on his tail."

"Why aren't you?" Shayne asked, curious and breathless.

It was getting harder and harder to drag her feet through the wet soil.

"Because someone was screaming at the top of her lungs." Gardner deposited Troy on the platform.

"Sorry I ruined your plans," Shayne said as Gardner plucked her out of the marsh. The muck finally claimed her sneakers with a loud sucking sound.

The agent remained in the knee-deep water. She stared at his face in the shadows of the moonlight. His jaw was square and he had a jutting chin. His eyes were set deep, but the color was a mystery due to the lack of substantial light. He no longer had a business cut. Instead, his wavy hair was long enough to tuck behind his ears.

"You'll be safe here until help arrives. I'll call your friends. Tell them where to find you."

"How do you know who to call?"

"Lady, there ain't much I don't know about you and your friends. I knew that bastard would realize you were a problem and eventually catch up to you. All I had to do was get to you and wait. If I don't apprehend him tonight, I'll be seeing you again soon. Wherever you are, he won't be far behind."

"Wonderful." Did her voice drip with sarcasm? She didn't care. "He must have been the one who attacked me on Sanibel."

"That was him."

"You were there? You knew he was going to show up there and didn't warn me? What am I to you? Bait?"

Ignoring her, he rolled Troy over far enough to retrieve the pistol from his waistband. "Keep this handy until help arrives," he said, handing the SIG Sauer to her.

"Maybe I should use it on you," she threatened, crawling over the wooden planks to Troy's lifeless form.

"You weren't supposed to get hurt. That wasn't my plan," Gardner responded.

"Is that supposed to be an apology? Bait is bait, regardless of your plan," she snarled but when she looked up, she was talking to air. The agent was gone. At least now, the man in her nightmare had a face.

41

I t took a second—one long, horrifying second—before Troy pushed aside the sounds and smells of Landstuhl Med Center in Germany. There was no soft bed beneath him or beeping machines ringing in his ears. His arms were free of needles, and a blood pressure cup wasn't manacled around his bicep. Instinctively, he reached up to cradle his throbbing head. A hand stopped him.

"Hey there." A soft voice filled with comfort. She stroked his forehead and held the hand he'd raised.

Shayne. Thank God. "Are you okay?" he asked, gripping her hand as he carefully turned his head so he could see her.

"Better than you, I'd say. You've been out for a long time." She caressed his forehead again.

The morning sun framed her face. Her wrinkled brow transmitted her concern. He pulled her hand to his lips and kissed the back of it. "I'm okay. Just a headache."

"You may need stitches. It's a nasty cut. Your shirt is toast. I used it to stop the bleeding."

Troy felt the wadded-up fabric beneath his head. "Where are we?" he asked, carefully rocking his head from side to side, doing his best to get a visual on the landscape.

"I'd say about a mile from the bungalow. Seemed like it took forever to get here."

Troy attempted to sit up but groaned when his head objected. "How did you do it?" He rested his head back on the bundled-up shirt and found himself staring at a thatched roof. He recognized the building style. He'd seen plenty of similar primitive huts in other parts of the world.

"Our savior returned, thank God. He'd gone after the man who set the fire but heard me screaming when you were knocked out. Gardner carried you out here."

"Gardner. Where is he?"

"He took off as soon as he dumped us here. He was hoping he could get back on the trail of the bomber. He sounded doubtful of a positive outcome." Shayne moved so she could block the sun from Troy's face. "You were right. He's been hunting him since his partner was killed."

Troy's second attempt at sitting up was a partial success. He managed to rise on one elbow, ignoring the discomfort in his head. "We need to move." He slowly scanned the area. "We can't stay here. We're too visible." The solitary open platform was easily spotted.

"We're not going anywhere," she replied, helping him into a sitting position. "You're in no condition to carry me, and I'm not going anywhere in this swamp without shoes."

Troy glanced at her bare feet. "What happened to your shoes?"

"The swamp monster claimed them."

He was still having trouble thinking clearly. "Monster?"

"Never mind my shoes. Help should be coming soon. Gardner was going to contact one of your friends and let him know where to find us."

"How the hell does he know who to call?" Troy asked, rubbing the back of his head. His hand came away crusted with dried blood.

"I asked the same thing. He seems to know a lot about us."

Troy perused the area around them again, the throbbing in his head waning a bit. "I still don't like waiting here."

"I don't see where we have any choice. Why don't you lie back and give that head a rest?"

He had no intention of closing his eyes again. Not until help arrived. "How do you know he called for help?" Troy asked. He spotted his gun in Shayne's lap. He reached out. She looked happy to be rid of it.

"Regardless of the fact that he's an ass, I'm sure Gardner is one of the good guys."

"If you believe he's one of the good guys, why is he an ass?" Troy adjusted his back so he was sitting as comfortably as he could against one of the four rough-hewn poles that supported the platform. The position gave him a good view of the area. The landscape to his back was a wide expanse of the river of grass. Anyone approaching from that direction would be easily spotted by Shayne. No one was going to sneak up on him from behind.

"Because he's been using me as bait. He's been watching me, waiting for the bomber to come after me."

"Wait a minute. Start at the beginning. My head is still clearing."

Shayne related the cryptic conversation she'd had with the DEA agent. When she was finished, Troy was torn between being grateful to Gardner for having seen to Shayne's safety instead of chasing after his prey. At the same time, he was furious that she'd never been warned about her status as a target.

"Did he give you any idea how the bomber located you?"

"I asked. I didn't get an answer, but he was certain the guy would eventually come for me. He's been sitting on his ass on Sanibel waiting for the bastard to show up. Gardner did admit to tracing us here after putting a GPS tracker in your bag, which I don't understand. Why the hell would he assume tracking you would lead him to me?"

Shayne's brow was furrowed and the corner of her lip curled. Troy, however, wasn't surprised at Gardner's assumption. If he was a good investigator, he'd have read the signals Troy was sending off regarding Shayne.

"Did our rescuer give you any idea why the guy waited so long to get to you? The bombing happened months ago." It remained a puzzle for Troy. Why wait so long to take out a witness?

"Gardner wasn't very forthcoming. He ignored half of my questions. Claimed I talked too much."

In spite of his headache, her obvious indignation at Gardner's comment made Troy smile.

"Colt's friend is going to be pissed his bungalow is gone. Hopefully, it's insured. Then there's the car."

"Stop worrying," Troy told her. "We were lucky. We got out, and if this was dry season, half the Everglades would be up in flames, and us with it. Look on the bright side."

"Since when did you become a Pollyanna?"

Troy cocked his head. "I'm not sure. You might have something to do with it."

Shayne gave him a knowing smile as she reclined against the pillar opposite from Troy. "I guess we wait and see."

"Rick said they'd have someone here. If Gardner is a man of his word, we won't have to wait long."

The buzz of mosquitoes and a light breeze that whistled through the grasses were the only sounds they heard. Shayne moved periodically to check the back of Troy's head. He let her fuss over him. It made her feel better, and the fact that she cared made him feel better as well. He wasn't overly concerned about the cut to his head. The bleeding had stopped and his headache was receding.

While they waited, Troy chewed on the question as to why Shayne had suddenly become a target. Sure, she could identify the man at the bar, but until recently, no one had known that the guy Shayne had seen that night and the man who'd been hired to tend that bar weren't the same. The ruse the bomber had set up had worked well with the authorities. But something brought Gardner's attention to Shayne as a target. He'd been watching her, possibly since she'd arrived on Sanibel. What did Gardner know, and why hadn't he shared it with his counterparts?

Then again, he might have but hadn't been taken seriously. Troy swatted a mosquito away from his face. The second option didn't seem feasible. One trained man might have gone unnoticed, but the team was too sharp and knew the island and residents too well. So why had Gardner followed Shayne to Sanibel? Why was he so sure she'd be the bait the bomber would take?

"You okay?" Shayne asked. "Something is bothering you."

"I'm trying to work out a puzzle."

"What puzzle?" Shayne scooted across the platform and settled in next to him. He rested his hand on her thigh and gave it a gentle squeeze.

"Did Gardner tell you if he'd been watching you in

Tampa? Before you arrived on Sanibel?" Troy pulled her hand into his.

"No." She looked out over the grasses. "I got the impression he'd been waiting on Sanibel for quite some time before that guy showed up. That would mean he had no idea how to find him, wouldn't it? I guess I was a crapshoot that paid off for him."

"Not entirely. As far as we know, he still hasn't got the guy."

"He seemed a bit perturbed that he'd been foiled again," Shayne added, her nose crinkling.

"If the asshole had let somebody in on his plan, things might not have gone south on him." Still, Troy understood why a man would go on a crusade to avenge the murder of a soldier in arms, especially if he felt his actions wouldn't be condoned.

"Gardner may have given us a clue," Troy said.

"How so?" Shayne asked, pulling her attention away from the expanse of grass to look at Troy.

"See if this makes sense to you. The authorities only recently began to look at the man you believed was the bartender as a possible suspect... And that was only after we told them what we'd discovered. The killer, apparently, did a very good job of covering his tracks. He continued to play the part of a witness as long as he could, so there had been no reason to suspect him."

"I'm with you so far," Shayne said.

"Gardner was removed from the case but was still with the DEA. We don't know how long it took him before he decided on a leave of absence. I'm assuming he didn't walk out the door the day after the bombing. If it were me, I'd have pushed for answers whether I was on the case or not."

He waited until Shayne's attention returned from her

periodic assessment of the landscape. Soldier or not, she was on guard.

"We know the initial focus of the bombing investigation was on the Congressman." Troy adjusted his position. The hardwood planks weren't the most comfortable to sit on but he'd been on worse. "Since the FBI hasn't been very talkative, I can only guess at this point. If Gardner suspected the investigation had taken a wrong turn, he may have decided it was time to go his own way."

"But the DEA would have been working the case." Shayne's eyes narrowed. "Wouldn't their focus have been on finding out who killed their agent?"

"They were working a case. I'm sure that upped the ante in solving it, but we have no idea where they were ordered to direct their resources. We also don't know at what point the different agencies got on the same page. Or if they ever did, for that matter. You have the ATF, FBI, DEA, and God knows who else all working together but following their own theories. I'm betting Gardner was working the case on his own time. At some point he came to the conclusion that one of those who walked away alive that night was behind it."

"Me and the bartender."

"Exactly. Since you weren't on Gardner's radar until after you arrived on Sanibel, I'm betting he worked the bartender angle until he ran into a dead end."

"Leaving me." Shayne stretched her legs out parallel to Troy and leaned back on her arms. "How did he know I wasn't the bomber?"

"We'll have to ask him. He may have had you pegged as the killer until you became a target."

"No. He made it clear to me the reason I was on his radar

was simply because I was bait to draw out the guy he wanted."

"For which he will pay," Troy muttered.

"Since he saved us both, I'll give him a pass," Shayne said, swatting at another mosquito. "I'm still not sure where you're going with this."

"He couldn't locate the bartender, which either made the man a victim or a suspect. That left you. It would have been easy for Gardner to locate you, since the feds had your location in their database."

"None of this explains how my stalker found me. Gardner was perplexed by that."

"You weren't exactly hiding out."

"No, but I didn't leave much of a footprint when I left Tampa. No one but my mom knew my actual address."

"Did you file taxes this year?" Troy asked.

"Yes, but before I left Tampa," she told him. "Copperhead had my new work address, but human resources assured me that my information was flagged. No one was to release that information to anyone. Trust me, I asked."

"Hell." Shayne threw her hands in the air. "Cat paid me in cash, so I didn't have to open a bank account. Utilities are included in my rent. My driver's license still has my Tampa address on it—not that I need it. I disappeared from social media altogether. Closed all my accounts. I could go on, but you get the picture. I'm nonexistent. I don't know how anyone could have found me."

"Yet somebody did. What about your phone?"

"I can only assume it was clean. The FBI arranged for it after mine was destroyed. It's prepaid in cash."

While she wouldn't be impossible to find, she'd made it damn difficult. "Yet Gardner gambled that he'd come after

you." Troy held out his hand, a silent request Shayne understood. She took it.

Troy heard the airboat before Shayne reacted to the
sound. He still swore his hearing had improved since the
loss of his eye. The swift watercraft darted out from behind
the hammock where the bungalow had been located. The
two of them got to their feet as the boat came into view.
Troy's gun rested against his thigh. It quickly became obvious, though, that he wouldn't need it. He recognized one of
the three men in the boat. Gib's ponytail whipped in the
wind created by the speed of the airboat. He wasn't the
backup Troy had had in mind when he and Rick had
discussed sending someone. Troy would trust Gib with his
life, but his skills didn't come close to measuring up to the
team's.

"I don't know who is driving that thing," Shayne said,
"but the guy sitting next to Gib is Gardner."

Was he now? Troy's hands fisted. He was looking
forward to meeting the mysterious DEA agent who used
women as bait.

The flat metal boat with its huge fan accelerated toward
them at a good clip. It was smaller than the airboats that
gave tourists a taste of the Everglades wilderness. This one
would hold six people max, in Troy's estimation. The logo
on the front lip of the boat wasn't familiar to him, but he
suspected it belonged to the local Miccosukee tribal police.

As the boat pulled up to the chickee hut and the engine
was cut, Gib hopped onto the wooden platform in his usual,
relaxed manner. Troy felt the muscles in his shoulders
loosen. Gib showed no signs of stress. He was comfortable
with the company he was in. The team had learned to trust
his instincts. Gib reached for Troy's hand and pulled him

into a shoulder hug. Just as quickly, he dismissed Troy and wrapped his arms around Shayne.

With Shayne preoccupied with Gib, Troy reached out a hand to the man who'd had Shayne under surveillance to help him onto the platform. As soon as Gardner had both feet firmly planted on the wooden deck, Troy pulled back and slugged the asshole.

42

"Troy, what the hell did you do that for?" Shayne asked. "He helped us." She noticed Gib's face light up. The cocky grin didn't make a damn bit of sense but dealing with Troy and Gardner was all she could handle at the moment.

"He set you up. He had it coming," Troy said.

"Stop it," Shayne snapped. Fortunately, Troy's clenched fists had dropped to his side. At some point, he'd returned his gun to the waistband of his jeans. Thank God for that, because the officer in the boat was resting his hand on his hip near his holster.

Troy took a step back from the target of his anger, who was vigorously rubbing his jaw. That small retreat must have been enough for the officer. He grabbed a rope from the floor of the boat and tossed it to Gib, who quickly tied off. The officer joined the rest of them on the platform, first-aid kit in hand.

"Let's get out of here." Troy brushed by the officer.

"Now you're being rude," Shayne said. "Damn it. Stand still, and let the man look at your back and head."

Troy glared at her over his bare shoulder but halted his stride. "Fine, if it makes you happy."

What the hell had gotten into him? She looked at Gib, who was still grinning, then at Gardner, who was studying them both.

"So we meet again," Shayne said to the agent. "I assume your prey escaped." Gardner's light blue eyes honed in on her. She was surprised he didn't appear angry at losing the target he'd been tracking for months.

"Chances were slim I could pick up his trail, but I had to try."

"We've got a BOLO out for the man fitting his description," the officer added, looking at Gardner. "There's a lot of land to get lost in out here, and there are only so many of us."

"He had a plan. He's gone," Gardner spat. "He's been one step ahead of me for the last six months."

"Maybe if you weren't such a renegade..." Troy said between clenched teeth as the officer pressed a dampened gauze pad to his back.

"And if you'd been on guard instead of being *busy*, I wouldn't have had to stop to warn you to get out of the house."

"Knock it off," Shayne said in concert with the officer. She didn't know the man, but they shared a mutual grin. "I'm Shayne Peterson. Thank you for your help."

"Nick Cypress," the officer said. "And this one-eyed tiger would be Mr. McKenzie, I assume."

Shayne raised her eyebrows at Cypress's frankness. She appeared to be the only one surprised. Troy was too busy hissing as Cypress directed his attention to another cut. Gib still hadn't lost his grin. Gardner kept looking back at the boat, apparently anxious to leave.

"Can we play doctor while we move?" he grumbled, confirming Shayne's assessment.

The tribal officer picked up the miscellaneous items he used to clean Troy's wounds and stuffed them in a Ziploc bag along with his latex gloves. "I've done what I can do here," he said, pulling a plastic pack out of his kit. He gave it a squeeze, then a shake. "Put this cold pack on the back of your head."

Cypress lithely jumped back into the boat then helped Shayne into the swaying craft. As soon as she was settled into a seat, Troy and Gardner followed. Gib waited. He tossed the line to Cypress before he joined them. Once the engine was engaged, the roar emanating from the large fan-like propeller made it impossible to converse. Cypress had a headset to cover his ears, which Shayne envied. Gib had also slipped on a pair. Both had mics attached to them and the two appeared to be talking. Shayne placed her hands over her ears, which had minimal effect.

Troy had obediently kept the ice pack pressed to his scalp. The noise had to be doing a number on his headache, but Shayne couldn't do anything for him. His firm jaw and frequent scanning of the area told her he was back on guard. When she glanced at Gardner, his expression was almost identical. She could easily see them both as predators. That should have frightened her, but instead she felt secure.

Their pilot knew his way around the waters. Shayne admired his ability to navigate the boat through the thick hammock once they reached it. As they got closer to the bungalow, Cypress cut the engine and pulled out a long pole. He used it to propel the boat toward its final destination.

When they reached the dry bed of land, Gib was the first to jump off the boat. He held the line until all but Cypress had disembarked. For the first time since they met, the officer used his radio to check in. "There's been no sign of your arsonist," he told the group standing in front of the charred remains of the bungalow. "I'm heading back to file a report. I expect you to keep us advised."

Gib nodded as he tossed the rope back into the shallow boat. Shayne forced herself to look at the burned debris. The fire had been doused. No smoke or embers remained, yet her skin prickled and her legs wobbled at the sight. She sucked in a breath through her mouth, trying not to inhale the familiar smell of charred wood. Both she and Troy had escaped death a second time. She dug her lower teeth into her upper lip, hoping to stop it from trembling. If Gardner hadn't chased them out, they would have been part of the scattered remains. Trusting her legs would hold her, she took a few steps and stood in front of the agent. His features were handsome, but his face was weary.

"Thank you." Rising on her toes, Shayne placed a kiss on his cheek. "We would have died if you hadn't warned us."

"I never intended for any harm to come to you." He looked past Shayne at Troy. "To either of you. I'd been watching the building, certain he'd show up. The man is as sly as a fox. I saw the flames before I spotted him." Gardner faced Troy. "You owe me more than a fist to the jaw for the danger I put you in. I wanted vengeance. I still do, but until I saw you both on the ground and heard the panic in her voice, I hadn't realized I'd lost something important in the process of avenging my friend and partner."

Troy stood in silence, staring back at Gardner. Shayne watched Troy closely, waiting to see if he would take another swing. Instead, his shoulders and jaw relaxed.

"I don't know if I can forgive you for putting Shayne in

danger, but I've lost people close to me. I know what it's like."

Surprised at Troy's concession, she stood open-mouthed as he took her arm. He ushered her past the remnants of the charred house and toward the large pickup truck parked several yards behind the pile of debris.

~

DUE TO THE height of the truck, Troy hefted Shayne into the rear seat before he followed. Gib got behind the wheel, and Gardner slid into the passenger side.

"You've studied him. What's his next move?" Troy asked Gardner as they made their way over the rough lane leading to US 41.

"He's got one objective. He'll be looking for her again."

"Why is she so damned important? He could disappear. Why take these risks? And how the hell is he finding her?" Troy asked. A pit opened up in the bottom of his stomach. Shayne wasn't safe, and his lack of attention last night had almost gotten them both killed.

"There has to be a leak," Gardner answered.

"Her location was never thoroughly buried," Troy reminded him.

"No, but she didn't make herself easy to find, either. I knew where she was, but I wanted to know how easy it would be for someone outside the system to locate her. I tried all the traditional means and came up dry." Gardner twisted in his seat so he could face Shayne. "I managed to locate your mother and called her."

"You what?" Shayne's eyes widened.

"It's all right. I explained to her that I was an old flame

and wanted to send flowers. I suggested you might need a lift in spirits. She said she didn't know your new address."

Shayne relaxed against the seat. "That was a stupid idea." A small smile appeared on her face. Troy was glad to see it.

"Why was it stupid?" Gardner asked, his brow wrinkled.

"Men." Shayne shook her head.

"What the hell is that supposed to mean?" Gardner asked. "I thought you'd appreciate the fact that I didn't frighten her."

"I do," Shayne agreed, "but no mother is going to give an ex-boyfriend her daughter's address. Think about it. You could be a stalker for all she knew," Shayne huffed. "Actually, you *were* a stalker."

Gardner was now the one wearing a scowl. Gib had remained unnaturally quiet but a glance in his direction told Troy he was enjoying the sparring. His gray eyes sparked with mischief.

"As much as I hate to admit it," Gardner continued, "I don't know how this guy is tracking Shayne. According to Gib here, your friends haven't had any better luck."

"Probably because it's an inside job. One of your agencies is leaking the information," Troy said.

"None of the agencies working this case knew she was out here in the swamp."

"You did," Troy pointed out.

"Only because I tagged your gear," Gardner shot back. "And I didn't tell anyone."

"Why were you so sure Troy would be with me?" Shayne asked, looking at one man then the other.

"It makes no sense that the leak would come from someone in the government," Gardner said, ignoring

Shayne's question. "The guy wouldn't have waited six months to come after her."

At least Gardner didn't out Troy as a lovesick pup. He'd obviously witnessed him mooning over Shayne while he had her under surveillance.

"This guy made the connection pretty quick to *this* relocation," Gib said. "Could you both have tracked her the same way?"

"No way of knowing for sure now," Gardner answered. "But I'd think it's unlikely. Unless someone advertised it, there wasn't a large window of time between the decision to move and moving her. I was lucky to get in and out of your place without discovery."

"We're going to discuss that later," Gib said, in one of his rare serious tones.

"Bottom line is that she's not safe," Gardner replied. "We need to catch this guy."

"If you intend to use Shayne to lure him in, think again. You're done baiting that hook." Troy felt every muscle in his body tighten. Shayne squirmed against his hold.

"Listening doesn't hurt," Shayne said, pulling away from Troy. "We can always say no. And personally, I'd like this nightmare to be over."

"This was never about the congressman, was it?" Troy asked.

"I never believed that it was, but the fact that he was there that evening had the others chasing leads in that direction."

"Then it was drugs?" Troy asked. "I need to be up to speed. Why was your partner at the country club? Why was he with Russell?"

"Russell. Now *that* was a fucking mistake," Gardner said.

"How do you mean? Why was a civilian involved with the DEA?"

"Copperhead," Gardner spat out. "The word came up a couple of times during the investigation. Just the word. It could have meant anything. The name of the operation. A code name for someone. The friggin' snake. Anything. The agency was working different angles, but we couldn't let the fact that there was a place in the county with the same name, no matter how unlikely it was.

"Russell had done some legal work for the Florida Department of Law Enforcement. He had a connection to the Copperhead Country Club through his dad. Some jackass somewhere knew that and had the harebrained idea that we could turn him into an undercover agent. The man was a goddamn lawyer. Not a spy. Whoever approved that plan ought to be shot, yet the idiotic scheme got the go-ahead.

"To top off this *clusterfuck*, Mark and I were assigned as his handlers, even though we were already working the docks."

"Why did Russell go along with it?" Troy asked.

"He never said, and we didn't ask. Mark and I never expected the lead to pan out. We met him once before that night. A few phone calls in between to check in. He seemed like a nice guy who wanted to help."

"Somebody didn't do their homework." Troy and the team had been in situations where intel was bad. He ran his hand through his hair. This was one of those times where the bad intel cost the lives of two men.

"I should have spent more time with Russell," Gardner said. "Gotten him pulled. He had no business being involved. He was anxious and he was green. A bad combination."

"Once the plan was approved, you had no say. Am I right?"

"Still..."

"Don't go there. Trust me, it doesn't do any good and it doesn't bring back the dead."

Troy locked eyes with Gardner. He hadn't just *said* the words to the man in the front seat, but had finally accepted the meaning of the words himself. He would never bring back the dead but he was alive, and he would do his damnedest to keep those he loved among the living. "So, Russell contacted you for a meet?"

"Yes. He texted me. We set up a phone call. He believed he was onto something but he was also smart enough to know he wasn't the expert. He wanted us to meet him at the country club. We decided on the gala because it wouldn't be unusual for nonresidents to be present. We were to blend in with the rest of the event supporters."

"He didn't give you any details when he called? Anything on what he might have found out?" Troy asked.

Gardner tilted his head back against the headrest. His exasperation was apparent. "I asked, but he wouldn't say. He seemed uneasy—unsure. He hadn't bothered us with stupid, silly shit before, so we agreed to meet. His hesitancy made me wonder if he might change his mind. I half expected a call from him to cancel."

"Obviously, you never got that call," Shayne concluded.

"No. So Mark and I transformed ourselves from dock-workers to businessmen and headed to the Copperhead gala. We made small talk with attendees, including Russell. We planned to talk with him privately after the event was over and everyone had left."

Gardner's face paled as he related the events closer to the moment of his partner's death. Shayne reached around the seat and gripped his right shoulder. They'd both been affected by that night. Their lives altered by the act of one man. They were connected.

Gardner's expression softened as he raised his hand across his chest and clasped Shayne's. He held on. Troy knew why. For the same reason Troy gripped her other hand. She anchored them both.

"Why did you leave the banquet room?" Troy didn't relish it, but the question had to be asked.

Gardner released Shayne's hand and looked out the window. He was gathering himself. The action had left him alive, but he'd lost a partner and friend. "I got a text from one of my snitches," he answered. "I left the room to make the call."

"Was it legit? Not a ploy to pull you away?" Troy asked.

"The bastard would be dead if he'd had any part in Mark's killing," Gardner said. "No. He had information. I passed it on to another agent. I had another target by the time the dust cleared.

"What the hell is that is asshole's problem?" Gib muttered, looking in the rearview mirror.

Troy turned in unison with Gardner and Shayne to look out the rear window. Some jerk was riding their ass.

"How long has he been there?" Troy asked.

"A few miles—with plenty of opportunities to pass," Gib answered. "I'm pulling over. Hang on."

Troy and Gardner both moved their hands to the butts of their guns, their eyes glued to the SUV. Troy released his grip on Shayne's hand and placed it on the back of her head. "Get down."

Their truck swerved to the right. Gravel and dust flew up behind them, blinding their view of the vehicle. Seconds later, the SUV flew past them and disappeared into the distance. They waited.

"Are we okay?" Shayne asked, raising her head.

"I think so," Troy told her. "Just another idiot getting his jollies by intimidating drivers." Troy patted the seat in front of him. "Give it a few minutes then take off."

"He didn't even tap his brakes," Gardner commented. "If he was after us, that quick move should have had him hesitating."

Gib glanced at Troy in the rearview mirror. Troy nodded in agreement to the assumption.

"You're planning to use Shayne as bait again, aren't you?" Troy asked Gardner once they were back on the road.

"Ultimately, it's Shayne's decision. Not yours, Troy," Gib said.

Troy heard the words but an invisible force fought to push them away. He was a soldier. A protector. Memories of the Afghani marketplace and the haunting look on the boy's face—a boy he'd failed to protect—slammed into him. He couldn't fail. Not again. Not with Shayne.

"Troy?"

The distant marketplace disappeared at the soft sound of her voice. His eye dropped to the small hand that clutched his. It was small, but tough and strong.

"Do you trust your friends? Do you trust me?" she asked.

His gaze traveled from their joined hands and met her eyes. Eyes that were round, brown, and, again, sparkling with gold dust.

"I trust you," she said. "Let's get this done and behind us."

He reached over and pulled Shayne into a deep, binding kiss. It melted the ice in his veins and warmed his heart. He'd been drawn to Sanibel and his friends. He'd found the help he needed and something more. Something he never knew was missing.

There was a cough, but it was Shayne pushing against him that broke the spell. Her flush as she pulled away brought a smile to his face at a time when nothing should make him happy. He stole one quick kiss then turned his attention toward the front seat.

"Do we have a plan?" Troy said.

"An outline," Gardener replied. "They should have the details ironed out by the time we get back. A lot of it depends on the answer to one question."

"What question?" Troy's eye narrowed at the agent.

Gardner twisted in his seat to look directly at Shayne. "Can you swim?"

43

Could she swim? Shayne hesitated. What the hell were they cooking up? Her heel tapped against the floor of the vehicle. When she answered in the affirmative, Gardner grinned—widely. The first true smile she could remember seeing on him. He picked up his phone and relayed the information to someone. Someone on Sanibel, she assumed. When pushed by Troy, Gardner pushed back. "Let them tie up the loose ends," Gardner told him. He had taken on the air of being one of them—one of the team. The lack of argument from the others in the vehicle appeared to cement Shayne's assumption.

An hour or so later, they approached the Sanibel Causeway. Shayne straightened in her seat when Gib pulled off the road before they reached the toll bridge. He turned into a marina just east of the island. The unannounced change in destinations had Shayne's heart skipping a beat. She reached for the edge of her seat only to have Troy take her hand. Shayne remembered to breathe. Shayne spotted Rick when Gib turned into the last row of parking spaces filled with trucks and empty boat trailers. She relaxed her death grip on Troy's hand. This torturous journey was coming to an end. A parking space remained open due to the orange traffic cone that had been placed in front of it. Rick moved the cone to let Gib pull into the space.

"Why are we here?" Shayne's eyes skittered around the sea of trucks and boats as Rick opened the rear door and lifted her out of the back seat. Troy jumped out behind her. "Where is everybody?"

They followed Rick halfway down the dock to a large cabin cruiser before he spoke. "Get in. Hurry," Rick said, his eyes gazing around the area.

Troy hopped onto the boat and helped Shayne get onboard, then quickly herded her into the cabin at the bow of the craft. Gardner followed the two below deck.

Shayne's eyes took a second to adjust to the lack of sunlight. The main cabin was spacious but felt much smaller with more than half a dozen large males circling her.

There was one new face in the group. The minute Troy saw him, his eyes lit up. "Adam. Thank God you're here." The men embraced in a barrel hug. The Sanibel crowd all smiled at the reunion. The smiles were genuine. Troy was one of them. He'd never stopped being one of the team, whether he had realized that or not.

"You haven't met Adam," Steve said, steadying Shayne as the boat lurched from its mooring.

Troy reached out, inviting her forward. He was still grinning, and it warmed her heart.

With Troy's arm anchored around her shoulder, he introduced the attractive man with black hair and coal-black eyes. Adam Lightfoot was the team's explosives expert. Her stomach dipped at that bit of information, but if anyone needed an expert in the field, it was them.

"Where are we headed?" Troy asked Colt.

Colt indicated the bench seats on each side of the hull. "We've got some things to go over and not a lot of time. It will be dark soon."

"You must be Gardner?" Colt turned to face the man who lagged behind.

"Garrett Gardner," the agent replied, offering his hand. Colt took it and introduced himself.

"Might have been nice to know you were lurking around the sidelines," Steve said. Shayne noted a bit of tension in his voice. Still, Steve offered his hand to the stranger.

"Hindsight is twenty-twenty. At the time, it seemed the right decision to remain in the background. I didn't know anything about your team, initially," Gardner explained. He introduced himself to the others then opted to stand, bracing his shoulder against the bulkhead.

The lateness of the day and the drawn curtains made the interior almost dark, yet none of the men had made a move to turn on a light. There was a small lamp above Shayne. She almost reached for the switch but stopped herself. She was surrounded by professionals. If they wanted to sit in the dark, there was a reason for it.

The boat was cruising at a steady speed. It wasn't blasting across the water, but they weren't trolling, either. Rick and Gib remained above deck.

"Where are we going?" Shayne asked.

"We'll be dropping anchor off the coast of Sanibel," Steve announced. He sat on the bench seat next to her and Troy.

"What do you guys have in mind?" Troy asked.

"We're working on the assumption that this guy is tracking Shayne somehow." Colt was the tallest man on the boat. He, like Gardner, had opted to remain standing. It made for a tight fit with Colt's head inches from the overhead compartment.

Shayne raised her hands in frustration. "I can't imagine how he could be tracking me now. I lost everything I owned in the bungalow."

"Except for the clothes on your back." Troy touched the pendant she wore around her neck. "When did you get that?"

"A few weeks ago," she answered. Out of the corner of her eye, she saw Adam moving toward a duffel bag in the corner of the galley.

"Did you buy it?" Troy examined the trinket.

"Hell no. Not on my budget." The martini-shaped piece was beautiful, and she suspected it hadn't been cheap.

"Where did you get it?"

"It was a gift from some of my customers at Copperhead," Shayne explained.

Adam stood in front of her, a small gadget in his hand. He waved it over Troy's palm where the pendant now rested. "That's it."

"*What's* it?" Shayne's stomach rolled. She looked to Troy for an answer.

"You're wearing the tracking device," Steve explained.

"Son of a bitch," Troy cursed. "How'd you get it? *Who* sent it to you?"

"It was sent by Copperhead's HR department."

"But who specifically?" Troy asked.

"I don't know." Shayne couldn't get the martini-shaped pendant off her neck fast enough. She dropped the chain and pendant into Adam's extended hand as if it were a snake.

"It was addressed to me in care of the garden center," she

explained. "Copperhead was the only one besides the authorities that had my new work address. They weren't supposed to give it out, so I assumed that was the reason they'd sent the pendant instead of one of the members. The message from the HR director said it was left on the receptionist's desk with a note asking if it could be sent to me. A farewell gift. I should have wondered about the large lapse in time since I left. I didn't."

"That means there could still be a link to Copperhead." Gardner pulled his phone from his back pocket. "We need to find out more about that handoff."

"Do not share this information," Troy warned Gardner. "If anyone gets wind of the fact that we've figured out how they were tracking her, we could lose Shayne's shadow."

"If you're insinuating that my team would leak info—"

"I'm not insinuating anything. Think," Troy said. "The minute Copperhead is contacted it could send up a red flag to the party behind this. We deal with this issue first then you can contact your people."

"Could they be one and the same? Could the bomber be the drug kingpin?" Shayne asked. "You might be wiping both out if you catch this guy."

"Unlikely," Gardner said. "Our bomber wouldn't have the time to run around the countryside chasing you and still have his finger on the pulse of an organization as large as the one we've been tracking. Besides, I've studied your stalker. He's a killer. The man, or woman, who runs the drug operation is a ruthless businessperson."

"There's still a decent chance when we get this guy, he will lead you to the head of the serpent," Colt said. "If he's contracted, he'll talk once we have our hands on him."

"This is a turkey shoot," Shayne mused aloud. Things were beginning to click. "You want my attacker before you tip your hand to anyone else who may be involved. You're trying to pick them off one by one."

"Yes, ma'am," Steve responded. His Southern drawl made her smile for some reason.

"Excuse the mixed metaphors, but that's why we're meeting on a boat, isn't it? You're baiting the hook —with me."

Troy was on his feet. "She is *not* going to be a lure for this killer again."

Shayne reached for his hand. "They're not going to put me in any danger. You know that."

He did. Every one of his friends would sacrifice themselves to protect her. Still, the idea of making her an easy target had his stomach twisting.

The engines on the boat went silent. Troy heard the anchor hit the water, then a few minutes later Rick and Gib joined the group. Rick opted to sit at the top of the ladder leading to the cabin. He wouldn't leave the deck unguarded any more than Troy would. From Rick's vantage point, he could participate in the conversation and still keep one eye on the horizon.

Troy began pacing within the tight confines of the boat's cabin. The muscles in his neck and shoulders tightened. Again, he could feel the scarred tissue along his jaw press against the bone. As he paced, the silence hit him. His head came up, and he scanned the faces of the assembled team and the woman who had accepted him into her arms. Although each expression differed, they all showed concern. He knew without question the worry was directed at him. He stalked the cabin like a caged, restless tiger. He took a deep breath. They had a mission to plan, and stressing wasn't going to help.

"Okay." He relaxed his stance then returned to Shayne's side. "What do you have up your sleeve?"

He listened to the outline of a plan that had been developed by members of the team during the foursome's return trip to Sanibel. The plan was based on the assumption the transmitter would be located. He questioned reasons for decisions, made suggestions, and silently thanked God for having these friends.

Adam had already attached underwater motion sensors to the boat prior to their arrival. The men who remained behind would know instantly if anyone approached the vessel from beneath the surface.

"Are you sure you can make it to shore?" Troy asked Shayne after the logistics were explained. Shayne, along with Colt, Steve, and Gib, would swim ashore, leaving Rick, Adam, Gardner, and Troy on board with the tracking device. But Shayne had been on the run for over twenty-four hours. She had to be worn out. It was a short swim to the isolated beach on the Sanibel side of Tarpon Bay, but swimming could wear you out quickly. She wouldn't be alone, he reminded himself.

His little beauty rolled her eyes. "I grew up in Florida. I was on the swim team in high school, although my coach will swear I should have taken up another athletic endeavor. Regardless, I managed to make it from one end of the pool to the other without drowning. Stop worrying, for God's sake."

"She'll be fine," Steve assured him, pulling a plastic sack from behind him. He tossed it to Shayne. "This should make things easier."

Shayne caught the bag and pulled out its contents. "A swimsuit. Perfect."

"An officer is meeting us at the beach," Steve said. "I'll text as soon as we're all safely ashore. Then it's a matter of waiting until our friend shows up."

"You're assuming a lot, aren't you? What if he doesn't show?" Gib asked.

"He'll show." Troy had no doubt. "He's not going to miss another chance to silence Shayne. He'll show up to finish what he started. The question is how soon?"

"As soon as he figures out how he's going to blow up this boat," Gardner said.

"Do you ever think before you open your mouth?" Troy asked Gardner before he looked at Shayne. Even in the dimming light, he could see Shayne's color had paled a bit, but she sat with her back straight, her shoulders square. He took a step toward her but stopped. She was holding her own. Battling her own demons. She needed to know she could do it.

"He may wait awhile to see if she's moved again," Colt said.

"There are a lot of possibilities," Troy agreed. They were gambling on this guy taking the bait—that he wouldn't try another method such as a rifle. Troy's gut said no. This guy got off on the big bang.

"I don't think he'll wait around too long." Troy was both anxious and nervous. Anxious for this to be over and nervous about Shayne's safety. "With two attempts on Shayne's life, he might not get another opportunity. He must know there's a chance the government will want to take her into protective custody. That's a gamble he can't afford to take."

"We're assuming he's not stupid," Shayne said. "He's got

to know this is a trap."

"Troy's right," Gardner agreed. "He may think this is his last shot. Plus, he's probably getting cocky."

"Cocky?" Shayne's eyebrows rose. "It was just pointed out that he's missed me twice. Why would he be cocky?"

"He hasn't been caught. Not even close," Gardner spat. "Two attempts on you. His success at the country club... And we don't know who he is. He believes he's too smart to be caught."

"We're going to find out just how smart he is," Colt said, moving the small curtain and peeking out the porthole. "It's time we got moving. Once we're out of here, Troy, turn on the galley light. Make something to eat...whatever. Look natural, but be sure that you're the only one visible from outside the boat."

"We'll make ourselves cozy in the berth," Adam announced, rising to his feet. "That's where I've got the equipment set up. If anyone gets near this vessel, we'll know it."

Shayne stepped into the head to change. It only took her a minute to slip into the swimsuit. "You ready?" Troy asked her when she stepped out of the bathroom.

"More than ready," she answered.

The men going ashore headed up to the deck. Those staying on board ducked into the berth, giving Troy and Shayne a few minutes alone.

Troy pulled Shayne into an embrace. He kissed the breath out of her. He felt her nervousness in the trembling of her lips—but more than nerves he could feel her strength.

Shayne broke the kiss. "We need to get this thing on the road. I'm tired of running."

Troy saw her to the top of the ladder, kissed the back of

her hand, and then handed her off to Steve. He waited near the entrance to the cabin, listening. There were no words said, but he could hear each of them as they slipped into the water. Now the waiting began.

Troy took Colt's suggestion and headed for the galley, which had been stocked with basics. They needed to eat. His stomach grumbled, reminding him of that fact. He hadn't eaten since sometime yesterday.

He quickly slapped together sandwiches and grabbed some bottles of water. The front berth had two small portholes, so Troy made sure the men were out of the line of sight before he flicked on the light. Adam and Rick sat on the floor observing the screen on Adam's laptop. Gardner reclined on the double bed.

"I promise not to get fresh," Gardner joked, as he reached for one of the sandwiches. "The floor was getting too crowded."

Troy had missed the camaraderie, the banter, and knowing someone had your back.

"Heard anything yet?"

"Steve texted before you came in," Rick answered. "Everyone made it ashore safe and sound. They'll take care of her. Let's concentrate on our end of the mission."

The muscles in Troy's neck and shoulders relaxed. He hadn't realized how knotted they were. Deep down, he'd known she'd be okay. His friends were keeping her safe, but hearing the news cleared his head and allowed him to focus.

"What about the sensors?" he asked, looking at Adam. "Anything?"

"Not yet," Adam answered, reaching for one of the sandwiches on the plate. His long legs stretched out in front of him. The small computer sat on his lap. "Got readings when the four left the boat but nothing since."

"You hadn't tested it?" Why the hell had Troy waited to ask them that question? This whole scenario depended on this equipment working.

"Red got his hands on this before I took off from Bragg," Adam told him. "He said this stuff works; that's good enough for me."

Adam was right. Gene Shannon, or "Red" as they called him because of his copper-red hair, was their team's gadget guru. If he swore by the equipment, then no one needed to question it. Again, Troy breathed a literal sigh of relief that he hadn't lost these friends during his efforts to destroy himself.

"Where did this boat come from?" Troy took a seat on the corner of the bed and bit into his sandwich.

"I've learned not to asked when Gib shows up with something we need. All I know is that it isn't stolen," Rick said.

"That man can come up with the damnedest things," Adam agreed.

"But no diving gear?" Troy asked.

"Just masks," Adam replied. "We wouldn't have time to get into full gear and it would be in the way. Besides, unless this guy has some way of getting his hands on a rebreather, he won't be using a tank. Too chancy to spot the bubbles in these calm waters—even at night."

After they ate, they moved surreptitiously into the main cabin so that they would be closer to the ladder leading to the deck.

Hours passed. The water around them remained quiet. Rick received a text that Shayne had been taken to a friend's cottage, where Gib would stay with her, and a police officer would remain outside. The others were returning to the marina. Additional tension drained from Troy's body.

Shayne was safe and protected. Once bastard was caught, they would talk about the future. But what if the guy didn't show up? He and Shayne would have to take off until her pursuer could be caught. Coming up with a plan wouldn't be easy. Neither of them owned a vehicle. He'd have to get ahold of some cash. He'd...

Rick nudged him. "Hey. She'll be okay." Troy looked at Rick. He and Shayne weren't alone in this. If they needed help, they'd have it.

"Showtime," Adam stated, setting the computer on the bunk.

"You sure?" Gardner asked.

"As sure as I can be without a camera. It's coming straight for us."

Troy felt a rush. *Damn.* They really might get the bastard.

Adam handed off the computer to Gardner, then he and Rick made their way to the deck. As soon as they were topside, Adam and Rick donned their masks.

"He's on the starboard side," Gardner told them from inside the cabin. "Approaching midship."

"He still there?" Troy double-checked before Adam and Rick went over the side.

"Yep. He's stationary. I'd get down there," Gardner said.

Adam and Rick slipped silently into the water from the opposite side of the boat where their visitor worked beneath the surface. The team was trained in free diving. The plan was for Adam and Rick to split up, approaching the man from both sides.

Gardner joined Troy at the railing, directly above the suspect's position. It was too dark to make out anything beneath the surface.

The water suddenly became turbulent. A second later,

Adam and Rick surfaced. Adam headed straight for the boat with a shoebox-sized object in his hand. Rick had their suspect in a chokehold. He was fighting to break free. Rick tightened his arm around the man's neck, a move intended to incapacitate him.

The man raised a knife and slashed out at Rick as Troy and Gardner hit the water.

Gardner reached the pair first. The agent twisted the man's arm then wrenched his wrist back. Troy heard the suspect's bone snap as he pulled Rick away from the struggle. The knife disappeared into the darkened water. The injury didn't take the fight out of their target. Gardner dropped beneath the surface as he wrestled with the man.

Troy reached for Rick. Blood flowed from a gash on his thigh.

"Go," Rick told him. "I can manage."

But as soon as Troy released his friend, Rick began to flounder. Ignoring Rick's request, Troy grabbed Rick under his arm. If he could get Rick to the ladder... He looked behind him and saw Gardner and his suspect break through the water again. Their prey wasn't giving up without a serious fight.

When Troy reached the boat, Adam was at the railing. "Can you get Rick out of the water? He's injured."

Adam jumped back into the bay. As he reached for Rick, he slipped Troy a knife. Troy swam back toward the men rolling in the water like two alligators in a wrestling match.

The men weren't aware of Troy's presence, too involved in a battle for life. A scissor kick propelled him toward them. When he reached the two, he managed to wrap his arm around the bomber's neck then jerked it back. He pressed the knife against the man's throat. Pushing off, Gardner raced toward the surface for air. The quick movement drove the weapon deep into their captive's flesh. The man went limp in Troy's arms.

"WHAT THE HELL did you do that for?" Gardner asked as they hoisted the body on board the boat. "He was our connection to the drug ring."

Troy remained silent. He had never intended to kill their target. The knife was meant to be a threat to get the man under control. Should Troy tell Gardner it was his powerful kick that had forced the knife into the dead man's throat?

"It was an accident. I wanted him alive as much as you did."

Adam poked his head up from the cabin below. Troy followed his line of sight to the dead man on the deck, but Adam didn't ask the obvious question.

"Where's Rick? Is he okay?" Troy asked.

"In better shape than that guy." Adam indicated the lifeless form. "He's in the cabin putting pressure on the wound. We've got the bleeding under control, but we need to get him to an emergency room and stitched up" Adam said, on his way to the helm.

"And the bomb?" Troy asked.

"In the galley. Disarmed, but don't touch it. Let the bomb squad deal with it."

Troy took a deep breath and dropped into the seat next to the captain's chair. The worst was over. He could see the emergency lights flashing at the marina as they headed across the waterway. No one had to tell him it was going to be a long night.

44

Shayne yanked weeds from the damp soil. It had rained last night. With her acute awareness of everything around her, she should have noticed. She didn't. She'd been fighting a panic attack since they'd received word that the bomber had made his attempt to blow up the boat. He'd been stopped but had been killed.

With the exception of Troy, Adam, and Gardner, who were still being questioned, everyone else was upstairs at Colt's. Even Rick who'd been stitched up and released from the hospital was back. Shayne had heard him griping about being capable of taking care of himself as Steve and Colt helped him up the stairs to Colt's unit. Now Rick had to deal with Cat and Josie playing nursemaids.

Shayne, on the other hand, needed some time to herself. She promised to keep her phone close and call if she needed help. With the danger gone, they gave her the space she requested.

She tossed another weed into the bucket. Fortunately, working had managed to offset the full-blown panic attack she'd felt coming on, but still her nerves danced under her skin. The insides of her garden gloves were wet with perspiration. She purposely worked in a secluded part of the garden. If she succumbed to the panic out here, she wouldn't have a witness if she dissolved into a puddle of fear. Troy hadn't been injured and was now being questioned. No amount of assurance the men had given her had been able to stop her imagining the worst for him.

What the hell is wrong with you, girl?

Dad? Her eyes welled up. She'd lost him. What would happen if she lost Troy?

Stop feeling sorry for yourself. Didn't I teach you better? She blinked the tears back and looked around her. She'd gotten used to her dad's little words of wisdom popping into her head, but a lecture? Maybe she really was losing it.

You're fine.

Shayne dropped back on her heels. She might be going nuts, but her dad always had something to say that made her a better person. She needed to listen. She closed her eyes, pictured sitting across the table from him in the morning—a cup of coffee in his hand. Silver sideburns and wire-rimmed professor glasses sliding down his nose. She smiled at the memory. He wasn't gone. He'd always be there for her.

In a whisper, she began talking to him as if he were there, telling him about Troy. How he made her feel. Imaginary dad or not, she skipped the intimate moments. When she listed her current worries aloud, they didn't seem so concerning. Her shoulders relaxed; her heart stopped pounding against her chest. The tingling sensation on her skin melted away.

Do you love him?

She'd never felt for someone the way she felt for Troy.

Her heart skipped a beat at the sight of him. Her heart burst when they made love. If that was love, then she was there.

She heard the back gate open then close. Troy! She took off around the corner of a planting bed but came to a halt, surprised by the visitor.

"Mr. Russell," Shayne exclaimed. "What are you doing here?"

"My wife and I are on vacation. Since we are staying on Sanibel, I wanted to stop by and see you."

Shayne led Russell to the small gazebo. "How are you and the family doing?" He'd lost his son that night. How did someone handle that?

"It's still hard, but we've managed. Do you enjoy your work here?" he asked, glancing around the tropical wonderland. If he wanted to change the subject, she wouldn't object.

"Actually, I do." Shayne smiled. "The people are great. They treat me like family, and it doesn't hurt that most of the guys are former Green Berets. We've had some trouble. I'm pretty sure I can't talk about it, at least not yet, but I was lucky to have them around."

"I'd gathered as much."

Huh? "How did you know to find me here?" She should have asked that question the moment she saw him. She didn't believe her old employer had given him her address. And there was still that unknown person behind the drugs.

"Lucky guess?" Russell smiled.

Not the answer she'd hoped for. Shayne absently reached for her pendant. She'd gotten in the habit of rubbing it between her thumb and forefinger when she was nervous. And there was a reason she no longer wore it.

"Look, I appreciate you stopping by," she said, getting to her feet, "but I'm very much behind in my work." She took a couple of steps toward the garden, not caring if she left him behind. Something was definitely off. Something that made her breath quicken and her skin prickle again.

"I see you lost your necklace."

Shayne froze. Her eyes closed and her stomach lurched. She took a couple of deep breaths, hoping he would disappear if she ignored him. Of course, he wouldn't.

"What do you know about the pendant?" She turned to face him. If there was going to be trouble, she might as well see it coming. Russell wore a windbreaker like most men wore when playing golf on a cool or rainy day. But it wasn't cool and it wasn't raining.

His hand came out of his pocket with excruciating slowness. Her heart sank. He had a gun.

"Come on"—he waved the pistol toward the back gate —"let's take a walk."

Her eyes caught the brilliant blue flash from his gun hand. She didn't walk as he demanded. She didn't move. Instead, she stared at his ring.

"I've seen that ring before."

"On my son." Russell's words came out slowly and dripped with vehemence.

"No. It was the bartender. I saw it on the bomber."

"Yes. My son," he repeated.

"But—"

"Move!" He directed her again with the gun in his hand.

Shayne resumed her trek, trying to make sense of Russell's words. Her feet, shuffling along the path, filled the ominous silence.

"Are you okay, Mr. Russell?" Her voice quavered. "Your son was killed. Maybe you're confused." Could he have suffered some sort of breakdown after losing his son?

"That was my youngest son, Mr. Law and Order," Russell

mocked. "I always knew he'd be trouble. Too much like his mother. Give him a shield with a star on it and he would have been Captain America. Such a putz. Keep walking." Russell gave Shayne a shove forward.

"When he moved to Tampa, I knew what he was looking for," Russell continued. "But *he* didn't know he was looking for me. Not until the end. Managed to kill two birds with one stone that night."

"You had your son killed—by his own brother?" Stunned, Shayne stopped moving, her feet frozen to the spot while her mind tried to catch up.

"No loss there. He screwed up everything," Russell said with disgust. "Poking his nose into places it didn't belong. Idiot. Now my operation here is done. Too many fucking agencies looking for the chairman of that board. Once they identify my son, they'll know it was me. Time to move on. Remake myself."

Slow him down. Buy some time. It felt like her dad was walking beside her, encouraging her. Shayne was going crazy, but what did it matter if she was going to die anyway? "And your wife? What about your wife?"

"I said, move!" Russell shoved Shayne again. "The world won't miss that righteous bitch. I know that *I* won't. It would probably be kinder to take her out before she discovers she's lost another son. It would save her the misery, don't you think?"

The rear gate was inches away. She inhaled slowly, warding off the panic. If she hadn't been so damned scared, she'd give herself a high five for not curling up on the garden floor.

"You figured out the necklace, didn't you?" Russell asked. "You used it to bait my son—to kill him."

"You sent it?" Of course he had.

"Yes, after my son wasted his time trying to find you. I should have handled it myself instead of trusting him."

"They'll know it was you. They'll trace it back to you."

"Unlikely. It was left on an unattended desk with an unsigned note. Besides, I'll be long gone."

"I still don't understand why I'm a problem?" Blood rushed through her veins. Her ears buzzed. She was getting dizzy.

"You were in the wrong place at the wrong time. Bad night for you, but unfortunately, you lived. Eventually, they'd have figured out who placed the bomb, and you'd become a witness—a protected witness. We would never have gotten to you after that."

"The ring," she whispered, understanding.

"Yes, the ring." He glanced at his hand. "The oldest son in the family is given the same ring with the family crest when he turns twenty. It's been a tradition in my family for generations. That all ends now. Because of you, my oldest son is gone."

"I didn't remember the ring. I might not have ever made the connection."

Shayne had her hand on the gate. Her heart beat against her breastbone so hard that it hurt. If she didn't do some-thing, she was going to hurt a lot more. She stared at the latch as the muzzle of the gun pushed against her back. A pebble skipped across the ground on the other side of the fence. A single pebble. Pebbles didn't move on their own. *Trust me*, she swore she heard her dad say. The words rang clearly inside her head. *Trust him*. A second pebble skipped by, passing to her left.

"I couldn't take the chance you wouldn't make the connection or identify my son. You had to walk down that fucking hallway at that fucking time, and then you fuck things up by living through it."

Shayne sucked in a breath and tuned out the chatter of the man behind her. Either her dad had come back from the dead or help had arrived. She'd take either one. She lifted the latch, saying a prayer that trust was the answer.

Troy was crouched outside the garden gate. The dense shrubs planted along the garden fence provided good cover. He wouldn't be seen as Shayne and Russell approached. He took some deep, slow breaths. No screwups allowed. Not this time.

Steve, on the left side of the gate, was doing his best Sean Spicer impression and hiding between the tall bushes of the neighbor's property. Cat had alerted them after hearing voices on her way to check on Shayne. Colt and Adam should be making their way through the center of the garden toward Russell. His continual chatter made him an easy find.

Whether Shayne realized it or not, she'd done a helluva job slowing things down, allowing them time to get into position. She had also gotten answers out of Russell that would not be coming from the man they now knew was his eldest son.

Troy heard the latch pop up. There was no "ready or not" part to this drill. He had to be ready, and he had to be right. Shayne's life depended on it.

As her foot hit the alley, she took a casual glance to her right. The pebbles had been a signal but one he wasn't sure she'd picked up on. Troy watched as she widened her stance, then slammed the gate open with her foot, simultaneously diving to her left. Steve grabbed her and shoved her into the shrubs behind him.

Russell raised his gun at Steve, but Troy tackled him to the ground before he could get off a shot. The older man landed hard, his face crushed into the rough ground. Adam vaulted over the fence. He pressed his foot onto the captive's wrist, which still held the gun.

It was all Troy could do not to snap Russel's neck. It would be well deserved. The son of a bitch had killed his own son, a DEA agent, and was planning to kill his wife. He would have done the same to Shayne had she not been smart and lucky.

Gardner, who arrived after they had Russell on the ground, wasn't privy to the plan the team had quickly thrown together. The agent wasn't stupid. He knew this was the man at the center of it all.

When Gardner looked at Troy, his eyes were as cold as steel. "Let me have him." The sirens coming closer didn't break his spell. "Let. Me. At. Him."

"Neither of us is going to jail. He's not worth it," Troy told him.

Colt appeared with a pair of zip-tie handcuffs. Rick's, Troy figured. Russell remained pinned to the ground by Troy's weight. His knee dug into the bastard's back. Adam still had his boot over his wrist.

Troy's gaze followed Gardner as he made his way toward Russell's head. A dark, menacing cloud surrounded him. "He's not worth it," Troy repeated.

Gardner pulled Russell's head back by his hair. "He's right," Gardner said. "You aren't worth shit." He slammed Russell's head to the ground then kicked dirt and crushed shell into his face.

Adam used his free foot to shove the gun a safe distance

away from Russell but leaving it for the police to handle. Colt nudged Troy aside and took over his position. He slipped the plastic cuffs over Russell's wrists and tightened them. Troy made a beeline past Steve and pulled Shayne into his arms.

"Are you okay?" he asked. He ran his hands over her, checking for injuries.

"I'm fine," she replied. "Once I stop shaking, I'll be great."

He pulled her back into his arms, pressing her head against his chest. "God, I was so scared when I saw Colt with his gun tearing out of the studio."

"How did he know?"

"Cat heard voices," Troy explained. "She was headed this way to check on you."

"God. If she'd come any sooner, she might have been killed. I'm so sorry."

"It's not your fault. Now hush a minute and let me hold you." He rested his cheek on the top of her head, eventually lifting her chin and kissing the life out of her. "I'm not letting you go. Ever. You understand what that means?"

Shayne was staring at him as Cat came running out of the office. Troy released Shayne. She knew what he'd meant, but he'd give her time to digest it.

He strode toward the arriving police vehicles. Several unmarked cars pulled in behind them. The alphabet agencies finally had someone they could take into custody.

NIGHT HAD FALLEN before all the outside law enforcement people left the island. Troy was glad to see them go. Two nights without sleep was catching up to him. Gardner and

Rick had joined them at Colt's place for a late-night dinner. Rick was there because Cat was keeping her eye on him until his stitches healed. Troy laughed at her sternness. She wasn't letting Rick go home. He would be spending the night at Gib's place next door.

Gardner had hung around to catch up on what he'd missed and to fill them in on what he could. Technically, he was still on leave. He would need to file paperwork to resume his duties. Duties he didn't seem all that enthused to be resuming. It was as if he'd completed his last mission for the DEA. Troy understood the feeling. When he accepted that he could no longer serve in the same capacity in the army, a sadness had settled over him, but there had also been a sense of freedom. Now that he had gotten past the guilt, the freedom opened up so many doors.

Shayne came in from the kitchen carrying two plates of food. She handed one to Troy then settled in next to him.

"What were you thinking about?" she asked.

"Freedom."

"Freedom? From what?"

"Freedom from my past. Freedom to choose my future." He smiled at her. "A future with you, if you'll have me."

He realized the room had gone silent. Everyone was looking at them. Shayne turned a lovely shade of pink. He leaned over and kissed her quickly. "We'll talk more tonight," he said.

"Speaking of which, where are we staying?"

"That Cracker-Jack box you've been living in. Any reason we can't?"

She laughed. "We'll be on top of one another."

"That's the whole idea." He smiled so widely he could feel it.

EPILOGUE

S*ix weeks later...*

SHAYNE BOBBED and weaved her way around her fellow passengers disembarking the plane. Since leaving Ireland, she'd been on three flights totaling over sixteen hours from start to finish, but she wasn't tired. She was bubbling. Straining her neck to find a familiar face at the end of the walkway, she almost broke into a run. Where was he? Troy was tall and not easily missed. She should have been able to spot him over the dozen or so people waiting to greet family and friends.

She'd spent a month in Ireland. She and her mom shared memories of her father and hopes for her future. Grandmama wouldn't be with them much longer, so Shayne was glad she'd made the choice to go when she did. Cat had texted Shayne while she'd been across the pond to tell her that Shayne had been accepted as a volunteer at the Sanibel Historical Museum and Village. She'd continue to work for

Cat but also put her degree to some use. Now if she could only find Troy. She was so excited she could bust, and he wasn't anywhere to be seen.

Rushing out into the main concourse, she made a three-sixty turn. That was when she spotted him. Her heart pounded. Troy had one foot propped against the wall. A large bundle of brightly colored flowers shielded his face, but there was no mistaking his build. "Troy!" She ran toward him. He straightened as she approached, holding the flowers out to her. She pulled up when she saw the bandages on his face. "Are you okay? Did something happen?"

He brushed her hair back behind her ears. She'd been letting it grow.

"I'm fine, honey." He gave her a lopsided grin due to the gauze pads and tape. "First of several cosmetic surgeries. Bandages will be off next week."

"Is that what you want?"

"It is. I had left the scars, in part, to remind me of what I'd failed to do. I did my best. I know that now. Besides, I'm working for Steve. No point in scaring his customers away."

"So long as you understand that I didn't mind," she told him.

"No, you never did, and that's one of the reasons I fell in love with you."

Her heart skipped a beat or two. She didn't count them. "You love me," she whispered, awed by the absolute thrill of it. Her eyes welled up. She wouldn't cry. Not here. They had talked every day while she was visiting with her mom and grandmama. Her heart knew how he felt, but this was the first time he'd said the words—and past time she did.

She brushed back a strand of dark hair from his forehead. "With or without scars, I want you to know that I will always love you."

He kissed her, lifting her off her feet when she wrapped her arms around his neck. Somebody let out a whoop, reminding her where they were. She wriggled out of his grasp, looked around, and saw that in addition to their friends from Sanibel, a small audience had gathered. Some individuals even applauded. She felt the blush. "Maybe the welcome home should wait until we get there."

"Honey, this can't wait—not a minute longer," he announced. He pulled out a jeweler's box from his pocket and took to one knee. He clasped her left hand and slipped a small green emerald on her ring finger. "It reminded me of the garden and of you. Will you marry me?"

She didn't try to stop the tears. She nodded and whispered, "Yes."

Neither of them was perfect. Both had their share of baggage, but together they'd begun to heal. They would finish the journey together.

ACKNOWLEDGMENTS

The absolutely amazing cover is the work of Elizabeth Turner Stokes of estokescreative.com. I look forward to future collaborations.

Aaron McNicol, editing720 & Chris Hall, The Editing Hall , thank you for your patience. Anya Kagan, Touchstone Editing who got me off on the right foot. I sincerely appreciate your tutelage.

To Romance Writers of America members Laura Drake and Lisa Nichols for sharing their expertise on PTSD and alcoholism.

To my friends, Steve, Mario, and Kim, who have all served this country. Thank you for being ready to answer any questions I might have. If references are off, they are entirely my error. Most importantly, thank you for your service. It is an honor to know you.

ABOUT THE AUTHOR

About the Author

C. F. Francis is a native Floridian who loves mystery, suspense and romance. Her favorite pastimes are reading, shelling and traveling. Her diverse background includes working in law, insurance, tourism and a stint with the Florida Legislature's Committee on Organized Crime. She is honored to have friends who have served in the Special Forces and Military Intelligence, who generously share their expertise when asked. Ms. Francis lives in Southwest Florida where she draws inspiration of her novels.

If you enjoyed this story, please consider leaving a review on Goodreads, BookBub or your retailer's site.

You can reach me through my website: www.cffrancis.com

Or email me at cffrancis@earthlink.net

ALSO BY C. F. FRANCIS

Lovers Key

Excerpt...

Just a few short minutes ago Josie Boussard had foolishly believed her torturous journey had finally come to an end. She'd stood at the door of *Island Images* and stared into the darkened photography studio. Her legs, already weak and unsteady, buckled as she read the *CLOSED* sign hanging above the names of the studio's owners: Gibson McKay and Colton James—Steve's former Special Forces Commander.

Daylight was hours away. Tears stung as they'd channeled down the open wounds on her face. Colton James, was the key to finding Steve. Without Steve, she had no one else she could turn to. Nowhere else to run.

The sound of tires on asphalt invaded her world of self-pity, bringing her back to a place of urgency and fear. She needed to get out of sight. After she'd wiped the tears from her eyes, she'd spotted the patch of utter darkness across the driveway and had painfully made her way toward it. A garden. *Perfect*.

It took every last ounce of Josie's reserves to navigate her battered body over the fence that surrounded the property. She crawled the last few feet to the massive potting bench she'd spotted once inside the small jungle. She shoved aside the bags of potting soil that rested on the lower shelf of the bench, then slid her long frame onto the rough wooden platform behind the wall she'd just created. Pulling her knees upward in the tight space, Josie clasped them to her chest, shivering against the unusually cool Florida night. Her eyes drifted shut as she said a prayer that no one would find her before morning.